Barbacoa, Bomba, and Betrayal

Also available by Raquel V. Reyes

The Caribbean Kitchen Mysteries

Mango, Mambo, and Murder

Calypso, Corpses, and Cooking

Barbacoa, Bomba, and Betrayal

A CARIBBEAN KITCHEN MYSTERY

Raquel V. Reyes

CROOKED
LANE

NEW YORK

Published in the United States by Crooked Lane Books, an imprint of The Quick Brown Fox & Company LLC.

Crooked Lane Books and its logo are trademarks of The Quick Brown Fox & Company LLC.

Library of Congress Catalog-in-Publication data available upon request.

ISBN (hardcover): 978-1-63910-524-3
ISBN (ebook): 978-1-63910-525-0

Cover illustration by Joe Burleson

Printed in the United States.

www.crookedlanebooks.com

Crooked Lane Books
34 West 27th St., 10th Floor
New York, NY 10001

First Edition: November 2023

10 9 8 7 6 5 4 3 2 1

To Viejo San Juan, the place where my spouse
and I found each other.

To my in-laws on the island, I wish we
lived closer to you.

To my sobrino Gabriel, thank you for always
asking "Hey, Tia, how is the book going?"

To la Isla del Encanto, I love you, Puerto Rico.

Chapter One

" **S** hould we take down the tree today?"

"*Noooo*," I replied, shaking my head but not looking up from my book. "You know the tree stays up until the kings come."

Robert and I had been married for almost six years. His family's Christmas traditions were very different compared to mine. The Smiths did Christmas morning stockings and presents, then had a formal late lunch that looked a lot like Thanksgiving minus the turkey. By five PM, the holiday season was over for them. On the other hand, my Cuban family stayed up on Christmas Eve, Nochebuena, cooked a whole pig, had a delicious meal, danced and sang, played games, and opened presents. Then twelve days later, the Three Kings came to give the kids more gifts.

This was our first Christmas in Coral Shores, a village within metro Miami. His parents lived three blocks away. Mine lived nine hundred miles away in the Dominican Republic, but they used to live a stone's throw away in Hialeah, another city within Miami-Dade County. We'd spent a joyous Nochebuena with my tíos and prima, who still lived in Hialeah, and then had a staid Christmas day with the Smiths.

"Plus, this is the first time we've ever had a big tree. I want to enjoy it for as long as possible." I closed the seafood cookbook and set it beside me on the blue sofa before admiring our tree. Our apartment in NYC had been too tiny for anything more than a fake tabletop tree. This year's evergreen took up the entire width and height of the front window. The deep woods pine smell wasn't as strong as the day it had come off the refrigerated truck from North Carolina, but if I got close to it and took a deep breath, it was still there. I also had a pine-scented candle that I lit to fill the living room with the crisp seasonal fragrance. But I had to be watchful that Camo, our calico cat, didn't get too curious about it like she was doing with an icicle ornament at that moment.

"Roberto! Get Camo before she gets in the tree again," I said.

My six-foot-tall husband got on all fours and crawled over to the tree. Manny, having heard his pet's name, came barreling out of his room to see what was happening. Laughing, he jumped on his father's back. The two crumbled to the ground in a tickle wrestling match. Camo darted away from the commotion and onto my pregnant belly for safety. Father and son ended up flat on their backs with their heads on the white faux-fur tree skirt. Probably not my wisest purchase, and maybe part of why Camo was attracted to the tree. She loved to sleep on the skirt's soft fur.

"Little man, what's that?" Robert pointed to something in the tree.

I hoped it wasn't a lizard. Camo loved hunting them when they got into the house, and that happened frequently.

"Is that a present we missed?" Robert asked.

"Is it for me?" The excitement in our son's voice was a holiday movie moment of wonder.

"I don't know, maybe. Let's see." Robert pulled the thin rectangular gift box from the low branch it had been perched on. He handed it to Manny, who read the tag with a bit of help from his father.

"Mami, es pa' tí." Manny scrambled over the area rug to present it to me. "Ábrelo, ábrelo."

I did as I was told and opened the gift. "Airplane tickets?" I read the folded printout. "Miami to Punta Cana! Robert, you didn't! Ay mi madre, we're going to see my mom!" I moved Camo from my lap and stood. "Get up. Get up. I need to kiss you!"

Robert lumbered up from the floor and embraced me. I kissed him deeply before doing a little happy bounce. "I can't believe you kept this surprise from me!"

Manny was caught up in the excitement too. He danced from foot to foot and shook his hips in a tick-tock fashion. "Vamos a ver a Abuela y Abuelo, yay."

He'd only seen his grandparents on video calls since they moved to the Dominican Republic. My parents were property managers for a small vacation rental company. They'd held him when he was little and then again when he was about two, but he didn't remember those visits.

"When are we going? Oh my go—" I looked at the paper more closely. "This ticket is for tomorrow and only for Manny and me. Why aren't you coming with us?" Tears welled up in my eyes. I was five months pregnant, and the hormone roller coaster meant the slightest thing could make me emotional.

"*Babe.*" Robert enveloped me in his arms. "I would love to go with you two, but they're about to break ground on the country club extension, and I need to be here. Listen, if I can get away, I'll pop over and fly back with you. Okay?" He stroked the back of my head.

I looked into his light-brown eyes and made a sad puppy face. He chuckled.

"Come on, babe. The time is what it is. You're pregnant and won't be able to fly in a month or two. Your parents can't come here because it's the busy season there. Manny's on vacation from preschool. I have this big work project—"

"Carajo, what am I going to do about work?" I asked. It hadn't been that long since I'd told them I was expecting. We'd doubled up on filming episodes of my cooking show, *Abuela Approved,* and my segment on the UnMundo morning show *La Tacita* in anticipation of my maternity leave. And I'd lost workdays to recuperation and a hospital stay thanks to having been locked in a freezer by a murderer. I couldn't afford to take off on vacation. My new career was still too new. It boggled my mind how I'd gone from wanting a quiet, studious academic career as a professor of food anthropology to being comfortable talking on camera about the foods of the African diaspora in the Caribbean to an audience of millions.

"Don't worry. I checked with Delvis. She said you are good until Three Kings. The network is doing something special for it. I figured you knew about it already." Robert grabbed Manny and turned him upside down. Giggles ensued.

"I don't know anything about a Día de los Reyes Magos special. But I'm sure Delvis has it bajo control like she always does. I'll show up and read whatever is on the prompter." I shooed away the worry with a hand swat to the air. "Ay mi madre, I'm going to Punta Cana! I can't wait to taste Mami's arroz con pollo again. And her pescado al escabeche. And I'll get her to show me the secret to her frijoles negros."

"And you'll relax! Right?" Robert gave me a stern look. "No more getting yourself into danger. No more m-u-r-d-e-r-s."

"Yes. Yes. Yes. Please, yes."

Chapter Two

The luggage carousel was empty but moving. Slowly bags began to spit out onto the conveyor belt. As we waited for our maroon suitcase to appear, I fanned myself. The baggage claim area had a high-pitched roof but was open to the outside air. Streams of tourists dressed for colder temperatures poured in, removing flannels and jackets.

"¡Ése!" Manny pointed.

I looked and informed him that, no, it wasn't ours.

"¿Ése?" he asked.

"Si, ése es," I replied, seeing the rainbow ribbon I'd tied to the handle to make it easier to identify. I stepped forward to lift it off the track but was intercepted.

"Here, let me," a man walking by with a rolling carry-on said. He was American but didn't look like he was on vacation. He had a Miami businessman vibe about him. Beige linen pants, no socks, expensive leather loafers, and a designer long-sleeve shirt that was trim-cut and tucked in. "A woman in your condition doesn't need to lift a heavy suitcase."

"Thank you," I said, truly grateful I didn't have to do it.

He extended the handle and offered it to me. I noticed his fingernails were manicured, and he had on a bulky and blingy watch. He also had a flat gold insignia ring. I looked up to smile another thanks for his kindness, but he'd turned and was on his way.

"¿Quién era ese hombre?" Manny asked.

I told my son I didn't know who the man was, but I was glad he'd helped me. Manny said he was strong and would have helped me if I had let him.

"Si, mi príncipe, yo sé." I kissed him on the head before we walked to customs. One of the uniformed agents motioned us to a short line. A flutter of panic hit me. *Miriam, chill. You don't have any contraband. And you are visibly pregnant and sweating, so maybe they are being kind.*

When Manny and I got to the agent's station, I handed him our passports and customs declarations. The man gave them a brief glance, passed our suitcase to the other side, and returned our passports to me.

"Bienvenidos a Punta Cana, Señora Quiñones. A mi esposa le encanta su programa *La Tacita*."

He hadn't called me over because of my belly. His wife loved my cooking spot on UnMundo's morning show. I grinned. Fame. It was wild. I could tell he was too embarrassed to ask for a photograph, so I volunteered one. Manny offered to take it, but a female guard stepped in to do it.

My parents were waiting for us outside customs. Mami y Papi took turns hugging me, then Manny. There was also a lot of marveling and blessing of my belly. Papi took my suitcase, and we followed him to the parking lot. Their minivan was an older model and came with their employment. When someone rented a villa, part of the package was transportation to and from the airport. They even had a variety of children's safety seats on hand. My mother had asked if Manny needed one, and I'd told her a booster would be good. I could see my father's care for the vehicle in the shiny polish and the vacuumed floor mats. As a kid, I'd helped him wax our family car under the shade of our Hialeah apartment's avocado tree. They'd been the property managers of that complex too.

"Mami, this place is super glitzy. Es casi como una pequeña Miami," I said. One by one, the airport shuttle vans peeled away from our traffic pack and into the grand entrances of beach hotels and resorts. The building style was minimal—clean lines, glass balconies, and statement landscaping. It had a very new feeling, just like the condos on Miami Beach, Brickell, and Edgewater.

"Ay, si. So many people from Florida own timeshares here," Mami said.

"Y, de South América too," Papi added.

"No, I'm talking about the architecture. It's the same style as so many of the luxury condos being built in Miami, ahora," I said.

"Everything here is new. But not where we are. Vas a ver. It is *very* pretty." Mami patted my shoulder from behind. She was seated next to her grandson, and I was in the front with Papi. I didn't know how much I'd missed my mother until that moment. The way her Vs sounded like Bs in English made me happy and warm.

In fifteen minutes, we were in a less beachy but still vacation-feeling district. The buildings had gone from eight and ten stories to two or three stories. Papi had given me the history of Punta Cana along the way. There was no history. The first hotel was built in the 1960s and another ten years later.

"There wasn't even an airport until 1984!" I loved Papi's "th" Ds. It was so good to be back with my parents. "Don't worry, nena. Santo Domingo is two hours away si quieres ver la catedral y la zona colonial," Papi added. He knew how much I loved history. I did want to show Manny the old part of the capital. The area was on the UNESCO world heritage list. The gothic cathedral was built in 1541. He'd like the forts and probably call them castles—because his Smith cousins Rae and Vanna were Disney fairy tale fanatics, and he loved anything they loved. But four hours roundtrip. I didn't know if I could handle it. *Gracias, baby bladder.*

Papi slowed to a crawl to turn into a driveway with a tall open gate. One side of the gate said Punta and the other Palma in a wrought iron script. Ahead of us was the most enormous Canary Island date palm I'd ever seen. It looked like a giant pineapple. A paver-lined drive encircled the palm. There were four villas. The largest was in the direct sightline of the open gate. To the right were two smaller villas.

"Uno es completo," Mami said, pointing to the one with a dark-blue sedan parked in front of it. "But the first one is two apartments. Top y bottom. The woman that rented the full house for the week arrived today. El mismo vuelo que tú. *Julies Howard*," Mami seemed uncertain about the name. "Pero, she said she'd rent a car. Imagínate—a three bedroom for only one person."

"Mejor para nosotros," Papi said. "Less people to clean up after. Y this way we got to talk and not worry what we were saying."

Papi was right. He did tend to clam up around strangers. *Umm, clams. I could eat. Are you hungry, mi sirena?* I laughed to myself. I'd started calling the baby mi sirena, my mermaid. I didn't know *or care* what the gender was, but I did know the baby craved seafood.

The carved wooden front door opened, and the man that had helped me with my luggage stepped out. The sun glinted off his fancy watch as he clicked the car's fob to open the trunk. I waved. The man smiled and gave a two-fingered V wave in return. Finally, getting a good look at his face—sandy-blond hair, very white teeth, no beard stubble—I could see he was handsome. But not in the macho-guapo way that my friend Jorge categorized my husband into. Jorge and I had the same type. This guy was more refined, and even though I had gotten a Miami vibe from his style, I didn't think he was Latino.

"I thought you said a woman rented it?" I asked my mother.

"Yes, Julies." She tapped the screen of her phone and then held it up for me to see it.

"Did you speak to the woman?" I asked as I read the email Mami had opened. The name was Jules. Which could be a man's or a woman's name, in my experience.

"No, mi'ja, todo es por el email. They even email us here cuando they could walk across and knock on our door." Mami chuckled.

Papi's slow roll took us past the grand villa, by an in-ground pool with lounge chairs, and finally completing the circle to a villa that was the mirror of "the apartments" one. My parents had the bottom floor. The top apartment had a sun deck and a spiral staircase to the pool area. Papi could have turned left instead of right when he entered the gate, but I guessed he'd wanted to show me the property.

"Abuela, yo quiero ir a la piscina." Manny piped up upon seeing the sparkly water. Half the pool was taken up by a giant blow-up swan. A bikini-clad blonde baked her ivory skin on it. She adjusted her oversized dark glasses and then took a sip from a straw that was in a can of sparkling rosé wine. I clocked it because it was my friend Alma's favorite brand.

"Ahora no, mi amorcito." Mami told him the pool was for the guests and that she promised to take him to the beach tomorrow. It was ridiculous, but I felt the beach was safer than a pool. *Reminder, Miriam, get Manny some swimming lessons.*

While Mami made us a late lunch, I freshened up. The two-bedroom apartment had tile floors, white walls, and a Jack and

9

Jill bathroom. The room Manny and I were staying in had a full-size bed for me and a pin-pan-pun, a rollaway bed, for him. My parents had already put sheets on it, and there was a stuffed teddy bear with a Dominican flag T-shirt propped on the pillow.

"Miriam y Manny, merienda. Come to the patio," Mami called. Her voice filled the hallway.

Despite having never visited my parents since they moved to the island, the patio was familiar, thanks to our weekly video calls. I'd seen it go from sparse to lush. My parents appreciated fruit trees, and I bet they'd planted most of the ones thriving around the patio. There was a guava, several fruta bombas, a banana, a guanábana, a passion fruit called chinola by the locals, and a patch of pineapples. A tamarind tree grew just outside the wall surrounding the Punta Palma compound. Its branches stretched over the property. The tea-colored juice Mami was pouring for us was probably made from the tangy fruit.

"Delicioso. Abuela me gusta," Manny said.

I took a drink to taste what Manny was raving about. "Mami, did you put a whole cup of sugar in this?" The juice was overly sweet.

"Sí, your father likes it sweet. Pero, you know that tamarindo is good for the morning sickness." Mami eyed my belly.

I wish I'd remembered that folk medicine a few weeks ago when I'd needed it. Gracias a La Caridad, that phase of the pregnancy had passed. "Where is Papi?" I asked.

"He'll be back en un ratito. He had to go to the store a comprar some tubería," Mami said. She put a set of long-handled spoons into the fruit salad. The rest of our meal was fresh farmer's cheese and Gilda-style crackers. I was pretty sure my mother had made the queso de campo too. I remember learning how to make it from my abuela the summer I visited her in Cuba. The salty white cheese was bland. It was almost like a hybrid of cream cheese and feta. It made a perfect accompaniment to something sweet like the salad and juice. I hoped my mother would make another batch of it while we were visiting so Manny could have the memory of it like me. He was young, but he really had a passion for cooking.

"¿Qué pasó? Did something break?" I asked her, wondering why Papi had gone to buy pipes.

"Sí, again. This is the third time." She put a forkful of papaya into her mouth.

"Tres veces. The same pipe? Where?" I built a cracker for myself.

"Atrás de la casa grande. The pipe that brings water to the house. Maybe we have to dig up the yard. Maybe it's a root breaking it. Don't worry. Your papá will fix it."

My phone beeped. "Perdóname, Mami. This is work, I need to answer it." I excused myself from the table and walked to the patio's edge.

It was a message from Delvis: *Sorry to bother you while you are visiting familia. But I need you to answer your email.*

Qué email I texted back.

About Three Kings. We need to know your flight # from DR to PR

I reread the message several times. What was she talking about? I didn't have an email app on my phone, and my tablet was still packed in my luggage. I had no idea what she meant. *Puerto Rico?* I decided to video-call her to get to the bottom of it.

"Hola, chica," I said.

"Hola." Delvis's blue hair was in her eyes. She flipped her wavy locks back. "¿Cómo está tu familia? I bet they were happy to see you."

"Yeah, super happy. Thanks so much for letting me go."

"Of course. I wish we could give you more time pero you know this festival is like one day and we want to film some local stuff before it. I think you are really going to love what we have lined up. Like, we don't really have you cooking. We have you, like, interviewing and stuff—you know, the whole food anthropology thing." The video buffered, and Delvis's nose-ring-studded face was frozen in mid-blink.

"¿Que, qué? What are you talking about? In Miami? What festival?" I hoped she could hear me.

"Check-check-check." The video had a stutter. I moved away from the house to get a stronger cell signal. "Check your inbox. It's all in the email. I told your husband about it. But he said not to ask you about it until later because your trip was a surprise."

"Email? I didn't get any email. What address did you send it to?"

"The Abuela Approved at UnMundo punto com." Delvis turned like someone had called her name. "I've got to go. Just reply before tomorrow. Okay. Abrazos. Bye."

The screen went black.

I grabbed the half-eaten cheese wedge from my plate and dashed into the house to get my tablet. It was between a pair of Manny's pants and one of my new maternity shirts. When I returned to the patio, Mami was showing Manny the guava blossoms that were buzzing with bees. I moved my plate to make room for the tablet. I found the Punta Palma Wi-Fi signal and asked my mother for the password.

"P, P mayúscula y guest minúscula y el número uno."

I typed the uppercase and lowercase letters, followed by the number one. Once I was connected, I logged into my UnMundo email account. The one I never checked because it was for fan mail.

Three hundred and seventy-nine unread messages! ¡Ay, ay, ay! I did a search for "Reyes," and four emails matched. I read them all quickly, then had to take a few deep breaths.

"¿Qué te pasa, mi'ja? Is it the baby?" Mami cuffed my wrist in a gentle squeeze.

"No, Mami, the baby is fine. Pero, I'm not. I have to go to San Juan in three days for work. Can I leave Manny with you for a week?" I grimaced. "I'm so sorry."

"Qué sorry. No te preocupes. El trabajo viene primero."

I could always rely on my parents to come at me with the classic first-gen immigrant work ethic. *Work comes before everything else.* "But I was looking forward to spending time with you," I pouted.

"We already spent years together. Now I get to *espoil* my nieto." She hugged her grandson tightly. "Isn't that right, Manuelito? Te quieres quedar con tus abuelos so Mami can work?"

"Sí," Manny shouted.

While my son danced gleefully with his abuela, I called his father to talk about his *communication problem.* After which I had to make a plane reservation.

Ay, ay, ay. Never a dull moment in my life.

Chapter Three

As promised, Mami took us to the beach the following day. The sun was mild and perfect. But the water was too chilly for our tropical blood. Manny played in the surf and dug rivers and canals that instantly filled with salty waves. He made friends with a German girl who shared her bucket and shovel with him. Together they built a sandcastle with a moat.

"Mami, this is divina. Thank you. I wish Papi could be here with us," I said, wiggling my toes into the white powdery sand.

"I know, pero he has to fix the pipe before the guests arrive. They can't stay there if there is no water to flush the toilets." She sighed. "It would look very bad. No queremos más problemas. The owner might want to sell if things are breaking."

More problems? What did Mami mean *more*? She started humming an old Cuban love song and didn't elaborate. She'd told me earlier that there was a party of eight arriving late in the day to stay in la villa grande. The largest of the four houses had an attractive arched entryway with purple bougainvillea growing through it. Papi had worked until dark repairing the broken pipe, only to have another leak in a different place in the morning. He'd shown me the PVC tube that went from the plastic storage tank, a dark green thing that looked like a flattened ball, to the pump that supplied the house with the rainwater for the four bathrooms. It was filtered but not potable for visitors. That type of catchment system was inexpensive and typical throughout the tropics, but foreigners were wary of it. There was a different system in the kitchen for drinking water that used reverse osmosis.

Papi had said the damage was probably done by an animal, like a mongoose or a hutia. Mongoose—*or is it geese*—have sharp needle teeth to kill snakes. It couldn't have done it. And the hutia was a short-tailed, tree-dwelling rodent that weighed about three pounds. Other than the tamarind tree, there wasn't a likely habitat for the endangered animal that liked mountains, not beaches. Plus, the creature was almost cute. Could its small beaverlike front teeth have gnawed through the thick plastic pipe? Maybe, but not likely. What I saw looked more like a nick from something metal or heavy. A machete? A saw? A cinderblock falling on it? Was someone sabotaging the property? If Mami wouldn't tell me about the "más problemas," I'd ask Papi.

"Come." Mami nudged me with her elbow to hand me a slice of watermelon. Since touching ground less than twenty-four hours ago, that had been her constant command: Eat.

I took a bite of the sweet melon while watching a paddleboarder lose their balance and splash into the clear, shallow water.

"Y toma esta melón para un ebo a Yemaya." My mother took a cannonball-sized watermelon from the cooler.

I looked at her like she had lost her mind, but she insisted. I was supposed to walk into the water and offer the fruit to the orisha Yemaya, the mother of the sea and the protector of pregnant women. She must have been talking to Tía Elba a lot because Mami wasn't a devout follower of la Regla de Ocha. I mean, we'd had a regular altar in our house with saints and candles and rum and tobacco, like most households in Hialeah. But lobbing a whole watermelon into the ocean was on another level. Mami would not take no for an answer. She said it was for my and the baby's protection. *Baby, you are certain to be a mermaid at this rate.*

When we got home, I checked on Papi and the plumbing problem. Manny and his abuela went al mercado to shop for the evening's supper—asopao de camarones. Before going to the big house, I went the long way around the circular driveway. I looked high and low for a creature with teeth strong enough to break a pipe. I found plenty of lizards and a bird with a banded tail that was hunting them. I saw a large hermit crab at the base of the huge central palm.

"Could that have done it?" I asked.

"Excuse me."

I jumped at the sound of a voice that wasn't my own. It belonged to Jules Howard. He was walking toward me. The door to his villa was ajar.

"Excuse me, but do you know anything about the Wi-Fi?" he asked.

"Do you need the password? It's P-P uppercase—"

"No-no-no, I have that. It's out. I was in the middle of uploading a property listing, and it went dead." Jules ran a finger across his throat.

"I'm sorry about that. I can ask my father. He's repairing," I fumbled for what to say or not say, "um, he's making a repair at the big villa."

"You're Mrs. *Keen-yo-ness's* daughter? I thought you were a guest like me."

"I'm visiting from Miami." I'd sped up my pace to close the gap between us. La Sirena kicked. I reacted by placing my hand on my stomach.

"Are you okay?" Jules asked with sincerity.

"I'm fine. Just the baby. Let's go ask my father about the Wi-Fi," I motioned for him to come with me. "Property listing? Are you a Realtor? In Miami?"

"Yes, um, are you?"

"Me, no. My best friend is, maybe you know her, Alma Diaz. She sells in Coral Shores."

"Sorry, no. I'm in commercial real estate. A little different than residential."

Did I detect a touch of snobbery? We'd stepped onto the sand and gravel path that led to the two-hundred-gallon water tank. A dark pink bougainvillea shrub camouflaged it.

"Perdona, Papi, pero el señor Howard dice que el Wi-Fi se cayó." I explained the situation to my father, who was wearing a green polo shirt with the property's name embroidered in gold. He wiped his brow with his forearm and instructed me on how to reset the router. Our conversation was in Spanish. I couldn't tell if Jules was following along or not. His eyes were on the house, examining it like an insurance adjuster.

"Come on, I think I can fix your problem," I said.

"How did you know my name? You called me Mr. Howard."

"Oh, my mother. The reservation. She thought you were a Julie." I laughed. "She and my dad manage Punta Palma."

"Okay, well, you know my name, but I don't know yours."

"Miriam Quiñones-Smith." I extended my hand. "Nice to meet you, Jules Howard. And thank you for helping me with my luggage the other day."

"You are very welcome, Miriam Smith," he replied, bowing his head. "So, what do you do in Miami?"

"I have a little cooking show with a Spanish language network."

"A cooking show like Food Network stuff? Impressive."

I blushed. "It's more than just cooking. It's about culture. Why do we eat the things we eat? Where did they originate? Many of the dishes we eat in the Caribbean have roots in Africa." I opened a hidden screened compartment in the foyer of Jules's villa. I unplugged the cord like my dad had instructed and silently counted to thirty.

"So, you're into food? What's the name of your show? Do you plan on opening your own restaurant?"

I reinserted the cylindrical plug and watched as the lights blinked to life. "A restaurant? I wouldn't know what to do with a restaurant. I'm an anthropologist, not a chef."

Jules looked a little crestfallen.

"My friend Marie is an amazing chef. She has a Haitian food truck. You should try it when you get back to Miami. I swear her pikliz is the best I've ever tasted."

"A lot of restaurants start as food trucks. Is she ready to make the move to brick and mortar? What did you say is the name of her business?" Jules had his phone out and his fingers poised to type in the name.

"Fritay All Day." The globe symbol on the router went from flashing to solid. "There. Looks like the Wi-Fi is back." I closed the nine-by-twelve painted screen frame, and the cubby disappeared. "If it goes out again, just try that trick. My father says it happens every once in a while. The island's internet isn't the greatest. Sorry."

His phone rang. "I need to get this. Thank you for the help." Jules stepped into the interior of the house. "Bonjour, monsieur."

Was he speaking French?

"Ne quittez pas." Jules held his hand over the phone's mic. "It was a pleasure to meet you, Ms. Smith. Thanks for the help. Maybe we can have a drink later."

A drink? Is he hitting on me? I am clearly pregnant. And married! As I left his villa, I twisted the band on my finger, which was getting tighter by the week. *Who is this guy?* I shot my BFF a quick message. Alma was video-calling me by the time I got back to Mami and Papi's apartment.

"Hola, chica. How's Punta Cana? ¿Y tus padres?" Alma's face took up the entire screen, and she was using it like a mirror to put on lipstick.

"Everything is good. I guess. I think. Well, there's this pipe problem."

"That's island life. So, what do you want to know about Golden Jules?" Alma primped her hair.

"Why do they call him that?"

"He has the Midas touch. He buys derelict properties, and his company, LPM, turns them into luxury developments. Mix-use. Lots of restaurants. LPM just bought a block over in Little River. That deco motel and that strip of tiendas on Sixty-Fourth. You remember it. It has that old neon flamingo sign."

"No, not really. But go on. Had it been for sale for a long time?"

"No, that's the thing. None of the properties he buys are on the market. That's why he is golden. He has a talent for finding them and getting the owners to sell. I drove by it yesterday, actually. The cyclone fence is already up, and the demo trucks are there. I think they have to keep the façade and the footprint, but they'll gut it and reno the whole thing."

A chill ran down my spine. *Was Golden Jules scoping out Punta Palma? Was he sabotaging the pipes so he could get it for a steal?*

Chapter Four

The flight from Punta Cana to San Juan, Puerto Rico, was shorter than the time it took us to get from the Luis Muñoz Marín Airport to Viejo San Juan. UnMundo owned a house in the old part of the city for visiting talent. I was still learning the entertainment world's lingo. Apparently, I was talent, and Delvis was production. My chauffeur was Delvis's cousin Welmo.

"Is it always this bad?" I asked.

We were at a standstill on the one-way road that led into Old San Juan. If I had to be in traffic, at least the view was nice. To my right was the Atlantic Ocean, and to my left was El Capitolio, the capital building with its large rotunda and columns. Behind the statue of San Juan Bautista, St. John the Baptist, the waves crashed. It added atmosphere to the blockish figure in a long robe. *I think the style is called brutalism.* It was quite the juxtaposition.

"There is always traffic. But it will be quick now," Welmo replied. "This was my, how you say, mi territorio, mi patrulla."

"Your *beat,*" I suggested.

"Yes, my beat. My patrol."

I heard a little sigh from my driver. He'd told me he'd recently been let go from the police force due to the austerity measures of the United States–imposed Financial Oversight Board. In the last year, 6,450 people had been cut from the Puerto Rico Police

Department. He was positive he'd get his job back eventually, but in the meantime, his cousin had gotten him this gig. Welmo had also informed me he was my security. I didn't think I was at the star level that needed security. *But if it keeps food on this father of three's table, I'm cool with it.*

Welmo's head snapped left to study an ambulance leaving the old city on the road behind the capital. I lowered the window as we got close to Castillo de San Cristóbal, the fortress on the northwest part of the islet. Distant sirens wha-wha-ed. If Welmo had been a dog, his ears would have stood up. I could sense he was on alert.

"¿Qué será?" I asked.

"Remember, I want to practice my English," he said with a laugh.

And you don't want to worry me. "Okay then, be my tour guide. What are we passing?"

"There is an old cemetery on the other side of the wall, and that road goes to La Perla." He pointed to a narrow paved street with walls.

I knew La Perla had the best views. It was a tiny strip of land outside the city's walls. In the 1700s, it was the mandated home to a slaughterhouse and the only place nonwhite servants and for-mer enslaved people could live. To this day, it remains a lower-income neighborhood with a strong identity.

"You know the video for 'Despacito' was filmed there," he said. I heard him sing a few lines from the Luis Fonsi crossover hit under his breath. He steered the car onto the narrow, cobble-stoned Calle Cristo. "This road is made from the stones of the ships."

I tilted my head out the window to take in their blue tint. They were ballast from the trade ships that had then been replaced with gold, spice, sugar, coffee, and rum for the return voyage.

Before we turned onto Calle Sol, we saw a crowd of curious onlookers blocking the road by the large yellow hotel.

"Algo está pasando en El Convento," Welmo said.

I guess he forgot he wanted to practice his English.

Calle Sol was narrower than Calle Cristo due to the residential parking on the left. I felt myself tensing as we came within inches of the parked cars. Old San Juan was a mix of businesses, homes, museums, and apartments. It was a micro-city on a hill with water views of the Atlantic Ocean and San Juan Bay. At the end of the street were the city wall and a bay vista. Continuing past a triangular-shaped plaza with a statue, we turned onto Caleta de las Monjas. Welmo beeped his horn, and a woman emerged from house number seven to remove an orange cone that had been reserving a parking space. A black-and-white cat reluctantly moved from its sunny spot by the cone.

I got out of the car and stretched. The cat stretched too. It made me miss Camo.

"Doña Santos," Welmo said before kissing her on the cheek. "Esta es la famosa Señora Quiñones." He motioned to me and made introductions in Spanish. We made the customary pleasantries about travel and welcome before Welmo popped the trunk for my suitcase. His attention was on the activity up the hill, and he nearly tripped over the curb.

"Cuidado," I said out of reflex as if he were Manny. This was only the second or third time I'd been away from my son, and I knew I'd enjoy the time away while also missing him tremendously.

"¿Qué pasó allá?" Welmo cocked his head in the direction of the hotel.

We all stopped and watched as a police officer told the onlookers to move along. The petite cop walked like a bantam rooster. He tied yellow tape to a grated first-floor window before unrolling it across the road to loop it around a sign pole. I had a weird feeling in my belly, and it wasn't coming from my sirena doing flips and kicks.

"No sé, hay una fiesta de locos esta semana. *El Bitcoin* o algo así," Doña Santos replied. She opened the mahogany door for us.

Our innkeeper thought the police activity had to do with the rowdy Bitcoiners in town for the week.

The black-and-white cat meowed at her. "Te daré tu leche en un ratito, Vaquita."

"¿Ella es tu gata?" I asked. The cat's name, Little Cow, was appropriate. Her markings resembled a Holstein.

Doña shook her head and denied ownership. In the next breath, she admitted Vaquita *was* her favorite of all the street cats. I looked around and noticed the sidewalk on the other side was dotted with felines. I bent to pet the friendly cat. *Little Cow, your person will bring you your milk soon.*

Stepping onto the worn and faded tiles of the foyer, it was like going back in history hundreds of years. The thick walls caused the temperature to drop a few degrees, and the sounds of the street were quieted. Welmo whisked my bag up the stairs to my room while Doña Santos gave me a tour. We were in la sala when we heard the front door open and close. Welmo called out that he'd be back in a second. The ground floor had a comfortable sitting room, a formal dining room, and a kitchen with a small round table. La cocina had modern appliances but with old-world cabinetry. The little breakfast nook sat by a window that looked onto a postage-stamp patio. A sun ray hit the crystal vase on the lace tablecloth, and the roses seemed to twinkle.

"¿Quieres un café?" she asked.

I pointed to my belly. "Si, pero no puedo."

"Dios te bendiga."

I smiled and accepted her blessing. She told me she would make coffee for Welmo and that she'd make me a hot milk with a drop of coffee. I asked for the bathroom, and she showed me a door in the hallway with a ceramic rose adorning it. After I'd freshened up, I headed back to the kitchen but stopped when I heard voices. Welmo was back. He was telling Doña Santos that someone had been shot. *That was the ambulance we saw leaving the city.*

"¿Uno de los Bitcoin locos?" she asked.

"No, un señor mayor. En la caleta atrás del Convento," Welmo informed her.

An older man was found in the alley behind the hotel. He'd been rushed to the hospital, but he'd lost a lot of blood.

Miriam, gracias a La Caridad that you didn't find him. I couldn't believe I was once again steps away from a crime. I put my hand on my heart and said a prayer of thanks. *I'll light a candle for the man's recovery.*

When I walked into the kitchen, their conversation stopped. Doña Santos placed a cup of off-white milk on the table and pulled out a chair for me to sit down. Welmo took his cup and sat opposite me.

"I will come by in the morning to pick you up. The first filming is at eleven. Y Delvis me dijo she would stop by later to take you to dinner." Welmo smiled. He jiggled a restless leg that made the cups and saucers chink. He realized it and stopped. "Doña Santos lives next door. So, if you need anything, call her or knock on the door."

"I will make you breakfast in the morning," she said, wiping the counter before rinsing her coffee cup.

"Are there any other guests staying in the house?" I asked.

"No, you have the whole place to yourself," Doña Santos replied.

Me, Miriam—crime magnet—all alone in a big house near where a person was just shot. Great. That's just great.

Chapter Five

D elvis came to number seven Caleta de las Monjas later that afternoon. We sat in the living room and went over the itinerary for the next few days. She'd included biographies of the local cooks I would be interviewing and places we'd be visiting.

"Qué bueno que vamos por el área de Loíza. I visited a few of the neighborhoods during a study trip for my master's. The community has such a strong pride and connection to their Yoruba ancestors. There is so much culture to explore," I said.

"I knew you'd be up for it," Delvis said. She gingerly put her hand over her bicep.

I could see a little bit of tape under her short sleeve. "New tattoo?"

"¡Ay! Yeah, I got it a few hours ago. It's starting to ache a little." She raised the fabric of her red T-shirt. "It's a Taíno sun."

From under the taped protective plastic covering, I made out the ancient symbol that I'd also seen in its petroglyph form. The sun had a simple face, eyes, and mouth, and the rays reminded me of a child's drawing of a daisy.

"Yo sé que es early for dinner, pero I want to take you to one of my favorite places before la rumba gets going," Delvis said.

"¿Qué rumba?" I tidied the papers into a stack with plans to review them before bed.

"Chica, it's New Year's Eve. Oh, I almost forgot." She unzipped her fanny pack and removed a lanyard. "The party is at El Morro. Just make an appearance. I know you might not want to stay pero Ileana y *La Tacita* crew will be there filming the fireworks. So, you know, it's good to show face. ¿Entiendes?"

I understood. It was advised, wink, wink, that I attend. I coiled the UnMundo necklace on top of the itinerary, with the VIP pass facing up. "Sí. I get you. I'll go early and leave before the fireworks if that's okay. Do I need to dress up? Because, like, I didn't pack anything."

"No, but I'll have wardrobe drop a few things off. Put on your walking shoes. The restaurant is a few blocks away."

My sneakers didn't go with my cotton bib sundress, but I was glad I had the comfy shoes anyway. Old San Juan was built on a hill. Although Manny and I did a lot of walking around our Coral Shores neighborhood, it was all flat.

The crime tape that had blocked the road earlier had been broken and now flapped in the breeze. The curious onlookers were gone. *But I'm still curious to know what exactly happened.* As we passed El Convento, I looked down the garbage can alley. There was a uniformed police officer standing guard by an employee door and one forensic person in a white jumpsuit kneeling on the ground. *Budget cuts? Or was the crime already solved? Maybe it wasn't a crime. Maybe it was self-inflicted.*

"Dame un segundo," I said. I put my foot on the hipped foundation of the building and untied my shoelace to retie it. Delvis checked her messages while she waited for me.

The officer was the same man that I had seen put up the no pase escena de crimen tape. He stood on the steps of the back exit. His eyes were on the tech taking samples. I tried to see what the tech was doing, but the half-sized dumpster blocked my view. A figure came from the other end of the alley. It was Welmo. He had two cans of soda and offered one to the police officer. Their body language told me they knew each other pretty well. Welmo moved to the top step and under the cover of the recessed doorway, but not before seeing me. He put a finger over his mouth and jutted his chin toward his cousin on the sidewalk. Then he slipped out of sight.

What is he up to?

"You good?" Delvis asked, her head still down.

"Yeah. I did a double knot." I wiggled my shoe for her to see. She put her phone in her pack, and we moved up the hill.

"How long ago was this a convent?" I asked. The hotel was directly across from a cathedral, and the lane where UnMundo had their guesthouse was named after the nuns.

"I think like 1650 until no sé 1900 o algo así. It became a hotel in the sixties." Delvis stopped in her tracks to face me. "Siempre es la misma mierda. Americans getting tax-free status to invest in the island, but the Boricuas get nothing but taxation without representation."

I'd never seen Delvis so emotional. She could be focused and intense about work but still always chill. This was anger. I knew a good bit about the colonial status of Puerto Rico. The United States had been taking advantage of the island for hundreds of years. If it wasn't using its beaches as target practice like in Vieques, it was using its people as guinea pigs for medicines and poultry growth hormones.

"They practically gave the hotel to one of the Woolworth heirs. It was called Project Bootstrap. *Pull the poor peasants up by their bootstraps.* Que malparidos. And the same thing is happening again. Un montón de americanos coming to the island, buying up property tax-free, and kicking out the locals. Ahora es los Bitcoin bros. Te lo juro." She inhaled. "I swear it makes me so angry."

I guessed my frozen face brought her back to her usual demeanor. She gave me a hug and then took a deep breath.

"Okay, I got that out of my system. Let's eat," Delvis said.

That is the second time in less than six hours that someone has mentioned Bitcoin. I need to ask Robert what the hell it is, and why people are so passionate about it.

By the time we'd hiked the four blocks up Calle Sol to the restaurant, my calf muscles were burning. The establishment had a mint-green exterior. There was a line of cruise ship tourists at the door. Through the street-level Juliet balconies, I could see the place was bustling.

"El Jibarito is your favorite place?" I asked. "I've eaten here. The food is good, but it's very touristy."

"I know, but some locals still eat here. And like you said, the food is good." Delvis excused us past the crowd and to the front of the line, where she gave the hostess a kiss on the cheek.

The hostess wore a sleeveless T-shirt and jeggings, and a frilly, old-fashioned apron was tied around her waist. Her earrings were flags, and her eyes smiled despite the fatigue that made her face sag. She pointed over her shoulder to an empty two-top and gave Delvis a menu.

"Gracias, tía," Delvis said.

"That's your aunt?" I asked.

"Yeah. Welmo's mom."

"I wish you had introduced me."

"I will when she comes by the table. What are you having?"

I looked at the simple laminated menu. It had all the standard fare; "standard," in this case, meant classic and delicious. Alcapurrias. Pasteles. Pollo en salsa criolla. Carne guisada.

Mofongo.

Mofongo.

Mofongo.

Trifongo.

They had all three kinds—breadfruit, plantain, and yuca—plus a trifongo that was green plantains, ripe plantains, and yuca.

"I know what I want. But I have to go easy on the fried foods because of the baby. Will you share some sorullitos with me if I order them?" I asked, referring to the fried corn sticks.

"Dale."

Delvis and the waitress, Welmo's sister, exchanged some friendly banter before we placed our order.

The sorrulitos came out first with a mayo-ketchup dip. I loved the sweet corn fingers and dunked one into the dip. The crunch of the crispy outside contrasted with the smooth, creamy insides, along with the mildly tart dip, was perfection. Sometimes they were made with cheese in the center, but I preferred the plain version.

"Does your family own the restaurant?" I asked.

"No, it's just my tía and prima that work here." Delvis took the last stick and bit into it.

"We should do an episode on sorullitos. I'll have to research their origin and development. Corn. Does Puerto Rico grow a lot of corn?" I looked around at the restaurant's décor. The interior walls had been brightly painted to resemble buildings around a town square. Above the small bar was a sepia drawing of a man in a straw hat with unwoven reeds instead of a wide brim. The hat, called a pava, was a national symbol of pride. So was the figure wearing it. A jibaro, from whence the place took its name, was a person from the countryside—a person of the land, a subsistence farmer. In the Cuban idiom, the equivalent was güajiro. Humble roots from a less industrial time.

"Miriam, earth to Miriam." Delvis waved a hand in front of my face.

"Huh?"

"What planet were you on?"

"Sorry, I went from corn to farmers to plazas to commerce and then back to the countryside," I replied.

"What, the jibarito? Yeah, the island is more than beaches, forts, and El Yunque. The mountains are beautiful. There's a little bit of everything, Caves, cows, coffee."

"Comida." Her alliteration was interrupted by the arrival of our food.

I'd ordered the chillo frito, a whole red snapper fried in a light dusting of flour. *La Sirena demands her fish.* For the side dish, I'd chosen mofongo de pana/breadfruit. Delvis's dish was pollo en salsa criolla with a side of arroz y habichuelas.

"Can I steal a taste?" I asked with my spoon over the saucy red beans. She pushed the small bowl toward me. The well-seasoned beans had a slight sweetness from the calabaza chunks used in the stewing. "Delicioso."

We chatted about the filming locations and personalities Delvis had lined up for me to interview. We passed on dessert even though they had a great selection of flans—coco, queso, vainilla, Nutella, almendras, y pistacho. *Pistachio? Maybe I should get it to go. I've never tried that flavor of flan. I'm curious.*

We said goodbye en la calle, and I promised to make an appearance at the event later. Instead of walking back the way I'd come, I found my way to Calle San Francisco and Plaza de Armas. The plaza was filled with people, tourists and locals alike. It had been the town center hundreds of years ago and still had that feel. There was a fountain with four sculptures that were either the seasons or the cardinal points. At an oblong kiosk that looked like it should be near the Paris Metro, I purchased a sesame drink called anjonjolí and a bottle of water. City Hall took up an entire side of the plaza. On its arched balcony were three large papier-mâché effigies wearing crowns—Gaspar, Melchor, and Baltazar.

I found a bench and sat to enjoy my sesame milk. A young girl fed a flock of pigeons. *I wish Manny was here.* I got my phone and video-called Mami.

"Hola, nena. ¿Come te ha ido en Puerto Rico?" my mother asked.

"Everything is fine. I met with my director. ¿Manny está cerca? I want to show him something."

"Un segundito." The video got bouncy as my mother walked onto the patio to find my father and son playing dominoes. Well, not playing the game but building with them. She passed the phone to my son.

"¡Mami!" Manny squealed.

"Mi príncipe," I replied with the endearment I'd called him since he was a baby.

He told me all about making a tres leches cake with Abuela and helping Abuelo move palm fronds. I showed him the Three Kings, the Christmas tree, and the other holiday decorations in the plaza. He asked about the bronze man on the bench with whom people were taking photos. I had to read the plaque to answer him. It was a sculpture of the salsa composer Tito Curet Alonso. The tourists were enjoying taking goofy photos with it. Then there was a sudden cacophony of beating wings as the pigeons took flight because of a running toddler. Manny jumped in his seat with excitement. *I wish he was here.*

"Te quiero. Besitos. Pásale el teléfono a tu abuelo," I said.

My dad took the phone. His face looked haggard. "¿Que te pasa, Papi?" I asked him.

"Nada, niña. *Just un long day.* Tuvimos un poquito de lluvia y parece que el agua entró en una de las casas." Papi scratched the stubble on his chin and let out an exhausted sigh.

Rain from the roof had gotten into one of the villas. And I suspected from his weary sigh that the guests had probably pitched a fit. Or maybe not, but it still wasn't good. I hoped the damage wasn't too bad and that it was easily repairable.

"Pero, *don't worry, be happi*. El año viejo has his suitcase packed y the new year viene. Feliz año nuevo, mi'ja." Papi turned the lens to my mother and Manny.

"No te olvides de tus uvas," Mami warned me. It was a tradition practiced in many Latinx and Hispanic homes. You had to eat twelve grapes for good luck before the clock struck to signal the new year.

"No te preocupes, Mami. Lo prometo." I promised her. *UnMundo will have them. Right? Probably in champagne flutes. I'll grab one to go.* I sent them air kisses before disconnecting from the call.

Throwing away my paper cup, I slipped the water bottle into my dress pocket and pulled my three-quarter sleeve white cardigan across my chest. The temperature had dropped a few degrees with the setting sun. Not knowing the exact street to take but knowing I wasn't too far from the guesthouse, I headed downhill toward the bay. As I passed restaurants and stores, there was a festive vibration in the air. A group with matching shirts that read *Dodson Family Reunion* shouted, "Happy New Year!" in a Southern drawl as they parted to let me through.

At the end of San Francisco Street, I turned onto Clara Lair, parallel to the city wall. To my left was the Puerta de San Juan. I wanted to rest my feet before the party, but the chance to take in the historic sites of the city won out. Walking through the sixteen-foot-high and twenty-foot-thick opening in the fortress wall gave me a chill. Hundreds of thousands of people have been through that gate, many of them in shackles. The name "Puerto Rico" translated to "rich port." It was named that because it was one of the busiest commerce ports during colonial times. People, gold, sugar, tobacco—it all came through the heavily guarded gate.

Barbacoa, Bomba, and Betrayal

All that wealth and none of it for the island's people. Coño. Igual que hoy. Puerto Rico is still being taken advantage of by outsiders. It's still a colony in practice, if not in name.

I took a few photos of the romantically lit Paseo de la Princesa promenade outside the wall. *I wonder if it was named after a specific princess. Pfft, probably a Spanish one.* Then I read the Latin inscription above the gate. Benedictus oui venit in nomine domini— Welcome those who come in the name of God. *Whose god? Not the gods of the Indigenous people. Or the orishas of the Yoruba enslaved.* My thoughts had taken a turn thinking about the plunder of the island. Papi's problems with the property were also worrying me. My sirena kicked, and I got out of my negative headspace.

"¿Qué quieres, mi sirena?" I whispered. "Do you want to see the water?" I walked a few paces to where I could see the bay. I thought about the watermelon Mami had made me throw into the ocean. As I listened to the waves lapping the patch of playita below, the chorus of a Celia Cruz song praising Yemaya came back to me. I sang it to myself as I walked through the gate.

Back on Clara Lair Street, I walked uphill two short blocks to Caleta de las Monjas. Stopping at the corner, I unscrewed the water bottle cap for a drink.

"¡No!" an angry and frustrated voice yelled.

Is that Doña Santos?

I looked around the corner of the building. It was her. She was arguing with a man on the sidewalk between the UnMundo house and her house. He shook his finger at her, but I couldn't hear his words. Doña Santos waved his hand from her face and turned a cold shoulder to him. The man reached to grab her as if to turn her back around. I didn't know what was happening, but I didn't like it.

"Tía, ya llege," I shouted with forced joy. Doña Santos looked confused at my calling her my aunt, but she played along.

"Por fin, nena." She moved away from the man and opened her arms for a hug.

I felt a hard gaze from the man but couldn't see his face in the dim and murky evening light. He spun around to leave and raised his hands as he mumbled something that felt like a threat. One of El Convento's wall lamps glinted off the man's watch as his arms came down.

"¿Quién era ese hombre?" I asked her.

"Nadie. Nobody. Don't worry about it." She took my arm and led me to the guesthouse door. "A package came for you. I put it on your bed." She tucked a stray strand of hair behind her ear. She patted my forearm before releasing me to unlock the door. "Buenas noches y felíz año nuevo."

"Felíz año nuevo," I replied, returning her new year's greeting. Then I watched her as she went into the adjacent property.

Who was that guy?

Why was he threatening her?

Who would want to threaten a sweet old lady?

Chapter Six

"Hey, babe."

"Hola, mi amor." I puckered my lips at my husband's face and sent him a kiss. "How's Coral Shores? How's Camo?"

Robert panned the lens to his lap. Our calico cat, Camo, was curled up and purring.

"Awww," I cooed.

"How are you doing? How's the baby?"

"I'm fine. La Sirena's fine. Do you know anything about Bitcoin?"

"That's quite a segue," he said, laughing. "Please tell me you aren't getting paid in cryptocurrency."

"*Umm, no.* Why, is it bad?" I combed my black hair back into shape after my disco nap. That's what a prof from grad school called a nap before going out clubbing. I placed the wide-toothed comb on the linen runner that adorned the small vanity.

"Well, environmentally, it takes a lot of energy to mine the coins."

"Wait, they're real coins? I thought they were, like, digital for video games or something." I propped the phone on a pillow and unzipped the wardrobe bag that had been dropped off to Doña Santos.

"They are digital. They're code hidden across the internet, and it takes a lot of terawatts to find them. Which means thousands of computers. Which means electricity. Which creates heat. And then there are the caustic batteries, which take scarce resources. One Bitcoin transaction uses more energy than the average household uses in seventy days. Seventy!"

"Okay, I get it, Mr. Environmental Engineer. You are becoming more and more green and less engineer-y." I chuckled. His expression signaled he was mildly hurt. "And I love it! I love the green Roberto." I blew more kisses, then held up a silver cocktail dress to my body.

"Pretty. Is that new?" He shifted in his seat and leaned into the screen.

"It's from the studio. There's a party tonight." I stepped over to the mirror. The silver-gray dress had long sleeves and a sparkly cord belt. It had a stretchy—*gracias a La Caridad*—slip under the gathered chiffon. The mid-thigh length made it youthful; otherwise, it would have been more mother-of-the-bride.

"You've been invited to a crypto New Year's Eve party?"

"*No*. It's for the UnMundo party at El Morro. But there is a Bitcoin convention at the hotel on the corner," I replied as I sat on the bed to finish our conversation. As I moved the black wardrobe bag, a pair of fancy sandals shifted out. The soles were like paper, and their strappy cords were like ballerina laces.

"I bet I know who it is."

I gave him a quizzical look.

"There's this guy named Brandon Pickles. He's like the king of Bitcoin. Drew's ranted about him. He says it's a pyramid scheme. The first tier makes all the money. The rest are just worker bees feeding the queen—in this case, the king." Robert raised his eyebrows in a silent guffaw.

Drew, the middle of the Smith brothers, was finance-savvy and a lawyer. I trusted his opinion.

"What are you doing tonight? The country club with your mother and the Smith clan?"

"No way. My mother is in time-out after the way she acted when you were in the hospital. You and the baby could have been *seriously* hurt. Marjory had no right to complain and guilt-trip you about the gala. You did an amazing job. The event was perfect."

Except for the part when the chef died, I got pushed into a refrigerator, and the killer got away. Except for that, the party was great. At least Robert was finally seeing his mother for the bitter, controlling woman she was.

Camo's tail filled the screen. She was awake from her own little disco nap and ready for her hunt-for-lizards party. *Poor little anoles don't have a chance.* After she leaped off his lap, Robert stood up.

"Espérate, something looks different," I said as I caught a glimpse of our living room.

"Yeah, I rearranged the furniture a little bit."

"*Why?*" It wasn't that I cared, but he'd never taken an interest in interior design before.

"Well . . . so . . . um, so you know how I love my Star Wars and Marvel movies, right? And you know that I *love* stringing up the sheet in the backyard for Manny and the cousins to watch a Disney movie. But, babe, it's just not cutting it for grown-up stuff."

"What did you do?" I asked, trying to control my boiling anger. We'd agreed not to have a big TV. A laptop was good enough if we wanted to watch something in bed together. But we didn't want Manny's childhood to be dominated by passive entertainment.

Robert slowly turned the camera to the wall. "Now, before you freak out, look. It's a piece of art when it's off."

"Que mier—"

He cut me off before I could get going on the string of profanity that was about to boil over. "Look-look-look." He turned the paused superhero movie off, and the screen became a replica of a painting complete with a frame. "See. It's one of Winslow Homer's Caribbean paintings. I picked it because I thought you'd like it. But if you don't like it, there are hundreds to choose from."

I actually did like it. I liked the red flowers against the blue sky and the sea at the horizon just above the white wall. It oozed island vibes. But I couldn't let him get off scot-free for not communicating with me about it. After he'd bought a Tesla without telling me, the new rule was no big household purchases without letting the other person know about it beforehand.

He'd made improvements in the mother department, but my husband's communication skills about money were still mierda.

Miriam, marriage is always a work in progress. At least it's not a putting green in the backyard. Cuidado, don't give him ideas.

I grumbled at Robert for a second but then chose to let it go. There were bigger problems in the world than a man who wanted a movie marathon.

"Feliz año nuevo, mi amor. I'll talk to you tomorrow."

"Night, babe. I'm going to call your mom in a few and talk to Manny. They'll still be up, right? I miss the little man. I miss you too," Robert said.

"They'll be up until midnight. Manny is getting Cubanized. By the time we get home, I bet he'll be slamming back espressos." I laughed at the image in my head—our little four-year-old with a drawn-on mustache and a pretend cigar playing dominoes with my dad and drinking Cuban coffee.

We ended the video chat, and I finished getting dressed. At ten, I locked the guesthouse and headed up the hill to the party. Passing the alley where the man had been shot, I remembered

Welmo's secretive behavior. Why hadn't he wanted his cousin to know he was there?

El Convento was humming with activity. Revelers with paper hats and plastic beads were coming in and out of the hotel. Electronic dance music escaped each time the door opened. I'd chosen to take the slightly longer but better-lit route to El Morro. As I passed Plaza San Jose, I saw a familiar figure.

"¿Jorge?" I called.

The man looked over his shoulder, recognized me, and did a turnabout worthy of an ice skater.

"¡Miriam!"

We closed the distance between us and hugged.

"What are you doing in Puerto Rico?" I asked.

Jorge was many things—a fitness instructor, a drag queen, an amateur makeup artist—but most importantly, he was a friend. He was Alma's friend first, but after he and I had saved a man, my neighbor who'd been poisoned, we had a bond.

"Do you remember Prince *Char*-ming?" Jorge gave a dramatic pause. "Well, I am now his princess." He showed off the new diamond and gold bracelet on his wrist.

"Wow. He bought you *that*. Coño, that's a chunk of change. I thought I saw sparks between you. *Sooo*—when's the wedding? I introduced you, so, like, I get front-row seats, no?" I took his arm, and we kept walking.

"Cálmate, chica. You know he is not out-out, yet. So, I'm keeping a low profile. We are in separate apartments pero only using one bed, if you know what I mean."

"Ay, Jorge," I said. I didn't want my friend's heart to get broken if Prince Charming was playing him. Y a la misma vez, I was sad that the young UnMundo celebrity didn't feel safe being his true self in public. Latin American culture was very gendered, but machismo was on the decline, and the rainbow flag was being flown proudly in most cities—the countryside, not so much. UnMundo was in 122 countries and had a viewership of 9.3 million. "Be my date tonight."

"Okay, pero no voy a decir que I'm the father of your bebe," Jorge said with a head waggle.

We both laughed loudly as we crested the hill. A few strides on Calle Norzagaray took us to El Morro's lawn. I stretched my arm high and took a selfie of us with the Spanish fortress behind us. The fort was lit dramatically, and people were laying picnic blankets on the long open space to watch the fireworks at midnight. I heard beer bottles clinking and cans opening. The moon and stars were bright about the dark ocean. White-capped waves lined the shore. I sent the photo to Alma and wished her good fortune and health for the new year.

A supersized golf cart with a magnetic UnMundo sign on its front came down the long walkway. Its driver noticed my VIP lanyard and offered us a ride to the party. I was thankful for the steps saved. In about two minutes, we were at the fort wall, giving our names to a woman with a tablet and a head mic. She must have been part of the local affiliate because I didn't recognize her as one of the Miami crew. She'd recognized me and marked me arrived on her screen quickly. But she was having difficulty finding Jorge's name. I could feel Jorge's mood changing.

"Si no se puede encontrar, márcalo como mi plus one," I said, offering her a quick solution to the guest list problem.

"No, no, no. Ya lo encontré. Jules Howard," the young woman said. She showed us the name on the glowing screen.

Jules Howard. Isn't that the name of the real estate guy staying at my parent's place? What is he doing here?

"No, mi nombre es Jorge Trujillo." There was an edge to my friend's voice. I felt like we might have a takedown moment brewing.

"Ay, perdóname. Aquí está tu nombre." She'd found Jorge's name. "Pasa y que lo disfruten." She undid the red velvet rope and let us pass.

We walked through the tunnel that had witnessed five hundred years of footsteps and into the rectangular muster plaza. There were bars at each end. In an archway that had once led to soldiers' sleeping quarters there was a smaller version of *La Tacita*'s living room set. There were potted palms, a white sofa with a matching chair, and a low coffee table decorated for the festivities. The sturdy tripod video camera was unmanned.

"I need a drink," Jorge proclaimed. "You want me to get you a water or a juice?"

"No, I'm okay for now." The bumpy cart ride had not been kind to my bladder. "Go find your prince. I'll catch up in a second."

I scanned the two hundred or so guests, looking for a sandy-blond head. Most of the rubias were women, but then I saw a paper-white smile. Jules was chatting with three tall men. One of them said something that caused the group to toss their heads back in collective laughter. I started to move toward them, but a hand grabbed my elbow.

"Miriam, que bueno que estás aquí," Ileana Ruiz, *La Tacita*'s host and my boss, said. We kissed cheeks and greeted each other warmly. "I want you on the couch."

Ileana snapped her fingers, and a woman in an apron materialized to powder my face. The plastic apron had rows of pockets filled with brushes, blushes, brow pencils, and more. Before I could protest, she was applying lipstick and darkening my eyebrows.

I tried to keep my eyes on Jules, but it was hard when I felt like my face was in a car wash with brushes flying and spinning around it. The makeup artist declared she was done, and I was led to the set by a PA, a production assistant. As I sat, I took another look at the jovial group. Jules and the tallest of the men shook hands. The man slapped Jules's back, and they headed toward the free-flowing liquor.

"Sorry, I didn't know she was going to put you on tonight," Delvis said from between the palms.

"Oh, hi. Yeah, um, what am I supposed to say?" I asked my director.

"I don't know what she's planning to ask you. But tease the locations we'll be visiting. You read the notes, right?" Delvis propped a pillow behind my back, forcing me to sit erect. Then she came around and fanned out the fabric of my skirt. "Okay, don't move too much. You look great. Just smile. I know you hate live, but you are going to be fine. You got this, chica. You're a star."

I'm a star that is about to explode. Where's the bathroom? I didn't know if it was nerves or the baby, but I squeezed my legs tighter and prayed the torture would be over soon.

The apron lady dulled Ileana's shiny forehead in a dervish of powder. Then the host sat on the couch. Our knees inches apart and our legs crossed at the ankles, we mirrored each other like a Rorschach inkblot. The hot lights popped on. Delvis stood beside the camera and looked at me with a toothy and scary grin. She used her index fingers to draw a smile in the air.

Oh! Me. You want me to smile. Okay. Got it. I probably looked catatonic as I did, in fact, feel immobile. What was it about live TV that freaked me out? I breathed in through my nose and turned up the corners of my mouth. Ileana asked a softball question—something like, Didn't I love Viejo San Juan's beauty, and what had I seen that day?—and stuck the mic in my face. Instinctually, I mentioned the gate and El Jibarito. I found that if I looked at her right earring—a long, drippy, chandelier-style

42

thing—I couldn't see the camera, and it was more like a conversation with a friend. She kept feeding me leading questions about the foods and local cooks we'd be visiting. She made it easy for me to sound knowledgeable, like I'd chosen the people and places. Her last question was a little personal, but she'd warmed me up so that I'd become comfortable.

"¿Y cómo está él bebe? ¿En cuáles nombres estás pensando?"

"No sabemos el sexo, pero por ahora yo estoy llamando al bebé La Sirena."

"¡La Sirena, mi encanta! Y la fecha de nacimiento?"

I told her the due date was May and that we were prerecording shows so that the audience would have fresh *Cocina Caribeña* and *Abuela Approved* content while I was on maternity leave.

Ileana announced the guest who would be taking my place on the couch after the break and reminded the viewers to prepare their grapes for the countdown. I joined her in wishing the audience a happy new year, and then the camera went to standby.

From the other side of the coffee table, Delvis said, "Good job. That was great. Here. I got you a bottle of water."

I took the bottle, which had the UnMundo logo on it, and stood. Delvis held my elbow as I stepped over the cables and off set. As my eyes adjusted to the lower light of the party, I was startled by Jules Howard.

"A little cooking show—I didn't know you were an *international* star," he said.

I swiveled toward him. "I didn't know you would be in Puerto Rico."

"Just for a few days, then back to my vacation. A colleague invited me to a party, and I couldn't say no. Bad for business." He tinkled the ice in his glass, releasing the vanilla and oak aromas of the Don Q añejo rum. "Can I get you a drink?"

I held up my water bottle and pointed to my basketball belly.

"Oh, I forgot." Jules laughed, embarrassed.

"So, you are friends with one of the UnMundo executives?" I asked. The men he'd been talking to weren't on-air talent, *at least that I knew*. "Are you developing a property show for the network?"

He looked at me glassy-eyed. How many drinks had he had?

"A property show—that's not a bad idea. I'll have to pitch that to Pablo."

"You're friends with Pablo Montoya, the CEO of UnMundo?"

"Yeah, he's an old buddy. We went to business school together," Jules replied.

I'd only guessed that his tall friends were execs. At forty-one, Pablo Montoya was the youngest CEO of a major entertainment network. A fact I'd learned from Delvis when she had fangirled over his portrait on the wall of our Miami studio.

"You'll have to excuse me. I see someone I need to speak to," I said. Welmo or someone that looked like him had just ducked behind a stanchion and into the darkness of a tunnel.

"Well, it was great seeing you. Happy New Year. Maybe we'll run into each other again at your parents' place. It needs a little work, but it has great potential. Carmen and Luis are so nice. That property is a lot of work for just the two of them."

How many rums have you had? Jules was rambling, and I was going to lose Welmo if I didn't move on.

"Okay. See you soon. Happy New Year!" I left him and his LED-bright smile.

When I got to the tunnel, I saw a figure, close to the wall, in the murkiest part, scurry down the steep decline. There was no way I was going to risk following him. My baby belly made my balance weird, and my sandals had no tread. Also, it seemed who-ever it was didn't want to be identified by me.

I returned to the party. Tatiana and Wichi, the network's dance show stars, were on the couch with Ileana. Music from a parranda band began playing. The holiday tradition of the travel-ing musical party was a vibrant part of Puerto Rican culture. The band had several tamboras (a two-sided drum), a cuatro (a four-string guitar), güiros made from gourds, palitos, a trumpeter, and a set of panderos (small, medium, and large) that looked like tam-bourines without the cymbals. The musicians crowded around the *La Tacita* set. Two PAs stealthily removed the coffee table so the dance duo could perform to the bomba being played. When the heavily percussive tune was over, the crowd erupted in applause.

The music had drawn all the partygoers away from the bars. The audience demanded "De Las Montañas Venimos" and the band responded with high energy. Feeling a little claustrophobic in the hip-shaking fun, I squeezed my way out of the pack. I saw Jorge and Prince Charming traipsing off into the shadows for a clandestine smooch. I texted him that I'd call him tomorrow and saw the glow of his phone when he read it.

With drumbeats resounding off the fort walls, I left the party. The golf cart and its driver were at the red velvet rope, and I asked for a ride. It was eleven thirty, and the blankets on the thirty-acre lawn had tripled. The fireworks would start at midnight, and the parties would go on until three or four. I hoped I'd be able to get some sleep so I'd be rested for tomorrow's shoot. *Welmo said he'd be by to get me tomorrow. Did I really see him at the fort?*

"Perdóname, señor," I said to the driver.

"Yes," he replied.

"Do you know anything about the shooting that happened this morning near El Convento?" Locals usually knew all the rumors.

"It wasn't a tourista. San Juan is *very* safe for touristas," the barely twenty-year-old guy said, a bit too practiced for my liking. "It was personal, un argumento. Don't worry. You are safe."

Personal. Yeah, shooting someone within arm's reach is definitely personal.

And I wasn't worried about my safety until just then.

My young chauffeur stopped the cart when we reached the street. I thanked him for the lift and got out. I took the same well-lit path home. The streets were filled with people. Musica urbana battled with salsa as revelers entered and exited the bars. At the corner of Calle Sol y Calle Cristo, I saw Jules Howard somewhat tipsily mount the steps to El Convento with Welmo a stride behind him.

What is Welmo up to? Could Jules have something to do with the man in the alley?

I was at the hotel door before I thought better of it. *Miriam, no seas boba. This is none of your business. Go to bed.*

I followed the pair through the courtyard and to a gate that separated the publicly accessible areas from the guest areas. Jules fumbled with his key but eventually opened the black gate. A second before it shut, Welmo jammed the toe of his shoe into the opening and slipped into the inner sanctum of the hotel. I looked through the rails and saw them disappear into an elevator. The electronic dance music I'd heard earlier was still going and seemed to be coming from a rooftop terrace. There were banners and posters in the courtyard advertising the Bitcoin conference. One of the banners was of a coin imprinted with a Japanese Shiba Inu wearing sunglasses. Around the dog's neck was a rapper's gold chain from which hung an emerald-encrusted pickle.

Is that what the coins look like? Like play money.

My sirena kicked, and I knew I needed to get back to the guesthouse. I went through the lobby and exited the hotel on Caleta de las Monjas. I shoved the key into number seven's lock, opened the door, and deposited my little purse on the hall table as I dashed into the bathroom. When I emerged, I heard a string of firecrackers pop and crackle.

No point in going to bed now!

I took my key and phone and went outside to watch the fireworks at the end of the street. A handful of people had the same idea. We all stood in the triangular plaza with the sculpture and looked at the sky over San Juan Bay. A woman about Doña Santos's age began counting down.

Doce, once, diez, . . .

Coño, I forgot my grapes.

The woman that was counting had plastic baggies with twelve grapes in each. She offered one to me, and I took it with gratitude. Quickly, I ate my uvas for good luck. As I stuffed the last one into my mouth, the sky lit up with red, blue, and white fireworks. There was a shared gasp of awe and delight from all of us in the plaza. A volley of pink and green pom-pom-style fireworks came next. The smell of sulfur and gunpowder drifted on the breeze. After a few more rounds of colorful magic, my sirena showed her displeasure with the sonic booms, and I called it a night. I thanked the grapes lady again and went to number seven, key in hand. Vaquita and her white-stocking companion crossed the street in front of me.

Stepping over the threshold, I saw a piece of paper had been slipped under the door. I looked up and down the street to see if its deliverer was still in sight. The only people I saw were the ones I'd just left. I opened the folded note. A single sentence was written in pencil.

You'll sell, or you'll be sorry.

Chapter Seven

Tocino. Yum.

It took me a second to remember I was in the UnMundo guesthouse. The smell of bacon frying had drifted into my room and tickled my nose. I got up and stretched. Last night's threatening and anonymous note, coupled with a strange bed, had made for a fitful sleep. The sounds of bottle rockets, singing revelers, and creaky stairs hadn't helped either. I'd gone so far as to block the bedroom door with the vanity's bench seat, as if such a minor obstacle would've impeded an intruder. Rubbing the sleep from my eyes, I noticed the bedroom door was cracked open an inch.

I'm sure that was Doña Santos giving me a gentle wake-up nudge. Right? Right.

As I did my morning routine, I checked my text messages. There were New Year's wishes from my friend Pepper, my sister-in-law Sally, and Robert's cousin Gordon. His message had a picture of him and Omarosa toasting with champagne flutes. I'd introduced the pair, and I was sensing that it was a true love match. Omarosa was the sister of my cousin Yoli's fiancée, Bette. That pair had also sent greetings.

Ayyyy, I miss everyone. Sirena, are you pumping out extra hormone weirdness today?

I dabbed my weepy eyes with a tissue. My fragile state was probably a combination of travel, a late night, work anxiety, and the pregnancy roller coaster. I needed to hear my straight-talking BFF's voice.

Bubble-tone. Bubble-tone.

"Dímelo cantando," Alma said. Her upper torso filled the small screen. It looked like she was at her kitchen sink with the phone propped on the sill. She had a prosecco bottle poised over a glass of jugo de naranja.

"Aren't you bright and bubbly this morning? Mimosa? Is the party still going, or did you actually sleep?" I asked.

"I slept like a baby." A wicked smile and a wink accompanied her statement.

"I wish I could say the same. Chica, this place is lovely, and I'm grateful and all, but it's big and old, and I'm the only one staying here y deja mi decirte que I got a little freaked out last night, you know, haunted house vibes. I wish you were here with me," I whined.

I heard bare feet on the tile in Alma's kitchen. She took the phone from the windowsill and smashed it against her chest so I couldn't see who she was *KISSING*.

"I'll call you back," she said.

The screen closed, and the call ended.

OMG, who was that? Alma had a date—a date who is still at her house!

My mind was spinning with questions. I was so happy to see her happy. I wondered if it was serious. My bestie was devoted to her career and didn't care about getting married. She'd also vowed to be a tía and not a mom.

Still on a cloud of giddy excitement for my friend, I went downstairs to breakfast. At the bottom of the staircase, I heard Welmo's voice coming from the kitchen. He and Doña were speaking in Spanish. Something about the man that had been shot. "Falleció." He died. As I shifted my weight off the last step, the wood creaked, and their voices dropped to indiscernible garble.

"Buenos días, bella. ¿Como dormiste?" Doña asked.

I lied and told her I'd slept great.

"Good morning, Señora Quiñones," Welmo said. He politely stood until I sat opposite him at the table by the window.

"Call me Miriam, please."

"Miriam." He cocked his head and nodded in acquiescence. "How was your day yesterday? Where did my prima take you for dinner?"

"El Jibarito," I replied.

Welmo shook his head and chuckled. "So, you met my mother and my sister, no?"

I nodded and smiled.

Doña put a plate of huevos fritos al caballo con tocino y uno guineo in front of me along with a milky café and a glass of guava nectar. She then added a bread dish with a fluffy Mallorca bun. Welmo waited for me to take a bite, then resumed eating his meal. I pierced the fried egg's yolk with the side of my fork and let the gooey yellow run into the rice. The rice and egg were cooked perfectly. I ate two hungry mouthfuls before crunching into the crisp bacon.

"Deliciosa," I said to the cook. "¿No vas a comer con nosotros?"

"No, nena. Ya come. Disfruta. Si necesitas algo me avisa." She patted my back and told me to enjoy my meal without her and to call if I needed anything. Then she disappeared into the front of the house.

I tore off a piece of the powdered sugar–topped bread and dunked it into my weak café con leche. "This Mallorca tastes like it was made this morning," I said.

"Yes, she gets them from La Bombonera bakery on Calle San Francisco. It is their special—" Welmo held the L, searching for its proper ending.

"Specialty."

"Yes, that is the word. Specialty. Gracias." Welmo wiped his mouth with his napkin and leaned away from his plate. "The restaurant has the original coffee maker from 1910. I will take you so you can see it and you must try the horchata de chufa. It is very good."

"Chufa, that's tigernut, a grain from West Africa. Interesting. What does the horchata taste like?" I asked as I cut a slice of banana to eat with a piece of salty bacon. Most home meals in Puerto Rico were served with a banana. The island had many varieties, but their catchall name was guineo.

"It has canela,"

"Cinnamon," I translated to help him. His English vocabulary was oddly inconsistent.

"And lemon. Very nice on a hot day."

"I'll ask Delvis if we can fit in an interview with the owners."

"I will give you her name." Welmo took out a palm-sized spiral notebook and tore off a page. "She is the granddaughter of the original owner, who came from Mallorca, Spain."

I loved a third-generation family business, and it would make a great segment for *La Tacita*. Welmo loosened the tooth-marked pencil from its spiral cage and wrote the woman's name down for me.

"Okay, so we go now," Welmo said, looking at his analog watch. I wondered if it might have belonged to his father, as the glass was yellowed and the leather band was cracked.

"Dame cinco minutos." I drained half the glass of juice and ate the last crumb of bread before hustling back to my room.

Doña Santos had smoothed the wrinkles from the bedspread and sprayed lavender on the pillows. She'd also tied the drapes back and unlatched the bi-panel window. A little breeze tickled the sheer lace curtain. I stuffed the dossier Delvis had given me, which I'd looked at before bed, into a canvas satchel. Last night's ominous note floated to the floor from under the stack of papers. *I should show it to Doña and Welmo.*

"Miriam, tenemos que salir pronto," Welmo called up the stairs.

I picked it up and tucked it into the bag's inner pocket. *Later. I'll show it to her when I get back.*

The day's shoot, on the other side of the island, was the farthest away of them all. The traffic was light, perhaps due to hangovers. Autopista 52 took us past Caguas and Cayey. On the way, I video-called Manny and my parents.

"Feliz año, mi príncipe."

"Hola, Mami. Mira lo que yo dibujé." My son held his drawing in front of his chest. It had three figures on blue ovals, four boxy houses, and a giant head with green hair. *Oh, that's the big palm.*

"Wow, que artista," I complimented him. He went on to tell me the story of his masterpiece. The biggest circle with legs was Abuelo. He had a toolbox and sweat. The medium-sized figure was Abuela. She was holding a rat by its tail. And the littlest figure was Manny, and he had a wrench.

"Mami, don't worry, el ratón está muerto," my son said.

"¿Dónde estaba el ratón?" I asked with some concern as to what kind of place I'd left my child. My mom stopped watering the patio plants and came closer to the tablet. She filled in the missing details. I asked if it was the hutia that Papi had suspected of causing the damage to the pipe.

"No, era jutía. Era gris como los que vienen en los barcos," Mami said. She and my dad had concluded that the gray rat must have chewed its way into the water tank and drowned. Mystery solved.

I shook off the heebie-jeebies and made a funny face to cover up my disgust. I could only imagine what Marjory, my mother-in-law, would say if the story got back to her. "Miriam, you are an awful mother. I'm going to call the authorities and have your child taken away." *She wouldn't. She would.* Truly, I was fond of most of my husband's family. I wished I could say the same thing about Marjory. And I wished she wasn't invading my thoughts even while I was a thousand miles away.

I brought my attention back to the video call. Manny weaved a detailed story of his adventure in helping (aka passing tools to my dad) drain and clean the water tank. He said they'd all gotten soaking wet. He pointed to his drawing with a brown crayon like a professor to a whiteboard. A breeze blew through the patio and flipped the paper, revealing its backside. At the same time, my parent's Wi-Fi slowed and froze my son in an eyes-shut-mouth-open expression.

Is that a grocery list? I looked at my small screen, trying to figure out if he'd used an important piece of paper by mistake. The letters were large print—not my mother's perfect cursive. Only half of the words were visible: ELL OUSE. *El mouse? El house? Someone's Spanglish needs work.* The screen went black, and the Call Ended icon flashed. *Wi-Fi problems, again.*

I considered calling Mami's cell phone to finish our conversation, but Welmo slowed down to take an exit. The rest stop had no restrooms. *Carajo.* It was just a parking lot with a scenic vista and a statue. El Monumento al Jíbaro Puertorriqueño was a white monument of a man and a seated woman holding a baby. It was alone on a pedestal with Las Tetas de Cayey behind them. The pointy mountains had exposed tips but were mostly green with trees. The mountainous area was a nature preserve, according to

Welmo. I appreciated the chance to stretch my legs and breathe in the herbaceous bosque air. I let Welmo take a few pictures of me, and I took some of the statue and plaques. Back in the car, I posted them to my *Abuela Approved* Instagram using the Puerto Rico flag emoji and the coffee emoji. Welmo had informed me that the chain of mountains was a coffee region. I knew that from Delvis's dossier, but I let him enjoy his pride in his country.

After Ponce, we took the coastal 2-Oeste highway. It was nice to see the calm Caribbean Sea, a stark contrast to its rougher and wilder sibling, the Atlantic Ocean, on the island's northern side. In the town of Yauco, we passed a multihouse macromural with bold colors and geometric shapes. At the town's plaza, a fleet of white vans with UnMundo logos took up all the parking spaces in front of the handsome 1930s Catholic church.

I was admiring the impressive tan-and-beige Nuestra Señora del Rosario and its single bell tower, which made it bothersomely asymmetrical, when Delvis tapped me on the shoulder.

"We need to get you into makeup. We have two locations to visit today and several establishing shots we need to get," Delvis yawned.

"Establishing shots?" I asked.

"Yeah, you walking by a mural, eating ice cream, sitting on La Escalinata—you passed it on the way in, the steps painted with the town's yellow-and-black crest. And maybe one by the statue of Agüeybaná."

"The Taíno cacique. Oh, I'd like to see it even if we don't film it." The literature I'd read about the town said it had been the capital of Borikén, the Indigenous Taíno name for the island. Agüeybaná, the Great Sun, had been their principal chief at the time of the conquistadors' arrival. "Um, where's the bathroom?" I accentuated my urgency by pointing to the cause—La Sirena.

"Come with me. I'll show you." Delvis yawned again.

"What time did you get to bed last night?" I asked.

"I didn't." She laughed. "Good thing we're in the coffee capital."

Back at the vans, I was introduced to the local crew, who were red-eyed but jolly. They were assembling equipment. One of the vans had a mini production studio in it. The guy at the console was playing a video game on his laptop. He closed it, and I noticed it had a Bitcoin sticker on it. It was the same one I'd seen in the hotel lobby of the dog with the pickle.

"And here is the makeup room." Delvis opened the panel door of a van with extra headroom.

"Surprise!" a familiar voice said.

"Jorge! ¿Comó?" I asked.

"No sé que paso pero Lucas got a text that someone was sick and if I could fill in," Jorge said. "So, close your mouth and get in the chair."

I did as I was told and listened to my friend tell me all about his and Prince Charming's evening. They'd gone to the Bitcoin party after the fireworks. Lucas, Prince Charming, was curious about the famous Brandon Pickles, so they'd crashed the rooftop soiree.

"Supposedly, the pepinillo guy is like superfamous or algo. Like, some people love him because, you know, money and celebrity, pero some people, like, think he is the devil—un nuevo Colón, a colonizer taking advantage of the island." Jorge brushed my hair and added some product to it to make it shine.

"¿Y tú? What do you think? Did you see him at the party?"

"I don't care about digital dog money, pero tiene que ser legit because that pickle necklace he wears is serious money." Jorge measured about ten inches using a makeup brush handle. "All diamonds and esmeraldas. Super tacky but the real thing. Nothing sparkles like real gems." He lovingly stroked the bracelet Lucas had given him.

"Espérate. The pickle on the dog is real?' I asked.

"Sí. The pickle y el perro are real. The dog was at the party too. They both have necklaces." Jorge raised one eyebrow and screwed his lips.

"Who are you talking about?" Delvis was at the van's door holding a large steaming coffee.

Yum, coffee. I want you. I miss you.

"Brandon Pickles," I said.

"*The Bitcoin king.* He's bad for the island. I wish people would see it. My friend is organizing a protest against him." Delvis took a gulp of her drink.

"What are they protesting?" I asked.

"He's buying up a lot of property, kicking out the residents, and raising the rents," she informed us.

"Ay Dios, was that what that was about anoche? Someone at the party tried to throw red paint on him pero *security,*" Jorge said security in an SNL skit voice, "caught the guy before they could do it." He undid the apron around my neck and spun me around.

"Yeah, that was my friend's friend," Delvis said. "Okay, enough chisme. Let's film."

Chapter Eight

The day's filming had been extensive. And I tried to nap a little on the long ride back to San Juan, but my head was popping and zinging with ideas for *Abuela Approved*. After the establishing shots, we visited a small coffee finca that processed the beans without modern equipment. Delvis purchased several pounds of their coffee for *La Tacita*. I knew I could make two segments from the videos we'd shot. *I'll do a coffee flan episode. That'll be cool.*

Then we visited Tomás Ortíz, El Jibaro 2.0. He wore a painted pava and made tostones de pana/breadfruit on his outdoor fogón for us. He gave me a bottle of pique and one of his artisanal wooden brew stands that held a cup under a cloth net. *That will make a good segment with the single source café. I'll talk about the history of the industry in the area. And I can do another show about pique, the not-hot hot sauce made with mild peppers and vinegar. Since it is almost always homemade, it will be an easy recipe for my viewers.*

Our last stop had been to Lara La Pasterlera, another food vlogger with a worldwide following. Her rustic take-out kitchen had an incredible view of the mountains and valleys. She'd made bacalaítos, salted cod fritters, for us. She was so sweet and personable that our ten-minute interview had turned into an hour. Lara and her family lived close to nature. Her sloping yard was rocky with exposed tree roots clutching the dirt like monstrous hands. There were fowl of all kinds and a rooster named Temblor. The gallo was named after an earthquake shake. Not only were his crows earth shattering, but he had been rescued after one.

I swiped through the snapshots I'd taken with my phone and sent Mami one of me with a chicken on my head. *Manny will roll on the floor laughing when he sees it.* I stopped on an image of the corrugated metal shed with its out-the-window sink. The camp kitchen was built on stilts. *Ay, ay, ay, it's basically hanging off the side of the mountain. I can't believe I didn't get vertigo.* I enlarged the image and looked at the exposed PVC pipes that supplied the water to the sink. *Could a rat chew through that pipe? NYC rats swim. They could survive a nuclear explosion. How did a rat drown in Papi's tank?*

My thoughts were in Punta Cana at my parent's place when I was jarred back to the moment by the lurch of the car braking. We were parked in front of a police station.

"I am sorry to stop. Te prometo que no voy a coger más que dos minutos," Welmo said. He texted someone and then got out of the car. A few seconds later, an officer came out of the building, sat on the metal bench next to Welmo, and lit a cigarette. A streetlamp behind the bench illuminated a circle in the otherwise dark patch of public space. It gave a moody glow to the scenario. The two didn't look at or speak to each other, but a white envelope was laid between them. *This is like a scene from one of those spy movies Robert likes.* Welmo took it, slipped it into his waistband and under his shirt, and returned to our idling car.

"Everything okay?" I asked.

"Just some paperwork I need." Welmo concentrated unnecessarily hard on the road.

Barbacoa, Bomba, and Betrayal

What is in that envelope? Is it about getting his job back? Or does it have to do with the dead man? Why is he so interested in the shooting?

A few minutes later, we turned onto the guesthouse's street. Welmo double-parked to help me to the door. On the step, there was a box.

"Were you expecting a delivery?" Welmo asked, his body tense and at attention.

"No, it's probably something from the studio." I was so tired and just wanted a hot shower. "It's probably something for the next shoot. Maybe a new pair of shoes." I looked at my canvas sneakers spattered with mud and dust from the day. Welmo bent and picked up the white box. He put it to his ear, sniffed it, then shook it lightly. I laughed. "Dámelo. I'm sure it's not a bomb."

I lifted the top off the gift box and tore the gold sticker that sealed the pink tissue paper seam. It was a mermaid plushie doll. "See. Not a bomb." I showed him the black yarn–haired doll with a blue and purple tail.

"Is there a note inside?" Welmo looked up and down the lane.

"No, I don't see one." I passed him the box. After I tucked the mermaid into my satchel, I unlocked the door.

Welmo took the tissue paper out and turned the box over, inspecting every detail. He read the name from the gold sticker. "I know this store. I'll find out who sent it to you. Yes?"

"Okay," I said, wanting to be done with the day. "See you for the Loíza trip. Gracias por todo." I smiled. Welmo intently looked up the street toward El Convento as I shut the door.

I heard water running in the kitchen. Doña was washing dishes. I hoped she hadn't made a meal for me. It was past ten PM, and I was still full from all the various foods we'd sampled during the day. *But a few bites of fruta bomba might help my digestion,* I thought.

"Ya llegue," I said, putting my bag on a chair.

"¿Cómo fue tu día? ¿Te gustaren nuestras montañas?" she asked.

I told her that I had very much enjoyed the island's mountains and I was sorry if I'd missed one of her delicious meals. I pointed to the dirty dessert plates on the table and the sliced brazo gitano. I wondered if she'd made the jelly roll or if it was from Mayagüez, the town to the west that was known for the cake.

Two dishes. Maybe she'd had a friend over.

"¿Quieres un poquito de postre antes de dormir?" she asked.

I politely refused her offer of dessert before bed. "Pero si tienes un poco de fruta bomba lo agradezco."

"Fruta bomba. Ay, sí, eres cubana," Doña remarked on how Cubans used the words *fruta bomba* instead of *papaya*. "Igual que la nueva visitante."

We had a new guest—another Cuban person. *Gracias a La Caridad. I won't be alone in the house anymore. I hope they are nice. I wonder which show they're on.*

Doña served me a bowl of fruit and continued to clean the remains of dinner. I moved my bag to sit at the table and recalled the note in the inner pocket. I took it out and showed it to her, explaining I'd found it New Year's Eve.

"No es nada. Otra solicitud para el zafacón." She crumpled the paper before tossing it in the garbage can. But there was something about the way she'd reacted that told me it wasn't nothing. She left agitated shortly afterward.

Otra. Another solicitation. How many have there been before this one?

And it wasn't a "Please contact me if you are interested in selling your house." It was a bit meaner than that. I took the note out of the garbage and smoothed the wrinkles. There was a grease spot, but it was still legible. *You'll sell or you'll be sorry.* I took a picture of it and put it back in the trash.

I rinsed my bowl and fork, then went to check that the front door was locked. *Funny, I didn't hear the door when Doña left.* I slowly climbed the stairs, yawning every few steps. The room next to mine had light coming from under its closed door. As I turned the porcelain knob to my room, the new guest stepped into the hall.

"Alma!" I shouted in surprise. "How did you get here?"

"En un avión, silly." She hugged me.

I rolled my eyes and hugged her back. "Duh, I know you took a plane. But how? Why? Don't you have work?"

"Well, actually, it was a private jet. And yes, I have work, pero Ana can handle it for a few days."

I looked at my work-driven BFF with skepticism. *"You. A vacation."*

"Jefas need vacations too. I mean, you told me you needed me, no? Que you were lonely and scared. So here I am. Chica, I can leave if you don't want me to stay." Alma acted like she was going to leave.

"Ay, stop. Of course I'm glad you're here. I just can't believe it. How did you know where I was staying?" I asked.

She pulled out her phone and showed me the selfie I'd sent her of me in front of the guesthouse. "There is no other pink house near El Convento with that Arabesque decoration above the door."

"Wait, did you say private jet?" I asked, kicking off my shoes and pushing them under the bed.

"Um, yes. So, um, my new friend has a jet. And since he was flying to San Juan today anyway, he told me to pack a bag and come with him." Alma's eyes were lovelorn.

Who was this guy? Alma was a don't-get-attached kind of woman—a serial it-was-fun-while-it-lasted dater. My friend was smitten, and I couldn't believe it.

I yawned. "I'm sorry, it was a superlong day. I need to take a shower and go to bed." I whined, "Promise me you will tell me *everything* tomorrow."

"I promise. Get some rest. I'm going to take a little walk around Old San Juan. It's so pretty. Maybe I'll get a drink at the hotel bar."

"Be careful."

"Don't worry. This is a tourist town, y hay luzes in the streets. It's well-lit. I'll be safe. Mi'ja you are such a mama hen. Igual como in high school." Alma laughed and kissed my forehead.

I didn't want to scare her by telling her about the guy that had gotten shot. And she was right. It was a tourist town. I'd walked around unworried last night.

But, Miriam, you came back to a threatening note.

And then tonight, you get an anonymous gift.

That's a little creepy.

And personal.

Not that many people know you call your baby La Sirena.

Except, of course, you said it on live TV.

Ay, Dios. Do I have a stalker?

Cálmate, Miriam. It's probably from UnMundo. Go to bed. You are loopy.

Chapter Nine

"Alma. *Alma.* You missed breakfast." I was in her room, gently nudging her to get up. "Levántate. *Mira, I saved you a Mallorca.* It's delicious. Nom. Nom. Nom." I'd used the plate as a lid for the coffee mug so that I could hold the banister on the way up the stairs. The size of my baby belly had me worried I was having a giant. My body had to recalibrate every day to keep balanced.

I put the plate on the marble-topped bedside table. The released coffee vapors did the trick. My sleeping BFF finally opened her eyes.

"¿Café? Oh, you are a lifesaver. Gracias, chica," Alma said. She sat up and fluffed the pillow behind her back.

"I didn't hear you come in last night. I must have been out like a light." I sat on the edge of the bed. Alma crisscrossed her legs and made room for me to sit further on the bed, which made the frame creak. *You too, bedframe? I don't need your unsolicited comments.*

"I went in your room and told you buenas noches. Mi'ja, you were snoring." Alma cut her eyes at me and raised her brow.

"I do not snore."

"Sure. You keep believing that. Um, this coffee is so good— like a nutty hot cocoa." She took another sip from the UnMundo mug. "Pilar made it, right? She's super. Last night we ate pastelón. You've had it, *no*? It's like lasagna, *pero* with maduros. Incredible."

I nodded that I had had it. "Yes, it's delicious. Wait, who is Pilar?"

"The lady that runs this place." Alma dunked a piece of the bread into her coffee and slurped it down.

"Doña Santos told you her first name?"

"Duh." Alma wiped a drip from her chin.

"Rewind." I put my hand out in a stop. "First, tell me about Mr. Private Jet. Then tell me what you said to Doña Santos that she just let you in, fed you, and gave you a room. And then I want to know where you got those." I pointed to the green-foiled chocolate coins next to a guesthouse key on the vanity.

"Well . . ." She took a dramatic breath. "I'll need more coffee and a shower for that story."

While Alma got dressed, I called my parents. After the third try, Mami answered my video call but passed the phone immediately to Manny. They appeared to be outside by the pool. A lounge chair with a striped beach towel was behind my son, and he had a big grin. I noticed the tip of his nose was a bit red, and his cheeks were sun-kissed. He was getting the full outdoor living experience while visiting my folks.

"Abuelo está en el techo como Spider-Man," Manny said.

"¿Que, qué?" I asked with serious concern and shock.

"Yo quiero subir también."

"¡No! Pásale el teléfono a Abuela." I was going to make sure my son didn't *get on the roof* with my dad.

"No puedo. Ella tiene la escalera." Manny turned the camera lens to show me that my mother was indeed holding a tall metal ladder against the side of their house.

"¿Qué pasó?" I asked. Manny took a step closer to hold the phone up to his abuela.

"No te agites. El viento daño el satélite. Pasa a cada ratito."
She smiled, but I wasn't convinced that it was nothing—that it
happened every once in a while. The wind damaged the satellite
dish. Sure, maybe in a hurricane, but the weather had been
extremely mild in the Caribbean this winter.

And did the wind put the rat in the water tank?

And what about the Wi-Fi that's dropping out daily?

Papi had come down from his perch. He patted his sweaty
forehead with a red bandanna before saying something to Mami.
Manny and the phone were too far away to hear what they were
saying, but I thought I had lip-read the word *arrancada*. *Torn.
The dish's cable was pulled.* Manny's arm got tired of holding the
phone out, and he turned it back to himself.

"Mi amor. Empuja las flechas en la esquina de abajo." I
pointed on my end to where I hoped the flip-the-lens arrows
were on his screen. He tapped the icon, and I could see that the
ladder was leaning against their townhouse at the edge of their
patio. It seemed it would have been easier and safer to have
accessed the roof via the second-story balcony. But maybe there
was a guest in the unit. It was impossible to tell. But what I
could tell was that my father looked worn out, and my mother
looked worried.

"Bye, Mami," Manny said as he flipped the lens back to himself. "Voy a nadar." He ended the call.

*Swim! You don't know how to swim. Mami better be getting in
the pool with you. Of course she is. Don't be a nervous Nelly.*

I self-talked myself out of a panic attack about Manny drown-
ing. My mother and father would, of course, be vigilant. And
then it dawned on me that if they were using the pool, there probably weren't any guests around. Mami had mentioned the pool
was exclusively for guests but that they could enjoy it when the
property was empty.

"Did all the guests check out? Or maybe everyone is just gone for the day."

"Chica, you are talking to yourself again," Alma said, entering my room.

"Oh, yeah, I guess I was. Some weird stuff has been going on at my parents' place."

"Weird like, qué? Like gross guests or like rude, privileged jerks?"

I shook my head in an absentminded way.

"Or do you mean like ghosts? *Woooo*. Like poltergeist stuff?"

"Alma!" I threw the closest and softest thing at hand at her, the mermaid doll. "You know that supernatural stuff scares me."

Alma fanned her fingers in the air like she was coming to tickle me.

"*Stop.* No, I mean like someone is trying to sabotage the property. Pipe problems, a dead rat, a broken satellite dish, and the Wi-Fi keeps going out."

"Chica, that could just be regular maintenance stuff. Do your parents think it's sabotage? Have they had any bad reviews?" Alma asked.

"Bad reviews? I don't think so. Where would we check?"

Alma took her phone from her silk jumpsuit. She was always the better dressed of us. "¿Cómo se llama el lugar?"

"Punta Palma," I replied.

"You know that's one of the tricks crooked real estate people use. They bombard a business with a bunch of one-star reviews until they lose so much money that they are desperate to sell."

Jules Howard! Is he behind this?

Alma's face went from neutral to furrowed brow.

"What?!"

"Nothing too bad. Mostly complaints about the weather or that people were speaking Spanish. The weather es el departamento

66

de Dios and *hello, people,* it is the Dominican Republic. But there is this one that was posted yesterday. It's kind of nasty. And it has photos."

I snatched the phone from her. There was a picture of the pool with green water. The caption read *Gross, algae.* Another one was of a planter littered with cigarette butts and Aluminum cans. That caption read *Trash everywhere.* I studied the cans. They were the same brand as the one the girl on the float had been drinking. The last image was of a dead rat with *Look what I found in the shower!!!!!* I counted the exclamation points. There were five.

"Ay, mi madre. I think the woman that was staying in the apartment by the pool planted those things. The pool was not green. I saw it two days ago. It was crystal clear. Actually, I saw it today when I was talking to Manny. It's pristine." I passed the phone back to my friend.

"It could be a filter," Alma said.

"My parents are super clean. You *know* Mami. She is sweeping and mopping all the time."

"Yo sé. Chica, don't worry. It's just one bad review. She probably wants to get a free vacation. People do that. They complain until they get a refund. Look, I'll report that the review is false."

"No, don't do that yet. Let me talk to my parents first and see what's going on." I found my sunglasses and got my purse.

"Cute mermaid," Alma said, placing the doll she'd had tucked in the crook of her arm onto the bed.

"It is cute, no? Someone sent it to me. Maybe I'll decorate the baby's room in an under-the-sea theme."

"Oh, I like that idea. *Pero, there wasn't a note.*"

We stepped out of the room and started down the stairs.

"No. It's probably from the network or Ileana," I said. "I'll ask Delvis about it tomorrow."

"You have a secret admirer," Alma said in a teasing tone. In grade school at St. Joseph's, she was always the first one to sing the K-I-S-S-I-N-G song at the first blush of a crush.

"Porfa." I rolled my eyes at her, but it made me wonder if maybe my Roberto had sent it as an apology for the TV. "So, tell me. Who is Mr. Private Jet?" I locked the guesthouse door.

The sun was strong, and it felt like early summer despite it being January. We watched the piragua man push his red-and-yellow cart to Plaza de la Rogativa, the place where I'd watched the fireworks.

"¿Quieres?" I asked, craving the icy cool of a piragua.

"Dale," Alma replied.

While we waited for the piragüero to set up, we took a few photos by the sculpture of a bishop and three women carrying torches and a cross. The bronze artwork commemorates a ruse that saved the fort from the 1797 British siege.

El viejito sang, "Piraguas. Frias y refrescantes," signaling he was ready for business. Alma asked for two. I watched as the man shaved the large block of ice and built a pyramid in the paper cups. He asked, "¿Qué sabores?" I looked at the rainbow of sugary syrups and chose two, parcha y crema. The man drizzled the bright orange passionfruit liquid over the tall ice cone then added the opaque cream syrup. Alma chose a single flavor, maví. It was the Caribbean equivalent of root beer. It had different names on different islands. But the flavor came from the bark of the Mauby tree that was fermented with spices like ginger, cinnamon, and sometimes star anise. The drink could be traced to the Indigenous peoples of the Caribbean.

We strolled along the Paseo de la Princesa, crunching and slurping our piraguas. I'd chosen my flavors well, and the cream balanced the tangy parcha perfectly. The waves were hitting the wall with a mid-tempo rhythm. Occasionally, a splash of sea spray would fly above the wall like a drummer hitting a cymbal. The broad waterside walkway made me think of el Malecón en la Habana. The ocean water was the same here as there, and it was filled with tears of longing and sorrow. Puerto Rico had lost so many to Hurricane Maria. Cuba's loss was continual. Every week there was a news headline about the Coast Guard finding rafters. Sometimes they were Cuban, sometimes Haitian, but always desperate enough to make a dangerous voyage on a homemade vessel.

As we passed La Fortaleza, the governor's mansion, my thoughts shifted back to Alma and her secret man. *A private jet. Tiene que ser rico. Like money-money rich.* The curiosity was killing me, and I couldn't take it another second. "Who is Mr. Private Jet? How did you meet? Tell me everything!"

Chapter Ten

"Okay. So, like, where do I start?" Alma said as she detoured to a garbage can.

"Basta. Enough stalling. Who is your mystery man?" I tossed my trash too.

"His name is Heriberto Chacón. I call him Herbie."

I made a face. My girl was not one for silly nicknames.

"Herbie like the Love Bug, you know." Alma doubled down.

I made another face.

"Don't hate on my cute, chica." Alma popped her eyes and wagged her pointer finger at me.

A few steps ahead of us, there was an artisan market—a dozen or so tents filled with anything and everything a person could put a Puerto Rican flag on. I spied a booth of beautifully crafted religious figures and went to it.

"*Soooo.* Spill! Tell me about him," I said.

"He's Venezuelan pero his abuela was Cuban. He's so handsome. And he treats me like a queen. Mira, if I text him, he will reply in like dos segundos. No important que he's in a meeting. He always has time for me." Alma sent him a selfie of her holding a carved wooden santo. Her phone showed a reply. She held out her phone so I could read it.

I saw that Herbie had replied with a heart. Instantly, there was another chime.

"He says buy it." She laughed and flashed her screen at me. It was a money transfer notification. Her new boyfriend had sent her $250. Alma recorded a short, coquettish thank-you video with a puckered-lip air kiss.

Who is this person? And what have they done with my friend?

Alma's phone pinged. Whatever he'd sent had made my friend blush.

"I can't show you this one."

"*Ew, gross.*" I slapped my friend's bicep. "So, where did you meet him?" I held a magnificently carved small statue of the Three Kings. Instead of frankincense, gold, and myrrh, they had traditional Puerto Rican musical instruments. I motioned to the seller that I was going to buy it.

"We met at that Christmas party I didn't want to go to. That new hotel slash residences place on Brickell. Remember? I was all like *not for my buyers*. You told me to take a Lyft, stop complaining, and enjoy the free booze. Gracias por eso." Alma winked. "Anyway, so I get there and, like, I notice him from across the room. Or maybe he noticed me. I don't remember. But our eyes locked, and the whole world just melted away. It was like we were the only two people at the party." Alma made a good-memory *mmm* sound as we moved to the next booth.

"Espérate. You've been seeing this guy for over a week and didn't say anything?" I said. "I'm hurt."

"*Por favor.* You kept Robert a secret for months before telling me."

"That was because he was a professor, and I was still technically a student, postgrad, but still." My bestie was never going to let me forget that insult to our friendship.

Alma pointed to a frilly folkloric baby's outfit hanging on display. I shook my head no in response to the over-the-top lace and ribbons. She then offered a bib printed with the words *baby's first pastelón*. I grinned and nodded that it was perfect. Alma bought it and a pair of cloth booties painted with tropical flowers.

"So, like I was saying, I didn't want to get too excited about him and, you know, jinx it. I mean, if it turned out to be a one-night stand, then I was going to be okay with that because it was, like, the perfect one-nighter. Pero, like, it turned into two nights, then three. He sent me flowers." Alma turned me around and spoke directly to me. "He had *a Rolls* pick me up and take me shopping in the Design District for a New Year's Eve gown. He bought me a six-thousand-dollar Dolce and Gabbana one-shoulder gown. He didn't want me to feel underdressed at the party. The party *on Star Island*. Half of the Miami Heat were there. The other half were Hollywood celebrities. It was like a TMZ hotlist—Drake, DJ Khaled, Diddy, Fat Joe, and a bunch of new rappers I don't know."

"Wow." I pinched my thumb and pointer finger together and fanned the air. "You are big league now. Will Drake be invited to the wedding? Can you put me at his table? You know I've always had a crush on him."

"Cállate." Alma pfted. "You know I'm never getting married."

Okay, at least my friend hasn't lost her mind completely.

"*Married*. Mi'ja, I'm the fun friend. And I work too hard for my money to share it with someone I barely know. Ya tú sabes." Alma laughed.

We were at the last booth of the little market when I realized I hadn't bought anything for my mom or Manny. Before I left, I planned to get Papi and Robert some good-quality rum. I took another look around and found an island-themed coloring book for Manny, along with a coquí plushie that made the iconic *co-kee* sound when the frog's front pad was squeezed. I bought a three-pack of locally produced seasoning blends for my mom and added a pack for me at the last second. *If it's good, maybe I'll mention it on Abuela Approved.*

"What should we do now? Do you have to work this afternoon?" Alma asked.

"No, I'm free today. Should we see if Jorge wants to meet for lunch?'

"Yes. And it's my treat. Well, Herbie's treat." She wiggled her phone in the air. She hadn't bought the craved santo, so I guess it was his money paying for lunch.

What does Herbie do for a living? Is he in real estate like Alma? She hadn't really said, had she?

We stopped at number seven Caleta de las Monjas to drop off our purchases and freshen up. Welmo and Doña Santos were in the kitchen having coffee when we entered.

"Hola," I said, looking at Welmo. "Do we have something today? I thought the schedule said today I was off."

"No, no, no, no. Don't worry. I am not here to drive you," Welmo assured me.

Remembering my manners, I introduced Alma to Welmo, at which point Doña Santos stood up and shifted into her hospitality role. She removed her and Welmo's dirty tazas and offered us something to drink and eat. Alma and I both knew it would hurt her feelings if we said no. So, we sat and accepted her offer of a pineapple drink she'd made.

She poured the sunset-colored drink from a refrigerated pitcher. I noticed chunks of pineapple along with cherries floating in it. The pineapple, cultivated on the island by the Taíno since way before Columbus, was local, but the cherries were from a jar. I took a sip and gave the proper appreciative comment. "Deliciosas. ¿Con qué está hecho?" I knew it was orange and pineapple juice with the sweetness of the cherry syrup, but I let her have the moment. She sopped it up and told me I could use it on my show. Then she went to the patio to water the plants.

Welmo swirled his glass before speaking. "I stopped by to have coffee con mi favorita mujer." He winked in Doña's direction. "And to tell you I found out who sent you the gift."

"Someone sent you *an anonymous* gift?" Alma's words dripped with suspension. "Like roses or like something creepy? Do you have a stalker?"

"The mermaid. You saw it. It's sweet—for the baby. Stop freaking me out." I turned from Alma to Welmo. "It *is* from the studio, right? I don't have an obsessive fan, *right*?"

"The gift shop girl says a man with a woman's name bought it," Welmo said. "He paid extra to have it delivered to 'numero siete de las monjitas' the jovencita told me."

"A man with a woman's name. Miriam, you have a mystery to solve." Alma rubbed her hands together. She was enjoying herself too much. "Pero, wait. Wouldn't the credit card receipt have his name on it?"

"He paid cash," Welmo answered. "She said he was a rich American con un Rolex—maybe with the Bitcoin party."

"Jules! It has to be Jules," I said.

"Who's he?" Alma asked.

"I asked you about him. Remember? You called him Golden Jules," I said.

"*The real estate guy.* I thought he was staying at your parents' place in Punta Cana." Alma scrunched her brow.

"Sí, pero, he flew over here for New Year's Eve. I saw him at the UnMundo party. He went to college with the CEO." I touched my forehead with my fingertips, a gentle *duh* slap. "He watched my interview with Ileana. I mentioned I was jokingly

74

calling the baby La Sirena. That's why he sent me a mermaid. See, harmless."

Alma and Welmo exchanged looks.

"So, how did he know where you were staying?" Alma asked.

"I told you, he's friends with the head of the studio. He probably just asked for the address of the guesthouse. He knows I work for UnMundo." I tried to fish out a cherry from the glass with my finger.

Welmo made a grumbling noise. He and Alma traded looks again.

"Pare. I'm sure it is innocent. He's a nice guy," I said. "The person you should be worried about is whoever wrote that note."

"What note?" The pair said in unison.

"Doña told you about it, no?" I pulled my phone from my pocket. I scrolled back too far and had to swipe past Manny's drawing, the jibaro monument, and my Yauco shots. I finally found the photo I'd taken of the note.

Alma looked at it as she passed it around the table to Welmo.

"You'll sell or you'll be sorry." Welmo squinted to read the penciled words.

"That sounds like a threat to me. *I told you* Jules is ruthless in real estate. I bet he wrote it. It's probably how he gets all those places before they go on the market. Be careful. He is not as nice as he makes out." Alma made duck lips.

Ay, Caridad. Jules wrote the note that Manny drew on. ELL OUSE is SELL HOUSE. Miriam, you are estúpida.

"When did you find this? When did you show it to Doña Santos?" Welmo asked.

I put my thoughts about Manny's drawing on hold and told Welmo the details about Doña's note. I stressed that I had shown the threat to her, but she'd dismissed it. He got up abruptly and went out to the patio. Alma and I watched the verbal exchange through the window. Welmo's prayer hands went from his forehead to his chest and then shook with the passion of a fervent monk.

"He is not happy," Alma said.

"And she is not bowing to the pressure," I said. Doña kept sweeping and refused to look at him.

"We should give them some privacy." I stood up to leave.

"No. I want to stay and watch."

"Alma." I tugged on her sleeve to stand up.

"Fine. Let's go to our rooms." Alma fake-moped from the table to the hall.

I stole a glance at the patio as I left the kitchen. I couldn't see Doña, but Welmo was staring at the vine-covered fence between the two properties. He threw his hands in the air.

"Are you coming?" Alma asked from the hallway.

We retrieved our purchases from the hall table and took them upstairs. In my room, we laid everything on the bed and consolidated it.

"I'm keeping this for the baby shower," Alma said. She took the bib into her room and returned promptly. "Want one?" She offered me one of the foil coins in her hand.

"No," I said. "But I'll take one for Manny." The green half-dollar-sized treats were embossed with a pickle on one side and a dog on the other. "Where did you get these?"

"Last night, when I left here, I went next door to meet Herbie for a drink. The bar had *pickle jars* of them." She chuckled.

"Mr. Private Jet is staying at El Convento?" I put the Three Kings carving and one of the spice sets on the bedside table, then packed the rest of the gifts into my suitcase. I wanted to remember to mention the spices to Delvis.

"No. He had a meeting there. Herbie is staying at the Caribe Hilton. He has a suite con una vista de la playa. I might visit him there tomorrow while you are away filming."

"Kind of late for a meeting," I said.

"The mega-rich don't live on regular schedules, chica." Alma primped her hair in the mirror.

My phone beeped. It was a message from Pepper asking if Sophia and Manny could have a playdate. "Oh, I forgot to get something for Pepper, Sally, and their girls. Do you think we could run back down to the market and get a few things for them?"

"There are plenty of shops around here. We have a little time before we meet Jorge. We will find something."

"You're right. Mind if we do a video call to Pepper?" I asked.

"Dale."

Pepper answered on the second ring. I explained I was out of town for work and that Manny was staying with his abuelos.

"San Juan," Pepper said in her Oklahoma accent. "I've never been. I bet it's pretty."

I went to the window and gave her a panoramic view. "You can see a little of the bay, and that's a historic cathedral at the other end. And here's Alma."

Alma waved with a cheesy smile. "Happy New Year, Pepper."

"Oh my God, I'm so jealous. A girl's weekend. I haven't had one of those in so long. Not since Elliot and I went to Bimini." Pepper tried to keep a positive tone, but sadness clouded her usual perkiness. She'd lost her best and first Miami friend, Elliot, less than six months ago.

I couldn't imagine losing Alma. I threw Alma a micro-signal, and she nodded in reply. "Pepper, we *have to* do a girl's trip. You, me, Sally, Alma, and Marie," I said.

"*Yeeesss.*" Alma squeezed into the screen with me. "And we should do it before the baby! Even if it's forty-eight hours. We can rent a big house and lounge by the pool with cocktails."

I elbowed Alma. Pepper had been trying to be careful about her alcohol intake. She'd spent the months after Elliot's death in a wine-o'clock stupor.

"How about mocktails in solidarity with the pregnant lady," I said. "My parents' place would be perfect. One of the villas sleeps eight, and it's just a quick drive to the beach. I'll ask about availability. What do you think?"

"Send me the link. I'll look into it and contact the rest of the squad. Oh, this is exciting! Something good to look forward to. *Yaas!*" Pepper's radiant joy had returned.

We ended the video call, and I sent her the link to Punta Palma. It was prime season, and I figured there would be no availability before my due date in May. I was wrong. Five minutes later, Alma and I were in the entryway about to leave the house when I got a message from Pepper.

Will you be back in DR Jan 6?

That's the plan

Perfect, the grand villa is available Jan 6–8. I'm booking it!! More details later.

"¿Qué te pasa, chica?" Alma asked in concern over my worried expression.

"Pepper said the grand villa is available. Mami told me they were booked solid."

"People cancel. No biggie."

"Yeah, but the property has been having some mysterious maintenance problems. That review, *remember.* I hope that there haven't been more."

Alma gave me a side hug. "Cálmate. I'm sure it's nothing. It's probably not sabotage or algo sinister. I'll check the review sites and report any outrageous ones I see. Okay?"

"Gracias, amiga." I put my head on my bestie's shoulder hoping she wasn't just humoring me. "Let me tell Doña that we're leaving."

I walked into the kitchen expecting to see her and Welmo, but it was ghostly quiet. The patio was vacant too. "I guess they left. Weird we didn't hear the front door." The heavy mahogany door let in the street noise when it opened. I stepped into the hall to join Alma, who was waiting in the entry, but baby bladder had other plans. "Voy al baño," I called.

"Good idea, mamacita," Alma said.

I kind of hated being called little mama. I was more than my current state of incubator. I reached for the doorknob but realized it wasn't the bathroom door with the rose on it. It was the utility closet. Or what I thought was the hot water closet.

"*Alma*, come look at this. I found a secret passage."

Chapter Eleven

"Those noises I heard the first night—the creaking stairs and doors. Do you think they were Doña Santos?" I asked Alma as we walked the few blocks to Jorge's holiday rental.

"Maybe. Pero también it's an old, *old* house. Old houses make noises. No te rompe el coco about it." Alma rapped her knuckles on my head.

"That door has to lead to her house."

"Well, if you had let me go through it, then we'd know. But no, you were all like, what if this and what if that. I think we are on the wrong calle." Alma stopped in the middle of the crowded narrow sidewalk. A pair of teenage tourists with their eyes on their phones bumped into us. The parents, who wore T-shirts with a Rasta man caricature and "Hey, mon." in a speech bubble, looked over their shoulders.

I pulled Alma into a gift store to get us out of the foot traffic. "What if it leads to an alley? Or a dungeon?"

"A dungeon? *Porfa*." Alma motioned to a framed print on the wall and made a what-do-you-think-of-this face.

"Oh, that's nice. Maybe for Sally," I said, then I noticed a packet of note cards with the same turtle and reef scene. "There *could be* a dungeon under there. Some of these buildings are five hundred years old and were built for Spanish admirals and stuff."

"Okay, sure, pero I don't think so. Come on, chica. It probably connects to Pilar's house." Alma was going through a rack of batik sarongs.

"Okay, yeah. But what was she doing in the UnMundo house in the middle of the night?" I asked. I selected a few beach cover-ups from the rack—one with a dolphin, another with a turtle, and a third with a red hibiscus. They'd make good gifts for Pepper and Daniela, the student teacher who lived with her and nannied for the family.

"Cleaning." Alma pointed to some colorful jewelry that Manny's primas as well as Sophia would like.

"*Cleaning* in the middle of the night. On New Year's Eve?" I added three sets of children's-size bracelets and necklaces to my pile.

"Viejitas are always cleaning. They love it. No sé porque but they do. And it's her job, right? She's like the innkeeper, no?" Alma tried on a floppy-brimmed hat that looked chic on her. "Puerto Rico is like Cuba, no? You have to throw out the dirty mop water at midnight, or you have bad luck in the new year."

"You're probably right. And you have to get that hat."

"Oh, I'm getting the hat. It will be perfect for my beach date with Herbie tomorrow."

We took our souvenirs to the register. My brain jumped from Alma in her hat on the beach with a VW bug to Doña Pilar Santos in a rough linen robe, ala innkeeper circa 1 BCE. I think it was the Christmas songs playing in the store that tipped my imagination to the biblical. Alma and I left the store singing the infectious carol about a little burro going to Belén/Bethlehem.

I checked my messages for the correct address. Jorge's B and B was around the corner. The slim building was on the high side of the islet, close to El Castillo de San Cristóbal. The apartment complex turned boutique hotel looked like it was in the middle of a remodel. One side of the lobby had swatches of paint colors and permit paperwork. The other side had an eight-compartment mailbox unit with a chipped-grout outline like it was about to be removed from the wall.

There was a tiny elevator that looked like a death trap. But four flights of stairs were too much to ask of my swollen ankles and bad balance, so I risked it. As we ascended, the elevator car's light bulb blinked with each slip of the cable.

"When do you think this was last serviced?" I asked.

Alma shrugged, unbothered by the sounds of grinding metal.

The doors opened, and we shimmied out of the tight box that had been too small for a pregnant lady, her friend, and their shopping. In contrast to the first floor, the fourth was bright and modern.

"I guess the remodel is from the top down," I said.

"And they are doing a nice job. Me like." Alma's eyes were taking stock of the details.

I imagined her real estate mind was writing the description for the spec sheet.

This historic property has been lovingly renovated with modern conveniences and period appointments. Each landing has Art Deco lighting fixtures. The rattan settee's vintage fabric pillows reflect a carefree and glamorous era. Each suite is whimsically named for a tropical fruit.

The yellow door with the word *Piña* in hand-lettered retro font opened. Our friend Jorge greeted us wearing snug Pride flag boxers and a pineapple-print beach towel turban.

"Chicas, gracias que you finally got here, because I am so bored," Jorge said, giving us each a fresh-from-the-shower hug. He unfurled his turban to reveal newly bleached hair.

"Blond!" Alma and I declared in unison.

"I told you I was bored, and when I'm bored, I get into trouble." Our friend slapped his chiseled abs and laughed. "Llegaste antes de la azul."

"*Blue.*" Alma raised her eyebrows.

"Just the tips. Un toquecito nada más," Jorge replied to her disapproving look. "Let me give you the tour."

We dropped our bags in a corner chair and let Jorge show us the apartment. The bedroom was small and tidy. The full-size bed looked like it had been sat on but not slept in. The only kitsch in the room was a pineapple bedside lamp. The rest of the décor was classy and chic. Alma and I each took a turn looking out the window at the view of the 1678 fort.

"The view from the other apartment is better. It's all mar. Come, I'll show you," Jorge said. He threw on a shirt and slipped into a pair of flat-front chinos. From the kitchen's eat-in counter, our friend took a key with a diamond-shaped tag, the kind from a 1950s motel. He opened another yellow door, which was one shade darker than the other one, and we entered the "Carambola" apartment.

It was twice the size, with two bedrooms and a much larger living room. Sunlight beamed through hurricane-impact windows that had to be new to the building. They dampened the noise from outside but not the gorgeous vista of the blue and white surf. The four-story building looked over a neighboring two-story building's roof with a plastic tarp weighed down by cinder blocks.

"This is where we sleep. Okay, not so much sleeping," Jorge said with a coquettish smile.

"Where is Prince Charming today?" I asked.

"Filming a commercial," he replied.

"Que cool. What is it for?" Alma asked, plopping onto the sofa.

"No sé. I think it's like an Instagram live or algo for TikTok. You know, like an interview that is sponsored." Jorge was in the open-plan kitchen. "¿Agua?"

"Sí," I replied. "So, like an infomercial."

"I guess. The opportunity just came up yesterday, and he said yes, porque they paid him in advance con Bitcoin. By this morning, he'd sold it or traded it or algo and made, like, double his money."

"El Bitcoin es everywhere," Alma said. "Someone put in an offer on a house with it. Can you believe it? I told Ana to try and talk the sellers into it, pero they said no. Until banks start giving loans in Bitcoin, it's cash or mortgage only."

I changed the subject. "Where are we eating lunch? I'm growing a baby, and I'm hungry."

"Hay un lugar cerquita. It has mofongo de mariscos. Do you want to try it?" Jorge asked.

"Yes to seafood," I said.

"I want to try some arroz con gandules. They'll have it, no?" Alma asked.

"Claro, I'm sure. It's casi the national dish," I reassured my friend.

To descend, I took the elevator while Alma and Jorge took the stairs. My logic was that the elevator was too small for three people, and they could call for help if I got stuck. I made it to the first floor safely and before them. I could hear Alma's voice commenting on the semifinished second floor like it was an open-house property. As I waited, the paint swatches caught my eye. I liked the light blue best. The building permit's tape was peeling, so I smoothed it back down, reading the paper as I secured it. The responsible parties for the renovation were listed as BPBP, LLC, with an Arecibo, Puerto Rico, address, and LPM/Belle Époque, with a Miami, Florida, address.

"This place is going to be hot when it's finished," Alma said from the first step.

"I saw AC," I said.

"No, hot like cool," she said, laughing. "Like super sexy."

"Oh." I was distracted by what I'd read on the permit. Something about the alphabet of initials was bugging me. "What was the name of the company that bought the hotel in Little River?"

"Jules's company?" My friend made a why-are-you-asking-me-this-now face.

"Yes."

"LPM," she replied. "Why?"

I pointed to the company name on the permit.

"Basta. Enough con el interior design blah blah blah," Jorge proclaimed. "This is vacation, not work." Jorge wagged his finger in Alma's direction. "Follow me. I have a secret to show you."

We followed him through the back of the B and B. The passageway was a bit of an obstacle course with five-gallon pails, stacks of floor tiles, and demolition debris. It was also dark, but conversations in Spanish could be heard ahead of us. We emerged into a freshly painted room with new industrial kitchen equipment covered in plastic sheets. A crew of eight workers was taking a break on the floor in various states of repose. A few were eating from Styrofoam to-go boxes. A woman in a hairnet and apron came out a door with another man's meal. She stopped and gave us a startled look.

"Jorge, I don't think we're supposed to be here," I said.

"No te preocupes. This is the shortcut," he said, and waved to the woman.

Our trio kept walking, and in a few steps, we were in a legitimate restaurant dining room. I could see the door to the street. The décor was Medalla beer signs and Don Q advertisements. A large ship's wheel with a fishing net hanging from it was on the wall. The woman we'd just seen delivering meals handed us menus and pointed to the sparsely populated room. We had our choice of tables.

I motioned to a table near the exterior door. We sat and were promptly served glasses of water. The place was called El Capitán, according to the menu, and specialized in seafood. I ordered a favorite of mine, ensalada de pulpo. Alma got her rice and pigeon peas as a side to a whole fried fish. Jorge got the mixed seafood mofongo. I looked out the restaurant's window to orient myself to where we were.

"Is this the building we saw from Prince Charming's apartment? The one with the tarp on the roof?" I asked.

"Sí," Jorge replied. He was sharing photos from his phone with Alma. "Mira how good we look together."

Alma pulled out her phone, and the battle of whose boyfriend was the most handsome began. While they one-upped each other, I excused myself to find the bathroom. I asked where it was and was directed up a set of stairs. The second floor starkly contrasted the brown and dated first floor. Like the building's taller sibling, it was being renovated from the top down. The tarp I'd noticed was covering a large skylight. The walls were finished in a high-end paper that had a plant motif. If the designer was going for a rain forest feel, they had succeeded. I could almost hear the trickle of a waterfall and the songs of Puerto Rico's beloved amphibian.

"Miriam, que boba eres," I whispered to myself. My imagination was good but not that good. The El Yunque sounds were coming from a speaker in the bathroom that a restaurant staffer had just exited.

"Perdona. ¿Qué van a hacer con este espacio?" I asked her what the space was going to become. The woman replied with a wave of dormant anger. Her family's restaurant was being kicked out. El Capitán's days were numbered. The new owner had quadrupled the rent. She hoped they'd get hired by the new management, but she wasn't counting on it. As she left me, she snarked about the soundtrack that they couldn't turn off. Now every croak of a coquí reminded her that her family business was gone.

Back at the table, Alma and Jorge had ordered cervezas and were planning a double date when the couples returned to Miami. Our food arrived shortly after. It was flavorful and well prepared. I tasted Alma's rice. Each grain was a delicate morsel of goodness. The gandules had texture but were not hard. Jorge's mariscos mofongo was aromatic and beautifully presented in a wooden mortar. The fried and mashed plantains took up half of the pilon, and the rest was packed with big chunks of flaky fish, shrimp, mussels, and a lobster claw like a flag on top. A sadness washed over me. I knew it wasn't my mermaid giving me a shot of melancholy. It was mourning that this culinarily talented family was losing its business.

I ate my meal, savoring each bite and mentally damning gentrification. LPM was behind this project, and LPM was Jules Howard. *Is he doing the same thing to Punta Palma? Will my parents lose their jobs?* The next time I saw Jules Howard, I'd throw that stuffed doll in his face.

Chapter Twelve

Welmo was at the kitchen table when I went down for breakfast. The day's filming location wasn't too far away—about eighteen miles. So, I knew I had time to enjoy my meal without Welmo rushing me. I'd read Delvis's notes before bed. One of the nonculinary things I was looking forward to was a visit to a vejigante mask maker for some establishing shots.

The masks, made from coconut husks, had brightly painted pointy spikes protruding from them, and the wearer carried a large threatening rattle. It was a Caribbean adaptation of a twelfth-century Spanish tradition. Ponce had a vejigante carnaval during the Lenten season. But Loíza's was a summer festival celebrating Saint James called the Fiesta de Santiago Apóstol. I'd attended it when I was twelve on a family vacation to visit Mami's prima Sandra. She'd married a Puerto Rican man, and they'd made their home in Luquillo, a neighboring town.

The costumed demons were meant to be scary. I'd had nightmares for weeks. Supposedly, the idea was to scare the wayward back to church. The trick hadn't really worked with me. I was more frightened of church afterward. *Demons.* I shivered at the memory.

"Are you cold? Can I get you a sweater?" Welmo asked.

"No, I'm fine." I chuckled. "I was thinking about how scary the vejigantes were when I was twelve. Now, I find them fascinating. Is that the coffee from Yauco?" I pointed to the brown bag with the hand-stamped logo.

"Yes, I bought some for Doña." Welmo dipped his toast in his coffee and took a bite.

"Buenos días, Doña Santos," I said as I slipped into my usual seat. A passing shower had left the patio glistening and fresh. I complimented her on the well-tended plants. I held up my juice and took a photo of it with the patio in the background to post on the *Abuela Approved* Instagram account. Doña served me a plate of eggs and rice. I took a shot of it and asked her if I could take her photograph to add to *my story*. Delvis had been after me to be more active on social media.

Doña blushed from the flattery but protested that she had work to do. She dusted some imaginary crumbs from the table and zoomed off like a flighty bird to the front of the house. *Did she just stop at the hidden passage door? Does she know I found it? Is it her secret to cleaning the guesthouse so eerily quick?*

I took a few more photos of the table, kitchen, and patio and combined them into a reel with music and text. I hoped Delvis would see it and be proud of my efforts. *Miriam, you are such a teacher's pet.*

After breakfast, we left Old San Juan. I lowered the car window and enjoyed the 70-degree morning breeze. The road off the islet took us past Alma's boyfriend's hotel. She was still in bed when we'd left the guesthouse. I assumed she'd had another late night of drinks at the bar with her boyfriend. I hoped it would warm up a few degrees for her beach day with him. I was seeing a whole new side of my BFF. She'd never acted this lovestruck in high school. It was all very weird, but I reminded myself to be happy for her and not judgy. Maybe when I met him, I'd see the attraction and chemistry. *Herbie, the Love Bug.*

Welmo turned on the radio. Between songs, the DJs gave their opinions on the latest political scandals and outrages. An American had bought an apartment complex in Arecibo and raised the rent. The residents, many of them old and on fixed incomes, were being forced out. One of the DJs made a vitriolic comment about Law 187 and Act 22 that Welmo agreed with.

"One hundred percent exemption on capital gains." Welmo slapped his palm on the dashboard. "Five years exemption on property tax." He raised a fist and shook it. "How is the island going to recover? The oversight board's laws are choking us." He clasped his hand around his throat in demonstration. "Sorry." He sighed and looked at me in the review mirror. "I get very angry. It is very wrong to take such advantage. I love Borikén."

"I get it," I consoled him. Puerto Rico kept getting knocked out by hard-hitting punches. Hurricane Maria had brought the island to its knees. They hadn't gotten a chance to get back on their feet. First, there was all the mismanaged aid, and then the corruption from inside and outside. Added to that was the US-backed electric company that was a joke. There were still blackouts that lasted days in some parts of the island. And if I understood the DJs and Welmo correctly, the fiscal oversight board had enacted legislation that allowed outside investors to avoid paying taxes on the premise that it would entice businesses to come to the island, which would, in theory, help the local economy. Outside investors were putting their money into projects, but the profits were not staying local. It was the same old colonial plunder and pillage song and dance but sung to a new tune.

Shifting to a lighter subject, I asked, "Do you think we will have time later to make a quick stop in Luquillo? My mother's cousin lives there." Sandra didn't know I was in town. I wanted to surprise her and find out how the cousins were doing.

"Claro que sí," Welmo replied, then grew quiet as he concentrated on traffic in Santurce. Before long, we were driving through Isla Verde and Piñones, popular beach towns.

"What a gorgeous day," I said as I looked out the window at the ocean.

We crossed a river and entered the town of Loíza. UnMundo's fleet of vans was crammed into a small lot by a one-story library. With no room for our car, Welmo let me out so he could find street parking. I saw blue hair and went toward it.

"Good. You're here early. We have an addition to the shoot. You aren't allergic to bees, are you?" Delvis asked.

"No. Why?" I asked with some concern.

"La Cueva María de la Cruz has the biggest bee sanctuary in the Caribbean. The beekeeper will show you the hives and honeycombs. It's an ecotourism project. You know, a feel-good segment. Come up with some culinary history spin to it. You like honey, no?"

Yes, I liked honey, but I didn't know how I felt about *thousands* of bees buzzing around me.

"Go to wardrobe and makeup," Delvis said as her headset crackled with a voice. She nudged me to a mini RV before leaving to solve whatever problem had surfaced.

I opened the slim door, stepped up, and saw Jorge. "You again? Why didn't you tell me? We could have driven in together."

"The makeup artist has the flu or algo. So, they called me this morning at like six. It's okay. I was awake anyway. Ay, mi'ja," Jorge said. He blew a puff through one side of his mouth and slumped his shoulders.

"¿Qué te pasa?" I asked. Jorge, usually the most sparkly and bouncy person in the room, was angsty and gloomy.

"Lucas didn't come back last night." Jorge showed me the outfit wardrobe had chosen for me. It was a gauzy white maternity shirt with marine-blue cropped pants. A drawstring bag of jewelry was tied to the hanger.

I chucked my purse onto a bench seat at the end of the cramped space, closed the curtain over the door's window, and twirled my finger for Jorge to turn his back.

As I changed, I asked him if maybe Lucas's commercial had run late. "Are you sure he wasn't in the other apartment this morning? Maybe he got in late and didn't want to wake you up."

"No." Jorge stomped his foot. "I checked los dos apartamentos. He hadn't been to his or mine. I'm super worried." Jorge undid the clip in my hair. "Do you think he met somebody?" He gripped a handful of locks and pulled a brush through them.

I tensed my neck muscle so my head wouldn't whiplash. "*Don't* think like that. I'm sure he just got stuck. Tech problems or lighting issues. I'm sure the shoot ran late."

Jorge pinned some hair on my crown and thankfully stopped his angst-driven hairstyling.

"Okay, pero then, why didn't he text me? Huh?" Jorge moistened a sponge with foundation and started dabbing my forehead with it.

I hoped I'd survive the not-so-gentle application. It felt like a bird pecking to get into my brain. "Chill. He probably ran out of battery. It happens. Especially when it's roaming. Where was the commercial being filmed?"

"I don't know. Mira, he sent me these pictures at like eight. His phone was working then." Jorge swiped away his Walter Mercado screensaver and opened his message app. "Does he look like he's at a party?" He handed it to me.

The selfies were cute and flirty. It was hard to tell much about the surroundings because half the photo was face. Lucas might have been on a balcony. There were five images, all very similar. I passed the phone back to him quickly. "He'll call," I said. I crossed my fingers under my thigh because I didn't want my friend's heart to be broken. *Lucas's eyes did look a little glassy. Maybe he did go partying.*

Delvis knocked on the RV's door and gave me a five-minute warning.

"Estoy listo." I replied I was ready. I gave my friend a hug. "Don't worry. He'll be there when you get back to San Juan."

Jorge pouted and then sat down to play with the makeup.

"Yes, distract yourself, Cha-Cha Minnelli," I said, calling him by one of his drag personas. "Lucas is probably already asleep in the apartment. Don't worry."

"Espero que sí." Jorge applied fuchsia shadow to his eyelid.

I hoped so too. I hoped I wasn't giving my friend false hope.

I mean, it is entirely possible that he dropped his phone and broke it. It is also entirely possible he is cheating on Jorge. I really hope it is the former and not the latter. Betrayal is brutal.

Chapter Thirteen

I was escorted to the town's humble plaza. Loíza's holiday decorations were dollar-store quality compared to Viejo San Juan's commissioned and extravagant ones. We took a few minutes of video. I posed on a sculptural bench that was a piece of public art. It had a mosaic depiction of a vejigante.

"We'll be back after the cave trip. I've arranged for some food vendors and musicians," Delvis said.

Booth tents and a couple of outdoor propane stoves were being set up. I saw a woman carrying a large aluminum pot with the bottom and sides scorched black from high heat. She set it by a yet-to-be-hoisted banner advertising empanadas de jueyes. Crabs. The river we'd crossed coming into town led to the ocean. The brackish environment was perfect for the blue land crab.

"Do you think we can find a local crabber?" I asked. "It would make a nice segment. The crabs in this area are caught and kept for several weeks. They're fed corn and rice to change the taste of the meat from funky to sweet. Crabs are scavengers, you know. So, if you were to eat the crab before changing its diet, it would taste kinda nasty."

"Yuck. I didn't know that. Really? That's a little gross. I will from now on have the image of a crabby crab with a cigarette in its pincher every time I eat jueyes. *Gracias, Dr. Quiñones,*" Delvis said sarcastically as we got in the van to go to the next location. "I'll work on finding a crabber. It shouldn't be too hard."

During the ride, my phone pinged with a message from Delvis in the front seat. It was a meme of a crab with a cigarette. "Very funny."

La Cueva María de la Cruz was a quick drive from base camp. It was bigger than I'd imagined. Even though I'd studied Delvis's info packet, 30 meters high hadn't impressed me on paper. Seeing the gaping mouth of the limestone cave, I did the conversion to feet. *98 feet, coño that's like nine stories high.*

"Okay, we are going to do the bee thing first. I think the apiary is over there." Delvis pointed to an area with a closed gate.

A woman in a keeper's uniform opened the gate and began walking toward our van. She unzipped the netting around her neck and let the hat portion fall to her back.

"¿Kharla?" I sped up my pace.

"¿Prima Miriam?" The keeper stopped in her tracks.

"*You two know each other?*" Delvis asked.

"She's my cousin that I haven't seen in, like—"

"Twenty years," Kharla and I said in unison.

"I thought you were in Costa Rica or Colombia or algo asi," I said.

"Sí, y Panama también, but I came back after Maria," Kharla informed me.

According to Mami, Kharla had been born with wanderlust. Over the years, I'd seen pictures of her feeding sloths, rehabilitating tamarins, and sliding down rain forest waterfalls. She was an idealist that put sweat equity into projects. It made absolute sense that she'd be involved in the bee project.

"Tienes que pasar por la casa. We need to catch up," Kharla said.

"There will be time for a family reunion after we shoot. We need to stay on schedule. Dale." Delvis pushed us toward the apiary with the crew following.

I donned a veiled hat and jumpsuit before entering the gated area. Between the smoke used to calm the bees and the hat's veil, I doubted the viewer could tell it was me in the shot. Even my baby belly was not obvious in the voluminous jumpsuit. Kharla opened one of the hives for the camera and showed the honey-dense combs. Each of the white boxes had a Taíno symbol painted on it. Archaeological evidence in the cave proved it had been used by Indigenous peoples as far back as 1000 BCE. The cave had also been used as a hiding place by enslaved Africans fleeing their captors. I hoped we'd cover that history and get a cave tour.

The next shot was away from the apiary near the wild colony of bees that made their home at the top of the cave. We stood safely beneath the hanging hives, this time in safety helmets in case of falling stalactites. Kharla did her spiel about the importance of honeybees and presented me with a jar of honey. Delvis called cut.

"It's supercool what you are doing," I said to my cousin as we followed the crew to a pavilion for the next segment. "Is this what brought you home?"

"No. Originally, it was just to help, you know. To clean, build, paint, whatever. It was como un mes after Hurricane Maria. Clean water was the biggest problem. The sewer water was everywhere. Y sin electricidad, the water pumps that run the filters didn't work. People were getting sick, and unos died de leptospirosis. That was the first project I got involved with—a solar-powered water system. Then when things were a little better, I left. I went to Jamaica to help with an eco-village. Todo vegan. It was bien chévere. Pero I couldn't stop thinking about home. Ya tú sabes. I'm back for good."

Kharla and I stopped and sat on one of the gargantuan roots of a ceiba tree. I took a few pictures of us and sent them to Mami. My cousin was no longer the skin-and-bones girl I remember from that family vacation so long ago. She was muscle and grit. She glowed with a vibrance that came from outdoor life. I hardly would have recognized her if it weren't for her dad's bulbous and wide nose and that joyful smile and cheek dimple that I remembered from when we were kids. Kharla and I exchanged phone numbers so she could send the shots to her mom, Sandra, who immediately demanded Kharla bring me home for dinner.

Delvis called my name and beckoned me to get to the pavilion for the next part of the shoot. My cousin and I moseyed in that direction. A bee buzzed between us, and I instinctually shied away from it.

Kharla laughed. "I'm used to them."

"*Bees*. Why bees? Why this project?" I asked.

"This? I wasn't even supposed to be here today. Imagínate. I'm just two or three hours a week aqui. The guy that was supposed to be here got the flu. No, I work con UPRI, Unidos para un Puerto Rico Independente," Kharla said.

"What's that? A government agency?"

"No. *Definitely* not government. I'll tell you about it tonight. I'll text you Mami's address." My cousin hugged me goodbye. I waved as she walked away.

I felt a tug on my sleeve. A PA gave me a bottle of water and pointed to the restrooms. She also gave me a two-minute call. After I'd freshened up, Delvis explained what she wanted me to do, checked my battery-powered mic, and gave me a silent countdown. The camera followed me from kiosk to kiosk as I admired the crafts. Then I stopped at the mask workshop to interview a seventy-five-year-old mask maker and his twenty-year-old grandson, who was learning the craft. I steered the conversation to the importance of the coconut to the inhabitants, past and present. It provided nourishment and was used in a multitude of dishes. And, of course, it was the base of the vejigante masks.

I purchased a small decorative mask to take back to Manny. Because it wasn't the size meant to be worn, it wasn't as scary. But it was still spikey. It looked a little like a psychedelic tarantula and about the same size as the arachnid.

Next, we filmed a short segment about headwraps. It was something the cave park offered to the tourists. The traditional headdress traced its roots to Africa.

"¿Qué color te gusta más?" the woman asked, showing me a large basket filled with strips of fabric.

"Azul o blanco." I suggested colors that would match my outfit.

"Claro, tú eres de Yemaya." The woman guessed I was a devotee of the orisha Yemaya, protector of mothers and children.

I wasn't, but Tía Elba had been encouraging me to be one. And I *was* wearing her colors. *And* I was pregnant. So, it tracked.

Maya is a nice name. What if we named our sirena Maya? Miriam, Manny, and Maya. Too many Ms.

The woman knotted a pretty swirl-patterned white-and-blue fabric around my head. The segment had nothing to do with food, but it did have everything to do with culture. The woman, Isa, told me and the camera about the enslaved Africans and free people of color that had settled in Loíza. Using the headwrap was about heritage and pride.

Delvis called cut, and the crew loaded back into the van.

"Jorge is going to kill me," I said.

"Why?" Delvis asked,

I pointed to my new do, and she laughed.

"Leave it. It looks good and will be perfect for the dance segment." Delvis grinned.

"You don't expect me to dance a Bomba, *do you*?" I knew she'd scheduled dancers and musicians for the plaza, but nowhere in her notes had it said *Miriam dances.*

Delvis avoided answering me by *suddenly* having to talk to the crew about next week's *La Tacita* special.

"Is that Jules?" I couldn't believe my eyes. Jules or someone that looked like him had entered one of the places that bordered one side of the central plaza.

"Who's Jules?" Delvis asked.

My head was turned so far over my shoulder that I could've been part owl. *Did I really see Jules in Loíza? Miriam, está loca. He is back in Punta Cana.*

"Who's Jules? Another prima?" Delvis inquired. The van pulled into base camp and jostled us as we changed surfaces from street to gravel and grass.

"No, not a prima, just some guy I meet at my parents' place. He was in town for the New Year's Eve party. He went to school with Pablo Montoya," I said.

"*Really?* Is he in entertainment? Does he work for a studio?" Delvis held her hand out for me to steady myself getting out of the van.

"No, mi'ja. He's in real estate. Sorry." I made a better-luck-next-time expression.

"Don't give me that face. This business is about who you know and who knows you. And I want to be known as more than *La Tacita's* segment director," Delvis said. She pushed her sleeve up her tattooed forearm before putting her fist on her hip. "Go to makeup, and we will call you in ten." She waved me away.

Before opening the mini RV's door, I got a text from Mami. She was five heart emojis ecstatic that I'd seen Kharla. Before I'd left Punta Palma, I'd updated her phone's program to improve our video calls. The upgrade came with an expanded emoji keyboard. She was texting like a Gen Z teen. I started to ask her if Jules was back but deleted it.

Miriam, you did not see Rolex-wearing, million-dollar-property-buyer Jules Howard in lower-income Loíza. This is not his scene.

I chuckled at my silliness and opened the door.

"¿Qué es eso?" Jorge asked. His one raised eyebrow judged my turban.

"Delvis said I had to keep it on for the next segment."

"Hmph. Okay, fine. Pero, let me fix it, so you look good. Porque ahora you look like," he exhaled a puff of breath, "um, no lo voy a decir."

"That bad?"

Jorge teased a few wavy curls from under the wrap. He reapplied my lipstick and dusted my nose and cheekbones with something. I looked in the mirror and appreciated his talent. He'd made the headwrap look like something I always wore. It looked natural and easy, not staged. Just a few wisps of hair made the difference. His phone beeped, and he practically dove onto the bench to get it.

"*Lucas?*" I hoped.

"No." Jorge threw his phone onto the bench. It bounced once and wedged itself between my purse and the back cushion.

"He's probably asleep. Don't worry. He will be there when you get back."

"No. He's cheating. He's not answering my messages porque he's with somebody else." Jorge flounced onto the seat, causing my purse and his phone to slip onto the floor.

A PA knocked and told me it was time to go to the plaza.

"Come with me," I said to my friend. "It will get your mind off of things."

Jorge started to protest but came along without much twisting of his arm.

The formerly dull plaza had transformed into a feast of sights, smells, and sounds. A regiment of drummers was warming up with slaps and slides on the skins of the barrile drums. I knew from previous research that the drums were originally made from discarded rum barrels. Some of the drums in the Bomba group were painted red, yellow, and green, while others were left in their natural brown. Isa, the lady from the park, was there too. She'd changed outfits. Her ensemble looked like the Puerto Rican flag. Her headwrap was white, her spaghetti-strap tank was blue, and her full skirt was red. She, too, was limbering up. When she swished her skirt, I saw she had on white leggings.

"Señora Quiñones," Isa called.

I waved to her, and she motioned for me to join her. Like a puff of magician's smoke, Delvis materialized between Jorge and me.

"You aren't expecting me to dance," I said to her frozen grin. She remained mute, meaning this was all planned, but she hadn't put it in my notes. "I'm a food anthropologist. Dancing is not food. Let me go over there and interview the lady frying alcapurrias." I pointed to the woman forming the yucca mash with a sea grape leaf before letting it gently roll into the hot oil.

"Anthropologists study culture. *This is culture.* You will be great," Delvis said.

"No jodas. Really? Mi'ja, I'm, like, seriously pregnant." I placed my hands on the sides of my belly.

"Por favor*rrr*, Miriam. Last week, you were at my Mambo-ize class, and you were fine. Mejor que fine," Jorge said.

"Mambo. You dance?" Delvis asked Jorge.

"Jorge does everything. Not only is he the best DJ, drag queen, costume maker, and maestro de yoga, but he is also the founder of Mambo-ize. It's like Zumba pero with Mambo. So, yes. He can dance. Have him dance instead of me," I said.

"Perfect. You can be in the segment." Delvis clapped her hands.

I fluttered my eyelashes at my friend.

"Both of you," Delvis added.

Jorge deadpanned and then stuck out his tongue.

"I will remember this. I finally get to be on TV pero with *no* makeup because of you," Jorge teased.

Isa gave me a white cotton skirt to pull on over my pants. The gathered elastic waist allowed me to accommodate it below my belly. When the man playing the cuá, a hollow wooden tube on a stand that, along with the maracas, maintains the rhythm for the dance, began striking the six-eight beat, my feet followed like they'd danced the steps a million times before. A song that sounded more like spoken word than lyrics boasted about the area's African heritage and resistance to oppression. A male partner joined Isa, and they danced around each other like roosters about to fight. Jorge and I were encouraged to mimic them and come to the circle's center. After some call-and-response between Isa and the primo drummer, the chorus of beats crescendoed and stopped in unison.

Delvis asked for a second dance so she could get some close-up shots. Isa whispered into the ear of the vocalist, who then said something to the lead drummer. I'd heard him called primo, as in first or lead. His job was to change the syncopation in response to the dancer and vocalist. A variation of the previous song's rhythm was played. Isa joined me on the dance floor. Instinct took over, and I began moving my skirt in waves like I'd seen practitioners of the La Regla de Ocha do. My tía Elba was one. Mami, not so much, but she'd attended a bembé or two when I was young and in tow. The enslaved Africans that had originated Puerto Rico's Bomba music were the same peoples that influenced the religious drumming used in Cuban Santeria, sometimes called La Regla de Ocha or Regla Lucumí.

When I stopped dancing, the plaza erupted in shouts and applause.

"Nena, you were candela," Delvis said. "You acted like you couldn't dance. Liar."

I wiped the sweat from my brow. "What do you mean?"

"You were doing a call-and-response about Yemaya with the drummer and singer. It was wild, like you were possessed. Like, wow," Delvis said. "Drink some water and rest a second. I found you a crabber. We will shoot the food stuff next, then go to the crab guy."

I looked for a place to put my feet up but had to admit I didn't feel tired. I put my hand on top of my belly and smiled. Maybe I had been visited by Yemaya, the protector of mothers.

"¿Qué estás pensando?" Jorge asked.

"I'm thinking I put mi sirena to sleep." I rubbed my belly. "Como en un rocking chair."

"More like a boat on an ocean," Jorge said. He pressed Play on the video he'd taken of me dancing.

"Ay, ay, ay. My tía Elba needs to see that. She'll say I'd been a caballo. Can you send me the video?" I wasn't a devotee of Tía's faith, but there was something to it. I'd visited a babalawo with her, and he'd been right about a lot of things. I mean, he hadn't predicted I'd get locked in a freezer and almost die, but the orishas speaking through him had warned me I'd be in danger if I wasn't careful.

Jorge sent me the video as well as a few still shots. There was one perfect image of me with my skirt's ruffles rolling like waves. I impulsively sent it to Mami and Tía. I enlarged the image and saw something in the background. It was Jules Howard. He was at the place I'd thought I'd seen him earlier. *That's his blingy, oversized watch. Is he taking a selfie?*

"Miriam!" Jorge yelled. "¿Pa' dónde vas?"

"To solve a mystery," I replied.

Chapter Fourteen

I crossed the street and went to the place. It was a casual restaurant with beer and a pool table. It advertised comida criolla. But it wasn't open for full service. There was a handwritten sign taped to the door. *Solo Bebidas. Evento en la plaza.* The bar was open but not the kitchen due to the event in the plaza.

I pivoted on my heels and smacked into Jorge, who'd followed me.

"Chica, are you still possessed? You just ran off como una loca. What's going on?" Jorge asked.

"This guy." I showed him the blurry enlargement. "He keeps showing up in places. Como un stalker. He helped me with my bag at the airport. Then he was at my parents' place. Then he was at the UnMundo party. Then he sent me a gift. And now he's here."

"Huh. Na-uh. No. You better call la policia," Jorge said.

"And." I poked Jorge's chest with my finger. "Welmo, an ex-cop, followed him that night into the Bitcoin party. Something is going on with that guy, and I'm going to find out what."

"Okay, Velma." Jorge removed my finger from his chest.

"Velma?"

"Velma. De Scooby-Doo, *you know.* The smart one. Always wears orange. It's her signature color. That's a hard color to do, but she does it." Jorge snapped his fingers for accent.

"I am not Velma."

"If you say so, Doctora Quiñones. *Perrrro*—You are super smart, and you solve mysteries like her. *Sooo*, I think that makes you a Velma."

I rolled my eyes at my friend. What was it with people giving me nicknames? Detective Pullman called me Jessica Fletcher and Veronica Mars. *Detective Pullman. I wonder if he could run a background check on Jules Howard for me.*

Jorge and I walked back to the plaza. Delvis and the crew were ready to shoot the food part, but I was still wearing the folkloric skirt. I returned the skirt to Isa and removed my headwrap. Jorge ran to the RV and came back with his kit. While my hair was fluffed and my makeup repaired, I texted Detective Pullman. I framed it as I thought I might have a stalker. *Can you run a check on a Miami businessman that keeps showing up everywhere I go?* He didn't reply.

"Ponte las pilas. I don't want to go into overtime, and we still have to do your crabs," Delvis said.

UnMundo had paid the exhibitors a generous fee to cook for the staged event. They'd also invited several organizations to be extras. A group of kids lined up to get pinchos, a skewered meat coated with a sweet barbecue sauce. Their matching T-shirts had the outline of a drum beneath the extracurricular club's name. I asked one of them to tell me his favorite thing about living in Loíza. The youngster smiled broadly and replied, "La Fiesta de Santiago." His mates all nodded in agreement, except for one slightly older girl who said she had a better answer. I asked her what that was, and she said, "El arroz con jueyes de Fela. Ella es famosa. Hicieron un documental de ella."

The tween beckoned me to follow her to the last booth in the short row, where an older woman stood, wearing a black hairnet over her silver hair. She introduced herself by her full name Juana

Felicita Teresa de Badillo I recognized that name from a paper I'd read on Afro-Taíno foods. A helper prepared a portion for me, and I tasted the rice for the camera. The rice dish was packed with flavors. There was sweetness from the crab and coconut milk. The sofrito was fresh and herbaceous. The pink beans called habichuelas had a nice tooth that balanced perfectly with the creamy fat of the pig's feet pieces. I loaded my plastic spoon with another heapful and savored its deliciousness with my eyes closed.

Fela, as she liked to be called, was over eighty but looked a decade or two younger. She told me about her cookbook and about the many historians and chefs that visited her kitchen. She insisted her restaurant was better than the booth because it had her burén. I let her talk. A burén, originally made of clay, was a wide, flat cooking surface used by the Taíno. Hers was made of metal, but it was the same principle. Coconut husks fueled the fire that heated the surface. She made cassava bread on it and a host of other artisanal and probably pre-contact dishes.

We ended the segment. Fela invited me to pass by her restaurant sometime. She'd let me see her kitchen and watch her cook. The anthropologist in me was excited at the prospect of doing some real field study. I chastised myself for not having done research about the area myself. La Barbacoa de Fela would have made a more interesting episode than this stage gathering.

"I'm going to let the crew eat, and then we'll go to the beach to meet the crab guy. *Okay*," Delvis said.

"No problem. I think I'll go back to Jorge's van and put my feet up," I said.

When I got to UnMundo's lot, the only person there was Welmo. He was seated in an aluminum beach chair, sharpening a pencil with a pocketknife.

"Did you get some food?" I asked.

"Later, I'm on guard duty," Welmo said. He blew the shavings off the pencil and tucked it back into the wire spiral of his pocket notepad.

"You have to try Fela's arroz con jueyes. I've never had anything like it. Incredible."

"No te preocupes. My prima will bring me a plate. She's good like that," he assured me.

My phone rang, and I excused myself to answer it. It was Detective Frank Pullman.

"What trouble are you in now, Veronica?" Pullman asked without a hello.

"I'm not in any trouble, thank you very much. I'm trying to keep trouble away from me, actually," I replied.

"Hmph. Well, tell me about this guy. You think he's stalking you. Why? Have you received any threatening mail?"

"No, but he seems to be at my every turn."

"If he's an obsessed fan, the best thing to do is to alert your network people. Ask for a security guard. Until he does something, the law can't do anything." Pullman covered his phone's speaker. Something muffled and unintelligible was said. Then there was a siren's wah-wah. "I've got to go. Don't risk your safety and the baby's. Tell your network about him."

"Okay. But can you run him through your system just in case he has a history of this kind of thing?"

"I've got to go. Send me the guy's name. If you get any threatening emails or anything like that, forward them to me. I'll see what I can do. You said he lives in Miami, right? I have to go." A car door slammed shut. Pullman ended the call.

Does a mermaid plushie count as threatening?

Jorge was smiling and laughing at his phone when I entered the caravan.

"Lucas?" I asked.

"No. Él es un comemierda. It's Alma. Mira." Jorge showed me his phone. It was a short video of our friend screaming expletives as she lifted into the air off the back of a boat. A multicolored chute pulled her skyward. Her hands gripped the harness lines. As she left the deck, her legs pedaled in a cartoonish panic. Then the boat sped up, and she was a dot on a cord.

"Ay, Caridad. I can't believe she went parasailing," I said.

"I know, right? Ese novio has her going wild, no?" Jorge played the video one more time and cackled.

"She has always been wild, but I guess *the Love Bug* has let the wild loose. Have you met him?"

"Who? Herbie? No. We're supposed to go out tonight on a double date. Pero ahora, I don't know."

"Hmm?"

"Lucas is cheating on me. Estoy seguro. Now the two apartments make sense. He's a player." Jorge cut his eyes at me.

"I'm sorry, papi." I offered in sympathy.

"Whatevs."

My friend put on a brave face, but I could tell he was hurt. And I wondered what the real story was with Lucas. Maybe something had happened to him. Dark thoughts entered my mind. Puerto Rico had its share of crime. Carjackings were often in the news. They were mostly drug-related, *but* if Lucas had been in the wrong place, that could explain the lack of communication. His phone was smashed or still in the car, and he was stranded by a sugarcane field. No one knows phone numbers anymore. They are all saved in our contacts. He might not have money for a ride back. So many people don't carry cash anymore. *His money is probably on his phone too.*

I wanted to say all the things I was thinking to my friend. But I didn't want to upset him either. Instead, I excused myself, claiming I needed the bathroom, and went to find my driver.

"Welmo, perdone," I said, seeing he was eating. "You still have contacts at the police, no?"

"Sí. Why?" He ate the last bite from his bowl, stood, and set the Styrofoam dish on the beach chair's woven straps. He cleaned a rice grain from his lips with his fingers.

"Can you discreetly check if somebody has been found? Maybe he doesn't know his name or is hurt," I said.

Welmo did the thing that Detective Pullman always did. His demeanor changed from warm to cold. He was in cop mode. Robert's cousin, Officer Gordon, did it too. *Do they teach that at the police academy?*

"Who? A friend? Are they missing?"

"Well, they didn't come home last night. They are in the same hotel as my friend Jorge, the makeup artist." I jutted my chin in the direction of the RV.

"Do you have a name or a photo?" Welmo took out his little notepad.

"I'll show you a picture." I went to the UnMundo website and found the show's promo page. "Him."

"Lucas Palo de *Gigi's Amantes*." Welmo raised an eyebrow. "Did you tell anybody at UnMundo?"

"No." I shook my head and lowered my voice to a whisper. "It might be nothing. Maybe he's at the beach having a good time. But still, my friend is a little worried because he isn't answering his phone. I don't want to make a big deal out of it, pero maybe you could ask around on the down-low."

"Leave it with me," Welmo said.

"Miriam," Delvis called from across the lot. "Get your things. You are going with Welmo to the last shoot. I'm sending the extra crew home."

I gave her a thumbs-up. I figured Jorge fell under the extra crew category. I went to get my purse and say goodbye to my friend.

"Text me when you get there." I hugged him. "I bet Lucas will be there with a good explanation. You'll see."

"Sí, the *ex-splay-nation* better be he is dead. *Or* someone in his family is dead. *Orrrr* something *berry* serious. Porque I do not put up with cheaters." Jorge talked fast and with buckets of drama.

I remember not too many months ago when I thought my Roberto might be cheating. He wasn't. There had been a perfectly logical explanation for his weird behavior. Okay, not perfect or logical, and we are *still working* on his communication skills. But the point was sometimes something innocent looked guilty when all the facts weren't on the table.

Chapter Fifteen

"Turn here!" I pounded on the back of Welmo's seat. A car had just passed us with someone familiar in the back seat.

"This is not the road. What is wrong? Are you sick?" He turned off 187 and onto Calle el Jobo.

"I thought I saw someone I know. Follow that red car."

"Lucas Palo?" Welmo queried.

"Stop here. I'll be right back." I unbuckled myself and had my hand on the door handle. The residential street didn't have a sidewalk and only had a few houses. The red car had let the person out. I waited while the Uber driver made a three-point turn to get out of the dead-end street. Welmo idled and waited for my instructions. I opened the door, slipped out, and shut it quietly. I heard protests and a warning from Welmo, but I ignored them as I stomped off. I wanted to know what Jules Howard was doing in Loíza on a street that came to a dead end at a dirt road that led to a tangle of trees and shrubs. It was not the place for a pressed-linen and fancy-watch Miami businessman who was supposed to be in Punta Cana.

"Señora Quiñones, please get back in the car. This is not safe for you. Get in the car, and I will see if it is Lucas Palo," Welmo said, creeping beside me at a snail's pace.

"Shh. It's fine. Come with me if you want."

I heard the brakes and then the door. Welmo was beside me in a few strides.

"We will be late to the filming. Let me handle this later. He might be intoxicated or violente," Welmo warned.

"Shh. It's not Lucas. It's the guy who sent me the gift." I put out my arm like a turnstile stop. It *was* Jules Howard. He was nosing around a bright-yellow cabaña.

What is he doing here?

I held Welmo in place and put a be-silent finger to my lips. We watched as Jules took a few photos of the wooden house. The structure was not plum, and there were air gaps between the corrugated metal roof and the walls. It looked a little like the jibaro cabins of old. Jules tried to look through the cracks in a louvered window. The horizontal aluminum slates were the type of inexpensive (and hurricane-safe) window used all over the island.

My sirena did a kickflip from the adrenaline pulsing through my veins. If I hadn't been possessed earlier, I certainly was now. I had to find out if Jules Howard was stalking me. *Miriam, it kind of looks like you are stalking him.* My inner voice was right. I quit spying and approached him.

"*Jules.* Is that you?" My acting was over the top, and I noticed Welmo looked at me with suspicion.

"Miriam *Key-known-es.*" Jules spun on his heels. "I'm afraid I have bad news."

Welmo grabbed my wrist to get me to stop my forward motion. I wiggled out of his grip.

Jules kept talking. "It's closed. I'm so disappointed." He pointed to the hand-painted sign I hadn't noticed. The red lettering was sun-bleached, and each word looked like it had been done by a different person, as none matched the other. It read *La Barbacoa de Fela.* "I really wanted to try the food. You're a foodie like me. Do you watch the James Beard nominated videos? I do. I've been obsessed with this place ever since. So unique. It would make a great restaurant in Miami. I'm thinking of this spot I have in South Beach, but something on Brickell would work too. Yeah, maybe near the Miami Circle. That could work concept-wise. Are you here to interview her for your show?" Jules's tone was boingy, like a kid's.

"Um . . ." I stammered. "Yes. I met her in the plaza not long ago. She invited me to see her kitchen."

"Oh, really. So, you know her. Could I get an introduction?"

"Actually, I thought I saw you by the plaza." I choose not to answer his request.

"I was there. There was some private event going on. I was looking for this place but was given the wrong directions." Jules paced in front of the locked door as if his desire to get in would will it to open. "I told the driver I was looking for good food, and he took me to his favorite place. It was closed too." Jules laughed sardonically. "But I stayed and had a beer. The waitress tried to get me to eat a papa *ray-in-ah*, but I passed. It looked greasy under the heat lamp."

Welmo cleared his throat. "Señora, we need to get to the location."

"Okay," I said to Welmo. Jules looked at Welmo, who'd been standing a few feet behind me the whole time. "Oh, pardon my rudeness. This is Welmo. He's with the studio. He's my chauffeur—" *That sounds so snobby, Miriam.* "And my security," I added.

Welmo shook Jules's hand. "Tenemos que ir," he said to me. Welmo acted as if he'd never once laid eyes on Jules Howard, but I'd seen him follow Jules into El Convento the other night. *What is going on here?*

"Speaking of drivers. Mine left me. Could I get a lift with you? Just to a major intersection, or this place." Jules looked at his phone. "It doesn't seem to have an address. It's a kiosk in *Pie-non-es*." He showed the screen to Welmo.

"It is not far." Welmo looked to me for the go-ahead. I nodded that it was safe. I no longer thought Jules was dangerous in the stalker sense. He was up to something, but I didn't think it had anything to do with me. There was still the worry that he was trying to buy Punta Palma for a steal, tear it down, and leave my parents jobless. But the only way I could find that out was to keep him talking.

Jules held the car door open for me.

"Thank you," I said.

"Of course. You're a lady, and a pregnant one at that. Did you get my gift?" Jules asked.

I waited for him to go to his side and join me in the back seat. I'd moved my purse and things into the front passenger seat to make it more comfortable.

"*The mermaid.* Was that from you?" I noticed Welmo giving me a quizzical look via the rearview mirror. "There wasn't a note."

"Really? I'm sorry. I did ask for one."

"Well, I'm just glad I now know who to thank. Thank you. It is perfect for the baby's nursery. That was very kind of you," I said.

"Think nothing of it. You and your parents are such nice people," Jules said, watching the scenery out his window.

"Actually, didn't you tell me you were headed back to the Dominican Republic to finish your vacation?"

He sighed. "Well, it *was* a working vacation. And now it's all work. Since I was in Puerto Rico, they asked me to check on our project in Old San Juan."

"They?" I asked.

"LPM, the conglomerate I work with. They do restaurants."

"What's the project?" I knew exactly what and where the project was. It was the family restaurant behind Jorge's place that had had their rent jacked sky high. A spike of anger hit me. *I swear pregnancy hormones make every mood and emotion increase by ten. Cálmate and keep him talking.* I fanned myself to chill my rage. "Is it something I might have heard about? Tell me about it."

"It's a new partnership, a restaurant attached to a boutique hotel. We got lucky with it. I had a handshake deal with the original owner, a nice old man, for the restaurant portion, but he died before I could finalize it. I thought we'd lost it. But the new owner approached us about a partnership. He is strictly vacation rentals and luxury second homes. He didn't want to do the restaurant part."

"Oh. Is he local?" I asked

"We are here," Welmo said.

He stopped in front of a trailer home on cinderblocks. It had a front porch made from pallets and a blue tarp awning that billowed like a lung. Delvis and a single cameraman were there. Welmo let me out of the car. He informed me that he'd drop Jules at his location and then return for me.

"Gracias. Okay, Jules. It was nice to see you again," I said with a wave.

That was a stupid thing to say. Nice to see you again. De verdad, Miriam. And you didn't get your question answered. Is the guy local, or is he an outsider taking advantage of Act 22? That poor family is losing their restaurant.

"Miriam, está es Gilberto El Rey de los Jueyes." Delvis introduced me to a man who was petite in stature but rotund in tummy. He wore a gray-and-navy striped button-up open over a white undershirt. The white shirt was stained with blotches of yellowed pink. *Fish guts. No. Crab juice, probably.* The undershirt's ribbing stretched over the man's belly, reminding me of a blue whale's chin.

We conducted the interview in Spanish. Despite his shaggy exterior, Gilberto was a gentle soul with a sense of humor. He patted his belly and joked he was in his last trimester and expecting a baron, a boy. I instantly warmed to him. We even took a silly photo in silhouette, showing off our panzas.

Gilberto's home and workplace were one and the same. We started filming behind the trailer by a canal that had a dense thicket of mangroves. He showed me two types of traps, a plastic tube and a wooden shoebox with a sliding door. Then we visited the limpeiza crates. The crabs stayed in them for about a month, eating corn and drinking tap water to clean/limpiar their flavor. Sometimes, he gave them a little coconut meat too. He moved the gym weight holding the top down, and opened the hinged lid for me and the camera. I wasn't prepared for the sound of hundreds of legs scurrying away from the light. I jumped slightly, and Gilberto laughed. He took out a big crab and displayed it for the viewer.

Gilberto said his was a simple life but a good one. He lived off the land like his ancestors before him but with better entertainment and transportation. He pointed to his satellite dish and a spotless and new Toyota truck with pride. To end the segment, we sat on his porch and ate salmorejo de jueyes made by his wife, Adela. I'd smelled the onion, garlic, and sofrito cooking as we'd done the interview and hoped we'd get a taste of whatever his wife was preparing. She hadn't invited us into their home, and I didn't want to push. So, when she emerged from the trailer offering me a castañita de pana filled with salmorejo, I eagerly accepted.

The stewed crab and the breadfruit tostone were a delicious combination. The tender meat went perfectly with the crispy saltiness of the fried starch. I tasted oregano and recao/culantro. The slight tomato flavor came from a restrained use of sauce—just enough to color and unite the ingredients but not overpower it.

The crab was the star of the show. Adela told me this was a popular dish during semana santa / holy week, when people refrained from eating meat. She'd learned to make it from her mother, who ran a fiambrera service from their home kitchen. I asked her to explain what that was for our audience. I knew the term meant a cantina service. My tía y tío had offered it from their Hialeah restaurant. It made life easier for working folks and elderly people who didn't have the time or energy to shop and cook. It was also very economical. The service provided cooked meals in a stacked and latched stainless-steel carrier. The fiambrera, as it was called in Puerto Rico, was returned the following day to be refilled.

Thinking of my tíos' restaurant that had been handed down to my prima Yoli steered my thoughts back to El Capitán. That family was losing their livelihood because of Jules Howard and LPM. It made my blood boil.

Chapter Sixteen

"You're riding back in the van. Welmo had an emergency," Delvis said after a fury of texting on her phone.

"Oh no. Is everybody okay? Is it his family? I mean, your family?" I asked.

"He didn't say. I think it's nothing major, just something important he needed to get to."

"Carajo," I said under my breath.

"Tranqui." Delvis used the Puerto Rican colloquialism for chill, "We'll get you back to the guesthouse. It might not be as comfortable, but we have better tunes." Delvis did a little perreo/twerk.

"It's not that. Welmo was going to take me to Luquillo to see my prima."

"The beekeeper?" Delvis checked the time. "I really need to get mi gente back to the studio."

"Give me a second. Let me see if she can come get me."

Kharla replied that she was nearby and would be there in ten minutes. I told Delvis it was handled and that my prima would get me back to the guesthouse after dinner. It was only a minute or two after the crew van had driven off that Kharla arrived. Gilberto y Adela had kept me company with stories of crabs getting loose, crabs found in their shower, and crabs fighting in the kitchen sink. I imagined Delvis's meme with the cigarette replaced with a knife.

"¡Prima!" Kharla yelled from her car.

"¡Prima!" I shouted back. I thanked Gilberto y Adela for their hospitality and said goodbye to them.

"Here, let me make room," Kharla said, moving a pile of papers to the back seat.

I took a single leaflet she'd missed and sat shotgun. The leaflet was two-sided and had a logo with a machete and pava. "Is this the group you were telling me about? U-P." I pronounced the initials in Spanish.

She corrected me. "*U-prree*. U-P-R-I. Unidos para un Puerto Rico Independiente."

"Wouldn't that be *u-poo-pre?* U-P-U-P-R-I."

"Prima, it was named before I joined it. If I had named it, I'd have called it M-L-C. Muerte a los Colonizadores." Kharla pfted. "We need to stop at the store. Mami said she was out of olives. She's making arroz con pollo."

"One of my favorites. Yes!"

I scanned the leaflet. It was for a planned protest in Old San Juan. *Bring your flags. Bring your water bottle. March starts at El Capitolio and finishes at La Fortaleza.* I flipped the page over. The date was cinco de enero.

That's the same day as the Three Kings festival.

I tucked the leaflet into my purse and planned to tell Delvis about it later that evening. I didn't know if the protest would march past the plaza where the Three Kings event was, but with the streets so narrow and the town so small, it might be a problem. And I knew Puerto Ricans took their civil disobedience very seriously. The turnout could be large. Marches on the island had shut down highways before. It had happened during the ousting of Governor Roselló. Before the government privatized all the utilities, union strikes were fairly regular and well supported. The voice of the people was a strong tradition in the island's culture. Their voter turnout was superhigh compared to the United States.

"If you are tired, you can stay in the car," Kharla said with one foot out of the car.

"Voy contigo," I said. There was no way I was passing up a chance to see food.

My cousin went straight to the aisle she needed but let me wander the produce and meat sections. My nose took in all the greenness of the fresh herbs before I sauntered to the butcher's display. All parts of the animal were available. There were pig's tails, ears, and feet. The store also made its own morcilla, blood sausage. It was made from pig's blood and fat, rice, mild peppers, and garlic. Morcilla was always made with animal blood, but which animal depended on the area. They used beef and veal in their sausage in Argentina, Uruguay, and Spain, where cattle husbandry was more plentiful. Puerto Rico's small landmass did not lend itself to large herds of beef cows. The island did produce its own beef, but a lot of it was from the dairy industry. I looked at the beef selection in the refrigerated case. It was mostly the tougher cuts for stews like carne guisada or thin slices for bistec encebollado or ground beef for picadillo. I didn't see any marbled porterhouses or top loin.

"Listo," Kharla said.

"Ready for dinner. *Yes.* I was thinking about beef recipes for *Abuela Approved,* and I might have made myself hungry." I laughed.

"Do you want to get a snack? Mami won't start cooking until you get there."

I looked at the baton of bread in my cousin's arm. "I could just have a piece of bread with cheese."

"Cool. I'll get some more pan. You get the queso."

I selected a queso fresco and checked that it was made on the island. The label said Hatillo, a town near Arecibo known for its dairy. We checked out. The cashier looked at me several times like she was trying to place me but was too shy to ask. Kharla noticed it too.

As we left the store, my cousin said, "I think she recognized you. Does that happen a lot? Do people ever ask for your autograph?"

"It is happening more and more. Yeah, it's a little weird but also cool. Mostly, they ask for a photo," I replied.

"Señoras," a voice called from the sliding glass doors. "Tu recibo."

The cashier waved the long receipt of mostly coupons and advertisements at us. It looked like a kite tail in the wind.

Kharla and I exchanged looks.

"I think she figured it out," Kharla said.

"Yeah. I'll go." I went and got the undulating paper. She sheepishly asked if I was on *La Tacita*. I told her I was and that I loved her island. We took a selfie with the red *Pueblo* grocery store sign above our heads. I told her to tune in to catch the Three Kings episode from San Juan.

"Dios te bendiga," the cashier said, blessing my pregnant state. "Y tengas cuidado. Hay una marcha ese día. UPRI es . . ." Her unfinished statement floated in the air before she turned to return to her line of customers.

UPRI es . . . ¿Qué? What about them?

In the car, Kharla was cleaning a large folding knife with one of the leaflets.

"Here, let me," I said, taking it from her. I cleaned the blade using a squirt of gel sanitizer and a paper napkin from my purse— moms are always prepared for dirty hands. Then I sliced open the round puck of cheese and cut a few pieces off. "That's a serious knife." I cleaned it again and gave it back to her.

"Yeah, it comes in handy." She closed it and started the engine. "Un vez, I was working as a tour guide at this banana plantation in Limón for a cruise line, tú sabes—because I needed the money, and the tips were okay. You know, work a few months, then live 'pura vida' for a few months. Anyway, this six-inch spider runs across the forest floor y una mujer de Wisconsin screams. I thought the woman was dying from a heart attack. Some instinct took over, and I threw my knife at the spider y *fua*." Kharla took her hand off the wheel and made a throwing action. "I stopped it like three inches from the woman's foot. Then I, like, unstuck the knife from the spider, wiped it on my pants and kept walking. I got the biggest tip of my life that day. It was so cool."

"Ay, ay, ay. I might have screamed too. I think those spiders are poisonous," I said.

"Yeah, the Brazilian wandering spider. Pero, they're like bees. They don't bite unless you mess with them."

"*Okay*, if you say so." I tore off a piece of the pan sobao, a semisweet pillowy bread, and made a mini sandwich with the cheese slice. "Want some?" I offered it to her.

We munched to the sounds of the road with the windows down to enjoy the cool winter air. The cheese in my snack made me think of my mother's queso de campo. I wondered if she'd made a batch with Manny or if the problems at the property had worsened and left them no time. I'd ruled Jules out as being the cause of the property's damages and issues. But I was no longer sure of that. Just because he wasn't physically there didn't mean he wasn't involved. He could have hired someone to sneak in at night, hack a hole in the water pipe, and drop in a dead rat. Or maybe he'd hired the woman that left the bad review? I got grossed out thinking about the picture of the rat in the shower. I rubbed my arms to get rid of the thought.

"¿Tienes frío?" Kharla asked. "We can roll the windows up."

"No, just an unpleasant thought worming into my brain. It's been a while since I was here. I've forgotten what the place looks like. Are we near?"

"Very." Kharla pulled into a three-story apartment complex with balconies. Almost every unit had its windows and doors opened. Sounds of dinner preparation and family conversations jumbled together into a comforting song.

"I remember the building being a peach color," I said as we walked away from our parking space.

"It was. They painted it blue last year." Kharla raised her arm that carried our purchases and motioned to the unit on the end. A rectangular table with folding chairs was on the cement pad outside the unit's sliding glass door. A hammock tied between palm trees rocked in the gentle breeze.

"La playa es por allá. ¿Verdad?" I pointed to a path in the greenery that I thought led to the beach.

"You have a good memory." Kharla put the bread batons on the table, entered the apartment with the large jar of green olives, and announced that we'd arrived. "Mami, llegamos."

Before stepping in to see Titi Sandra, I seared the updated image into my memory. The blue building matched the fading dusk sky. The breeze felt salty on my skin. I inhaled deeply. My olfactory senses smelled garlic and sofrito. My sirena responded to the dopamine, and I felt her move in my belly. It felt good to be *home*. Puerto Rico wasn't my home, and I hadn't spent a ton of time with Titi Sandra, but it felt like home. It felt warm and familiar. It was just what I needed. I'd spent three days away from my son, and it had been a week since I'd had my husband's arms around me. I was missing them.

"Nena, ven acá," Titi Sandra called to me.

I entered the kitchen and hugged her tightly. She put a cutting board before me and told me to slice the bell peppers and onion.

Sandra poured some olive oil into the Dutch oven pot and cooked the chicken thighs. I added what I'd cut. Then the spices went in: cumin, culantro, cilantro, oregano, garlic, and a packet of Sazón con saffron.

"Don't forget the olives," Kharla joked.

Sandra looked at her daughter in a fake angry way and dropped in twelve to fourteen of them, plus a few drops of the salty brine. A small can of tomato sauce was next, then the rice. The chicken stock was added along with two bay leaves, then the final liquid, a can of beer, went in. The lid went on the pot. After we'd cleaned the counter and washed our hands, we sat on the porch to wait for the one-pot meal to cook.

"Okay, nena, tell me everything. How is Miami? What's it like being on TV? I watch you every week." Titi Sandra's voice was music to my ears. She sounded so much like my mom. And her mannerisms were similar too. They'd grown up together and left Cuba close to the same time.

"I'm getting used to being on TV. But, you know, it isn't what I thought I'd be doing with my diplomas." I chuckled. "I thought I'd be giving lectures and traveling to do research and writing a book about foods of the diaspora."

"Mi'ja, you are traveling and giving lectures. I learn something new every time I watch you. You are very smart with the history. And the cookbook, it will come. Todo a su tiempo, poco a poco." Sandra patted my forearm. "Now, tell me all about Manny and your husband. Esa nunca va a casar y tener hijos." She motioned with her lips to her daughter.

Kharla rolled her eyes at her mother. The *when are you going to give me a grandchild* microaggression was a guilt trip Latin women of a certain generation kept up like a scared tradition. My prima had the same mantra as Alma. Neither of them wanted to get married or have children. However, I felt like maybe Herbie was changing Alma's mind about the marriage thing. I'd never seen my bestie so gaga over a guy.

"Gracias a dios, mis otras tienen hijos." Sandra referred to Kharla's two older siblings. They had two children each, all of whom were playing a video game in the living room. The grandchildren were staying with their abuela so the parents could have a break.

I loved the Latinidad culture of the extended family. After the way my mother-in-law had been acting, I knew we'd never achieve that level of comfort and security with Robert's side. I had built a kind and helpful village with my friends in Coral Shores. My village was great, but my heart ached to have my parents close by— to have them over for weekly dinner, to seamlessly have them as part of our daily routine.

"Show me pictures," Titi Sandra said.

I reached into my purse to find my phone, and the leaflet came out with it.

"Por favor, no me digas que te estás enredado con UPRI. Ten cuidado que son comunistas."

Titi Sandra's tone had changed. Her shift to purely Spanish was an indicator that she was serious. And if I was reading Kharla's sigh right, it seemed like a sore spot.

"Mami, not every organization working for dramatic social change is communist," Kharla said.

"Socialism es communism. Es lo mismo." Sandra was talking with her hands. She pointed and waved her finger like she was writing the words in the air. Her whole body expressed her strong stance and belief. "No escabemos de Cuba para converternos a Fidelitos."

"Mami, tranqui. I'm Puerto Rican."

"Half puertorriqueña y half cubana," Sandra interjected.

"I'm not a little Fidel Castro. UPRI is about empowering los puertorriqueños to have a voice and to govern themselves. It's social democracy," Kharla said with practice and calm.

Titi Sandra gave up and went to check on the arroz con pollo. Kharla leaned toward me and asked, "Is that a Cuban thing?"

"Yes. Any mention of social programs and Cubans in Miami immediately jump to the big bad *red* wolf. And then, after Chavez, with all the Venezuelans that fled to Miami, the talk radio got worse. It is still very, very visceral. Sixty years is nothing when you can see your homeland ninety miles off the coast but can't be there."

"But you've been there, *no*?"

"Yes, I went to visit my abuelos. Mami hid dollar bills in the lining of my suitcase. All my clothes were two sizes too big and new so I could leave them for Abuela. Abuelo showed me the farm that used to belong to our family but was taken by the state and redistributed. Some other family lives in Abuelo's childhood home. I stood in line at the grocery," I made air quotes around the word, "waiting hours with Abuela for one pot's worth of café and a small bag of rice. The dollars I'd brought helped her buy stuff on the black market, but even there, the food selection was meager. The island is not the utopia that was promised—people are suffering, buildings are falling down, basic needs are not being met."

"Okay, but why can't Mami see that rich Americans are stealing our land? Isn't it the same thing? I know Brandon Pickles is not a dictator, but he's stealing land from Puerto Ricans," Kharla said.

My ears prickled at Pickles's name. He was the Bitcoin guy that kept popping up. I was about to ask Kharla for the dirt on him when her dad walked up from the beach path. He had a towel around his neck and sand on his feet. After a hug and a blessing, he sat catty-corner to me. He asked if I'd met any superstars yet. I told him Marc Anthony and Enrique Iglesias had been to a party I had organized. I left out the part about not meeting them because I had been locked in a freezer by a murderer.

Titi heard her husband's voice and joked that his nose was better than a dog's. He always came home just as dinner was being served. She put a folded towel on the table and returned with pot holders on her hands and carrying the Dutch oven. The grandchildren rumbled out of the house. Once everyone was settled, she lifted the lid off the pot. Steam curled, lit by the porch light against the evening dark. It was like a scene from a movie.

Before Sandra disturbed the presentation, I took a picture of the arroz con pollo. She'd adorned the top with red pimento strips, canned asparagus, and defrosted peas. It looked like a compass rose. Mami decorated hers in a similar fashion. I hated asparagus growing up because I'd only ever tried the mushy limp ones from a can. It wasn't until I was in college and had fresh asparagus that I learned to like it. I pushed mine to the side of my plate. We all talked and ate and laughed. I had seconds. The grandkids woofed theirs down and then begged to return to their video game. The girl of the quartet backtracked and gave me a kiss. She whispered in my ear that she loved my *Abuela Approved* show because it helped her practice her English. My heart swelled with pride. I asked her if she wanted to be on my Instagram. I took a photo of us and posted it along with the arroz con pollo image. I hashtagged it with #FamilyDinner #PuertoRico #Relatives #Familia #FeelsLikeHome #AbuelaAp-proved #TiaApproved.

I offered to help clean plates, but Kharla said we had to get going. She had something to get to at the community center, and San Juan was about a forty-five-minute drive. Along the way, she told me all about Brandon Pickles and the real estate empire he'd amassed. He was even trying to buy one of the little islands off the coast to build a members-only beach.

"All beaches are public. It's the law. Cabrones. He has to be stopped. He will be stopped. The people are starting to realize it. It's a ripple effect. Pickles buys a place, and then all his Bitcoin wannabes snatch up the properties around it. They raise the rent. People can't afford it, and they have to move. But where do they move to? They are being pushed out of their hometowns. The UPRI march is going to be big. You'll see. La revolución is coming." Kharla's words were strong, but her tone was calm. She was giving off serious don't *bleep* with us vibes.

I could understand why her mother associated it with communism. You didn't throw around words like *revolution* lightly in the presence of an exiled Cuban. Kharla was more connected to her father's Puerto Rican roots since she'd grown up on the island. Having studied the Caribbean for my degrees, I'd read cultural references to historical events, people, and uprisings like El Grito de Lares. I trusted Kharla when she said the march would be big. It was in the Boricua nature to push back against colonization. Brandon Pickles was the equivalent of King Ferdinand of Spain in Kharla's mind.

"What street are you?" she asked.

"Just drop me here. I can walk the two blocks. I need to stretch my legs a little anyway."

"Are you sure?"

"Yes, prima, I'm sure." Actually, I didn't want her to see the Brandon Pickles Bitcoin banners on the hotel. Titi Sandra's worry was infectious.

"Okay. Pero, don't tell Mami, or I'll be in more trouble." Kharla laughed.

We kissed goodbye, and I got out by El Morro. I walked the same path I'd taken on New Year's Eve. This time there wasn't a tipsy Jules Howard by my side. But there *was* a Welmo acting suspiciously. I watched him duck into the shadows. A policeman was talking to a sunglasses-at-night guy.

Is Welmo spying on the cop or on the sunglasses guy? What is up with him?

Chapter Seventeen

I was tempted to ask Welmo why he was lurking in the shadows, but my sirena had other ideas.

"Please stop kicking my bladder, mi'ja," I whispered as I doubled my speed.

I rounded the corner and saw Alma and Jorge in front of the guesthouse with suitcases.

"What's going on? I'll be right back. Don't leave." My words were fast, but my feet were faster. I dashed into the house and made it to the hall bathroom in the nick of time. No longer a water balloon about to burst, I dried my hands and gave myself a quick glance in the mirror. "Do I hear whining?" I tightened the faucet, and the faint sound stopped. But then I heard the sound again in the hallway. I told myself old house, old pipes and went back to my friends outside.

"Okay. ¿Qué está pasando?" I asked.

"I'm moving into Alma's room," Jorge said.

"The bed is big enough for both of you, but I'm sure there is another room down the hall," I said.

"No, I'm moving in, and Alma's moving out. She's going to Herbie's hotel." He looked haggard as he lifted his bulging suitcase up the front steps.

"Alma, you're leaving me?" I asked.

"Don't say it like that. You were gone all day, and I was with Herbie all day. And well, his hotel is super nice and—" Alma took a beat to accommodate her things into the trunk of the idling car.

"And you want to be with your boyfriend," I said.

"Yes. Don't hate me. We'll do lunch tomorrow and spend the afternoon together. They have a spa at the hotel. Oooh, let's get massages," Alma said. "My treat."

A massage didn't sound bad. My back *was* a little achy. "I think I'll take you up on that, actually." I rubbed my lower back.

"Chévere," Alma said with a smile.

I checked that Jorge wasn't coming down the stairs. "Did Jorge and Lucas break up?"

Alma leaned in conspiratorially. "I don't know, pero Jorge está seguro que he is cheating. He doesn't want to stay there and have it flaunted in his face when Lucas comes back with some new guy."

"Wait. Lucas hasn't come back yet?" I asked.

"I don't think so." Alma shook her head. "Please tell Pilar gracias for me. I thought she'd come out of her house. Jorgecito *was* a little loud con *el cheater this* y *cheater that*, pero maybe she's already asleep." Alma kissed me and got into her waiting car.

I looked at Doña Santos's house. It was a little odd that she hadn't noticed the loud arrival. It was only nine at night. *Maybe she's eating dinner.*

"Did she leave without telling me goodbye?" Jorge asked. He stood in the doorway with his hand on his hip.

"She told me to tell you for her. The car had to move. They were blocking the road," I said.

Jorge sat on the step, and I joined him. He put his head on my shoulder with a sigh and leaned on me like a heartsick teen. Vaquita slinked out from behind a planter, crossed the narrow ballast stone street, and meowed at our feet.

"Is it time for your cream?" I scratched under the cat's chin. "I don't know where your lady is, but I can get it for you." I patted Jorge's bare knee for him to move.

"Cute cat. It looks like a cow," Jorge said.

"Yeah, her name is Vaquita. I'll be upstairs in a few minutes if you want to talk."

"I'm going to take a shower and cry myself to sleep. Maybe tomorrow I'll be ready to talk, pero ahora I'm still mad and sad y ya tú sabes." Jorge held out his hand to help me step up and into the house.

He went upstairs, and I went to the kitchen to find Vaquita's food dish. It was by the sink. I poured milk into it and tore off a few strands of cold chicken from leftovers in the fridge. As I walked by the door to the secret passageway, I heard the whining pipes again. *I guess Jorge is in the shower already.*

I fed Vaquita her treat. While I waited for her to finish, I relished the night air and the magic of the old city. The cathedral at the top of the little street was postcard perfect. The sky gradated from dark blue to black, and the church's facade was lit to show off the Three Kings banners—one king per door. The purple, burgundy, and green robes of the astronomically minded royals were decorated with gold stars. I could make out the flickering candles of the votive table through the church's tall open doors. The devout were entering for prayer. On the sidewalk, a couple stopped to kiss before crossing the street to the little park with the whimsical sculptures. Neither the church's nor El Convento's lights reached all the way to the park. It was the perfect place for a bit of privacy.

I took a few steps in that direction and saw the couple on the park bench beneath the bronze giraffe-cat sculpture. *How romantic.* My heart pined. I stared into space, thinking about when Roberto and I first dated. *So hot and heavy. We couldn't keep our hands off each other.* I caught myself gravitating toward the park.

Miriam, get a grip, girl. Don't be a creeper. Give them their privacy. You are not watching a Hallmark movie. I blinked a few times to shift from fantasy to reality. The couple, a dark-gray blob, wriggled like a Jell-O mold. *Young love.* I gave a happy sigh and turned to go. A slim gray blob shifted on the far bench in my periphery. Someone else was in the park. A prickly feeling flushed the back of my neck. *Someone is looking at me.*

Meow.

Vaquita strutted toward me. The prickly sensation dissipated. I looked over my shoulder and saw an empty park. Had it been my imagination?

"Are you finished, chiquita?" I asked the cat.

Meow.

The cat weaved between my legs as I walked back to number seven. As I picked up the empty dish, Vaquita leaped to the top step. She purred and butted her head to my hand. I petted her until she grew tired of it. Her soft fur made me think of our calico, Camo, which, in turn, made me think of Manny and how inseparable the two were.

My phone vibrated in my pocket. I withdrew it and pressed the Accept button. The screen filled with Camo's furry face.

"I think she misses Manny. She's been on me like glue since I got home," Robert said.

"Did you read my mind? I was literally just thinking about them." I chuckled. "Look, I seem to have become a cat magnet." I pointed the lens to my feet, where Vaquita was lounging, and then to the cautious feline onlookers that had gathered. "I'm not feeding all of you." Two of the five cats meowed. "Take it up with Doña. Look at me talking to cats like they understand me." I took the dish inside and locked the door.

"Cats *are* smart, but Puerto Rican cats probably understand Spanish better than English." Robert smirked.

"Ha-ha. I'm sure they are bilingual." I rinsed the dish and put it back where I'd found it. With a glass of water in hand, I sat at the dinette table and propped the phone on the bag of coffee still there.

"I miss you and Manny. I don't know if I can make it four more days," Robert said.

"It *does* feel like I've been away a long time."

"How's the show going?"

I relayed the day's filming to my husband and told him about dinner at my cousin's house.

"Babe, that's awesome that you got to see some of your family."

"Yeah, it was great. But I'm a little worried about my prima. She's involved with this *political,* for lack of a better word, group that is doing this big protest." I took a sip of my drink.

"Are they unhappy with the new governor? Or is it like a we-want-better-pay-for-teachers type thing? Didn't you tell me she was like a hippie environmentalist type? Is it about land usage?" Robert rubbed his nose to keep from sneezing. Camo was on his chest, the tip of her tail tickling his chin.

"Kind of about land, actually. I mean, they have a point. It's a bad law that puts Puerto Ricans at a big disadvantage."

"Okay, so what has you worried? It sounds like a protest is the right thing to do."

"Yeah, I guess. I don't know. I think Titi Sandra got in my head. Let's move on. Tell me about your project. How is it going?"

Robert grumbled. A delay had pushed back the groundbreaking. As I half-listened to him complaining about the Coral Shores building department's antiquated permit system, I noticed the newspaper on the table. It was folded to an article—an article about police corruption. The FBI had been ordered to form a task force to investigate. I flipped the paper open to read more, but the article continued on another page.

"Babe. Babe. Are you listening?" Robert asked.

"Sorry. I dazed out on you. It's been a *long* day." I faked a yawn that became a real one.

"Get some rest. We can talk tomorrow. Maybe we can do a three-way video call with Manny."

"I like that idea. Maybe before you go to work?"

"Okay, I'll call you at seven. Is that too early for your parents?"

"No, that will be perfect. They will be up. Besos." I sent kisses.

"Love you, babe. Get some rest." Robert disconnected.

I opened the newspaper to find the continuation. Maybe Welmo didn't lose his job. Maybe he was fired for being corrupt. We did go to the police station for a secret rendezvous. I had seen Welmo take a fat envelope from a police officer. *What was in the envelope? Money? Miriam, where is that coming from? Welmo is a good guy. He's not a bad cop.*

I found the rest of the police corruption article. It was scarce on facts about what kind of corruption and vague on the depth and scope of the FBI investigation. Did it go all the way to the top? Or was it only a unit, like the drug squad or something? The article ended by stating it would report the story as it evolved. I skimmed the rest of the paper and found something else that piqued my curiosity. The man that had been shot in the alley and later died had a majority ownership in El Convento. My thoughts went back to that day. Welmo had been very, *very* interested in the crime scene. He'd talked to the cop on duty. *No*, he'd clandestinely done it. The same one I saw him spying on a little while ago.

Had Welmo shot the man in the alley?

Don't be estúpida, Miriam. Welmo was at the airport waiting for you when that man was shot.

Maybe he shot him and *then* went to the airport. The man could have laid in the alley bleeding for an hour or more before

135

someone noticed him. *Really, Miriam? This town is compact and busy. But not in the mornings! It's sleepy until the cruise boats disembark.* I checked the newspaper for the exact time of the shooting. The article didn't report the hour, but it did mention the injured man had been discovered by an employee of El Convento. *I could find out who and ask some questions. No, Miriam, you should just go to bed.*

I tidied the table and turned out the light. As I passed the hidden passageway's door, I heard the whining again. I put my ear to the door and listened. It sounded more animated than old pipes expanding and contracting. *Could it be a trapped animal?* I put my hand on the porcelain knob to open it a crack for a better listen, but it was locked.

Let it go, Miriam. Old house equals old pipes equals weird noises.

As I climbed the stairs, I argued with my inner voice like I was defending my doctorate. My dungeon theory wasn't ridiculous. Old San Juan was a walled city with forts and a bloody history. The house might have once belonged to an admiral. Or it could have been used by the Spanish Inquisition. After all, it was on a street named for nuns that led to a Catholic church. Colonial Puerto Rico was brutal.

Miriam, go to bed. You are making up ghosts.

Chapter Eighteen

Our family video chat was filled with giggles and laughs. Manny told us all about making queso con Abuela. It was messy. And then Manny described cleaning up palm fronds with Abuelo. My dad had put a frond on each shoulder and had pretended to be a giant bird.

"We made a bohío," Manny said before taking a gulp of his breakfast juice. He bit into a banana and talked while he chewed. "Want to see?" He grabbed the tablet from its perch and zipped out of the patio to show us. Papi had used three chairs to form the walls and then laid the fronds on top like the roofs used by Indigenous Caribbeans. The bohío, as it was called in Cuba and other places, was a thatched hut. My heart swelled with joy. I loved that Manny was building connections to his Cuban roots.

"Manuel Quiñones, ven pa' cá y termina tu desayuno," we heard my mother say in a loving but I-mean-business way. Manny ran back to finish his breakfast, and we said our goodbyes.

I tossed the phone on the bed and swung my legs over the edge to stand. It was 7:15, and I smelled Doña's breakfast bacon from upstairs. When the phone rang, I answered it before I looked, thinking it was my Roberto. It was not.

"Miriam, how dare you. What were you thinking? Well, obviously, you weren't thinking, were you? You've abandoned your child in a *foreign* country. Have you lost your mind? And why? To film some nonsense for that Spanish station."

Marjory's tirade was too loud for my ear. I mashed the speaker icon and moved the phone away from me, as if distance would lessen the assault. Jorge knocked on my cracked door and stepped inside. He made a WTF face. I put a finger up to my lips, telling him to stay quiet. I knew from experience that my mother-in-law wasn't looking for an explanation. She was asking and answering her own questions.

"You have your priorities wrong. A good mother would be with her child," Marjory said.

I took the bait, gnawed on it, and spit the hook back out. "Are you calling me a bad mother because I left Manny with his grandparents? Or because those grandparents aren't you?"

"*No*, that is not what I am saying. My concern is that you left him in another country and ran off to do your silly little cooking show."

"It's my job, Marjory. It is not silly. It is educational," I said, keeping my tone neutral but my voice strong.

"You need to stop chasing stardom and start focusing on your family. You were nearly killed because of it. Think of the baby."

I screwed up my face and looked at Jorge. His face reflected mine. Was she trying to say my job was the reason I was locked in a freezer? I wouldn't have been in that kitchen if it hadn't been for Marjory. She was the reason I had been organizing the Women's Club gala in the first place. I did it as a favor to her—trying my best to be a helpful daughter-in-law.

She kept goading me. "Has Douglas had all his shots?" *She is the only person that calls him by his middle name. I know she does it on purpose.* "He could get sick with some foreign disease like ding-ee."

"Dengue is already in Miami. He is with his abuelos," I said.

"Is there even a hospital where your parents live?" Marjory asked.

My nostrils flared. Jorge put up a stop hand. He made a series of staticky sounds with a few digital-esque beeps, then hit the red End button.

"Your suegra es una bruja," Jorge said with extra sass.

"Witch?" I laughed. "I wish she was one. I could deal with the crystals, sage, and tarot cards," I said.

Jorge talked over me. "She needs to be saged."

"Pero, no. She's an angry, scared xenophobe that hates that her son married a brown-skinned woman who speaks Spanish. Gracias a La Caridad that the rest of the family isn't like her." I moved us toward the stairs.

"You should block her number. Block. Block. Block. Block. Block. Seriously, block her." Jorge looked over his shoulder to accentuate his message.

"I can't block her. She lives three streets from us. And I'm married to her baby boy. Pero, trust me, I am practicing boundaries. I will never let her bully me into doing another club event."

"Okay, if you say so." At the bottom of the stairs, Jorge hooked his arm into mine.

"I mean it." I play-slapped his bicep as we walked toward the kitchen.

"You are *too* nice, Miriam. You have to cut her off. Just like I did with Lucas. No second chances."

"Did you talk to him last night?" I asked.

"No. He's ghosted me. So, I blocked him. I don't want to hear his excuses. I'm not going to waste esta maravilla"—Jorge made curvy waves with his hand from head to toe—"on someone who doesn't appreciate me."

"But what if something really did happen to him? Has he posted anything to social media? I mean, you know he's alive, right?"

Jorge stopped and turned me by my shoulders to face him. "Do you think something serio pasó? Like, for real, bro. Do you think he's in trouble or hurt? Ay, ay, ay. I should call the hospital, no?"

My friend's bravado had crumbled, and I could see he was still worried about Lucas.

I hugged him. "It is a *little* weird that you haven't heard from him. I think we should let the network know and maybe call the police." I released him from the hug and patted his back as we moved down the hall. "Or at least talk to Welmo about it."

"Escuché mi nombre," Welmo said, having heard his name mentioned.

He was at his usual spot, and Doña was seated near him enjoying a taza de café. Beside the stove, there was fried bacon cooling on a paper towel. She got up and asked if we were ready for breakfast. She also offered breakfast to Welmo. He accepted, and she told us to go to the dining room.

The three of us sat clustered at one end of the long table. The windowless room was too formal for my taste. It made me feel like I'd been called into the dean's office. I chose to sit facing the entrance to avoid seeing the grim portraits on the wall. The oil paintings looked like they might've been commissioned by the house's first occupants. The man, in military regalia, had a joyless face. The woman, much younger than her mate, had thick black eyebrows and pale skin. She wore a lace scarf over her hair and a high-collared dress. The three-quarter profiles faced each other on the wall. The artist had caught something deep in his rendering. The woman's eyes and mouth told an emotional story. She missed wherever she'd left and knew she might not live to see it again. I began to wonder if she'd been married to the man as a business exchange between wealthy families. She looked trapped, and his compassionless stare kept her fixed.

"Buen provecho," Doña said after serving us.

We thanked her for the hearty breakfast. She came back a moment later with a pitcher of juice and filled our glasses. She left it on the table in case we wanted more. On the hall table, I saw a plate with plastic wrap. Doña picked it up and went out the front door.

Is that her breakfast? Why not eat with us? Is she taking it to a family member at her house?

"Welmo, does Doña live alone?" I asked.

"Yes. She is a viuda, a—" He searched for the word.

"A widow. Que triste." It was sad.

"Hay una nieta that stays with her sometimes, so she doesn't have to drive late at night." Welmo took a doughnut from the pyramid of them. They were rolled in sugar that glistened like glitter. "She is a bartender. I think."

The plate of food must be for the granddaughter. Or Vaquita!

I laughed to myself. Jorge cut his eyes at me. His leg was anxiously bouncing and rattling the silverware.

"Ask him," Jorge said in una voz baja.

I put my hand on the silverware and whispered back. "Ask what?"

Jorge mouthed Lucas.

"Of course, I'm sorry." I nodded at my friend. "Welmo, remember yesterday when I told you we were worried about Lucas Palo?"

Welmo affirmed he did and took a second doughnut.

"Did you find anything out?" I prompted him.

"He hasn't called you?" Welmo directed the question to Jorge.

"Nada. No texts. No DMs. Nada." Jorge crossed his arms over his chest. "I can take a hint."

"Are you sure? Check your voice messages again," Welmo said.

"Mira, nada." Jorge opened his phone's text message app. He scrolled through their chat. All the bubbles were on the right side. There were no replies. And the bubbles were all green. Meaning the receiver was out of cell range or had their phone off. Jorge dropped the phone on the table and pushed it across the lace tablecloth to Welmo. "See? Nothing."

Welmo closed the app and pointed to the telephone icon at the bottom of the home screen. "It says you have twenty-five voice mails."

"They are all spam. Car warranty y scams y mierda. Lucas never leaves me voice messages porque he knows I don't listen to them."

I reached across and dragged the phone to me. "Let me see. You never know." I tapped the icon. Yes, most of them were from numbers labeled unknown or from small-town middle America. I was reasonably certain that Jorge didn't know anyone from Lebanon, Kansas, or Belle Fourche, South Dakota. "Did you listen to this 787 one?"

"Seven-eight-seven. ¿Qué es eso?" Jorge asked.

"Puerto Rico," Welmo and I said in unison.

"Tch. As if, pero fine, I'll listen to it," Jorge said.

I couldn't make out the words in the message. But judging from Jorge's facial expressions, I knew it was a message from Lucas.

"So, what did he say? Where is he?" I asked.

Welmo scooped up the last forkful of egg, rice, and bacon on his plate. He leaned back in his chair and chewed.

"Here, listen for yourself." Jorge pressed Play and turned on the speaker.

"I'm going to a wellness retreat for a few days. No te preocupes. We are fine. I just need—" There was a pause, like Lucas was making up the story as he went along. "I have to look my best for the camera. This place has a special facial, como un botox sin needles. And there is yoga y un vegan chef. But it's, like, secret secret. I can't tell you the location because they don't want paparazzi to find it. Don't stay at the B and B. You can stay at the UnMundo house with your friend."

"Good thing I'm already here," Jorge commented.

"I'm fine. We *are* fine. I'm at a spa." Lucas's voice was extra. "I'll see you in a few days." The message ended.

"Your friend is safe. That's good," Welmo said.

"Pfft. Un wellness retreat. Claro. Sure," Jorge said.

"You don't believe him?" Welmo asked.

I didn't entirely believe Lucas either. But the time stamp on the message was yesterday evening, and it was Lucas Palo's voice.

"I mean, I'm glad he's alive, pero he is *not* doing yoga and eating vegan. *Porfa.* He's with some guy and wants to keep me como sopa en bajo." Jorge lifted one eyebrow and fluttered his heavily mascaraed lashes.

"¿Sopa en bajo? What's that?" I asked.

"You know, soup ready to heat up. Like for when you get hungry, you have something ready to go. Pero mi'ja, let me tell you, yo no soy un side chick. Not me." Jorge tore a doughnut in half and stuffed it in his mouth.

I took the other half away from him and ate it. It was soft and fluffy, like a cross between a sponge cake and a regular cake. I bet they were from the same bakery as the Mallorcas. Welmo began clearing the table.

"Okay, I say take him at his word until you know otherwise. Pero, no importa, because today we are having our own spa day, and you will not have a chance to think about Lucas because you will be having too much fun with Alma and me." I winked at him.

"Can we get mani-pedis, tambien?" Jorge made a pleading puppy-dog face.

"I'm texting Alma right now." I quickly typed that she needed to add Jorge to our reservation. I heard Welmo stacking the dirty dishes in the kitchen. I texted Alma a question mark and waited for a confirmation.

Duh, Alma texted. *Mani-pedis and facials for three. And a massage for you.*

Gracias, chica. I texted back. *What time?*

Soon. Let me finish breakfast and get dressed. Alma sent a photo of her current view. There was a room service tray, a carafe of mimosas, her knee, and Herbie's hand on it.

Eww. Is she naked? Oh, no. I see the edge of a bathrobe. Still, TMI.

I told Jorge we should get ready to leave. We went upstairs to brush our teeth and get our bathing suits.

"Déjame saber when you want me to call for a ride," Jorge said at the door of his room.

"Um, maybe Welmo can give us a ride. Let me ask him." Not wanting to yell down to the kitchen, I opened the contacts on my phone. Before I tapped the text option under his name and number, I hesitated. *Why is his number molestando me all of a sudden?* "Jorge, can I borrow your phone?" I asked.

"Mujer, I told you I got you on the ride."

"No, it's not that. Just give me your phone. Unlock it, porfa." Jorge handed it over.

I checked the 787 number Lucas had called from against the 787 number I had saved for Welmo. They were the same number.

Qué carajo is he playing at? Welmo knows where Lucas is. So, why isn't he telling us?

Chapter Nineteen

Because I was back to being suspicious of Welmo, we called a ride. I invented a thousand scenarios during the short drive to Alma's hotel. The only one that made sense was that Welmo's *emergency* yesterday was *actually* Lucas.

But why keep it secret?

I reminded myself that he was Delvis's cousin, which put trustworthy points in his column. Maybe Lucas had gotten into a compromising situation. Maybe it was something that would embarrass the network. Welmo worked for UnMundo, and he *was* an ex-cop. Of course, they'd have called him to clean up a sticky mess. I didn't want Jorge to be right about Lucas cheating on him, but maybe he was. Maybe Lucas had been caught in the act. Maybe there was video. I inhaled sharply.

"¿Todo bien? Is it the baby?" Jorge asked.

"Hmm?" I replied.

"You went," Jorge mimicked my inhale, "y put your hands on your stomach."

"Did I? I didn't notice. I'm okay. I rest my hands on my belly now that I don't have a lap." I laughed to ease his worry, but it didn't ease mine. Lucas was somewhere. Welmo knew where. I knew that Welmo knew, but I couldn't tell that to my friend yet. I stared into the distance, more in my head than ever.

"Hel-lo, earth to Miriam. Llegamos." Jorge waved his hands in front of my face.

"Sorry. La vida sin café has made me—" I started to say but didn't finish because I was stunned when I got out of the car.

Alma and Herbie were there to greet us. Heriberto Chacón did *not* photograph well. In person, he was magnetic. He was handsome—like, really, *really* handsome. He was a few inches taller than Alma. He was fit without it looking like he spent hours in the gym. He was not the slime monster I'd made up in my head. I was the one that had been the monster, a green-eyed one.

"Bienvenidos, I am so happy to finally meet Alma's friends," Heriberto said. He greeted us with hugs and cheek kisses. I could hear more Venezuelan than Cuban in his accent. "I'm sorry I can't join you for lunch. A business obligation has come up. But I've arranged for a private chef. I hear someone likes seafood." He winked in my direction. "Enjoy the spa." He kissed Alma on the lips and then jumped into a waiting car.

He was gone before I could thank him for planning lunch with me in mind.

"Isn't he great?" Alma asked.

Jorge and I nodded in agreement.

"Okay, massage for you." Alma pointed at me. "And mineral whirlpool for us." She side-hugged Jorge.

The spa smelled of eucalyptus and sounded like a stream flowing through a moss-floored forest. It put me in a peaceful state almost instantly. We were given locker keys, robes, and towels. Alma was already in her bathing suit and chancletas, but she put her cover-up in the locker. My locker had someone's lost and forgotten scrunchie in it. I picked it up like it was a biohazard and deposited it by the mirror and sink area for a staff person to find. That was just the sort of not-great-but-not-terrible kind of detail a petty reviewer would exaggerate about. As I stored my purse and slipped into the robe, I remembered the harsh and false review that had been left about Punta Palma.

"Alma, did you get a chance to search for those reviews?" I asked.

"I did. Pero, I didn't find any others. So, that's good, no?" Alma fluffed her hair, smiled at herself in the mirror, and licked her lips.

"Yes, I guess that's good news."

"You look worried. Don't be. It's one review and it's *obviously* an attempt to get a refund. So, stop thinking about it, mi'ja, and go enjoy your massage. See you in an hour," Alma said. She gently pushed me out the door. We met Jorge coming out of the men's changing room. They both threw kisses at me as I was escorted down a tile and bamboo hallway to a massage room.

The masseuse introduced herself and let me know she was trained in prenatal massage. She had me select a scent and put a few drops into the almond oil she would be using. She turned her back so I could disrobe and get on the table. Then she pressed Play on a small black cube, and the room filled with the mellow vibrations of singing bowls. I felt like I was drifting on a cloud. Before I knew it, the massage was over. I felt relaxed and rejuvenated. She instructed me to hydrate and gave me a glass of cucumber-orange-mint water before showing me to the whirlpool room. Hot tubs were a no-no while pregnant. And even though my friends assured me the water was a tepid 80 degrees, I situated a teak lounge chair near the edge of the pool to converse with them.

"Sigue," Alma said, undulating her fingers at Jorge.

"So, like I was saying, supposedly the old man that owned the building died on the stairs. Like, maybe he tripped over something or lost his balance or algo. I don't know, but he, like, died, you know, with, like, unfinished business. Like, he wasn't sick. He was just old and used un baton, a cane. Like, he could have

147

lived another ten years, right? So, like, that's why it was too freaky to stay at the B and B alone. I swear the ghost of el viejo was there. Like, I swear I could hear him talking outside my door." Jorge pushed off his perch and made a water ballet move. The rolling waters added flair to his performance.

"Señora Diaz, it's time for your treatment," said a woman dressed in the spa's uniform.

Alma and Jorge got out of the pool, dried off, and donned their robes. We followed the woman to a room that looked out onto the beach. There were three white recliner chairs that belonged in a sci-fi movie. I took the middle position with Jorge to my right and Alma to my left. We each had an attendant. We were given hair bands and instructed to pull our hair from our faces. Soon after, the cleansing and moisturizing began. The attendants commented that our facials were specific to each of our needs. Jorge got the enzyme one that smelled fruity, Alma got the detoxifying one that began with a coffee scrub, and I got the hydrating one. Once we'd been sufficiently lathered and slathered with goop, the manicurists descended on us. Our feet were wrapped in steaming towels, and our hands rested in warm, oily water.

"This is how I should be treated every day," Jorge said. "The reina life."

I chuckled. I was not used to this level of indulgence, and it made me a bit uncomfortable, if I was being honest. But Jorge and Alma seemed to be in their element.

"Queen Alma, Queen Miriam, qué dices?" he asked.

"Make sure my crown has lots of diamonds," Alma said. Her clay mask was drying, and she tried not to move her face too much.

The attendants came back and wiped away our masks. Then creams and oils were applied, whichever was appropriate for our skin type. Once our faces were dewy and glowing, the chairs' hydraulics were engaged, and the backs righted. A spectacular ocean and beach view filled the floor-to-ceiling windows. We were each given a glass of water with sliced fruit beautifully lining the lower half of the tall vessels.

"This is exactly what I needed. Gracias, amiga," I said to Alma. "I love my show, pero I'm only in front of the camera once a week." I tried to talk with my hand, but the manicurist caught it before it could fly into the air to accentuate my every word. "This week it's been constant and corre corre, you know, y de verdad, it's more draining than you think. I don't know how actors do it."

"*Pfft.* Lucas loves the camera. He says you have to make it your dance partner. Why am I *even* talking about him? I need to forget him. It's time to day drink. I need a *pea-chair* of piña colada. Like, seriously." Jorge said.

"There will be alcohol with lunch. See that cabana?" Alma jutted her chin in the direction of a palm-thatched hut. "That's ours for lunch. The chef is going to grill the seafood tableside," Alma said.

"That is very nice of Heriberto." *I couldn't bring myself to call him Herbie.* "I hope he can get away early and join us."

"No. I think he went to see The Pickle," Alma said.

"*The Pickle.* You mean the Bitcoin guy?" I asked.

"Sí. Algo paso the other day, and Herbie has been helping him with something big. *And* someone kidnapped his dog," Alma said. "It's a mess. Pickles loves his dog."

"How much are they asking?" Jorge asked.

"¿Qué?" I turned toward him.

"You know, how much money to return the dog?" Jorge clarified.

"Oh. Is there a ransom note?" I turned to Alma.

"Que yo sepa, no. Pero Pickles would pay it, whatever the cost. He could transfer a million in Bitcoin with the push of a button," Alma replied.

"Maybe they want cash," I said.

The manicurist gave me the color choices board. I picked a fruta bomba color. Jorge took the color samples from me and picked an iridescent shade that went from blue to purple. His manicurist smiled. Mine gave him a confused look like it was the first time she'd seen a man ask for colored nail polish. I passed the board to Alma, who picked a neutral taupe.

"Cash would be hard to get, *right*? Bitcoin is all digital, so it's traceable," I said, musing aloud. "*Maybe* that's why he needs Heriberto's help. I mean, if he had to convert the digital into hard currency, he'd have to go to the bank and withdraw it, no? Didn't you say Heriberto has financing connections?" I didn't wait for her to answer. "Who would steal Pickles's dog?" I sucked my lip as I thought. "Maybe the person that crashed his party and tried to throw paint at him." Delvis had said she knew the protester. I immediately thought of my prima Kharla. *Is she involved? Did her group dognap Pickles's perro?* "But why? What point would that make?"

"Velma, basta. I'm sure Scooby-Doo is fine. We are relaxing, not solving mysteries, porfa," Jorge said. He admired his one finished hand, then put it up to show it off to us.

"*Velma*. I like that. She's the one with glasses. Always wears orange," Alma said. "Kind of like the color you picked." She narrowed her eyes at me in a teasing manner.

I looked at the polish being applied to my nails. "Don't you start too."

"Velma. De verdad, it's perfect," Alma said.

"I know, *riiight*?" Jorge said. "Los dos are smart. They both need fashion help. And los dos are always solving crimes. Miriam es una Velma, one hundred percent. She just needs the glasses."

"Je-je-je. You two are hilarious," I said. "You should be comedians. Get a special on Netflix."

"I like that. Yes." Jorge used his hands to paint the picture. "It's like Queer Eye meets Property Brothers. Alma finds the houses, and I give the buyers a makeover." He paused. "And there's a party at the end."

While the two of them riffed on their imaginary show, I thought about the paint thrower.

Did they change course and kidnap Pickles's dog when the paint protest didn't get the results they wanted?

Is my prima involved?

Is there a ransom?

And is the Love Bug paying it?

Chapter Twenty

My friends were still fantasizing about their show as we walked to the lunch cabana from the locker room.

"En serio, we should propose it to Ileana," Alma said.

My BFF was friendly with the *La Tacita* host. That connection had gotten me my on-air job. Ileana did have a lot of UnMundo pull. Their crazy idea could sprout wings.

"I have the perfect name!" Jorge stopped in the middle of the path.

Alma and I stopped too. It was then I noticed Jorge had applied mascara, eyeliner, and lip gloss while in the changing room. I'd barely managed to look in the mirror to fix my hair.

"*Casa Party*." Jorge moved his head in an arc as he said it.

"I like it. House Party," Alma said. She snapped with both hands and did a little shimmy.

We resumed our procession to the cabana. The table was set with white plates and decorated with conch shells. It was so pretty that we all took out our cameras to take photos of it. I squatted to get a table-level shot with the waves in the background and almost lost my balance. Thanks to the massage and pampering, I'd temporarily forgotten my belly was a beach ball. Then, as if unhappy with my critical observation, my stomach growled. *Okay, mi sirena, you will get to eat in just a second.*

Barbacoa, Bomba, and Betrayal

The grill off to the side of the cabana had heat mirages coming off it, but there was no food on it nor a chef behind it. We sat. Jorge and Alma continued developing their *Casa Party* pitch. I took a moment to post an image of the tablescape to the *Abuela Approved* Instagram. I used the hashtags #ChefsTable, #Seafood, #SeeFood, #PuertoRico, #BestLife, #BlessedLife, #SaltLife, and #Playa. *I think I'm getting the hang of this.* I put my phone facedown on the seat cushion. It chimed a notification. I grinned, pleased with myself and thinking it was Delvis approving of my post, but it wasn't. Instead, it was a text message from Detective Pullman.

Veronica, call me when you get a chance. I have info on your man.

My man? Jules! I'd asked him to run a check on Jules Howard. I was pushing my chair away from the table, about to excuse myself to make the call, when the chef appeared. It was a battle between my curiosity and my hunger. La Sirena won. She wanted to eat. The call had to wait.

"Bienvenidos, soy Chef Tito a su servicio. Today, I have prepared a fresh ceviche de camarones for your appetizer. Please enjoy."

A waiter brought a tray of martini glasses filled with the chilled chopped shrimp salad. I took a bite, worried the acid from the lime, orange, and tomato juices might have made the shrimp tough. But the chef was serious when he said fresh. The ceviche had probably been made no less than thirty minutes prior. The refreshing seafood salad had cucumber, red onion, cilantro, red and green peppers, seedless tomatoes, and garlic. But there was another flavor I couldn't put my finger on. There was a little brininess to the marinade. *Clam juice, maybe.* I asked the chef.

"You have a very good tongue," Chef Tito said.

I knew what he meant even though it was lost in translation.

"I use un poco de clam juice." He pinched the air and disappeared down the path to the hotel.

Jorge got his day drinking started with a passionfruit daiquiri. Alma opted for a *Medalla Light*. "I can't be on the beach in Puerto Rico and *not* have a *Medalla*," she said.

"This daiquiri is delicoso," Jorge said, slurping it through the paper straw. "They invented it here, no?"

"The daiquiri was invented in Daiquri, Cuba. The piña colada was invented in San Juan, Puerto Rico." I informed him.

"Bueno, next round is piña coladas for all of us. Sin ron for mamacita," Jorge said.

The chef returned, rolling a cart. On the top shelf was a red snapper, head and all. He lifted the oiled and seasoned fish by its tail with a spatula under the weight of its midsection to place it on the grill. The sizzle it made carried the herbs and spices to my nose. My mouth watered. The spectacle for the senses got Jorge's and Alma's attention too. They stopped talking about *Casa Party* to clap.

Chef Tito cleaned his prep station and shuffled a few things on the middle shelf. He flipped the fish and then wiped his hands on the towel slung over his shoulder. He pushed up the sleeve of his chef's jacket, revealing brightly inked tattoos on the inside of his forearms. One was of a machete slicing a coconut. The machete had a Puerto Rican flag on its handle. The other arm had a collage of green peppers, garlic, onion, and herbs. I saw the distinct flat leaf of culantro/recao.

"Is that a sofrito tattoo?" I asked.

"Sí." Chef Tito laughed. "I have one of fruits on my back. Mango, papaya, guineo, todas las frutas de la isla." He tapped his bicep. "Up here, I have casaba, pana, batata, y plátano."

"*Wow*. So, all the island's native starches. Qué cool like food groups. Are all your tattoos food-related?" I asked.

"Casi todos. I just got a new one that is but isn't." He rotated his arm and showed me a Wizard-of-Oz-green pickle curved around his elbow.

"Pickles are food," I said.

"Sí, pero, I don't cook with them. This is my lucky pickle." Tito gave me a lopsided smirk. "It's to commemorate my first restaurant. It's in Viejo San Juan. It will be open in a few months. I will put you on the guest list as one of Heriberto's friends."

Tito squatted behind his cart. He took three pilons from the bottom shelf and placed them on the prep area. I knew what was coming next. I tapped Alma's thigh to get her attention. "He's making mofongo. Watch." He removed the tinfoil from a large metal bowl. I smelled plantains, fried green plantains, to be exact. He poured a glug of olive oil into each wooden mortar, then added two roasted garlic cloves and a large pinch of salt. After he'd pounded and ground the flavor base with the pestle, Chef Tito placed three chunks of plantain in each and mashed them. Next, he added chicharron to the mix. The fried pork belly was the umani of the dish. He packed the mofongo in the pilon and made a dimple with the pestle. From the grill, he took octopus tentacles, shrimp, and a lobster tail. Using cleavers, he chopped the meats in a showy fury. He portioned them in thirds and scooped them onto the mashed plantains. Obscured from our table's view, he had a small pot on the grill, which he removed to pour its hot contents over the mofongo. It was a red criolla sauce. The thin but flavorful sauce warmed the cooling mash. My friends and I thanked the chef by digging into the masterpiece with oohs and aahs of satisfaction.

A waiter from the main kitchen came to the grill carrying an oval dish. It had a bed of white rice on it. Chef Tito placed the cooked snapper on it. He poured the remaining criolla sauce over it and set it on our table.

"Chillo con salsa criolla. Buen provecho," the chef said with a slight bow.

"Gracias. It looks and smells delicious," I said.

Chef Tito left us to our feast. The waiter brought piña coladas. My mocktail had two pineapple slices and a paper umbrella to distinguish it from the rum ones.

Jorge was about to serve himself some of the chillo when I stopped him.

"I need a picture first," I said.

My friends made fun of me but then encouraged me to take photos of them eating their mofongo. I did and then slipped my phone under my napkin. We ate to the sounds of crashing waves. The scrumptious food was enhanced by the setting y amistad.

When the waiter came to clear our plates and offer us dessert, I excused myself to the restroom. I took my phone with me. After freshening up, I stood outside the bathroom to make a call.

"Detective Pullman."

"Hi. It's Miriam. You texted me saying you had some information," I replied to his gruff bark.

"Oh, it's you. Are you staying out of trouble? You haven't tripped over any dead bodies, have you?" he asked.

"Funny, not funny," I replied. I grit my teeth and let Pullman get his jabs in.

"And no international drug ring either, right?"

"No. I'm working. When would I have time?" I poked back at him.

"I hope that's true, Señora Fletcher," Pullman said with a perfect ñ his Colombian wife would be proud of. "So, tell me about this guy again. You *think* he is stalking you. Did you alert the studio?"

"Okay, I no longer think he is stalking me. But I *am* worried about him stealing my parents' place. I think, or at least thought, he was sabotaging the property to get the owner to sell, but now I'm not sure."

"They manage a vacation property, if I remember correctly. Is it on the market?"

"No."

"So, why are you worried?"

"I just am. From the little I've found out about him, he buys properties before they go on the market," I said. "I don't want my parents to lose their job and home." I pushed my back against the wall.

"I don't think you have anything to worry about in that department. Jules Howard filed for bankruptcy last month."

"Really? Interesting."

"Financial loss can make people emotionally unstable. Are you sure he's not a stalker threat?"

"Yes. I'm pretty sure he only stalks restaurants."

"I still think you should mention it to your people."

The silence went on a beat too long.

"*Veronica,* promise me you will tell the studio about this guy," Pullman said.

"I will. I will. Thanks for the information."

"I know I tease you with nicknames, but I'm serious, Miriam. Tell the studio."

"I promise I'll tell someone. FYI, Jorge is crimpin' your nickname game. He has started calling me Velma, from Scoo—"

Pullman finished my words. "—by-Doo. Aww, that's a good one. I wish I'd thought of it. Bye, Velma. Stay out of trouble."

I groaned. "Bye, Frank."

When I got back to the table, Alma got up. She hurried past me.

"¿Pa' dónde va ella?" I asked Jorge.

"She had to go to the room and do something on her laptop. Sell a property or buy a property. I don't know. Algo así. *Maybe* take something off the MLS. I don't know. Something to do with a house. No houses." The rum had gone to Jorge's head, and his speech was languid.

"Ana couldn't do it, huh?"

"Ana isn't supposed to know. Shhh." Jorge put his finger to his mouth, and his elbow nearly slipped off the armrest.

I waved to the waiter and signaled for coffee.

"Why isn't Ana supposed to know?" Ana was Alma's very capable assistant. Alma trusted her implicitly.

"Because its cryp-toe-cur-rent-c-c," Jorge whispered loudly. "Ana dice que el crypto es spooky." He disintegrated into giggles.

"How many of those have you had?" I asked.

"Tres. Pero, they were strong." He grinned.

"Ay, ay, ay. Here. Toma agua." I pressed a glass of water into his hand.

When the coffee arrived, I had a sip and then told Jorge to drink mine and his. Alma hadn't returned yet. I stole the white chocolate starfish from her untouched dessert and bit off a piece.

Why is Alma hiding a sale from Ana?

I took another bite. It wasn't chocolate. It was coconut flavor.

Why does Ana think Bitcoin is spooky?
Maybe not spooky. Maybe Jorge means scary.

Chapter
Twenty-One

Alma came down from her room, bathed and with freshly applied makeup. She wore white pants and a green-and-black split-sleeve tunic. I could see her laptop sticking out of her black leather carryall.

"I hate to cut our day short, mis amores, pero I have work to do," Alma said.

Jorge and I sighed.

"*Staaaay.* Enjoy the beach. Charge everything to our tab," she said.

"No. I should get back too. I need to check in with Delvis." I remembered that I'd meant to tell her about the protest. Did the studio know about it? Had they made contingency plans if it got unruly?

"I'm going to stay," Jorge said. "I like the view." He motioned with his mouth toward the hotel's lifeguard that had taken up post on the beach. "I think I'll go for a swim."

"Here, take my room key in case you need it." Alma tossed the keycard onto the table.

"Gracias." Jorge blew her an air kiss.

"Chica, you ready? Want to ride together?" Alma asked me.

"Are you going my way?"

"I'm meeting Herbie at El Convento. He's convinced Pickles to buy some property in Miami." My BFF's eyes sparkled with dollar signs. *Or were they bitcoins?*

On the short car ride, I had a bombillo moment. *Duh! Chef Tito's pickle is for the Bitcoin King, Brandon Pickles. I bet he's the money behind the restaurant. Restaurants cost a fortune to open.*

"Can you drop me at El Capitán?" I asked.

"Are you still hungry?" Alma looked at me with raised eyebrows.

"No! Ay, Caridad, no. That meal was incredible. I ate plenty. Please tell Heriberto how much I enjoyed it. No, I'm not hungry. I want to interview them for the show tomorrow. Delvis just gave me the green light." I waved my phone as if I'd gotten a message from my director, but I hadn't. What I wanted was to talk to the same woman I'd chatted with before. I wanted her to know Chef Tito was taking over El Capitán. *And maybe ask her about how the old man died. And possibly ask her about Jules Howard.*

Pullman's voice echoed in my head. *Stay out of trouble, Veronica.* I told myself I wasn't snooping. *I'm not a Veronica or a Velma or even a Jessica.*

"Mentirosa," Alma said.

"Did you just call me a liar?" My BFF could always read my mind, but this was beyond her normal, eerily accurate insights.

"Yes." She chuckled. "It's okay if you are still hungry. You're pregnant, chica."

"You're right. Chef Tito's seafood feast has my sirena craving more. I think the baby really is a mermaid."

"Or you have an omega-3 deficiency." Alma shrugged. "Pero, I still like the idea of an ocean theme for the nursery."

"We haven't decided on a theme yet."

"*We* have." Alma pointed to herself. "Soy la madrina. And I'm throwing the shower and decorating the nursery as my gift to you."

"Okay, but by we, I meant Roberto and me, not you and you. Robert is an equal parent in this partnership."

"I have great taste. Trust me. Let me be the baby's fairy godmother."

"As if I've ever won an argument with you," I said, chuckling.

"I'm so glad you see it my way." Alma bumped her shoulder into mine.

At the crest of the hill entering Old San Juan, I directed the driver to turn left and drop me off near El Capitán. I wished my friend good luck, then shut the car door and waved goodbye. On the sidewalk, I put my thoughts in order. It was well after lunch and nowhere near dinner. So, it was the perfect time to catch the waitress for a chat. But under what guise? I didn't want to get her hopes up for an UnMundo interview that I couldn't deliver. I decided honesty was the best policy. I wanted to know if Chef Tito was taking over and what, if anything, she knew about Brandon Pickles. Was the Bitcoin King as terrible as my prima Kharla claimed? If the new restaurant's chef was local, did that make it less outsider-Americans-taking-over? Maybe Tito would hire the current staff to stay on.

My foot was on the threshold to go inside when I noticed Welmo and the cop from the alley sharing a beer at a corner table. I quickly withdrew from his sightline.

Miriam, que qué, what are you doing? Why are you hiding from Welmo?

I had to be truthful with myself. I didn't want to hide from him. I wanted to spy on him. There were plenty of other places to grab a beer with an ex-colleague. *Why here? And why him, the bantam cop?* Welmo was being clandestine. The day the body was found in the alley, he'd been very keen to talk to the officer but not be seen talking to him.

I went around the building and into the B and B. As I passed the staircase, Jorge's story about the old man's death came to mind. The stairs didn't look particularly dangerous. An elderly person with a cane *could* miss a step and lose his balance, especially if the lights were off. I thought about my own recent trepidations with stairs and balance.

Shaking off the what-ifs, I continued down the hallway. It and the room the workers had used for their break had been tidied. Big black bags of construction debris lined the passageway, ready for the dumpster. The only thing left on the floor was a Styrofoam to-go box. I picked it up to add it to an open bag. Its contents rolled and clinked.

Food doesn't make that sound.

I opened the boxed and saw that it held a bottle of face serum, a toner, and a cream. I'd seen the brand before. It was expensive, according to Viviana from UnMundo's Miami studio. "No toca, eso es exclusivamente para Lucas Palo." I remember her scolding me not to touch a bottle I'd reached for, thinking it was eye makeup remover.

¿Qué? What are Lucas Palo's skin care products doing in a to-go box? Did Jorge toss them out in spite?

I heard someone approaching from the restaurant. Setting the to-go box back where I'd found it, I made three long, loping steps and squeezed, *literally squeezed*, between a glass-front chiller and an industrial dishwasher. Whoever the footsteps belonged to, they stopped by the construction bags. I held my breath and made a silent plea to La Caridad y Yemaya that my belly wasn't visible from their vantage point. As badly as I wanted to peek around the corner of the chiller to see what the person was up to, I didn't dare. There was no plausible excuse for me being where I was.

I heard the clink of the rolling bottles and then the distinct sound of the plastic bag filling with air to open it wider. *They're putting the box in the bag like a take-out meal.* The room went silent. I imagined the person's eyes searching every shadow and space. I stopped breathing and waited. *Once, doce, trece*—Finally, on count fourteen, I heard them walk back to the restaurant. I counted to twenty and unwedged myself from my hiding place. The Styrofoam box was gone. I looked down the hall into the dining area. Welmo was at the front door with a take-out bag in his hand.

"Señora." The waitress's voice startled me. "¿Quiere una mesa?" she asked.

"Yes," I replied, trying to formulate a strategy quickly.

She led me to a table and placed a menu in front of me. She informed me the kitchen was closed until five but that coffee, postre, and cold items were available.

"Perfecto. Un flan y una taza de café con leche que es más leche que café. And let me buy you a coffee. I'm alone, and you are not busy." I fanned my palm at the empty restaurant. "Keep me company, please."

The woman seemed unsure.

"We met the other day. ¿Recuerdas?" I motioned upward to the second-floor bathroom. "I was with my friends. One of them was staying at the hotel."

She nodded with pursed lips.

"I think I know who is taking over the restaurant." *Honesty is the best policy.*

That had gotten her off the fence.

"Dos cafés y dos flanes," she said.

She returned with our coffee and desserts. The restaurant was quiet enough that the rain forest sounds from the upstairs bathroom became our background soundtrack.

"Where is everyone else?" I asked.

"Mami is in the office doing bills. Papi and my brother went to Pueblo for bread. They left me to watch the front," she said.

"This really is a family restaurant."

She nodded. "So, you know about the new cook. Is he going to hire us?"

I put my spoon down. The cheap metal utensil rocked in the syrupy caramel. "I don't know. I pray he does. His specialty is seafood, like yours. I met him today. Chef Tito. Have you heard that name from the new owners?"

She shook her head.

"What do you know about the owners?" I asked.

She took a draw from her cup. "I know I don't like them. Ramoncito, el viejito, the owner that died," she clarified for me, "he didn't like them either."

"But he agreed to sell to them, no?"

"I guess. He was eighty. The building needed repairs." She shrugged.

"He fell down the stairs, no?"

"Yes. From the fourth floor to the third. Which was un poquito raro."

I made a face for her to elaborate.

"Because he always took the elevator." She laughed to herself. "He would joke that if the elevator ever broke, he'd be stuck in his apartment, and we'd have to go back to the old way." She hand-over-hand pulled an invisible rope.

I knew she meant the basket and pulley system. It wasn't so old. People still employed it. I'd seen someone use it the other day at a corner bodega when I'd gone to the plaza. The person at the top puts money in the basket and lowers it to the person on the street level. That person takes the money, puts the food item in its place, and then hoists the basket up. The basket I'd seen had a bell on it. It was the analog version of Uber Eats and DoorDash.

"I miss that viejo. Did you know he was a famous musician when he was young? I'll show you." She went into the kitchen. A few moments later, she emerged with a newspaper article in a sealed plastic bag. "See?" She handed it to me to read.

The article was a full page. There were photographs of a young man with a trumpet with various well-knowns like Celia Cruz, Willie Colon, and a few others who looked familiar, but I couldn't name them. But the photo that caught my interest was one of the apartment building with a slight-of-stature police officer standing guard. There was no doubt that it was the bantam cop. I pointed to the man in the black-and-white image. "Do you know who this is?"

"That's Vega. He found Ramoncito. He was just here too." She cocked her head toward the table that hadn't been cleared. One Medalla bottle was empty, and the other was practically full.

"What was he doing here?"

"Having a beer." She looked at me like I was Juan Bobo. "He comes here a lot now."

"No, I mean, when he found Ramoncito, what was he doing here then? Were they friends? You said he found him. Did he find him on the stairs?"

"I don't know. I guess. It was a Sunday, so we were closed. Like I said, the building needed to be fixed. Kids were breaking into the apartments to have parties. They were spray-painting the walls. Everybody had moved out expect for Ramoncito on the top floor. He liked the view. And Luisa on the first floor. She was sordo." She tapped her ear to signal hard of hearing. "Maybe Ramoncito called la policia because he heard or saw something. Then he went out of his apartment to stop them and fell." She shrugged.

Maybe.

An older version of the waitress stepped out of the kitchen. Her worried face brightened when she looked at me. She recognized me from *La Tacita*.

"Mami, venga pá cá," the waitress said.

Her mother came over. I introduced myself, and she embarrassedly acknowledged that she knew who I was. The daughter didn't watch the UnMundo morning show. I told her about the Spanglish YouTube channel. She said she'd look it up.

"¿Mami, tú recuerdas cómo fue que Vega encontró a Ramoncito?"

The mother made the sign of the cross. She then sat and told me about it like we were old friends. Vega was a tenant. He'd moved into apartment 303 about six months before Ramoncito's accident. The building was nice before his arrival. Then there were a series of robberies. Ramoncito complained to her, 'what good was it having a policeman in the building if he brought trouble with him.' After that, the pipes started to break.

I thought about my parents' pipe problem.

When the second-floor ceiling fell in, the residents left. They said the building was falling apart, and Ramoncito wasn't going to fix it. But she knew he'd already called for the repairs. He'd called from her office phone. She'd helped him find a new repair company after the first three he'd tried didn't show up. It was Vega that suggested he sell the place. Ramoncito didn't want to sell. He had the money to fix it. It was his home. He loved it.

"So, qué pasó?" I asked.

"No sé," she said, shaking her head. "Pero yo ví el contrato. El nombre en la firma era *Ramón Ferrer*."

She'd seen the contract. The name on the dotted line was his. What changed his mind?

I wondered if the signature on the contract she'd seen was really Ramón's. Was it a forgery? Or did someone force him to sign it and then push him to his death?

Someone that walked like a little rooster.

Chapter
Twenty-Two

My head was dizzy from all I'd discovered at El Capitán. The picture was still missing a lot of jigsaw pieces. And I felt like maybe I should heed Pullman's advice to avoid trouble. Was I sticking my nose where it didn't belong?

Yes, you are, Veronica!

But there *was* something fishy going on with the restaurant's and apartment building's new ownership that had me concerned for my parents. El viejo, Ramoncito, had the money to fix the sudden avalanche of problems. He hadn't wanted to sell. And he always took the elevator. The building started to decline when Vega, the bantam cop, moved in. *And* he was the person who found Ramoncito.

Was Vega the person that found the man in the alley too?

I should ask Welmo.

Welmo. He was a riddle. My gut told me he was a good guy, but why was he always hiding in the shadows. Was he friends with Vega? Was he trying to get his job back via back channels? Or did he suspect Vega of something, and like a good (ex) cop, he was pursuing it? He *had* followed the police officer the other night. *But* I'd also seen him following Jules.

Jules. Recently bankrupt Jules. I needed to figure out how he fit into all of it. How was he investing in new restaurants and properties if he had no money? *Remember, Miriam, Jules said he works with LPM, not that he is LPM.* Was he trying to break out on his own? Or had he already broken away from them, and that's what got him into financial trouble? Maybe that was why he was on the island. Maybe he needed money and was looking for investors. Did he ask his college buddy, UnMundo's CFO? Did he get turned down? I bet that's why he was so keen to go to Brandon Pickles's New Year's Eve party. Pickles was rolling in coin, and he was buying up properties all over the island.

Pickles. I needed to warn Delvis about the march, which wasn't about Brandon Pickles but was kind of about him. UPRI was protesting colonizers controlling Puerto Rico's future. The Bitcoin King fit that profile.

I stopped under a tree in a plaza to call Delvis.

"Hola, Miriam. What's up? I'm in the studio editing yesterday's crab footage. There is some good stuff. Super glad you suggested it."

"Cool. Gilberto and Adela were fun, and they're such sweet people too. Listen, I'm sure you know about it, but I just wanted you to be aware that there is a protest march tomorrow in Old San Juan," I said.

"Yo sé. I know, I know. I think we will be okay. They aren't expecting more than a hundred people. And we will probably be done with filming before they get anywhere near La Fortaleza. We start early on El Morro's lawn with the camels and the kings. All of *La Tacita* will be there to help pass out presents to the kids. Then you and I and our crew will go to El Museo del Indio to do your thing. I'm still working on getting the cooking demo approved by the museum. Están bien tercos sobre el concepto. So, be prepared because things might change."

"Only a hundred? Kharla told me like a thousand."

"Kharla? Your prima is going to the protest?"

"Yeah. She's involved with UPRI. They are expecting a big turnout."

"Hmm. Let me call my friend and see what he has to say. You aren't worried about violence, are you? Puerto Rico has protests all the time. It's no big deal. It's actually going to be more like a street party. My friend said that there is a parranda band marching. And I know there will be bomba y plena too."

"Okay, pero, are you sure? I mean, UPRI did crash a private party to disrupt it. And the protest route goes by that hotel again. What if they want to make a statement and, like—"

"*The red paint thing at the Bitcoin party?* Eso era una bobería. It was a harmless." Delvis paused. "Yeah, okay. I see your point. I'll find out more. But don't worry. Even if three thousand people show up, it will just be a big street party."

"Three thousand sounds like a lot for these narrow streets."

"Mi'ja, that's nothing. In two weeks, it will be San Sebastián. That is, like, two hundred thousand people. THAT is a party. Super fun. Trust me, the *narrow* streets can handle it. They've survived casi five hundred years. I bet the protest will look like a party to the cruise boat tourist and the Bitcoin gente también." Delvis laughed. "I have everything bajo control. Don't worry."

We ended the call, but I kept my phone in my hand. *I have everything bajo control. Don't worry.* I'd begun to realize that was Delvis's automatic response to everything. She had it under control, and I shouldn't worry. I appreciated that, but from my park bench, I could see the corner of the nunnery-turned-hotel-turned-Bitcoin-party-central, and I felt like I didn't want to be anywhere near there tomorrow. If it was a parade stop on the protest's route and if they were planning a bomba on the front steps, what was going to happen when Pickles's groupies wanted to join in? I'd seen them with their only-good-vibes attitude and swagger, and their life's-a-party privilege. They were capitalist hippies, which was an oxymoron. Maybe Coachella was a better analogue. Pickles's followers believed in the Bitcoin free lunch. *Mi'ja, there is no such thing as a free lunch.*

Thinking about Bitcoin reminded me of Jorge's exchange with Ana. It was as good a time as any to call her and find out what she meant. Why was el Bitcoin spooky? I pressed the Call button.

"Hola, Miriam. How is Puerto Rico?" Ana asked.

"It's beautiful. How is Coral Shores? Are you managing okay without Alma?"

"Yes, I am showing lots of houses. I think we have a buyer for the big bayfront house on Mahi Street."

"Awesome. Is that the house Alma told me about? Didn't someone want to buy it with Bitcoin?" I hoped I sounded excited and not like a snoopy Velma.

"Don't get me started about Bitcoin. Pft. Alma has gone loca."

I very much wanted to get her started. "You don't like Bitcoin? It's just another form of money, isn't it?"

"Okay, let me put it to you this way. When Kostas has money to clean, he gets a bunch of people who owe him *favors* to buy Bitcoin with it, and then he cashes it out a few days later and deposits it in a real bank. *You see.*"

Kostas Borisova was a billionaire with ties to the Russian mafia. Ana had owed him a favor that had gotten her interrogated by the police last year.

"Do you mean money laundering?"

"Exactly. I don't want to have anything to do with crypto money. It's dirty. Keep me away from anything the bravata touch. I told Alma to be careful with her new boyfriend. I get a Fyre Festival vibe from him."

"Fyre Festival?" I'd never heard of it.

"It was supposed to be like a Coachella. You know what that is?"

Celebrity watching wasn't one of my pastimes, but I knew it was a music festival with a unique fashion vibe.

"So, like Coachella but on an island in the Bahamas. All the trust-fund kids and wannabes bought VIP tickets and flew to the middle of the ocean to an undeveloped island expecting five-star treatment, but instead, they got school lunch sandwiches and a tent. Well, the lucky ones got a tent. It was a mess. There are a couple of documentaries about it. You should watch them."

"Maybe I will. Did the festival have anything to do with Bitcoin?"

"No, but I'm saying if it is too good to be true, then it probably is.

"There are no free lunches."

"Exactly. They paid a thousand dollars for cheese on white bread."

We both laughed.

We said goodbye, with me promising to keep an eye on Alma's lovesickness. If Ana was worried about Herbie, the Love Bug, then I should be too. I wondered if Detective Pullman would run another background check for me.

Miriam, you've lost your marbles. I tucked a stray hair behind my ear as I laughed at myself. There was no way I'd get another favor out of Pullman.

I got up from the bench and crossed the plaza at a diagonal. In the center of the plaza was a statue of Juan Ponce de León. The conquistador stood with his weight on his back leg and his arm outstretched. His finger pointed at something. The other hand was on his hip. The pose, the thigh-high boots, and the feather in his jaunty hat felt like humor. If the boots had had stiletto heels, it could have been an advert for *Kinky Boots*, the musical.

I read the four panels at the base. The conquistador was long dead when the statue was erected in 1882, but it seemed his publicists were still doing their job. The chiseled inscriptions were boasts of the man's *great* deeds. I understood that it was futile to be angry at the tone-deaf words in stone. All I could do was shake my head at the grotesqueness of "Visitó la ysla en 1508. Volvió á poblarla en 1509. Terminó su conquista en 1511." He visited the island in 1508. He came back in 1509 to populate it. He finished his conquest in 1511. I clenched my fists.

There were people here before you came!

My phone vibrated in my pocket. I slung my purse to the side and reached in to get it. It was a text from Jorge.

I read his text out loud. *"You are not going to believe lo que encontré en el closet de Alma.* Okay, what did you find?"

The answer was in the subsequent text. It was a photo—a photo of a Louis Vuitton *keepall*. Inside the bag, there was money, a lot of money. Jorge's next text was "WTF" with the bulging eyes emoji. Those were my thoughts exactly. What in the world was Alma doing with that much cash? Jorge was right; I almost didn't believe him.

I texted Jorge to not touch anything else and to get back to the guesthouse stat. The money had to belong to Heriberto. *Right?* What kind of business was he in that he'd need to carry that much cash? Alma had said he was in finance. The Christmas party where they'd met was at a multitower condo complex he'd helped finance. I knew he was a millionaire, but that didn't mean it was necessary to carry around millions in a duffel bag.

When someone bought a house with cash, it wasn't literally cash. It just meant it wasn't borrowed money. It meant the buyer had liquid assets. *Right?* Did I really know what I was talking about? *Maybe* Heriberto flew to Puerto Rico to buy property. *Maybe* he planned to deposit the cash into a Puerto Rican bank. The banks were on odd hours due to the holidays. *Maybe* he just hadn't made it to the bank yet.

Really? Miriam, stop reaching. Only bad guys carry around that much cash.

Chapter Twenty-Three

"Miriam."

I'd been talking to myself so much, trying to decipher what exactly was going on, that I was hearing my inner voice using its outside voice to call me.

"Miriam!"

I looked around to make sure someone wasn't actually calling for my attention.

"Miriam. Mujer, mira pá arriba."

The voice telling me to look up sounded like Alma's. My eyes scanned the windows and roofs of the buildings around me, but I didn't see her. I kept walking down Calle de Cristo. As I passed the steps to El Convento, Alma barreled through the decorative iron gate.

"Chica, I was calling you," Alma said with alcohol-tinged exuberance.

"Were you on the roof? I looked but couldn't see anyone," I said.

Should I say something about the bag of money?

"Yes, we're on the roof. It has a great view. I saw you, but I guess you couldn't see me. Come up and celebrate with us."

"What are you celebrating?" I asked. I checked that her ring finger didn't have a rock on it and quietly sighed with relief that it didn't.

"I just made my biggest commission ever! I sold the penthouse floor to Brandon."

"Really? Que cool. ¿Dónde? What building?"

"Duh, Herbie's development. The one on Brickell. But the whole floor! The two units. Thirty million each! Chica, that is so many zeros." Alma lowered her voice. "My commission is three point six."

I was doing the math equation in my head. $\$60,000,000 \times 3.6\%$. I thought her usual commission was 6 percent, but maybe it was normal for it to be lower if the price of the property was higher.

"Million." Alma put me out of my misery. "Three million six hundred thousand dollars. Do you know what I can do with that? I can expand the business. I can help so many charities. I can start an addiction awareness program in the schools."

Alma's brother, her only sibling, had died of an overdose when we were in high school. I knew it would mean a lot to her to be able to help other families avoid such tragedy.

"Come and have a glass of bubbly with us," she said.

I pointed to my belly and made a don't-you-remember-I'm-pregnant face.

"Chica, one sip of prosecco isn't going to do any damage. Come on. I want you to meet Brandon." Alma pulled me by the hand to the steps. "Come on. For me."

"Okay, okay. Pero, I can't stay long. Jorge is on his way back and doesn't have a key to the guesthouse," I said.

"Pilar will let him in. She's always around. Don't worry."

We got in the elevator and rose the four floors to the top. A simple outdoor table rested under a bougainvillea-covered pergola in the corner near the pool. Beneath the thorny branches sat Heriberto Chacón and Brandon Pickles. A freestanding champagne bucket was between them. It had two bottles in it. One of the black bottles was upside down.

"Miriam, I'm so glad you could join us," Heriberto said. "Let me introduce you to our associate, Brandon."

I took the man's extended hand. Brandon Pickles was lean and a few inches shorter than Heriberto. He had pale skin and a splatter of freckles. A lock of his shoulder-length, light-brown, almost-red hair fell onto his face, and he finger-combed it away. The open neck of his shirt showcased an emerald pickle on a Cuban link chain. The promo posters had exaggerated its size, but it was still an eye-catcher.

"Nice to meet you, señorita," Pickles said.

I saw Heriberto react with a micro-grimace at the man's terrible Spanish. His businessman's smile returned instantly, and he waved to a waiter to bring another glass.

"Un placer," I said. It wasn't really a pleasure to meet him, but I had been curious about who the man behind the royal moniker was. "I hear congratulations are in order. You're moving to Miami."

"I'm in Miami a lot—Ultra, Rolling Loud, Art Basel, CryptoCon. It makes sense to have a place to crash," Pickles said.

Alma patted the chair next to hers. I looped my purse over the metal chair's finial and sat. The waiter placed a fresh glass on the table along with a charcuterie tray. Brandon popped one of the cornichons into his mouth. Not only was the man's surname a fermented cucumber, but he apparently liked them too. He took the bottle from the ice and dripped water as he reached to fill my glass. I noticed the label on the bottle had a winking dog.

"Do you own a vineyard?" I asked, pointing to the bottle.

"I own a share in one. Scooped it up for a steal when Spain's economy was tanking. *Cava, Spain's answer to champagne.*" He pointed to the Spanish on the label that read denominación de origen, proclaiming the grape's provenance. "I always travel with a couple of cases of my private label." Brandon Pickles had a laid-back cadence to his voice. *California? Or affect?*

175

"Salud," Heriberto said.

"Cheers to Miami," Alma added.

We all clinked glasses. I took a token sip and set my flute down. The bubbly wine had a floral scent with a lemony finish. It would go nicely with flan. I'd have drunk the whole glass in a second if it weren't for the baby. The self-control I exerted over alcohol was easy compared to keeping my mouth shut. I had so many questions that needed answers.

What was the deal with that bag of cash? That was for Heriberto. Did Lucas shoot a commercial for your Bitcoin? That was for Pickles. Are you in business with Jules Howard? Also, for Pickles. And then for my BFF: Have you been kidnapped and brainwashed? *Because you are acting a little weird.* Actually, that was not a bad place to start. The kidnapping or, rather, the dog-napping. Had UPRI taken the dog? Was there a ransom note? What were their demands? Was there going to be trouble tomorrow at the protest?

"Is that your dog on the label?" I asked Pickles. "What breed is he? I don't think I've ever seen a dog that looks like him. Or is it her?"

Alma gave me a stop-it-that's-a-sensitive-subject glare. I ignored her.

"Yeah, that's my girl, Dill. She got out the other day and hasn't come back. A firecracker scared her, and she bolted. I'm a wreck about it," Pickles said.

"Don't worry, we will find her soon," Heriberto said.

"She's used to bottled water and Wagyu beef. She has to be miserable. My poor *Dilly-Willy* is lost and scared down one of these little streets." Pickles waved his drink at the city.

"Does she have a tag with a phone number? Have you offered a reward?" I asked, wondering if Dill always wore her emerald pickle collar. It was probably worth a month *or three* of rent for someone on the island.

"We've got the local police looking for her. But a reward is a good idea. Herbs, my man, an old-school paper flyer might be the ticket. Is ten thousand cash too little?" He looked at us for guidance. "You're on TV, right? One of the Spanish stations, yeah? It broadcasts on the island, yeah? Maybe we should put it on the news." He looked to Heriberto for his opinion. "And social. We need to get it out on social."

"Brandon, we will find your dog. Let me handle it. You don't need to give those socialistas any free publicity," Heriberto said.

"Socialists?" I knew he meant UPRI but played dumb.

"Some activists have targeted Brandon with a smear campaign. They are the ones that set off the firecrackers," Alma said. "No es nada serio. Let's have another drink to Miami." She motioned for Heriberto to pass her the bottle. "Brandon, you are going to *love* your new condo. Miami is the gateway to the Caribbean and Latin America. It is the perfect place for your headquarters." She refilled the glasses. "Salud!"

I faked a sip of Cava and then listened to Heriberto and Alma stroke Pickles's ego. It was disgusting. So was Alma's new zeal for Bitcoin. *What is she saying? She wants to have a real-estate Bitcoin brand. ¿Que qué?* My phone vibrated. Jorge was locked out of the guesthouse. Doña was not answering his knocks. I was glad to have an excuse to leave. I thanked them for including me in the celebration and wished Pickles happiness in Miami. Alma walked me to the elevator.

"Are you serious about a real-estate Bitcoin?" I asked.

"*Porfa.*" She laughed. "That was me keeping him hooked. Heriberto is trading my Bitcoin commission for real dollars. It will be sitting in my bank account, collecting interest, before I get back to Miami. I made money plus some. Chica, I am not Juan Bobo." Alma pulled me toward her and kissed my forehead.

"Don't worry about me. I'm a smart Latina making jefa moves."
Boss moves. What?

Alma's words had not convinced me that there wasn't something
to be worried about. It all seemed too good, too easy. She might not
be a Juan Bobo, the titular character from the Puerto Rican folktales
about a naïve boy that gets into avoidable troubles, but that didn't
mean that love and greed weren't clouding her judgment.

I waved goodbye as the elevator doors closed. I thought about
what I'd learned as I moved through the lobby. UPRI had set off
some fireworks that had scared Pickles's dog. And Pickles was
moving his headquarters into Heriberto's luxury development in
Miami. I'd basically learned nothing. And Jules Howard's name
hadn't come up.

I exited via the door that faced the guesthouse's street. The
little park across the street was empty except for a few birds. A
pigeon was perched on the back of the giraffe-cat sculpture. It
pecked at a piece of bread. Could Dill be hiding in a park scroung-
ing for scraps? Old San Juan had a lot of little plazas and parks.
Maybe the dog was outside the wall on the Paseo de Princessa.

"Por fin. I thought I was going to be cat food!" Jorge motioned
to the cat meowing and pawing at his leg.

"Vaquita, are you hungry? Is it time for Doña to give you your
snack?" I cooed at the feline. "¿Tocaste su puerta?" I pointed to
her door.

"Yes." Jorge cocked his head and made bulgy eyes.

"Okay, okay. It's just weird. She is usually here at this time of day,
cocinado." I'd assumed she'd be in the kitchen preparing dinner.

I unlocked our door, and Vaquita snaked through my legs
into the house.

"Vaquita, come back. I don't think you're supposed to be in
here." I set my bag on the hall table. "Jorge, can you get her out of
the kitchen? I have to pee. Bad."

"Sorry, chica, this girl needs her afternoon beauty nap." Jorge was at the top of the stairs.

I sighed and went into the half bath. Baby bladder handled, I made sure the faucet was tightly closed before turning the little room's light out.

Meeeooooow. Meow. Meow. Meow.

Vaquita's mews were rhythmic. A long one followed by three short ones like she was telling me to hurry the bleep up.

"I'm coming," I said to her.

The cat was at the back door, frantically pacing its width. The kitchen lights were off, and the last bit of the sun's glow barely illuminated the table by the window.

"Do you want to go to the patio?" I asked the cat. "Does Doña let you back there?" I turned the ancient skeleton key in the door and pulled the door to me. "Well, at least you'll be outside. Hopefully, Doña won't be too upset."

Vaquita darted by me and into the gray evening. She let out another string of desperate meows.

"Doña!" I hurried to the figure on the ground. Doña was on her stomach, her face turned to the side. I knelt beside her. There was a dark mass of goo in her silver hair. *Blood.*

"Doña!" I yelled. She was breathing but not responding to me. "Ay, Caridad. Doña responda."

I got up and ran into the house. I shouted to Jorge for help, then grabbed my phone from my purse. As I went to the patio, I turned on every light switch I could find. Thankfully, one of them was the back door sconce. It wasn't a lot of light, but it was better than darkness. Vaquita sniffed Doña, then sneezed. The cat leaped onto a wobbly round café table and bounded to the outside wall.

"¿Qué te pasa, chica?" Jorge said from the threshold. "Oh my God. Is she okay?"

"No. It looks like she's been hit on the head. She's bleeding and isn't opening her eyes," I replied.

Groan.

"Oh, thank goodness. She's making sounds. What do we do?"

"Call somebody! Call 911," Jorge said.

I felt stupid that I didn't know if Puerto Rico used the 9-1-1 system or had another number. I called Welmo instead.

"Welmo. Doña is hurt," I said.

"Hurt? What do you mean?" Welmo asked.

"She's bleeding. Please help. Hurry."

"I'll be there in two minutes." Welmo ended the call.

I sat beside the older woman and stroked her hand. "Viene ayuda." Help was on its way.

I told Jorge to bring me a few pieces of ice wrapped in a clean dish towel. While he did that, I got the seat cushion from the garden chair. I gingerly lifted her head and slipped the thin foam pillow under it. Her eyelids fluttered, and she moaned. It was weak, but at least she was conscious.

"I got this instead." Jorge passed me a frozen bag of mixed veggies and a cotton towel.

I put the folded towel over the bloody cut and gently applied pressure. The bleeding had stopped, but the gash was gnarly. Doña winced. I broke the frozen chunks of peas, carrots, beans, and corn apart before delicately placing the cold compress on the towel. She was probably going to use it for arroz chino. Chinese fried rice. The Chinese, mainly Cantonese, had come to the island in the nineteenth century as indentured laborers, and then later, there was a wave of Cuban-Chinese in the 1960s, escaping Fidel Castro. A unique style of Chinese fast-food restaurants developed in the last half of the twentieth century. Fried rice was served with a side of French fries. Often, there was a freezer case of mantecado at the take-out counter, and the establishment did double duty as a Chinese restaurant and an ice-cream parlor.

"Hel-lo. Miriam." Jorge snapped his fingers. "Is she okay?"

"Sorry, I was thinking about—never mind. Um, what do you think happened?" I asked Jorge.

He was beside the vine-covered wall separating the guest-house from Doña's side. "I don't know, but there's a gate here." Jorge opened a section of the vined wall. Unoiled hinges squeaked. Jorge looked into Doña's patio. "There's a broken pot on the ground."

"¿Una cazuela?" I asked.

"No, not for food. For matas. Like terra-cotta—a plant pot. It's big. Come look." Jorge let the gate swing shut and helped me up.

I felt guilty for leaving the innkeeper's side, but I was curious about what could have happened. The gate was completely cam-ouflaged, which explained why I hadn't noticed it from the kitchen table's window. Doña's patio was better lit. There was a floodlight by her back door. The smashed pot was large and looked heavy enough to have caused the damage to her skull. I toed a piece of the terra-cotta and saw a dark blood spot. The plant's roots looked like worms crawling free from the clumps of soil.

"How did a pot fall on her head?" I asked, mainly to myself.

"I don't know. But that pot looks just like those on the wall." Jorge pointed to the pots on the back wall. The guesthouse side had three—one at each corner and one in the middle. Doña's side was missing its middle pot. "Do you think the cat could have pushed it over by accident? Maybe that was why she was so agitated."

"I don't know." Jorge made duck lips. "That pot is heavy. I don't think cats are that strong. Mira." He pointed to Vaquita, who was on the cinderblock wall watching us. The cat meowed, then jumped and disappeared down the other side.

"Where did she go?" I asked. I went to the wall as if I'd be able to look over it. Even on my tippy toes with an outstretched hand, I couldn't reach the top of the wall. The wall of the adjacent building, a small apartment complex, looked like it was flush with the patio. "Step up on this and look over the wall." I motioned for Jorge to use the lip of a large potted palm as a step. "Is there an alley?"

"I wouldn't call it an alley, pero there's a space." He made a narrow gap with his hands. "I see the cat. And a rat! *Gross.*" Jorge gagged. He put his hand on the wall pot closest to him, the one on the shared corner. It didn't move or rock. "I think these things are permanent."

"What do you mean?"

"Like glued con cement or algo." Jorge got down from his perch with a graceful ballet spin.

"Where is she?" Welmo called from inside the house.

Jorge and I hurried over to where Doña lay.

"Estamos en el patio," I called.

"Pilar, Doña Pilar. ¿Qué pasó?" Welmo knelt beside her. He put his mouth close to her ear and whispered.

Doña, with the last of her energy reserve, answered, "Sí." Her eyelids fluttered and then she mumbled a cuss. "Fue ese maldito cabrón."

Who did she mean?

Chapter
Twenty-Four

Welmo and Jorge had carried Doña Pilar to the car and taken her to the hospital. Jorge caught a ride back to the guesthouse soon after. Of course, Welmo stayed with Doña in the emergency room. I'd seen how protective he was of her.

Jorge knocked to be let in the house. I'd locked all the doors and checked them twice after they'd left. Something about Doña's accident didn't seem accidental. *A cemented planter doesn't just jump off a wall and onto a person's head.* As I reached for the lock, I got a text update from Welmo.

"They are keeping her overnight for observation," I said, giving Jorge a welcome-back kiss.

"Mejor. Because she woke up once or twice, but then, you know . . ." He pantomimed a faint.

"Did she say anything when she woke up?"

"The first time, no, pero the second time, cuando we were in the waiting room, she said algo to Welmo, and he got, like, mad, you know? Like, biting his teeth."

"*Clenching his jaw.*"

"Eso mismo."

"Did you hear what she said?"

"Venga. Vete. Deja. I don't know, algo con un V or B or D."

"Are you sure it wasn't Vaca? The cat. Was she trying to tell him the cat pushed the pot over?"

"Maybe, pero chica, even if the cement was loose, I don't think un gato could knock it over. Maybe the cat was in the plant, you know, doing caca"—Jorge waved his hand under his nose—"and like she tried to get it to stop. Maybe she pulled it down from the wall."

But that didn't explain why she was in *our* patio, and the broken pot was in *hers*. I felt like there was something missing to the story. *If I couldn't reach the pot, how could she? She is shorter than me.*

"I'm going to change. I'm going out."

"Where are you going?"

"Hay un club gay that the lifeguard from the hotel told me about."

"Ooooh, you have a date. I'm glad to see you getting over Lucas."

"No estoy over Lucas." Jorge shook his head. "It's not a date. El lifeguard is straight *pero* his brother is gay y el bartender del club. So, *maaaybeee*," Jorge stretched out the word and grinned wickedly. "If he looks as good as el lifeguard, maybe I can start to get over that cheating cabron." He kicked up his heel as he stepped onto the stairs.

"Okay, I'm leaving you my key." I put the key on the hall table. "Make sure your phone is charged. Y por favor be careful."

"Okay, Mami," he said, leaning over the second-floor banister.

"Not funny."

"*A little* funny. Bye, I have to go get more gorgeous."

I didn't relish being in the house alone. Seeing Doña helpless and hurt had rattled my nerves. "I should make dinner and get my mind off things," I said. As if on cue, La Sirena punched, and my stomach gurgled. "Let's see what we have to work with." I opened the refrigerator and then the cabinets. I could have easily reheated something, like the arroz con gandules in the tinfoil-covered bowl, but cooking was my zen. It was like meditating, and I needed to clear my mind. My day had been like a preschool cartoon—full of "Look at this." "Oh, look at that." "Is that a clue?" "Follow the map." But unlike one of Manny's TV shows, there were no obvious answers here. And there definitely was no happily-ever-after final scene with singing and dancing muñequitos.

Sigh.

I missed my son and my house and my husband. I missed our predicable rhythms of the week. *Miriam, in just a few more days, you will be home.*

"Dinner, then bed. You are tired, chica," I said, closing the refrigerator I'd been staring into.

I found a can of garbanzo beans in the cabinet. From the counter, I took an onion and two tomatoes. It was the makings of a simple vegetarian meal. The pan on the stove was a good size for what I had planned, so I turned the heat up to medium and poured in some olive oil from the rectangular can by the spice rack. I sliced the onion and put the tangle of transparent strings into the warming pan. Next, I crushed several cloves of garlic and added them. The next layer of seasoning was oregano, cumin, and a heavy dash of adobo. I drained and rinsed the legumes and set them aside. Then I chopped the tomatoes. Ideally, I would have deseeded them but didn't bother with it. They and the garbanzos went into the sauté. I combined and stirred it so that the onions wouldn't burn. The last ingredient was a squirt of ketchup. The sugar, condensed flavor, and color brought the dish together. I sliced some bread into one-inch rounds and popped them under the broiler for a minute. As I was plating my dinner, Jorge galloped down the stairs.

"Do you want to eat before you go? I have extra," I said into the darkened hallway.

"It smells delicioso, pero *garlic*. I have fresh teeth, gracias. Bye."

I heard Jorge take the keychain from the hall table and close the door behind him.

I was alone and while, usually, that wouldn't have bothered me, tonight it did. The house was just too quiet. I'd even have welcomed the creepy whining pipes. Instead, I opened my phone and put on some music. Marc Anthony's voice filled the dining nook. It was one of his older tunes. As I crunched my bruschetta-like garbanzo and onion toast, I laughed at the synchronicity of the lyrics. "Yes, Marc. I need to know too!" I was seated at Welmo's usual chair because I didn't want to look at the spot where I'd found Doña. Facing the opposite direction, I mainly saw the vine-covered wall between the properties.

The change of perspective had me noticing things I'd overlooked before. I could see the springs to the garden gate. Now that I knew they were there, they were apparent. *That must have been how Doña disappeared the other day when Welmo was arguing with her.* Along the top of the wall, a feline shadow moved. Vaquita. The weak light from the outdoor sconce barely reflected in her green eyes. *She probably wants her evening meal.* The cat stopped her amble. At first, she was a gray mass, but then her black-and-white patterned fur became obvious. Doña's patio light had turned on. *Wait, when had it turned off? Was it on a motion sensor? It was on when Welmo took her to the hospital.* The light turned off again. Vaquita froze. She was laser-focused on Doña's side. She crouched flat and then jumped down into the guest-house patio.

I turned off my music and opened the door for the cat. *She's already been in here once. What's the harm?* While I prepared a dish of cream for her, she purred and circled my ankles. "Venga, Vaquita. Tienes que comer afuera." She ran to the door like she'd understood me. I placed the dish outside at the bottom of the steps. I smelled cigarette smoke. I tiptoed over to the gate. *Someone is in Doña's patio!*

Carefully and slowly, I cracked the gate open to peek in. There in the back corner was the unmistakable fiery cherry of a cigarette. *Is it Doña's grandkid, the one that stays over sometimes? I should tell her what's happened.* I opened the gate fully and stepped into the other side. Something knee-high ran at me.

"Dill?"

It was Brandon Pickles's dog. The dog seemed to smile. Its tail wagged at helicopter-blade speed. The dog wanted to be petted. I looked into the corner and watched the smoker move into clearer view.

"Lucas?!"

Chapter
Twenty-Five

"*L*ucas. ¿Cómo? How? Have you been here the whole time?"
I asked.

"Shhhh." Lucas blew smoke with his admonishment. He put
the cigarette out and signaled me to go into Doña's house.

Inside, he locked the door and checked that the curtain covered all the glass. Dill lapped from a bowl of water on the floor.
Then she sprinted down the hall. I followed Lucas, who was following the dog. The layout of Doña's house and the guesthouse
mirrored each other. There were two doors in the hallway under
the stairs. Lucas opened one of them and told Dill to go to bed.
We watched as she made circles and pawed at the blanket on the
floor until it was suitably comfortable. The dog curled her body
and put her head on her paw. Dill let out a pitiful whine. That was
the sound I'd heard. It hadn't been the pipes. It had been the dog.

"Shh. I will come back later, and we will jugar," Lucas said.
He closed the door to the passageway that connected the two
houses. "Gracias a Dios, the dog doesn't understand Spanish.
Because when I say"—his voice dropped several decibels—"play
fetch, she goes crazy."

"Did you kidnap Brandon Pickles's dog?" I asked.

"*No.* Okay, maybe. Pero, I had to. You don't understand. I
needed protection." Lucas tapped his chest with his fingers. "The

dog is safe. Nobody is hurting the dog. The boludo dog is eating like a king. Doña cooks for it. ¿Dónde está Doña?"

Lucas and I were in the windowless dining room. It was less formal than the one in the guesthouse. It was more like a den. There was a love seat, a small desk with a computer, and a round dining table with an unfinished game of solitaire on it.

"Doña is in the hospital."

"¿Qué le pasó?"

"I'll tell you what I know after you tell me why you're hiding." I sat on the maroon love seat, crossing my ankles as I lifted them onto a small footstool.

Lucas paced. He fiddled with his packet of cigarettes before tossing them onto the table, which caused two cards to glide off and land on the faded rug. They were the ace and five of bastos. He hadn't been playing solitaire. He'd been playing brisca, an old European game. La baraja, as it was called in Spain and most of the places they colonized, was a forty-eight-card deck with four suits: copas/cups, oros/coins, bastos/clubs, and espadas/swords. As a child, there had always been a pack about the house. I remembered looking at the ornate cards and making up stories about the men in tights with their puffy shorts and feathered caps. The deck had no queens, which had made me sad.

I'd only seen the game played a time or two. One time was when a couple of neighborhood families were waiting out a hurricane together. Papi and his friends had gotten tired of dominoes. The men were drinking rum and smoking cigars. I remembered Papi taking out the eights and nines of each suit because brisca was played with forty cards. He'd given me the extra cards so I could pretend to play a hand like the adults.

The deck usually only came out at our house when Mami and Tía Elba sat at the kitchen table worrying about a problem. Each card had a meaning and could be used to tell the future. Supposedly.

Hold on, Lucas and Doña weren't playing brisca. They were fortune-telling.

Lucas chuckled as he picked the cards up from the floor. He fanned out the pair with his thumb. "Lies and deceptions," he said. "That's what Doña Pilar says these cards mean. And I think she is right."

Of course! Doña is old school like Tía. She's seeking guidance in the cards.

Lucas slid the two cards into the cigarette pack's cellophane.

"I didn't know you smoked," I said.

"Only when I'm stressed."

"Why are you stressed? What's going on? You told Jorge you were at a spa."

Lucas sighed. "Let me start at the beginning."

I listened as he told me about meeting Brandon. Lucas was a fan. Brandon Pickles, a self-made billionaire, was the celebrity to be seen with. Lucas wanted in. Brandon asked him to make a Spanish-language video for him. Pickles wanted to win over the Puerto Ricans and stem the tide of the bad press.

"Bad press?" I asked.

"Sí. Parce que there have been some news reports that he kicked people out of their homes in Arecibo."

"Are the reports true?"

"I mean, yes and no. He bought some apartments. He remodeled them into little hotels. Pero, it wasn't like he threw people on the street. He gave them notice and followed the protocol, you know. The hotels are cute. They are like the one Jorge and I are— were—staying in. That's why I didn't go back and why I told Jorge to move in with you. How is he? Is he really mad?" Lucas bit his bottom lip.

"Yes, he's mad. And hurt. He thinks you left him for another man. Pero rewind, why couldn't you go back to your hotel?"

"Because Brandon owns it."

"Okay, and—"

"I'm getting there." Lucas took a deep breath and cracked his neck like a boxer waiting for the bell.

The story came pouring out. Lucas and Pickles had filmed an interview-style video in the VIP lounge. After the taping wrapped, they'd celebrated on the rooftop with his private-label Cava. *Sounds familiar.* Pickles invited Lucas to stay and hang out with his inner circle. Pretty soon, the party that was part of Bitcoin conference events got pumping. Dill, who'd been with them the whole time, needed a walk. Lucas offered to take her.

It was dark, but the streets around the hotel were lit. Lucas took a few pictures of Dill with plans to post them on his social media. He also made a video to send to Jorge, a look-what-I'm-doing kind of thing. Dill pulled him around the corner, chasing after a cat, and they came upon a pair of police officers arguing. One was telling the other that he needed más dinero, more money. "Si los accidentes continuan alguien va a hablar." If the accidents continued to happen, someone was going to talk. He needed more payoff money to keep the rank and file quiet. When they noticed Lucas and the dog, the cops gave him a get-out-of-here look and went into the service alley.

"You see, I still had the camera going. I didn't know what I had until I returned Dill to Pickles's suite." Jorge jiggled his leg and spun the cigarette pack with his thumb and pointer finger. "I put the dog in the room and went to use the bathroom. When I came out, I heard the door unlock. Dill went to the door. I didn't want it to look like I was going through Brandon's private suite, so I stepped onto the balcony. When I heard the voice of the police officer from the alley, I closed the balcony door and prayed he didn't come out there. I was cagando. I was so scared. That's when I realized he wasn't alone. The officer told the person he was with about seeing one of Pickles's groupies walking Dill." Lucas rolled his eyes. "I am not a groupie."

"What happened next?"

"It was a little hard to hear because of the street noise, and I didn't want to be seen, so I watched them with my camera. You know, I just put the lens in the corner of the window." He demonstrated with his hand as a wall and his pointer finger as the phone. "The guy gave the cop a roll of cash from a bag in the closet."

Cash in a bag. That sounds like what Jorge found.

"Did you record it?"

Lucas nodded. "Claro, and that's why I'm scared."

"Can I see the videos?" *Is the other guy Heriberto?*

"I dropped my phone when I was running away. The whole screen shattered." Lucas crossed his legs and jiggled his foot on his knee. "Welmo is having it fixed for me."

So, Welmo knows, and I was right about the face serums. They were for Lucas.

"How did you get out of there? ¿Y la perra?" I asked.

"She followed me. I waited for the men to leave. I counted to sixty, then took the stairs because I figured they were taking the elevator. Pero, I'm on the stairs and see the dog following me. I guess one of them went back to the room, and she got out. Miriam, I was terrified. I ran out of the hotel so fast because whoever let the dog out had to be chasing the dog. Brandon loves that dog. She is like his mascot, you know?"

"How did you get here?" I waved my hand to indicate Doña's house.

"So, I ran out of the hotel and down to the park with the sculpture of the priest."

"La Rogativa?"

He nodded.

"Pero, Dill wouldn't leave me alone. So, I ran through the big gate. That's when I dropped my phone. It flew out of my hand and bounced twice. I grabbed it and then hid in some bushes with the dog. We stayed there for, I don't know, like, five hours. I had to keep petting the dog to keep her happy and quiet. She fell asleep eventually. Pero, I didn't know what to do. My phone was dead, and seguro que those guys knew who I was. Anyway, right before the sun came up, I told myself I had to find a better hiding place. I thought about going to El Morro because Jorge and I had found a private place there during the New Year's party." Lucas opened his eyes wide to mean *you know*. "Pero, as we were walking in that direction, past the priest park, Dill saw a cat and ran up the caleta after it. It was like fate. I chased after her because she is, like, my bargaining chip, no? I saw Doña Pilar feeding the cat, or trying to, but Dill wanted to play with the cat. She recognized me from when I'd stayed at the guesthouse antes. I told her I needed to hide the dog for a few days. She let us into her house because she didn't want to wake you up. Then when I told her the rest, she called Welmo."

"Because he is UnMundo security?" I said with a question in my voice.

"No, because he is FBI."

Chapter Twenty-Six

"Welmo is working with the FBI," Lucas said.

"I don't understand," I said.

"Perhaps I can explain." Welmo and Dill were in the hall.

I stood up and walked toward him. "Did you come through the secret passage?" I poked my head into the hall and looked both ways as if I could solve the mystery.

"Yes. When I saw your unfinished dinner in the kitchen, I thought you might be in the patio, but you weren't. And with Doña's back door locked and you not answering my texts and calls, I became worried."

"Sorry, I left my phone," I said.

Welmo nudged the dog into the room and slid the pocket door closed. "We need to keep her and you"—he pointed to Lucas—"away from the windows. And we may need to move you. I don't know if they know you are here, but the attempt on Doña was too close for comfort."

Lucas became more fidgety. He gathered the cards and cut them multiple times from one hand to the other. The dog gave him a concerned look before hopping onto the love seat. I joined Dill, and she put her head on my thigh.

"How is Doña? And what do you mean attempt? *Someone hit her with that flowerpot*," I said.

194

"Yes, there is a police officer I've been monitoring. I can't go into details. But I'm part of an FBI special task force investigating police corruption on the island." Welmo sat at the table across from Lucas. "Doña confirmed that someone hit her. He jumped over the back wall when this one"—he pointed at his tablemate—"turned the light on. Did he see your face?"

"No!" Lucas said loud enough that the dog looked up in alarm. "No. I thought I heard Doña cursing at someone. I turned the outside light off and then on again. I waited and didn't hear any voices, so I peeked through the curtain. I didn't see Doña, only the broken pot. I figured that was why she'd cursed and that she'd gone to the other patio to get a broom or something. If I'd known she was hurt—" Lucas left the rest unsaid.

"She must have crawled through the gate during the brief cover of dark, trying to get away from her attacker," I said. "Is she going to be okay?"

"Yes. They gave her some stitches. Because of her age, they want to monitor her overnight. I have someone stationed in her room in case they decide to come back and finish what they started," Welmo said.

"But why attack Doña?" I asked.

"Is it because of me?" Lucas asked with dread and guilt.

"No, they want her to sell the houses. And when she said no, they went with plan B. Make her death look like an accident and forge the contract papers," Welmo said.

"Like the owner that *fell* down the stairs?" I asked.

Welmo affirmed my guess. "And the man in the alley," he added.

"I need my phone. I need to show you something," I said.

I went through the connecting space and into the guesthouse. While I was in the kitchen retrieving my phone, I checked that the back door was locked. It was, I assumed by Welmo. My brain

195

was popping with a million questions and revelations. Welmo's "I need to practice my English" was an act. And Delvis had to be in on the subterfuge. Was he *ever even* a real police officer? Or had he always been FBI? I put all my questions aside and opened the text exchange between Jorge and me. Sliding the pocket door open a crack, I went into the room.

"Here." I held out my phone to Welmo. "Jorge found this in Heriberto Chacón's room."

"Where is your friend now?" Welmo asked.

"He is at a dance club." I turned to address Lucas. "You know he thinks you left him for another guy. He's really heartbroken."

"It wasn't my fa—"

"Shhh." Welmo interrupted Lucas's justification. "I need to talk to him. Tell him to come back."

"What do I tell him? I don't think he'll leave the club just for me." I raised an eyebrow.

"Tell him que yo estoy aquí," Lucas said.

"No. I don't want anyone to know where you are. That is too risky. And we don't know if someone is with him. Brandon Pickles's followers will do just about anything he asks. He might have put a tail on him."

"Are you serious?" I asked.

"Very." Welmo's eyes expressed the gravity of the situation.

"Is Alma in danger?" My heartbeat went into hummingbird speed.

"Maybe. Heriberto Chacón is well connected in the money laundering world. He knows a lot of people that want to protect their secrets. I think your friend Alma will be safest if she doesn't know anything about this." Welmo pointed to Lucas and then Dill. "Unless she is part of Chacón's business. Is she?" He pinned me with a steely glare.

"No! Alma would *never*. Nunca, nunca, nunca." I sunk my fingers into Dill's thick coat. *Buuuut, she did just sell one of Herbie's penthouses. Actually, two penthouses. Does she know? No! She's stupid in love with the guy. But I can't believe she'd risk her career for a guy. No. No. She doesn't realize what he has gotten her into. No.*

"Miriam. Miriam," Welmo said.

"Huh," I replied. "Sorry."

"Text Jorge that the studio needs him for a job. Get his location, and I'll go get him," Welmo said.

"A job at this hour?" I said with uncertainty.

"Tell him that Ileana is freaking out because she burned her nose," Lucas said.

Welmo and I exchanged confused looks in silence.

"A sunburn. Say she went on a boat ride or algo. Say it is a makeup emergency," Lucas said.

"Will that work?" I asked.

"Yes. It will work. My Jorge is serious about skin care. I'm sure he has a cream that makes sunburns vanish," Lucas said.

During the time it took Welmo to get Jorge and return, Lucas and I played fetch with Dill in the hallway to tire her out. I also went through every Alma and Heriberto scenario in my head. The only logical explanation was that he had targeted her. *And how do I broach that awful subject with my bestie?*

Welmo alerted me to their return with a text to meet him in the guesthouse.

"Miriam, do me a favor and make me un poquito de café," Jorge said the moment he stepped in the house. "I had *a few* Cosmos." He laughed.

"I promise to make you some coffee, but first, you need to see this," I said.

"Is Ileana here?" Jorge spun around in horror.

"No, it's something else," Welmo said.

"Someone else," I corrected.

Jorge gave me a what-are-you-talking-about look. I took him by the wrist and led him through the secret passage. Dill, asleep on her blanket, opened her eyes. The dog's tail thumped against the wall in a hopeful wag.

"Go back to sleep, puppy," I said.

In a low voice, Jorge asked if that was Pickles's perro.

"Yes. We will explain all that later," I said.

I opened the dining room door, turned into the den, and made a flourish with my hand. Lucas, at the table attempting a three-story card pyramid, looked up.

"Hola, mi amor. I can explain," Lucas said and stood.

"Es-plain! Es-plain me qué. Que you lied. Que you cheated. Qué-qué-qué-qué-qué?" Jorge's Cosmos and his hurt were stirring up a tornado. His hands flew around, and his head was swiveling like a child's top.

"Shh! Siéntate," Welmo said with authority.

We all found our seats like we'd been caught goofing off by the teacher.

"This is a serious situation. Lucas was not cheating on you. His life is in danger, and I fear yours and Alma's might be too," Welmo said.

He hadn't signaled to me, and to be honest, I'd felt left out. *Really, Miriam? You have FOMO? Remember almost dying in a freezer? It is good that you are not in the sights of the baddies this time.*

Welmo confessed his true identity and explained the last few days' events. Jorge went from angry, spurned lover to doting and concerned partner. The pair moved their chairs closer together so they could hold hands.

"Jorge, I need to know about the money you found. Where was it? How much was in the bag?" Welmo leaned against the doorjamb, occasionally surveying the hall.

"I was looking for a fresh shirt. Alma had given me the key to her room and told me I was free to, you know, and so, like, I looked in the closet, and there it was. It wasn't hiding. It was just there. Rolls of bills. Like, literally, I was looking for a casual shirt, like an AX or algo," Jorge said.

"Armani Exchange," Lucas said for the fashion deficient.

"For the record, I didn't take any money. I was tempted. I had a little angel on this shoulder and a little devil on this one. I mean, it was so much money. He wouldn't miss a few hundred. Pero, I didn't. Okay?" Jorge rambled.

Welmo quieted him with a stare and an exacerbated snort. "Your fingerprints are on the bag. I hope they aren't on the money too. You don't want to be incriminated in this when it goes down."

"What exactly is 'this'?" I made air quotes around the word.

"Police corruption, bribery, forgery, money laundering, and possibly murder. That is the short list. I've been undercover for six months. They suspected Vega was dirty."

"Vega, the little one?" I interrupted Welmo.

"Yeah, that's the one I saw in the alley when I was walking Dill," Lucas said.

"Ay Dios, is that why you are hiding?" Jorge asked Lucas.

Lucas acknowledged his conjecture with a nod.

"I thought it was mostly evidence *disappearing* from lock-up and bribes from the drug gangs in los caseríos. Public housing. But then Brandon Pickles came on the scene, and things changed. He already had a reputation as a rich American using the island as his playground. He'd bought several apartment buildings in Arecibo and Luquillo. Then he turned his attention to Old San

Juan. But los viejos de San Juan didn't want to see their town become a mini Miami. No offense."

"No offense taken," I assured him. "But how do Vega and Heriberto fit into all of it?"

"Pickles needed a local to persuade the old timers to sell. Vega fit the bill perfectly. He's a police officer. The locals trust him."

"Did he push Ramoncito down the stairs? I asked.

Jorge gasped.

"Probably," Welmo said.

"And the guy in the alley the day I arrived," I said.

"Looks like it. His house is the first after the alley. It seems that Pickles wants to buy the entire block."

"Doña! The letter!" I said.

"What letter?" Jorge asked.

"That's enough. I've told you more than I should. Everybody go to bed." Welmo clapped his hands and made sweeping movements.

"But what about Heriberto and Alma?" I asked. "Is my friend in danger?"

"I have someone watching her. She is safer not knowing. You must not warn her." Welmo glared at me.

Ignorance is bliss.

Except Alma is not ignorant. She's going to see something or hear something, and then her rose-colored glasses are going to crack.

Chapter
Twenty-Seven

There had been a bit of an argument last night. Well, more like children whining to a tired and not-having-it parent. *Is Manny going to go through that phase? He is such an angelito. Ay, Caridad, I bet La Sirena will be my defiant child.*

Jorge and Lucas wanted to share a bed. Welmo said Lucas was not to leave the windowless den. It was too risky. *Good thing we didn't tell him about the patio smoke break.*

I didn't want to sleep in the guesthouse alone. Looks had been exchanged. Huffs and snorts had been issued. I might have used the vulnerable pregnant woman alone card. I'd pointed out that the den's convertible love seat was twin-bed size and not very comfortable for two adults. Jorge finally acquiesced but stomped up to his room like a petulant child.

Welmo had informed us he would check all the doors and windows of both houses before taking up watch in the dark front room. He'd planned to sleep one hour, patrol the joined houses, and repeat. I'd done the math. He'd get, maybe, four hours of sleep.

I'd slept about as well as I imagined Welmo had. But without Doña to make breakfast and my needing to be on set at seven in the morning, I got up, got ready, and got to the kitchen. There were no specialty pastries from the bakery, but I managed to make a delicious breakfast for the four of us. Tortilla Española. I substituted sweet plantains for the usual potatoes in the crustless skillet quiche.

"Buenos días," I said to Jorge as he entered the kitchen.

"¿Café? I need caffeine," he said with a yawn and a stretch. "I'm your makeup artist again today. I love you, mi'ja, but I'd rather stay here with Lucas."

"I know, but we have to trust Welmo." I flipped the pan onto a plate and admired the sunburst pattern I'd achieved with the maduros. It was like a pineapple upside-down cake but with eggs and ham instead of flour and cherries.

"Mamacita, I want to be with my boyfriend. Like, never let him out of my sight again. He is like a magnet for trouble." Jorge spiked his hair while talking.

"I know. Obviously. He attracted you," I said with a laugh.

"Oh no, you did not go there, Miss Steps in Crime Caca everywhere she goes."

"Ay, cállate." I told him to shut his mouth. "Here, take these plates and forks."

Jorge opened the passageway. I expected to see Dill, but the dog wasn't there. We found the canine in the den. She was pouncing on the floor with her front paws like those videos of foxes in fresh snow. It was similar to Lucas, who was fighting to fold and push the bed into the love seat.

Welmo came down the stairs. He'd changed shirts and was freshly showered.

"Can one of you clear the cards off the table?" I asked.

Jorge set the table while Lucas stacked the cards into a deck. I put the tortilla in the center and returned for the coffee and cups. Welmo insisted on carrying the tray for me. It had a sugar bowl, four cups, a ceramic pitcher of hot milk, la greca of coffee, and a serrated knife to cut our egg pie.

Barbacoa, Bomba, and Betrayal

Lucas fed Dill in her quarters while I served the humans. Our first sips and bites were in silence. We all looked worse for wear, but the worst of us was Lucas. He had sunken half-moons under his eyes, and his nails were bitten to the quick.

My phone buzzed with a message. "Excuse me," I said, pulling it out of my pocket. It was Delvis.

See you in fifteen minutes? I have wardrobe for you.

I texted back. *Are you coming to the guesthouse?*

No, at the museum.

"Apúrate, Jorge. We need to get to set," I said.

My friend sighed deeply but did, in fact, hurry up. Welmo promised to do the dishes before he left to get Doña from the hospital. Jorge gave Lucas a long kiss and whispered something into his ear, resulting in a grin.

"Come on, we need to go." I pulled the lovebirds apart.

As we exited the room, I heard Welmo instructing Lucas not to leave his confines.

"Here. If you hear someone at the door, call me. I programmed my number into it," Welmo said.

I took a step back to spy. He'd handed Lucas a small, cheap phone.

In five minutes, Jorge and I were ready to leave. Before I could open the door, Welmo had to check the street from the guesthouse's living room window like we were in a spy movie.

"Should we be worried?" I asked.

"No. But watch your surroundings. Take Calle del Cristo. It will have people on it. If anyone follows you or is watching you, stay in plain sight. Keep to public areas, don't go down alleys, stay together, and call me if something feels strange," Welmo said.

The deadbolt clanged behind us. It wasn't loud, but in my head, it boomed like the Law & Order *chung chung*. Robert loved that show. Before Manny was born, he'd watched it regularly.

Roberto, mi amor. I wish I was home with you now.

Chapter
Twenty-Eight

As we turned the hotel's corner, perspiration moistened my brow. It was not from exertion but from worry. *Has Heriberto gotten my bestie involved in money laundering? Is Alma in danger? Did Pickles really order those people killed? Or does Vega kill old people for his own sick kicks?*

I cradled my belly as Jorge and I ascended the hill the long way to the museum. A group of Día de los Reyes parade participants were in the pointing Ponce de León square. Their bold and bright costumes hung over the park benches. Giant papier-mâché heads sat on the plaza floor like Alice in Wonderland mushrooms. Most were human faces, but there was one animal, a pig. I stopped and snapped several pictures, momentarily forgetting about the Bitcoin King and his criminal entourage. I wanted to ask the lively group about the characters and their significance, but Jorge tapped an imaginary watch on his wrist and drew me away from my anthropological mission.

Municipal workers were barricading Calle Dr. Francisco Rufino from car traffic. A flatbed truck with blue porta-potties beeped that it was in reverse. We could see the back wall of the three-story museum but were stopped from taking the direct route to our destination. I told the worker blocking us that we needed to get to the museum.

"Está cerrado," said the worker in a go-away-tourist tone.

I told him I knew that the museum was closed, but we were with UnMundo and recording a special in the museum. The man was *not* impressed. He was *not* going to let us through.

"Crucen la plaza y entren por el otro lado," the man said.

I rubbed my hand on my belly, hoping to gain some sympathy, but the man's attention was on the forklift with the teetering porta-potty. I grabbed Jorge's hand and started to skirt the barricade while the guard was distracted. I quickly changed my mind when thirty feet ahead of us, I saw a pair of police officers emerge from the reddish building. One of the cops was petite. Vega, maybe. I didn't waste time finding out.

"We need to go this way," I said to Jorge. I led him past the tall clay totem on the top tier of the plaza. Jorge went before me at the stairs, and I used the green rail to steady myself as I hurried down the steps as fast as possible. At the bronze lamb sculpture, I stopped to take a breath.

"Mamacita, stop the sightseeing. Pick up the pace," Jorge said.

"Bro, this is not your Mambo-ize class. Give me a second." I fanned my heaving chest. Had I really seen Vega?

I pushed off my perch, and we walked across the flat lower tier of Plaza del Quinto Centenario.

"Do you see an entrance?" I asked Jorge.

"No. I don't even know where we are going," he replied.

I looked across the street as we walked beside the museum searching for a door. Red streamers tied to wooden stakes marked a queue on El Morro's lawn. A few early and eager families were already lined up. A local radio station was there interviewing them. Farther away, on the grass where hay had been placed for the camels, I noticed an UnMundo T-shirt on a man rigging a star onto a cable. I slowed my pace and watched him hoist it into the air.

"Where do you think the camels are now?" I asked.

"Qué sé yo. Maybe they bring them by boat." Jorge shrugged.

A golf cart with a blue-haired driver sped toward us.

"There you are. Get in," Delvis said.

"Gracias a La Caridad," I said, taking the front passenger seat. Jorge sat on the rear-facing bench. Delvis made a U-turn, and I held on for my life. "Baby on board!"

"Oh, sorry," Delvis said. "I promise no more fast curves."

At the end of the block, she turned the corner slowly and parked the cart next to the UnMundo van. The street in front of the museum was blocked from vehicle and foot traffic.

"Jorge, Ileana is in the makeup van waiting for you. Do her, then I'll send Miriam to you," Delvis directed.

I followed Delvis into the building to a ground-floor bathroom commandeered to be a changing room. Hanging from the stall's crossbeam was a maxi dress that went from red at the bottom to orange to yellow. The halter top had a gathered neck on a stiff ring-style collar. Delvis leaned her back against the door while I slipped out of my cropped khakis. I folded them before slinging them over a stall door. Next off was the aqua-colored shirt that Alma had given to me. *Bestie, I hope you are okay.*

I put the dress over my head and let it fall around me. I looked in the mirror and shifted my weight from foot to foot. The fabric swung with my movement. I wasn't feeling the look. The dress's shape reminded me of a flor de campana/angel's trumpet. But the color was not as subtle, and then it hit me.

"I look like a mango," I said, glaring at Delvis.

"What? *Noooo.*" Delvis stifled a laugh.

"All I need is a little green."

"Stop. You look fresh and vibrant. And juicy like a—"

"Mango!" I put my fists on my hips.

Delvis bent over with laughter. "Okay, you do look a little mango-y, pero you can rock this dress."

"It's a tent. I'm a mango tent." Tears welled up in my eyes. Was it a shot of La Sirena's hormone jet fuel? Or was it stress about Alma? Something had me hypersensitive. I usually didn't care about clothes or my appearance.

"Deep breath. No te agites. We wanted you to be comfortable. That's why wardrobe picked out something loose, but it does have a belt. So, let's try the belt. Okay?" Delvis took the belt from a bag and handed it to me.

I tied it above my belly to make an empire waist which improved it slightly.

"Unhook theses bra straps for me," I said with my thumb under one of them. Once the tension was released, I undid them in front and stored them in my purse. I'd learned to always wear a convertible bra on film days.

"You look radiant. Very Beyoncé. Like when she wore that yellow dress in that video," Delvis said. "The one where she walks through the door with the water." Delvis acted it out as we exited the bathroom.

"Do you mean the video where she takes a baseball bat to the car?" I asked.

"Yeah. And also like that maternity shoot where she was Oshun. Puñeta." Delvis stopped. "I knew I forgot something. The jewelry. There are some big gold hoops with beads from a local jeweler. I'll grab them from the garment bag. Get to makeup. I have to go check on the crew. I'll bring the earrings to you when I come get you in a second." Delvis let me out of the building via the twelve-foot-tall entrance doors.

Outside, I saw the same pair of policemen. *Coño, that is definitely Vega.* They were walking toward me. I turned and tried to retreat to safety, but the doors were locked. As they closed in on me, I froze in a panic. *Do they know that I know? Are they here to kill me?*

"Señora, una pregunta," the taller one said.

A question. I have a question for you too. Are you the one that hit Doña with a flowerpot? I checked my surroundings for terra-cotta weapons.

"Sí, como no," I replied like any good law-abiding citizen.

"¿Ha visto este perro?" Vega showed me an image of Dill on his phone.

I shook my head. *Can they tell that I'm lying? Ay, Caridad, they can tell. I gave the dog a little piece of ham this morning. They can probably smell her on me.*

"¿Está segura?" Vega asked if I was sure.

"He visto muchos gatos pero ningún perro," I said. *Why did I say that? I told them I'd seen a lot of cats. He is going to know I've been on Caleta de las Monjas.*

"Si ve este perro por favor avisa una policía," the taller one said.

No way am I going to alert the police if—ha ha, when—I see Dill.

The police let me go, but Vega gave me a hard stare as they walked by me. He grabbed his partner's arm to stop him.

"Juan, tenemos una personalidad famosa aquí," Vega said.

Oh no, he's recognized me from TV.

"¿Me permites una foto?"

He wants a photo. Ay, Caridad, what do I do? I can't say no. That would be suspicious.

I smiled as best I could and let them each take a photo with me. I thanked them for watching my show. Vega told me he didn't watch me, but his daughter did. *He has a child! That's terrifying.* Juan, the tall one, informed me his wife watched *La Tacita*. They finally went on their way, and I bolted for the makeup van.

"Why are you so sweaty?" Jorge asked.

"I was just interrogated by the police. The bad police. The ones that tried to kill Doña. And probably killed Ramoncito. The ones Lucas is hiding from."

"Chillax, mi'ja. No one is going to kill anyone in the middle of a Three Kings festival." Jorge put a cape around my neck and began combing my hair.

I texted Alma while he applied a glossy frizz-control serum to my locks. The someone-is-writing dots didn't appear. I gripped my phone and willed her to reply.

"Look at me," Jorge said, lifting my chin with his finger.

"Is that green eyeshadow?"

"Sí. It will make your eyes look hazel on camera."

"No. No green. I'm already mango enough, gracias," I said.

"¿Qué?"

"Never mind. Just give me natural-looking makeup, please." My phone vibrated. "Ay, thank God, she replied." I held the screen up like I was taking a selfie so I could read while Jorge applied blush and contour.

After your shoot, come to the hotel and watch the parade with us. Alma texted.

Which hotel? I texted back.

Pickles. 😊 *We are watching from the roof.*

I'll try, but the studio might have plans for me.

There was no way I was going back into the pickle jar after what I'd learned about him and his associates. I needed a way to get Alma away from Heriberto and Pickles. I needed to talk to my bestie face-to-face and sans rolls-of-money boyfriend.

I texted Alma again. *I miss you. Maybe we can meet for some girl time.*

There were no dots. My message went from blue to green. Images of Alma being thrown off the roof filled my head. *I have to get her away from them.*

Chapter Twenty-Nine

"Here." Delvis dangled a pair of hoops from her fingers. "The museum director's name is Francisco Ferrer. We are set up in the El Indígena de América collection. It has been closed since Hurricane María and is almost ready to reopen."

"Why was it closed? Did the museum get damaged?" I asked.

"It got some water, but he said the worst damage was from mold."

"Oh, wow. No electricity meant no power for fans or AC," I said. My mind immediately went to my cousin Kharla. She'd come back to the island to help after Maria. She'd helped with the skills and interests she had. I bet I'd have helped at the museum. We each followed our passions in life. I'd gone the books, study, and school way. She went the plants, animals, and direct-action route. Her current involvement with UPRI made sense in that light. She wanted to help the island and her people. *Is UPRI going to protest peacefully, or do they have a civil disobedience action planned?*

Snap. Snap. Snap.

"Oye, Miriam, atención." Delvis got my attention. "Francisco will give you a tour, then stop in front of a diorama of Taíno people cooking. That's when you do your thing. Don't get too nerdy. Keep the language layperson, not academic. Remember, we want to keep the audience's attention. We've got permission to film some B roll in La Herencia Africana exhibit for later use. This should all take about an hour. Then Jorge will touch up your makeup before going over to the kings."

"Perfecto. Tengo un break. So, like, I can go away for an hour?" Jorge asked.

"Yeah. Get a coffee or watch the crowds but stay close by, please." Delvis motioned for me to exit the van.

"What are you going to do?" I ask Jorge.

"I might go back to the house and—" Jorge winked, then dropped a slim box of fake nails into the black bag on his shoulder.

I knew he was going to see Lucas. "Be careful," I whispered. "Lock the doors—door to the van. I'm leaving my purse and phone in here." I used my normal voice.

The three of us exited. Jorge practically skipped away. I watched him as long as I could. He was taking the quickest but quieter route to the guesthouse. My palms got clammy. *Please don't run into the police.*

Delvis knocked on the museum door, and a museum staff member let us in. We were escorted to the newly restored exhibit hall. Francisco Ferrer, a couple of years my senior, was younger than I expected. He'd done his graduate work in the United States and his Ph.D. in Mexico. We instantly took a liking to each other and manifested Delvis's fears—we got nerdy.

"The Taíno resisted colonization in many ways, but one way was food," Francisco Ferrer said, pointing to a conical mound in the diorama. The statue, a short, muscular man with stripes of red and black dye on his skin, crouched beside the heap of soil. He held a batata/sweet potato. The mound, called a conuco, was a passive way to grow large crops of root vegetables and corn. Vegetable debris was gathered into a pile, the crop planted, and the decomposing compost fed the growth. Nature tended to itself and freed the Taíno from time-consuming farm labor.

"Like in La Isabela, Hispaniola," I said. I knew the account of the 1493 farming strike. It, like their method of growing, was passive. The natives of the area simply didn't plant any crops that year. The Spanish had relied on the Taíno for most of their food. So, once the invaders had depleted the stockpiles, not knowing or caring to learn how to feed themselves, hunger set in. The tribe's actions had unimaginable repercussions, namely the extinction of several native animal species that the Spaniards killed to satisfy their voracious appetite. A few of the extinct fauna were depicted in the diorama, like the "mute" dog accompanying one of the humans and a small rabbitlike rodent called a cori, which was on a spit by a fire.

"Many foods could be cooked on the barbacoa, a wooden grate over a flame. The modern etymology of the word is, of course, *barbecue*. Coastal tribes with diets of fish and crustaceans, like whelks, sometimes used a baking method to cook their fish. They'd coat the fish in mud and place it in a pit of embers. When the dried mud was removed, so were the fish's scales. It was an adaptive way to scale their catch," said Francisco.

As we walked to the African heritage section, I thought about other stories of Indigenous resistance—Hatuëy in Cuba, Agüeybana the second, whose statue I'd seen in Yauco, and the countless others whose names were lost to genocide. My cousin Kharla was continuing the tradition. UPRI was pushing back against the Bitcoin invaders. In my head, I saw a brigade of pickles clashing with the protestors chanting Borikén. I placed a hand over my mouth to hide my grin. *Marching pickles.*

Delvis directed me to walk by a wall with a triptych of two fully costumed vejigantes and one white-clad bomba y plena dancer. The images were on citrus-colored backgrounds. She had me stroll in front of it half a dozen times. And then she had me mimic the dancer's pose, holding the hem of my dress similarly. *Ay, ay, ay. If I'd only known I was going to need dance moves, I'd have taken that elective instead of bowling, which I've never used in any practical way.* The crew took a bunch of B-roll close-ups of the masks and instruments. We were done by five after nine. The museum director led me back to the main entrance while Delvis stayed with the crew to pack up.

The noise volume outside the museum had changed. I could hear the din of people gathering and the distorted squawks of megaphones. I looked for Vega and his pal before crossing the barricaded road to the UnMundo van. The handle turned, which gave me relief. It meant Jorge was back, and I would not be alone.

"How was—?" I stopped mid-query in shock. *"Lucas?"*

Seated in the makeup chair was a woman in a yellow sundress with Lupita Nyong'o–level toned arms. *I think that's my dress.* She had black hair, and Jorge was applying press-on nails.

"Esta es mi amiga Lucy," Jorge said with conviction.

"Lucy?" I made sure each syllable dripped with incredulousness.

"Hola." The voice was nervous and too high.

"Shh, mi amor, don't talk. Remember, you have *laryngitis*," Jorge said.

"Lucas, you are not supposed to be in public," I said.

"Don't worry, nobody saw us," Jorge said.

"How did you get around Welmo? Does he know?" I asked. The pair shook their heads.

"He called me. He took Doña to her daughter's house in el campo because the traffic into Viejo San Juan was bad," Lucas said in his regular voice.

"Is he coming back here?" Anxiety cracked my voice. I didn't want to be in the vicinity of a murderous police officer and his cryptocurrency overlord without some protection. Any doubts I'd had about Welmo's alliance had been quelled. Welmo was with the good guys, and Vega was on Team Bad Guy.

"Yes and—"

Jorge interrupted Lucas. "And I promise to have him back in the house soon. Okay?"

"It's so boring being alone," Lucas said.

I grumbled. "No me gusta ni una gota." *No. I don't like this one bit.*

"Someone is going to recognize you. *Ileana* is going to recognize you," I said.

"Not when I'm done working my magic," Jorge said, selecting a lipstick color from his palette.

"Where did you get the wig? Did you pack one?" I asked.

Jorge pointed to a hairless Styrofoam head on a shelf under the makeup mirror. "That's what gave me the idea. I slipped it into my bag when you were talking to Delvis."

"I don't see how this is going to work." I sighed deeply and slumped onto the bench seat. I watched as Jorge put the finishing touches on *Lucy's* makeup. He was a true artist. If I hadn't known it was Lucas, I wouldn't have given the woman he'd become a second glance.

"Miriam, let me fix your lipstick and darte un poquito de powder," Jorge said.

The van's interior was small, and Lucas and I had to dance a little to switch places and get around each other.

"Stop," Jorge said.

We both froze and looked at him.

"You two could be hermanas. Look at me." Jorge took a picture of us.

"Do not post that on your social!" The command in my voice surprised me.

"Cálmate, mamacita. I won't. I just want to remember it. Mira." He showed us the image.

He was right. We could pass as relatives. It was primarily due to similarities in hair and dress, but Jorge's signature contouring makeup added to the familiar illusion.

Delvis opened the door and gave me a two-minute warning without stepping into the van. Jorge introduced Lucy, and Delvis didn't bat an eye. I slipped my phone into my pocket to take pictures with the three kings. Manny's mind would be blown. Los Tres Reyes were like Santa Claus to Puerto Rican and Cuban kids.

"So, this is how it's going to go," Delvis said, helping me step out of the van. "Ileana is already over there. She *witnessed* the kings' magical arrival. Now they're filming the camels eating breakfast."

I gave my director a strange look.

"Hay. They are eating hay."

"That look was for the magic part," I said.

"Oh, it's a special fade-in effect with stars. The kids love it."

"Can we come too?" Jorge asked. Half his body was hanging out the door.

"Claro. I'll get you crew passes when we get there and put you to work. There are a lot of presents to pass out, and the faster we can move the line the better. No kid meltdowns is the goal," Delvis replied.

I don't like this. Jorge, this is a bad idea. Muy, muy, MUY mala idea.

Chapter Thirty

Delvis led us to the taped-off UnMundo craft service area. She forced me to drink some water and eat a corn muffin. "You are growing a baby. Eat. I don't want you fainting on camera," she said.

A few people gave Lucas/Lucy looks. But that stopped as soon as Delvis handed us all lanyards. She stationed Jorge and Lucas/Lucy along the get-a-gift path. The large containers of unwrapped toys were camouflaged with potted plants, and so was Lucas, thankfully. I mimed to them to put on their sunglasses. *Let's hope no one spots them. No gotcha videos, please!*

The containers were gendered. Barbies and babies for girls. Basketballs and build-y things for boys. I stopped Jorge before he ranted.

"I know. I know. It's stupid. Boys need dolls too." I gave my friend a hug.

"It's about to start," Delvis said, waving her arm at the golf cart coming from the fortress. She pulled me to the spot where she wanted me. Ileana got out of the cart and smiled at the crowd of parents and kids. A crew person handed her a wireless mic. Ileana hyped the arrival of the kings.

A parranda began singing Puerto Rican Christmas songs. I filmed a snippet of it to send to Mami y Papi later. Then a boy about Manny's age, who was on his father's shoulders, screamed, "Camellos." Three camels could be seen coming over the grassy ridge. Each beast was led by a magi. I got goose bumps. It was truly magical. I wished Manny was there to witness it. I told myself maybe next year. *Roberto can come with me and take care of the kids. Did I say kids? Ay, ay, ay. We will be a family of four by then.*

The kings and their mounts took several minutes to cross the lawn. The singers and musicians kept the crowd engaged. When I finally saw their faces, I was glad they weren't all white and European-looking. Each costume represented a different ethnicity. The Black king had kente cloth trim on his cape. The Asian king had a Chinese emperor's hat. And the European king looked like Spain's red-and-yellow flag. I took a selfie with me close in the corner and Los Reyes over my shoulder. I sent it to Mami, knowing she'd show Manny, then tucked my phone away.

The plastic garland barricade was lifted, and the organized chaos ensued. All kids under ten got a gift, then moved down the line for a photo with the three wise men and exited. I was on baby duty. If I saw a parent carrying a child under one year old, I gave them a board book and a teething rattle. The line went quickly. Several women recognized me from my *Cocina Caribeña* segment on *La Tacita* and asked to take photos with me. I held a few newborns, which made my sirena kick and flip. *Jealousy?* I witnessed a boy with long hair and tattooed, artsy parents go up to a girl in an Arecibo Capitanes jersey and swap gifts. The boy got her brown-skinned Barbie, and she his basketball. Both children were much happier after the exchange. I winked at Jorge, who was watching it too.

The gifts had all been handed out by eleven thirty. But the crowd had tripled, not with children and families but with celebrants. I saw lots of people in folkloric dress. Some were carrying drums. The official start of the parade was noon. *The exact time of the UPRI protest.*

"Great job, mi gente," Delvis said. "Miriam, take your friends to craft service and get some lunch, then go back to the van. I'll drive you to the guesthouse. It will be safer for you than walking in this crowd."

Craft service had tripleta sandwiches cut on the diagonal, bags of chips, and various canned drinks. We each grabbed a refresher, water for me, Coco Rico for Lucas and Jorge. The coconut-flavored soda was too sweet for my taste. The boys took chips and sandwiches. I took only the sandwich. The beef, lechon/pernil, and ham sandwich was on a pan dulce–style bread. It had shoestring potato chips like a frita cubana, but it wasn't a burger. The tripleta was to Puerto Ricans what the Cubano was to Miami Cubans, but with mayo-ketchup and sliced steak. I asked a local crew member where the trash can was to throw away the sandwich's wax paper. They moved aside and motioned to it, calling it a zafacón, a word distinct to the island. The etymology of the word was up for debate. It was either a Spanglish-ization of *save a can*, a WWII campaign to save metal for ammunition, or an adaptation of an Arab word brought over with the Spanish colonizers.

A megaphone squawked with orders to move onto the sidewalk. The parade would not start until a path was cleared. The parranda band struck up an improvised song, and the assembled crowd slowly moved downhill like ants on a sugar trail.

"Let's get you back to the house," Delvis said, putting her hand on my back. "Welmo will find a safe place for you to watch the parade."

"Is Welmo there?" I asked.

"Not yet. But he will be soon. He had to park his car and walk in. The traffic is backed up for miles," Delvis replied.

I looped arms between Jorge and Lucas and whispered that we needed to go. Lucas, as Lucy, was foolish, but if we got home before Welmo, it might be no harm, no foul.

Delvis drove the UnMundo van with me in the passenger seat. I watched the crowd for Vega and his police officers. *Stop worrying. Lucas is behind the curtain and out of sight.* It took a bit of convincing, but Delvis finally got the man in the reflective vest to move the safety cones and let us pass. The street and sidewalks were empty except for a few parked cars. I thought I saw Vaquita move from a car hood and into hiding. We were at our little street in a minute, but it was too narrow for the van to turn into.

"Hurry up and unlock the door," I said to Jorge.

"Chill, chica. You are e-stressed 'pa nada," Jorge said.

I scanned the mass of people up the street. Sawhorses on steroids blocked the public from the residential area at the small park. No Vega, but I thought I saw his tall friend. Jorge and Lucas dashed to the house, keys in hand. I thanked Delvis and was about to get out when she held me back.

"Is there something I should know?" Delvis asked.

Ay, Caridad. "What do you mean?"

"Is there something I should know about Lucas?" She cocked her head toward the guesthouse door.

"*You knew* that was Lucas this whole time," I said.

"Pft. Claro. The arms. The eyes. The name. Is he, I mean she, or is it they . . . are they transitioning?"

It took me a second to understand what she was talking about and then another second to decide what to say.

Delvis took my silence as a protective wall and jumped in. "I want to be supportive and use the right pronouns. We will need to educate some of the more conservative staff at the network."

Her sincerity and kindness were a knife to my heart. I hated it, but I had to tell a white lie.

"Lucas was worried about his fans seeing him and wanting photos." *More like Pickles and Vega.* "He thought it would distract from the children. So, Jorge helped him with a disguise," I said.

"Oh, so Lucas is still Lucas, not Lucy."

"As far as I know, yes. Do you think anyone else noticed?" I was still worried about some random video or photo from the event going viral. Internet sleuths were like a dog on a scent trial. They would follow it up a tree, down a hole, and to its end. I was sure Pickles and his people were monitoring social media for Lucas and Dill. Jorge and Lucas had taken a stupid, stupid risk

"No creo. Most of the crew are local and haven't worked with him much. Jorge's makeup was perfection, and the wig helped. Lucas looks good as a brunette." Delvis laughed.

I played along and laughed too.

"Go enjoy the parade. Someone, either me or Welmo, will get you to the airport tomorrow," Delvis said.

I scanned the area and then clumsily climbed out of the van. The curtain in the front window of Doña's house moved. Had Welmo made it back before us?

Better Welmo than Vega.

Chapter Thirty-One

Jorge and Lucas were in the hallway doing the happy dog dance with Dill. I triple-checked that I'd secured the door, then dropped my bag on the entryway table.

"Was the dog out when you came in?" I asked.

"Sí," Jorge said, giving Dill a rub on the scruff.

"But we locked the door to her room, *right*? So, who let her out?" I put my hand on my hip.

"Yo." Welmo ducked under the frame and stepped into the guesthouse.

Anger and disappointment pulsated off him.

We are in deep caca.

"You and you. Go to the sala. Now!" Welmo's words came through clenched teeth.

Jorge and Lucas scurried through the connecting passage. Dill moved to my side and sat.

"You too." Welmo pointed at the dog. Dill followed his finger and galloped after the boys. He closed the door and turned to me.

Deep caca.

"What were you thinking?"

"It wasn't my idea, lo juro," I said, raising my palm in an oath. It didn't take long for me to throw my friends under the bus. I

221

wasn't proud, but it was the truth. It had been Jorge and Lucas's stupid idea.

My phone rang. I took my phone out, saw who it was, then showed the screen to Welmo. He nodded and told me to put it on speaker.

"Chica, where are you?" Alma asked. "The parade is about to start."

"I just got back to the house from my UnMundo stuff," I said.

Welmo gave me a you-didn't-just-say-that look. I volleyed back an I'm-sorry grimace.

"Cool. So come to the hotel. Brandon has the whole roof for us."

Welmo shook his head vehemently.

"I don't know if I can get in. The street is blocked. Are they even letting non-guests into the hotel today?"

Welmo gave me a thumbs-up.

"Chica. Brandon practically owns the hotel. I'll meet you at the side entrance in dos minutos to let you in."

"Okay." I shrugged in resignation, to which Welmo fumed. As soon as I disconnected the call, he let me know his dissatisfaction. He mumbled cuss words in Spanish between giving me instructions on how to get out of the hotel if there was trouble.

"Your phone lock is a code, not a thumbprint, correct? Disable it. I want you to be able to call me and let me listen in if anything seems weird." Welmo leaned on the hall table. "If you feel trapped or in peril—"

I interrupted him. "Peril?"

"Yes, peril, it means—"

"I know the word. Pero, like, do you really think I might be in danger? I don't want to be there, pero tambien, I'm just watching a parade with my friend. *And* I'm visibly pregnant. Come on, don't scare me. Expectant mothers usually get respect and reverence. We are treated casi like saints—people open doors for us, offer us seats—"

"I don't want to frighten you. You will probably be fine. Stay in public view, and don't be alone with *anyone*," Welmo said.

"Even Alma?" I asked as I walked toward the door.

"We don't know if your friend has been corrupted. Better safe than sorry."

Welmo checked the street and let me out. Our end of the road was empty. There were no cats sunbathing, and the air was still like it had been sucked up by a big bad wolf about to blow a house down.

Vaquita, where are you? I wish you were out here asking me for milk. It would make me feel better, like things were normal.

At the top of the street, where it intersected the parade route, there was an orderly crowd emitting a low murmur. It felt similar to that moment right before a concert started or the curtains were opened for a play. It was a held breath of anticipation.

"Chica. Mira. Over here." Alma was at the service entrance waving to me. "Come through here. Hurry, it's about to start."

I gripped the pipelike handrail and stepped into the sheltered space where I'd seen Welmo that first day when he'd brought a drink to Vega.

"Come on. Herbie showed me the secret elevator the cleaning staff use," Alma said.

I looked back at the alley where the man had been shot as the heavy steel door closed behind us. We were in the hotel's laundry room. The pungent smell of industrial detergent made my nose drip and my eyes water. Alma led me to a utilitarian elevator and pressed the button for the top floor. We were alone, and it couldn't be helped. Welmo's warning echoed in my mind.

"Hey, chica, are you okay?" Alma turned her face to me. "Are you crying?"

I dabbed my eye and sniffled. "I guess I'm allergic to laundry soap."

"Okay, cool. I mean, not cool, but it's not labor pains, right?" Alma squeezed my hand. "I can't wait to hold her. I mean, claro, I can wait. I'm not wishing for her to be born early, pero you know what I mean."

"I know." I squeezed her hand in return.

"I love you, bestie. I don't want anything to happen to you or the baby."

"I love you too."

Ding.

"We're here. Follow me." Alma sidestepped a few paces, waving a *come here* hand. "We've got the best seats in Old San Juan."

The short service corridor opened onto the Jacuzzi area. Neat rolls of plush towels, stacked in pyramids, stood like a terrycloth version of Giza on a teak table. A foursome, in animate conversation, was in the bubbling tub. Bottles of Brandon Pickles's private-label prosecco bobbed in the melting ice of a topless cooler.

At least there are other people here.

"There you are, mi bella," Heriberto said. He kissed Alma, his whiskey glass on her shoulder.

A sensation like someone had poured the cooler's icy water down my back chilled me. Mi bella. My beautiful. I didn't like the possessive tone Heriberto was using with my friend. I knew I was being critical. I called Roberto mi amor all the time. *But this is different, Miriam. He is a criminal. Money laundering is a crime.*

"Miriam, I'm so glad you could join us. What can I order for you? I know. A virgin piña colada," Heriberto said.

"Water will be fine," I said, but he was already telling the server the order.

I stood next to Alma and looked over the edge. The sidewalks on both sides of the blue ballast stone street were packed five people deep. The smaller children were on the shoulders of fathers and tíos. A trumpet blew a fanfare, and all heads turned uphill. The parade was starting. A group of men in pavas was at the head of the pack. They all had cuatros, a lute about the size and shape of a viola.

"You can probably see the strings on the instruments with those binoculars," I said to Brandon Pickles.

He lowered them and looked at me. "I'm hoping to spot my dog. She's still lost. I've tripled the reward to one hundred thousand but nada." The man sighed wearily. "Here. Use them. I need a drink." Pickles handed me the compact Leica binoculars.

The view from the roof was fine, but with the lens, I could see the brushstrokes on the cabezudos prancing behind the band. I recognized Juan Bobo and his pig from the plaza. I knew that character from the folktale, but the other heads were personalities I wasn't familiar with.

"¿Quiénes son los personajes?" I asked the server delivering my frozen drink. It had a straw, a paper umbrella, and a pineapple wedge.

She answered in Spanish and told me they were local characters. She identified the characters as a well-loved schoolteacher, a poet, a general, a painter, a revolutionary, and a comedian named Don Cholito. He had glasses and a happy, open-mouthed smile. The moon-faced head with the orange tone was a lottery ticket seller. The head next to him was in honor of the Afro-Latino musician Toribio, el Rey del Güiro. A few paces behind them, there was an abuelita type, which made me think of Doña Flora. The server pointed to a grumpy-looking face with white hair, big eyebrows, and a mustache. "Ese es Ricardo Alegría. Él fue antropólogo." *An anthropologist!* I used the binoculars to take a closer look.

I absentmindedly took sips from the piña colada while enjoying the big caricature heads on small bodies. Pickles returned to his post, and I passed him the binoculars.

"Did you see Dill?" he asked.

"No, I'm sorry, I didn't." I pursed my lips. The man looked miserable. *Miriam, don't you dare pity him! He's not a good person. He's forcing people from their homes and ordering flowerpots to be smashed on the heads of little old ladies!* Despite myself, I said, "I'm sure your dog will be home soon, maybe even today."

"What's this about the dog?" Heriberto asked. "Do you know where she is?"

I shook my head and avoided his eyes. "Look, here come the vejigantes," I said.

Their masks had pointy horns the size of an alpha buck's antlers. A troop of thirty or more folkloric dancers accompanied them. The vejigante costumes were bold and voluminous like parachutes. They taunted the bystanders, and the crowd loved it. As the troop passed the hotel, some dancers peeled off and went to the church steps.

"Mira, mira, mira. Los Reyes," Alma shouted. Her drink sloshed as she waved her arms, giving someone below us a prosecco baptism.

The three kings were sans camels. I imagined what it would look like if those huge creatures got loose in the streets of Viejo San Juan. Supposedly they were ornery beasts that spat and kicked. I thought the kings were the tail of the parade, but I was wrong. The people on the sidewalk funneled in after them.

"That was shorter than I expected," I said.

The server cleaning the table near us told me the parade wasn't over. It had just started. The route made a square—down to Calle

Fortaleza, up Calle San Justo, then it turned left at Calle Luna and finished back at the cathedral steps. Some of the performers would get off at Plaza de Armas. There was a stage there and entertainment for the children.

"¿Y los Reyes?" I asked her, wanting to know their final stop.

"Entran a la iglesia a visitar al niño Jesús," she replied.

I turned to Alma. "Do you think we could go to the church and wait for the kings to return? I'd love to film the kings visiting baby Jesus for Manny."

"Claro. I'll go with you," Alma said.

Heriberto's head popped up from whatever he had been looking at on his phone. "Go where?" He moved toward us with a shark's smile. Was he curious, or was he hunting?

"Miriam and I are going to the church to see the visitation," Alma said.

"I'll go with you," Heriberto said, wrapping his arm around Alma's waist and pulling her close.

"No, stay with Brandon. He is so sad about his dog. He needs a friend. I won't be gone long." Alma pecked him on the cheek.

Heriberto's displeasure cracked his handsome, nice-guy mask. Daggers flew from his eyes. But just as quickly as the anger had surfaced, it receded. He caught himself and turned on the charm, kissing Alma's cheek. "Okay, but I'll miss you. Don't be gone long. And be careful in the street. There are a lot of people; your friend could get pushed and trampled on. I don't want anything to happen to her baby." He looked at me when he said it.

Miriam, he just threatened you. He knows something. The question is, what?

"Ahh, Love Bug, you worry demasiado. I always watch out for my best friend. I'll keep her safe. Chica, maybe the kings will give you a blessing too." Alma swirled her pointer finger at my belly.

"Loca, you know they aren't actual kings, right? They're not even priests," I said. I hoped my nervous laughter didn't give away my very real anxiety that Vega had told Heriberto something.

Calm down. Vega doesn't know you know where Lucas and the dog are hiding.

"Duh, pero all blessings are good luck, and everybody, especially you, can use some good luck."

Chapter Thirty-Two

Alma turned her flute up and drained the last drops of prosecco. She then locked arms with me and started us toward the elevators. I stopped to adjust the belt on my dress. I wanted to hear what Heriberto, Brandon, and the cryptocurrency crew were talking about. When Brandon Pickles spoke, the crew hung on his every word. All breaths were held until Pickles finished dishing out his fiscal tip of the moment.

"Puerto Rico is a tax haven, man. Dudes, you need to get in on it. I've bought all the townhouses next to the hotel. I'm turning them into a private club with suites. *It's gonna be hype.*" Brandon Pickles mugged a rapper pose to accompany his stereotyped inner-city intonation.

Did he get to Doña? Have they killed her and forged her signature?

"Come on, let's go. You look fine," Alma said.

"Oops, I left my phone." I pretended to feel in my dress pockets for it. "Hold on, I'll get it." I walked close to Pickles's table to hear more.

"Dudes, it is going to be dope. VIP only. And hey, if you need a loan to get in on it, my man Herbie can hook you up. He's like Bank of America." Brandon chuckled. "More like Bank of *South* America."

I acted like I'd found my phone on the tall cocktail table we'd used by the wall. As I hurried past the crypto crew's table, I felt Herbie the Love Bug's eyes on me. From my periphery, I registered it wasn't pink bubbly hearts shooting from his eyes. It was razor-sharp cuchillos, again.

"Got it, vámonos," I said, punching the button to the guest elevator. Once we'd stepped inside it, I pondered what I'd heard.

What did Pickles mean by loan? Was Heriberto giving out cash loans? Welmo had said he was money laundering. How much money did he have access to? How did it work?

Bing.

"Oye, chica, get your head out of the clouds," Alma said, standing in the lobby.

I blinked and stepped out before the doors slid shut. "Oh, sorry. You are flying home to Miami after our girls' weekend, right? Have you booked your flight to Punta Cana?" I was worried about her being on Heriberto's private plane.

We walked on the black-and-white checkered floor to the doors.

"I couldn't get a seat on your plane, but I'm catching the afternoon flight," she said.

"Okay, good. As long as you're not taking your boyfriend's jet."

"What do you mean, good?" Alma threw me a side look.

"Just, you know, small planes are always crashing into the Everglades or over the Bermuda triangle." I deflected from my true worry.

"Chica, don't curse me with mala suerte." Alma's phone pinged.

I had my hand on the handle, about to pull the door open.

"Give me a second. I have to take this," Alma said.

She lowered herself into a flocked fabric chair. She listened to the caller, replying with hmms and uh-huhs. Different emotions passed through her face, like she was flipping through Instagram filters for the right one.

"Everything okay?" I asked when she'd finished and joined me.

"No sé. Let me get back to you on that." She patted my arm. We moved from the quiet lobby into the electric street.

"Okay, well, at least tell me who called," I said. *She looks shook.*

"Pullman."

"Pullman? My Pullman? What does the detective want with you?"

"*Your* Pullman." Alma's mood lightened briefly. "I asked him to run a background check on a buyer. I told him he owed me at least one favor for all that house arrest stuff he put me through."

I'd asked for a check on Jules and gotten nothing. But her face indicated that hers had been more fruitful. "Who's the buyer? Your boyfriend?"

Alma looked at me, biting her upper lip. "Sí,"

A chorus of drumrolls from a dozen barriels reverberated between the cathedral and the hotel. It got the attention of everyone on the street. Alma and I crossed the blue stones and got closer to the performance. The drums stopped in unison. A voice as complex as an aged rum called for a bomba. The crowd knew what was required of them. We clapped the staccato rhythm until the man silenced us like a conductor with a baton. Dancers in white pushed through the audience and climbed the stairs to stand on their marks in front of the drums. The musicians slapped the skins like soldiers marching to battle. The singer's caramel and smoky baritone sang about African roots and land.

The Three Kings Parade had finished its loop. Its participants and followers found spaces, and the audience tripled. It was then that the featured dancer came on stage. It was Isa from Loíza in her Puerto Rican flag dress. The bomba intensified. The crowd was like a gongoli, a millipede—one body with many legs. I held my phone above my head and pressed Record. I rotated to capture the performance and the pulsating crowd. It felt modern, like a music festival, and ancient, like a tribe around the village fire, all at the same time.

When the view frame got to the hotel, I stopped my rotation. I zoomed in. Pickles, Heriberto, and Vega, were pointing at the little park. Vega snatched the binoculars from Pickles. He moved south along the wall closer to the area they were studying. I shifted my lens that way too. It was hard to see anything but the tops of heads.

"Help me get to the stairs. I need to see something," I said.

Alma cleared a path for me using "the pregnant lady needs air" card.

With the height of the church's steps, I could see what they had seen. It was Dill. Brandon Pickles's dog was in the park. She was jumping on the legs of the people standing on the benches and creating a stir.

How did she get loose?

Jorge and Lucas were coming up the empty and barricaded Caleta de las Monjas. Close behind them was Welmo. I yelled a warning, but there was no way they could hear it over the singing and drumbeats. Alma stepped up beside me.

"What's wrong?" Alma asked.

I leaned close to her ear and spoke. "Too much to explain, but we need to protect Lucas from that guy." I pointed at the hotel roof. Vega was gone. Heriberto too. Only Pickles and his binoculars remained.

"Brandon?" Alma asked.

"No, his cop friend and your boyfriend," I replied. "I'm sorry, amiga, but your man is bad."

"I know. That's what Pullman called to tell me."

While our heads had been together, I hadn't paid attention to the crowd. It was parting like the Red Sea with a four-legged, reddish-gold furball playing the role of Moses. Dill was running toward me. Her tongue lolled out of her grinning mouth.

"Ay, no, no, no, no," I said.

I sat down on the step as quickly as possible to avoid being knocked over like a bowling pin. Dill galloped up the steps and lathered my cheek in doggie kisses. My panic and concern were momentarily abated. The crowd's attention returned to the words and beat of the bomba. I keyed into the *English* lyrics being sung by a new voice, a female voice.

> *You can't take our land.*
> *Our homes are not for sale.*
> *Go home, yanqui.*
> *Rise up, Borikén.*

I stood and looked at the singer. It was my prima Kharla. She pointed to the top of El Convento, punctuating her every sentence. The crowd responded to her call to action with its own spontaneous chorus.

Abajo con el yanqui. Down with the Yankee.

A vejigante joined the dancers on stage. He rolled his masked head from side to side like a bull sending a warning. I took Alma by the wrist.

"We need to get out of here," I said.

"¿Y el perro?"

"She needs to go back to Pickles. Can we get her to the hotel lobby and leave her?"

"Yeah, let's try," Alma replied.

Jorge, Lucas, and Welmo had gotten swallowed by the crowd. I scanned the masses and spotted Lucas's Lucy wig. Jorge was with him. By luck, we locked eyes. I mouthed "go home." Alma played the pregnant woman card again. I heard at least five Dios te bendiga blessings as we moved through the tight but clear passage. With Dill between us, we were able to cross the street. We went around the barricade to the hotel's side entrance.

At the lobby door, Alma waved her passkey and tried to get the reception desk staffer's attention to let her in. I leaned against the wall with bent knees to keep ahold of Dill's collar.

"Miriam!" The shout came from Lucas/Lucy. He and Jorge were at the edge of the audience, trying to get to us.

Dill broke loose from my grip and bounded toward the familiar voice that had played fetch with her the last two days. I went after her, leaving Alma at the hotel's door.

My cousin's protest song continued. She was working up the crowd. I could see the dancers whirling and the horned mask punching the sky.

I reached Jorge and Lucas/Lucy a moment after Dill. The dog wasn't fooled by Lucas's disguise. She knew it was him and pawed at the side of his dress like she knew there was a treat in the pocket.

"Hold on to her," I told him.

"I got her," Jorge said, reaching for Dill's neck.

"How did she get out?" I asked.

Jorge looked past me.

"It was an accident. Pero, like, I think we have bigger problems." Jorge's eyes widened. He pointed over my shoulder to Alma.

Heriberto was in the doorway. He had an arm around Alma's back. In his other hand, there was a gun pointed at my BFF's waist. He moved his hostage down the steps and onto the sidewalk.

"Give me the dog, and I will let your friend go," Heriberto said. He tried to kiss her on the temple, but Alma strained to tilt her head away.

Worried that she'd do something brave, I looked at Jorge to tell him to let the dog go. But it was my turn to be wide-eyed. Vega was cutting through the crowd from uphill.

"Let me have her." I took Dill from Jorge and pushed her toward Heriberto and Alma. Then I told Jorge and Lucas to separate and get lost in the crowd. "Find Welmo."

Vega changed directions to track them. I looked back at Alma. He still had her.

"Let her go," I yelled.

"Put the dog in the lobby," Heriberto said in a hard voice.

Dill was stopped in between us. She looked from Heriberto to me. *Dogs know. She knows he is not nice. She doesn't want to go to him.*

"Okay," I said. "Come here, Dill. Come on, Dilly Willy." Dill obeyed and came to my side.

As I got closer to them, Heriberto kept a distance between us. He poked the automatic weapon deeper into Alma's side. She winced.

"You're going to let her go, right?" I said.

"After you put the dog inside," Heriberto replied.

The lobby door was ajar. I pushed Dill inside and closed the door.

"Miriam! ¡Cuidado!" Alma screamed.

I turned around, but it was too late. Heriberto had let Alma go, but he was coming for me. I was trapped.

Chapter Thirty-Three

The bomba dancers, the drumming, and my cousin's rally cries had the people's focus. No one was aware of the drama behind the barricade.

I felt my sirena do a kick-flip. My heart was beating hard and fast with the fight-or-flight dilemma. I couldn't believe I'd put my baby in peril *again*.

"Don't hurt me. I'll do whatever you tell me," I said.

"Cállate," Heriberto hissed. He pressed the gun nozzle to my back.

"Herbie, let her go," Alma said. Her voice was calm and loving. She inched toward us. "You can't hurt a pregnant woman. Come on. Tell me what you want."

Alma had her arm stretched out. She beckoned me to reach for her hand.

"Get me that mamarracho's phone," Heriberto said.

"¿Quién?" I asked. He'd used a vulgar Venezuelan slang, but I was pretty sure he'd meant Lucas. *Or did he know about the photos on Jorge's phone?*

"El chamo de la telenovela," he replied.

"Let my friend go, and I promise I will bring you the phone," Alma said. Her fingertips were brushing mine. She moved an inch closer. "She's pregnant. You need to let her go."

Heriberto loosened his grip on my upper arm. I stepped down one step.

"Not so fast. I am coming with you," Heriberto said.

Alma took my hand. What happened next felt like La Caridad was watching over me. The lobby door opened into Heriberto's face, pushing him backward. A pair of crypto bros came out of the door, laughing and joking. They were oblivious to what they'd done. Alma hurried me down the last three steps to the sidewalk. While Heriberto yelled at the men, Alma and I disappeared into the crowd.

"We should separate," I spoke loudly. "We need to find Lucas before he does."

I looked around, but the audience was too thick. I couldn't distinguish more than a few bodies ahead of me.

"I think I see Jorge," Alma said, jumping above the heads to see.

"Go. Get him. Take this. Call Welmo," I said as I passed her my phone. "I'm going to try to get to my prima."

Alma pushed her way through the sea of people. The bomba alternated between Spanish and English. Kharla sang in English, and the male singer in Spanish. The choruses were like waves of percussion, gaining storm surge force. Between each wave, there was a silent lull. I used those moments to progress toward the stage, saying "Permiso, embarazada." I switched between languages. "Excuse me, pregnant."

I was one row from the church's steps when someone yanked at my dress.

"Ven acá Lucas Palo."

I turned to see a slim arm attached to a fistful of my skirt. *Vega.* He'd mistaken me for Lucy/Lucas. Our dresses and hair were similar.

Does that mean Lucas is safe? Is he with Welmo?

I jerked the fabric from his grip and propelled myself forward. The row parted for me, and the young woman beside me helped me up the first step. Behind the microphone stand, Kharla looked at me. Concern riddled her face. I was almost at the stage when I felt a pull.

This stupid dress!

"Bad cop," I shouted.

Kharla either heard me or read my mouth. In an instant, there were two dancers beside me. They closed around me like a curtain. Vega was left alone and steaming at being foiled. Isa was one of my rescuers. She'd used her skirt like a swan threatening to attack, giving me cover to get to Kharla.

"¿Qué está pasando?" Kharla asked. Our heads were cheek to cheek.

"Too much to explain, but we need to keep my friends away from the cops. They are corrupt," I answered.

The other singer gestured to Kharla. She needed to get back on the mic. Kharla tapped Isa's shoulder and relayed that she needed to stay with me.

"Busca a mi amigo, Jorge," I said.

Isa, who'd never stopped moving her feet and hips to the ritmo, scanned the crowd for Jorge. When she saw him, she pointed at him.

"Por fin llegaste," Isa said loud enough for the first few rows to hear. She acted like he was a tardy dancer. "Deja que mi compañero de baile pase." The men and women around Jorge pushed him to the stage. She threw him into the dance. Jorge didn't take more than a beat to find his flow.

Vega paced on the lowest step like an angry rooster. The vejigante mirrored his moves, not letting him advance.

I finally spotted Lucas/Lucy and pointed them out to Isa. She was about to command the crowd again, but someone grabbed

Lucas/Lucy from behind. It was Vega's partner, the tall cop. He ripped the wig from Lucas's head. Lucas fought back. He stepped on the tall cop's foot, then rounded and kneed him in the groin. Lucas managed to get a few feet away while the cop doubled over in pain. But then Lucas's head whiplashed. The cop must have grabbed the hem of the dress. *Stupid dress!* When the man stood up, he had his gun in his hand.

BANG!

He discharged the gun into the air. The crowd screamed and cleared a space around him. All the drumming stopped. The cop was panting, clearly ticked off. Lucas was ashen with fear.

Where is Welmo?

Vega tried to get to Jorge.

They must know he knows something too.

Where is Alma? I hoped my best friend had called Welmo and made it to safety. But she hadn't. Heriberto had nabbed her again. He wasn't waving his gun about like the tall cop, but from the panicked look on my bestie's face, I knew he was threatening her with one.

I need to save her. And Lucas.

I took the mic from Kharla.

What can I say to defuse this situation?

I swept my eyes over the audience. I didn't want to put anyone in danger.

Just tell the truth, Miriam.

"Este policía es un corrupto," I said pointing to Vega. From my elevated vantage point, I could see that the unfolding events were being filmed. One of those with their camera held out was a twenty-something in a rainbow-striped American flag shirt. *I hope she is live streaming. I hope David Begnaud sees this and reports on it.* "These police officers are taking bribes."

"Stop spreading lies," Vega said. "Surrender. You are under arrest."

There was a collective gasp.

Miriam, you have the mic. Tell them everything.

"He is working for Brandon Pickles," I said. My cousin side-eyed me, and I nodded that I was sure. Kharla looked toward the hotel's roof.

Welmo!

Welmo was on the roof taking Pickles into custody. And then I noticed the snipers. At the corner of the roof, a person in full SWAT regalia had a rifle trained on the tall cop. Another sniper zeroed in on Heriberto and Alma. The gravity of it all hit me. I felt my blood pressure dip. My knees weakened. I leaned against my prima. She took the mic from me, and I felt Isa behind me. Isa had one of the drummer's chairs. She told me to sit.

"The Bitcoin King is dethroned," Kharla said.

Murmurs rippled through the crowd. Then there was another gasp. The sound of boots and armaments filled the air. Looking around, I saw more snipers. There was one behind the church's scrolled decoration. There were others on surrounding roofs. Officers in beige fatigues with bulletproof vests moved into the crowd. They surrounded both hostage situations and disarmed them quickly and without resistance. I watched Vega be zip-tied and escorted to a prisoner van backing up to the barricade.

An FBI agent brought Lucas to the church stage. Jorge embraced him. "Ay, papi. I was so worried," Jorge said. The two kissed.

Phones were still recording. *Ay, ay, ay.* That was probably not the way Lucas wanted to come out to his fans.

Soon, Alma was escorted to us. Then, my friends and I were moved into the church. We sat in the pews and were told not to move.

"Are you okay?" I asked my bestie as I squeezed her hand.

"Are *you* okay?" Alma asked.

"I think so," I replied. I put my hand on my belly. I took several deep breaths. La Sirena seemed to have calmed down.

"Amiga, you need to retire from crime-fighting," Alma said.

"Yeah, Velma," Jorge said.

"No more, Nancy Drew," Alma said.

"Me?" I was shocked. "Ningún parte of this was me. Nope. This wasn't me. This was you and you and you." I pointed to my three friends. "I was minding my own business."

"Whatever you say, Jessica Fletch," Alma said.

"It's Fletcher. And I am not, nor do I want to be, Jessica Fletcher," I said.

"I thought Veronica Mars was your code name," Welmo said, coming into the sanctuary from the center door.

"Miriam Quiñones is not your real name?" Lucas's face showed his utter confusion. He scratched his head and removed the stocking over his natural hair. "Are you undercover FBI too?"

We all burst out laughing.

"Detective Pullman is going to love that," Welmo said.

Chapter
Thirty-Four

The streets had been cleared but hadn't been opened to the public. Jorge, Lucas, Alma, and I were being taken to Doña's house, which had been commandeered as an FBI field office. I saw two news crews as we crossed the street from the church. One was interviewing bystanders near the little park. The other, an UnMundo crew, maybe the one from the Three Kings gift-giving event, was filming at the uphill perimeter. Thankfully, Caleta de las Monjas was cordoned off by guards and FBI vehicles.

Vaquita greeted us at Doña's front steps.

"I bet she misses Doña," I said to Welmo. "How is she?"

"Worried about her guests and refusing to stay in bed," he replied.

Vaquita's motor was running. Her purrs were louder than normal. The cat circled my ankles and bonked her head into me.

"I think she's hungry. Let me get her some food. Her dish is in the other kitchen." I pointed next door.

"I promise I'll feed her. Interviews are a priority." Welmo tapped on the mahogany door. It opened about a foot, and Vaquita zoomed into the house. The person at the door, a Latina in a suit, didn't go after the cat but did give Welmo a raised-eyebrows query. "Don't worry about the cat. She belongs to Doña Pilar."

Welmo put us back in Doña's windowless first-floor room to wait to be interviewed. After realizing we weren't going to the kitchen, Vaquita followed us into the room. Jorge and Lucas sat on the love seat. Alma and I took the table. Lucas brought the footstool over to me. I wrestled the shoes from my swollen feet and put them up, leaving just enough room for Vaquita to curl up on the stool.

"I can't believe what just happened," I said.

"Incredible, *verdad*," Lucas said in agreement.

"No talking," said the agent at the door.

Looks were exchanged between us. Alma mouthed something to me, and I shrugged that I didn't understand her.

After ten minutes of excruciating silence, someone knocked at the door. Our agent cracked the door open. My friends and I craned to try and see who he was talking to, but the gap was only an inch or two wide.

I heard a familiar rusty-pipe whine. Dill put her muzzle through the crack and widened it so she could come in.

"Dill, come here, girl," I said. Vaquita raised her head, hissed a warning, and then back to sleep. "Why do you have Dill?" I scratched the dog's scruff. Dill then pranced over to Lucas, wagging her tail.

"She's evidence," Welmo said.

"*Evidence*. She's a living, breathing animal. Where will you keep her?" Lucas asked.

"One of our K-9 handlers will take good care of her. Don't worry," Welmo replied.

"Not the police, *right*?" I said.

"No. FBI. Bomb-sniffing unit," Welmo informed us. "Miriam, we will interview you first because I know you have a plane to catch tomorrow. But for the rest of you, it will be a long night. We'll get you food and drinks and try to make you as comfortable as possible. But I want to prepare you for a long wait. You can't use your phones or talk about the events, but you can watch TV, play cards, and move about freely in here.

"Can Dill stay with us?" Lucas asked.

"Until the handlers come, sí." Welmo motioned for me to come with him.

Brring. Brrring. Brring.

"That's my phone," I said. "Alma has it." I stuffed my feet back into my shoes.

Alma withdrew it from her pocket. "It's Robert." She put it on the table screen up.

"Can I answer it?" I asked.

"No, I'm sorry. But you can text him that you will call him later," Welmo said.

"What do I tell him? Do you think he knows what happened?" I asked.

"Does he watch Spanish-language news?" Welmo asked.

"No," Jorge, Alma, and I said in chorus.

My phone pinged with a text message. I looked at it but didn't pick up the phone.

I can't wait to see you tomorrow. Talked to Manny. He is excited. Getting on the plane soon. I'll call when I land in DR.

Welmo read it too. "Problem averted for a moment. The agent doing the interview will let you know what you can and can't say about the investigation."

"You aren't interviewing us?" Jorge asked.

"I'll be in the room, but as an informant, I'm not officially FBI." Welmo looked at Jorge, then each of us in turn. "Don't worry. I know it is scary, but you will all be fine."

"What if Herbie gets out?" Alma asked. "What if he comes looking for me?" Alma ran a nervous hand through her dark hair.

"He's not getting out," Welmo said.

"And what about Vega? What if one of his cop friends *conveniently* mishandles the paperwork and lets him go?" Alma rolled her head from side to side.

"This is federal, not local. The Feds don't *let* people go," Welmo said.

The agent at the door cleared his throat.

"Don't worry. Watch some TV." Welmo handed the remote control to Alma and took my phone from the table. "Come on, Ms. Quiñones."

"Miriam," I said.

"Alright. Come on, Miriam. Let's get your statement."

Vaquita slipped out of the room after me. *Cats have a sixth sense.* The interview was going to take place at Doña's kitchen table.

"Can I feed her?" I asked.

"Go ahead," the agent at the table said.

I got a saucer from the drainboard. In the refrigerator, I found some cooked chicken and milk. Vaquita got on her hind legs, stretched, and tried to reach her paw to the counter. "Paciencia, Vaquita."

"Would you prefer we speak in Spanish?" the woman at the table asked.

"Whichever is best for you. I'm fluent in both," I said as I put the cat's dish on the green-and-black tiled floor.

"Okay. Please sit. I'm Special Agent Ivette González."

The woman offered a handshake. Her hand was smaller than mine, but from her confident grip, I suspected she could take down a six-foot-tall man easily. She wore a blue windbreaker jacket with the yellow FBI initials on it. Underneath, she had on a white polo shirt.

"You already know Welmo."

I nodded.

"He will take notes for us," Special Agent González said. "Let's start with Jules Howard. Tell me what you know about him."

"Jules Howard? I thought you told me he wasn't involved in any of this." *Are my parents in jeopardy? Is Manny in danger?* I looked at Welmo for reassurance, but he didn't or couldn't say anything. González was clearly in charge.

"We don't think so, but your interest in him brought him to our attention," she said. "Tell me what you know about him. You asked your friend Detective Frank Pullman to run a criminal check on him."

"*Pullman.* You've been talking to Frank?" I gripped the table's edge and rubbed the nubbly tablecloth to self-soothe.

"¿Quieres un poquito de agua?" Welmo asked.

"Yes, please," I replied.

Welmo got me a glass of water and put Vaquita's dish in the sink. The cat went to the patio door and meowed.

"She wants out. She's an outdoor cat," I said.

Welmo unlocked the door, and the three of us watched the black-and-white cat bound onto the wall and into the alley.

"Here." Welmo set the glass before me. "Back to Jules. Tell me why you were following him."

"I wasn't following him. I thought *he* was following me," I said.

"Is that why you asked Detective Pullman about him?' González said.

"Yes. I thought that maybe he was trying to buy the place my parents manage in the Dominican Republic. And then when I found out about the Bitcoin King, I was certain he was part of that scheme."

"Tell me about the scheme," she prompted.

"You know, Americans buying property in the islands. I know Brandon Pickles was promoting it to his followers. Jules is in real estate. His company was on the work permit for the hotel and restaurant renovation. And then there were the threatening notes that looked the same." I took a sip of water.

"Notes?" Welmo asked.

"Yeah, I showed you the one that was slipped under the door. Let me have my phone, and I'll show you the other one," I said. Welmo gave it to me, and I showed them the fuzzy screenshot of the writing on the back of Manny's drawing. "See? They kind of look like the same handwriting. And they are both in pencil."

"We don't think he's involved, but your interest in him had us curious. Do you have the paper in the image?" González asked.

"No. But Mami probably kept the drawing. I can get it when I see her tomorrow," I said.

"Follow up with that," she said to Welmo. "Okay, what do you know about Heriberto Chacón?"

"Not a lot," I said.

"How did Ms. Díaz meet him?" González asked.

"That was my fault," I said. *Carajo, I wish I'd never told Alma to go to that party.* "Alma met him at a holiday party. For a condo development on Brickell. I encouraged her to go. I feel so guilty about it now. If I hadn't pushed her, she wouldn't have gone and met that basura of a man. It's my fault she met him."

"Mmm, I don't think that is accurate," she said.

"I'm telling you the truth," I said.

"No. I mean, I think your friend was targeted by Mr. Chacón. He's done it before. He identifies single women in the real estate business to romance and manipulate. It's how he launders money," González said.

My jaw went slack. My poor bestie. That was going to sting.

The interview continued for at least an hour, if not two. I told them everything I could remember—Jorge finding the duffel bag of money, my talks with El Capitán's waitress, finding Doña injured, and then discovering Lucas and Dill.

"Detective Pullman was right about you," Welmo said.

"Yes, and she follows hunches," González added.

"What did Frank tell you?" I asked.

"He called the studio to alert security about a possible stalker. He told me trouble liked to find you and that you have a knack, his word, for being in the wrong place and at the right time," Welmo said.

"Have you considered changing careers? The bureau is always hiring," González said with a smirk.

Chapter
Thirty-Five

I woke up the following morning tired and concerned. Jorge's room was the same as he'd left it yesterday, and the other guest room was also empty. Where were my friends? I'd thought they'd put Alma in the third guest room.

Brring.

Brring.

Welmo had returned my phone after the interview with instructions to not talk about what had happened. If anyone asked about it, I should reply, "I'm not at liberty to discuss it." If I ever saw Alma again, I was pretty sure that would be the first thing we talked about. At least Jorge and Lucas had each other. *I hope they didn't separate them.*

Brring.

I hit the green video chat icon on the screen.

"Feliz Día de los Reyes, mi príncipe," I said.

"Mami, Mami. Mira," Manny said.

"Wow, little man, the three kings came," Roberto said with a wink. He pointed the lens at the hay strewn around the walkway.

It was tradition for children to put a box of hay or grass outside for the camels on Three Kings Day Eve. In the morning, the box would have a gift in it. Usually, it was a toy, but depending on the family's financial health, it might be an essential item like a new pair of shoes or something. My parents had put a green toy truck in Manny's box.

"Un camión de fruta," Manny said. His smile was to his ears.

Roberto kept our son in the screen so I could see him play with the truck. Around its bed, molded plastic had been made to look like wood. It had removable boxes with fruit decals on them.

"Banana, piña, naranja, güayaba, pana," Manny said examining each little box.

"Pana? What fruit is that?" Roberto asked.

"¿Mami, cual es el nombre en inglés?" Manny asked me for a translation.

"Breadfruit. We make tostones with it. Maybe we can have some with dinner," I said.

"Sí, me gustan los tostones." Manny loaded his truck and pushed it on the patio floor toward one of Mami's fruit trees.

"Robert," I said in a conspirator tone.

He flipped the lens to him and lowered the speaker volume. "What, babe?"

"How are my parents?" I asked.

"They are right here. Do you want to talk to them?"

"No, not until I can see them in person." Last night, I'd told Robert the bare minimum about what had happened. It was a loose and stretchy truth—I was a bystander in a police corruption incident. I hadn't mentioned the FBI or guns. "Have you been keeping them away from the news?"

"As best I can. They were pretty busy yesterday getting the grand villa ready for your friends," Robert said.

"Okay. Let me say goodbye to Manny. I'll see you in a few hours." I blew kisses and told our son I couldn't wait to hug him. Robert pointed the phone at my folks, and I waved to them. *Weird. Mami usually starts talking and takes the phone. She and*

Barbacoa, Bomba, and Betrayal

Papi barely gave me two seconds of attention. They must be focused on Manny.

Placing the phone in my purse, I gathered the last of my things and zipped my suitcase closed. I heard a noise downstairs.

"Welmo?" I called out from the top of the stairs.

"No. It's your favorite director, Delvis. I'm taking you to the airport. I brought you a Mallorca for breakfast," Delvis replied.

"I thought Welmo was driving me." I lowered the telescoping handle of my bag. "Can you give me a hand with this?"

"Claro," she replied, setting the box of baked goods on the hall table.

"Has Welmo told you anything?" I asked as we went down the stairs.

"No. I don't think he can, really. Ya tú sabes. I didn't even know that he was undercover until a few days ago."

"Wow." That was an understatement.

Delvis took my bag to the car parked by the barricade. As my suitcase rolled by, Vaquita jumped off the hood of a black SUV.

"Dame dos minutos," I said in Delvis's direction. "I need to give Doña's cat her morning cream."

I prepared Vaquita's dish and put it on the sidewalk by the steps. "Where are your friends?" The other street cats were noticeably absent. "Take care of yourself, and tell Doña I'll miss her delicious meals." I stroked the cat's back. She lifted her rump but didn't stop eating. "Oh, I almost forgot the Mallorca." I got the pastry box from the hall, locked the door, and left Caleta de las Monjas.

It was early enough that there wasn't too much traffic. I took in the views as we left the old city. Delvis was chatty about ideas for upcoming episodes of *Abuela Approved*. I gave her uh-huhs when appropriate but didn't pay close attention—my mind was on Alma, Jorge, and Lucas. She gave me a tight hug when we got to the airport.

"Disfruta con tu familia. I'll see you Monday at the studio," Delvis said.

In the terminal, I ordered a milky coffee and ate my breakfast. The rich sweet bread was now forever linked with Viejo San Juan for me. *I wish I'd gotten to see Doña before I left.* I checked my phone before turning it off for the flight. There were no messages. Sigh.

The landing was bumpy, with a fuselage wag and screeching brakes. When we came to a complete stop, the passengers exploded into applause. The communal happiness was infectious. My anxious mood lifted. The same guard as before signaled me to come to his short lane. He asked me with concern how I was doing. He'd seen the viral video on the evening news. One of the bomba drummers had live streamed the standoff. *Great. That means Mami will see it on the morning news, or one of her friends will send it to her on WhatsApp.* I thanked him for his concern and told him I had just been in the wrong place at the wrong time.

"Babe!" Robert shouted as I exited the secured zone. As if I could have missed him. He was at least a head taller than most in the small waiting crowd.

"Mi amor," I said as I reached him. He kissed me, then hugged me tightly, then kissed me again.

"I have missed you so much," Robert said. "Ten days is too long." He rolled my bag with one hand and held my hand with the other. "The van is this way."

"My parents didn't come?" I swiveled my head, looking over my shoulders like maybe I'd missed seeing them. "Is Papi in the car?"

"Nope. They stayed with Manny. Carmen is making something special for your friends, and Luis said he had to do some work on the computer." Robert steered us through the parking lot.

"He just *let you* take his van?"

"Yep. He gave me the keys and told me to park in the hotel van section."

"Papi is on the computer. My dad, the one with a toolbox the size of a suitcase, is on the computer. Why?" I asked.

"I don't know. Does it matter? He said he had to look for something." Robert leaned in and awkwardly kissed my head as we continued to walk. "He's probably looking for a part. Or maybe a large toolbox."

"Ha. Ha. Ha." I gave him an I-am-not-amused look.

During the ride to Punta Palma, we chatted between directions from the disembodied British lady's voice. Robert had his Siri set to James Bond mode, as he liked to call it. I told him I needed to tell him more about what had happened yesterday, but I wanted to hug Manny and chill a bit before I got into the details.

"Whenever you're ready, babe. No rush. All that matters is that we're together. Seriously, next time you have a work trip, I'm coming with you, if that's okay."

"More than okay. I was thinking the same thing. Manny would have loved Puerto Rico. And he could have met some of his cousins," I said. *Coño, Kharla. I wonder if she is okay. Did the FBI question her too?*

"What about me? Didn't you miss me even a little?"

I tsked. "Ay, mi amor, of course I meant you too." I shot off a quick text to Kharla. It was a wonder that Tía hadn't called my mom with the news.

"Uh-huh," Robert said with great exaggeration.

"I missed you. *Really!*"

"I know Manny's your number one guy."

"Oh, stop it." I gave his bicep a love tap.

He parked Papi's van and turned toward me. He took my face in his hands and drew me into a deep and long kiss. "I love you.

I missed you. I saw the video. I know you'll tell me when you are ready. But, babe, that was some scary sh—"

"But I'm fine," I said, interrupting him. "I'm fine."

"Are you sure?"

"I'm. Fine." I gave him a peck on the lips and got out of the car.

Am I fine? Or am I compartmentalizing?

Robert rolled my suitcase to our room while I walked through to the patio.

"¡Mami!" Manny sprang up from playing with his truck and ran into me with a gentle headbutt. His little arms didn't reach around me, but it was the tightest and best hug. And it was just what I needed.

"Mi príncipe." I stroked his thick glossy hair. I could tell my mother had treated it with oil like she'd done to my thick black locks when I was a kid.

"Hola, Mami. Hola, Papi." I kissed each of my parents. Papi had their laptop on the table but closed it as I approached.

Robert joined us.

"Thank you for letting me take the van, sir. Here are your keys back," Robert said.

He passed the key ring to my father. It had a Caridad de Cobre image in a resin dome with an enameled Cuban flag on the metal back. I'd had to make a special trip to Navarro drugstore to get it for him when his old one had cracked. Papi had had a Caridad key chain for as long as I could remember. It was like his good luck charm.

"Muchas gracias. You had no problem with the parking, no?" Papi said.

"No. Your friend, Pepe, let me through the gate. I told him I was your *je-er*—" Robert tried to pronounce the Spanish word for son-in-law.

"Yerno," I said, filling in his hesitation.

"Jer-no," Robert repeated.

"Close enough." I smiled at him and kissed his cheek.

"Very good." Papi slapped Robert's back. "Carmen, you want to go to the store, no?" My dad asked my mom.

"Sí. Sí. Sí. Sí. Sí." Mami picked up the coffee cup beside the laptop, gave Papi directions with her eyes and a mouth jut, and then hurried away. Papi scooped up the computer and followed her.

I watched them disappear into the house.

"Well, that was weird," I said.

Robert had lowered himself onto the floor beside Manny to play farm with the mishmash of animals assembled. "What's weird?"

"My parents. Mami didn't try to feed me. She didn't ask about the baby. And Papi hates to go to the grocery store with my mom."

"I think they just want things to be perfect for your friends. *Mooo.*" Robert moved a realistic-looking brown cow closer to Peppa Pig and Dora the Explorer's monkey.

"No. They are hiding something from me." I sat in the chair Papi had vacated. The smell of gardenias drifted on the breeze.

"*Oink. Oink,*" Robert said.

"That's not how Peppa talks," Manny told his dad with a giggle.

"How does she talk?" Robert gave the figurine to his son.

"She talks like this." Manny put on a terrible British accent and made Peppa talk to the cow. "I can run faster than you. I win!"

Robert chuckled. I smiled.

Manny continued in character. He had Peppa organize the animal workforce to load the boxes onto the truck. "Monkey, move the bananas, but don't eat them. We have to find a new house just like abuela y abuelo."

"¿Que dijiste de tus abuelos?" I asked Manny.

"Abuela y Abuelo tienen que mudar," Manny replied.

"¿Mudarse? ¿Por qué?"

"Porque el dueño está vendiendo." He tried to put Peppa into the cab but couldn't make her fit. So, he put her on the truck's roof with Dora's monkey as copilot.

"*Babe*. Are you okay? You look pale. What's wrong?" Robert put his hand on my knee and jiggled my leg lovingly.

"The owner is selling the property, and my parents have to move," I said.

Chapter Thirty-Six

The reason for my parents' weird behavior made sense. They still thought of me as their little girl and wanted to avoid telling me bad news. I had to admit I was doing the same thing with my news. *Miriam, you learned it from somewhere.* Although my news wasn't bad per se, it *was* scary because of the guns. Guns are always scary.

"Actually, their news isn't bad either. It's just unexpected," I said.

"Babe, did you say something?" Robert asked.

"I'm just thinking out loud." I pinched my lips to keep my thoughts from escaping. *Does this mean they can come back to Miami? They could come back! Manny and La Sirena could have their grandparents nearby!* I moved my hand away from my chin. "Ay, Caridad, that would be great!"

"What would be great?" Robert asked.

"Huh?"

"You said that would be great."

"Oh, yeah. It would be great if I gave Manny his present," I said, projecting my voice at our son, who was driving his truck under the guava tree.

"¿Los Reyes dejaron más regalos?" Manny's curiosity was piqued.

I told him yes, that when I'd seen the three kings in Puerto Rico, they had given me a gift for him. I went to our room and unpacked the gifts. *Coño, I forgot to get the rum for Roberto and Papi.* "I mean, I would have gotten it if it weren't for the Bitcoin King and Herbie, the Love Bug. And let's not forget Vega! Grrr."

"*Babe.*" Robert was standing at the door. "Are you really okay? You tend to talk to yourself when you're worried and stressed."

"Do I?"

Robert opened his arms and invited me in for a hug. I accepted.

"Where's Manny?" I asked.

"Your parents just pulled up. He went to help them. I think he heard there would be cake and ice cream." Robert leaned his head back to look at me. "So, are you going to tell me what's got you stressed?"

We sat on the bed, and I gave him the condensed version of the past week. He, at first, suggested I speak to his father, Senior, since he was a judge and had had dealings with FBI and federal cases. I nixed that immediately. Even though Senior had always been nice to me, he was married to Marjory, and I didn't need any more condescending remarks from her.

"Okay, well then, talk to Drew or Sally. It's always good to have legal counsel," Robert said.

"You understand I'm not involved in the case. I was just a bystander. Alma, Jorge, and Lucas are the ones that really saw stuff. Ay, ay, ay. Do you think they'll need to go into witness protection?"

"No. That happens more in the movies than in real life. But like I said, talk to my brother."

"I'll ask Sally when she gets here. Speaking of Sally, when does her plane land?"

"I'm the airport taxi today. I'm picking up everyone, except for Alma, at one o'clock. They're all on the same flight. I thought Alma would probably fly in with you. Have you spoken with her?"

I fished out my phone. Still no messages. "No. Let me try and call her."

Alma answered on the third ring. "Hola, chica. How's D.R.?"

"Forget about me. *How are you?*"

"Todo bien. I mean, as good as a bad situation can be. For real, I might need some therapy. But in the short term, I want our girls' weekend."

I sensed that our call had listeners nearby.

"You're coming? I mean, they are letting you loose soon. *Right?*"

I heard her cover the mic. There was a muffled exchange of voices. "Of course. I'll be there. Just a little later than planned. I'll text you the info when I have it. They are trying to get me a flight tonight."

"Who is they? The FBI?"

"Uh-huh." Alma paused. "Miriam, let me ask you this. Is Jules there?"

"¿Que, qué?"

"Jules Howard. He was renting one of the villas, no?"

"Are you saying he *is* involved?"

Robert gestured quizzically. I waved an I'll-tell-you-later hand flutter.

"Hold on, I'll find out." I went to the kitchen, where my parents were unpacking their purchases. Manny was sitting on the counter, putting the canned goods into the cupboard by color and with the labels facing out. Papi was gathering the plastic bags and stuffing them into the half-round storage and dispenser thing attached to the the sink cabinet door. "¿Mami, todas las villas están alquiladas?" I asked my mother if all the units were rented.

"No. You and your friends tienen el grande. Y Señor Julie, sigue en el número cuatro," Mami said.

"Is Julie—" I stopped myself. "Have you seen Jules today?" My mom could not get used to Jules as a man's name. *Mr. Julie. Ay, ay, ay.*

"Si," Papi said. "He helped me with the computer today."

Mami side-eyed him with a don't-say-more glare.

I furrowed my brow. *What the what? Sleeping with the enemy.* It wasn't the time to go into it all—especially with Manny there. I huffed and left the house.

"Where are you going?" Robert asked, following me.

I'd forgotten I still had Alma on the line and the phone resting on my shoulder, close to my ear.

"Where are you going?" said the voice on the Puerto Rico end of the call. It was Welmo, not Alma. "Do not approach Mr. Howard. Do you understand?"

I stopped halfway across the circle by the huge palm. "I'm not going to talk to him about—you know. But I do need to talk to him. He sabotaged my parents' place and messed with their livelihood. I need to have a few words with him." *No, more like a string of coño carajos. Arrrgh! The lying bleep-bleep.*

"Miriam. Do. Not. Approach. Him," Welmo said.

"I'm not going to talk about Pickles or Heriberto," I said.

"Do. Not. Approach. Him," Welmo repeated.

"Don't worry. I'm not alone. I have my husband with me." I grabbed Robert's arm.

"What's going on?" Robert asked.

"Shh," I replied to him.

"Miriam, please, listen to me. Do not talk to him. It might tip him off. We are on our way there. We only need to know that he is there. Is he there? Have you seen him?" Welmo was using his pseudo-calm and controlled voice.

"I'll tell you in just a second. I'm going to his villa now."

"No, you are not," Welmo said.

I kicked the gravelly sand by the palm and sighed a sigh worthy of a high school drama kid. Then I stomped in a little circle and let out a grumble.

"What's going on?" Robert asked.

"*Miriam*," Welmo said.

"Fine," I said after I had a moment to quiet the urge to pummel Jules.

"Promise," Welmo said.

"Lo prometo," I replied.

"Thank you. We will be there soon. Please stay away from him until we get there," Welmo said, ending the call.

"What was all that about? Who is Jules?" Robert asked.

We strolled back to my parents' apartment with our arms linked. I leaned my head on his shoulder. "He's a real estate guy. He's renting that villa, but he went to PR for a few days. For a second, I thought he was stalking me—"

Robert interrupted me. "What? Why didn't you tell me?"

"I didn't want to worry you, and it turns out he wasn't stalking me. But then I thought he was involved in the murders."

"Murders! What murders?" Robert stopped us on the path to the front door.

"Did I skip that part?" I made an apologetic face at him. "The Bitcoin King hired a dirty cop to pressure elderly property owners into selling, and then when they didn't take the offer, he'd kill them and make it look like an accident. But Jules supposedly wasn't involved in that. Just like he supposedly didn't sabotage the water tank and pipes. Jules told me he was all about the food—restaurants, not vacation properties. Now I don't know what's true. You've been here almost a day. Have you seen him?"

"No. I've been with Manny most of the time. I brought a copy of *Treasure Island* to read to him since we're on a Caribbean island. I thought it would be perfect. Last night, he kept asking for one more page. And then this morning, first thing, he asked me to read him some more." Robert laughs. "Pirates. Buccaneers. Parrots. Hidden treasure. *Yo ho-ho.*"

Robert was so proud of himself that I hated to squash his joy. "Maybe you could ask your old school librarian for some better suggestions. That book has a lot of stereotypes like the noble savage," I said. His high school librarian, an English ex-pat, lived in our Coral Shores neighborhood and was the reason he loved British detective novels.

"Gillian was the one who recommended it to me," Robert said. "It's a classic."

"He'll get to the classics in college. Hopefully, in a critical comparative literature class. He's a four-year-old. Let's fill his head with positive depictions of Black and brown folks. Please."

"You're right. I didn't think of it from that point of view. I just wanted to share an adventure book with my son."

"I know." *Patience, Miriam. He is trying.*

"Book! Is it story time?" Manny said, standing in the doorway.

"Maybe later, little man. I think now is Three Kings present time," Robert said.

"Yes." I'd forgotten all about the gifts. We went into the house, and I got the coquí plushie and coloring book from the bedroom. Robert covered Manny's eyes until I had the unwrapped gifts on the patio table.

"Una rana!" Manny squealed.

"Sí, esta es una rana de Puerto Rico que se llama un coquí. Presiona aquí," I said, pointing to the button sewn into the frog's hand.

He pressed it. *Co-kee.* Then he pressed it again and again and again. Silently listening to *Treasure Island* was looking better and better.

Chapter
Thirty-Seven

After an early lunch, Robert went to the airport to pick up my friends. I stayed behind for a few reasons. One, there wouldn't be enough room in the van if I went. Two, to be honest, I was a little tired. Three, I wanted to confront my parents about the news they were hiding from me.

I got my chance while Manny colored a rain forest scene spread across two pages. He was as meticulous with his coloring as he was with his can organizing. His crayons were arranged in gradation.

"Mami, qué es eso about this place selling?" I asked my mother en voz baja.

"No vamos a hablar de eso. Yo lo tengo bajo control," Papi answered.

"So, the property is sold? Will you get to keep your jobs?" I prodded.

"Your father said he has it under control. No te preocupes," Mami said. "Pero you have some esplaining to do."

"Sí," Papi concurred.

Mami curled her finger in a "come here" gesture. Papi and I followed her into the sala, leaving the sliding glass doors open so we could monitor Manny.

"Prima Sandra me llamó. ¿Qué pasó esta vez?" Mami asked.

"*Yes*, what happened *this time*? Do you work for UnMundo or la policía?" Papi crossed his arms and leaned back in his white rattan chair.

"The police? Me? *Nooo.* I work for UnMundo. No es mi culpa que trouble finds me," I said. "I was just doing my job and minding my own business." I felt sixteen again, like the time Alma convinced me to stay out past curfew and lie that the car had had a flat tire. All my teenage infractions were Alma's doing. Come to think of it, Alma was at the root of my current troubles too.

"Mi'ja. This is *very* serious. Tiene que pensar en él bebe. I called Elba y ella me dio una receta para un despojo." Mami got up from her position next to me on the couch. "But first, el huevo."

"Mami, you don't believe in that," I said. Mami wasn't a regular La Regla de Ocha practitioner like Tía Elba. But I remember having an egg cleanse when I was very young with a high fever. Tía Sandra had passed an egg over my forehead, chest, and arms. The fever was supposed to transfer into the egg. I was pretty sure the Tylenol had helped, but my fever did break afterward.

"Mi'ja, it works," Mami said, coming back from the kitchen with a fresh egg. She rubbed the egg over my head, arms, and legs while repeating a phrase that was part Spanish and part Lucumi, a Yoruba-derived language spoken in Cuba and the diaspora. Once the egg cleanse was complete, she had me follow her out of the house and past the driveway gate. She threw the egg on the road and said some words to Eshu and Eleguá. "Today is the perfect day to do this. Six is their day."

Mami had me place a plate of food outside the house and put a caramel candy by her Santo Niño de Atocha statue, the saint synced with Eleguá.

"Ahora el despojo," Mami said.

I looked at my dad for help. He poured a glass of juice from the fridge and shrugged as if to say don't fight it. Then he took the small jugo de piña out to Manny.

Mami carried a soup pot of herb-infused water to the bathroom. She had me get undressed and get in the shower.

"Mami, tell me that's not hot," I said.

"Cálmate. It's not hot. It's warm pero not hot. I went to la botánica this morning for the last yerba. The apasote. Everything else is from mi jardin." She stirred the tepid tea with a plastic one-cup measuring cup.

"What's in it? It smells fo." I pinched my nose.

"Tienen zaragüey, rudó, perejil, paraíso, alacrancillo, y apasote," she said. "Here, cover your face."

She gave me a washcloth, which I held tightly over my eyes, nose, and mouth. Mami poured cup after cup of the stinky tea over my head and body. I felt wet leaves stick to my skin. When she was finished, she handed me a towel.

"Mami, let me rinse off. This stuff stinks," I said.

"No. You dry, but no rinse. Vamos." She clapped her hands. "This is protection for you and the baby."

Ay, ay, ay. What is that smell? It's like paint-thinner, oregano, citrus, and pine rolled into one. Yuck.

I picked herbs and twigs from my hair, dried off as best I could, and dressed. I went to the patio to be with Manny and air-dry some more.

"Fo-fo. Mami, se tiró un peo," Manny said, fanning his hand in front of his nose.

"Nooo." I acted shocked that he thought I'd farted. "Es un nuevo champú de tu abuela."

Manny told me he didn't want me to use that same shampoo on him. I told him I hadn't wanted it either.

I got a text from my husband that they were pulling into Punta Palma and to meet them at the grand villa. Mami, Manny, and I walked over. I kept an eye on Jules's townhouse but didn't see any activity. *He's probably on his laptop, wheeling and dealing and ruining someone else's job security. I bet he'd sell the shoes out from under his own mother. Arrgh!*

Robert unloaded the bags from the back of the minivan as my friends dismounted from it. Each one stepped out, spun around like a Disney princess, and took a deep breath of the verdant air. I called out their names and gave them hugs. "Sally. Pepper. Ana. Marie. You don't know how good it is to see you," I said.

"Marie?" Mami asked. She tilted her head, and her jaw went slack. "From St. Joseph's?"

"Hello, Mrs. Quiñones. It's so nice to see you again," Marie replied.

"How is your mother?" Mami asked. Marie's mother and mine had been on a few fundraising committees together. This basically meant they procured incentive rewards to give the students who sold the most boxes of the World's Finest Chocolate. I earned a gift certificate to Carvel ice cream once. But Alma usually got the top prize, a season pass to Santa's Enchanted Forest, the holiday-themed amusement park that opened after Halloween and ran until about Three Kings Day.

"She's good."

"Tell her hello from me."

"I will."

I introduced my mother to the others. Manny bounced between Sally and Pepper, asking if they'd brought his cousins, Rae and Vanna, and his bestie, Sophia. He couldn't remember Marie's daughter's name, Zora, after Zora Neale Hurston, so he asked if Zo had come. I'd paid her to watch him once at the park, and he'd taken a liking to her. She wasn't babysitter-age-older than him, but she was big-sibling old enough to keep an eye on him at an event or park.

"Little man," Robert said. "This is Mami's time to play with her friends. You'll see your friends in a few days. Come help me with the bags."

Robert gave Manny the lightest bag to carry, a lilac tote that matched one of the suitcases. It was almost too much for him, but he was determined to get it up the stairs, even if he had to stop and rest on each step.

"Come, I show you the villa," Mami said, inserting the key into the lock.

My friends followed her into the house. There were oohs and aaahs. Mami showed off the kitchen that she'd stocked with breads and snacks. She had juices, fruit salad, and homemade farmer's cheese in the fridge. Pepper hung back and walked with me.

"Sweetheart, you have something in your hair," Pepper said in her Oklahoma accent. She picked a limp parsley leaf from my hair. "What's that smell? Have you been painting?" She took a sniff of my still-damp hair. "Smells like turpentine."

"Long story. But if you see my mom boiling a pot of herbs, run." I grimaced.

Chapter
Thirty-Eight

It was early afternoon. After Mami's mandatory merienda of fruit salad and farmer's cheese, everyone wanted to go to the pool. I didn't want to squeeze into my swimsuit, but I did want to de-stink myself. Chlorine smell was better than eau de industrial pine cleaner.

"I'll meet you at the pool in five. If you look out the window, you'll see it. It's by my parents' apartment," I told them as they rolled their bags down the hall on the second floor.

"Okay, see you there," Ana said.

From the landing, I viewed Punta Palma from a different perspective than I had before. It was a lovely property. I could see my parents' care and pride all around. The grand villa was spotless, with not a speck of dust on the windowsill. Every corner had been swept and mopped. The trees, scrubs, and plants were lush. No weeds were poking through the gravel. I could see over the large palm in the center of the drive to the decorative gates. This place was supposed to be my parents' last gig. This was as close to the Cuba they missed as they were going to get—island life with a similar Spanish-Caribbean culture as they'd grown up with. Mami had even mentioned they might apply for Dominican citizenship.

La Sirena kicked and brought me back to task. "Bebé, I hear you. You want to be in the pool. We're going," I said out loud. Using the handrail, I descended the tile stairs as quickly as was safe.

As I closed the villa's front door, I heard the beep of an automatic car lock. Jules was leaving his townhouse. *Now's my chance.* I marched over to him.

"Ms. Keen-yo-nes! I'm so glad you're safe and back with your family. I can't believe Brandon Pickles is associated with those kinds of people," Jules said. He was dressed casually in a linen shirt and canvas slacks.

"You lied to me. You sold this place out from under my parents' noses." My voice had teeth.

"*What?* No." He put his hands on his chest and shook his head vehemently. "I had nothing to do with the sale. I don't know who bought it. I've been trying to find out for your dad. The Dominican real estate system is different than the US system. I don't have access to their MLS."

"Sure. *You expect me to believe you.*"

"Ms. Quiñones, I swear." He held up his hand in an oath. "It wasn't me. It wasn't LPM, the conglomerate I work with. I promise. We do restaurants, not vacation rentals."

"Uh-huh. Like El Capitán! That family had run that seafood restaurant for generations, and now they have no place to go." I put a fist on my hip.

"I wasn't part of that deal. That's Belle Époque. They're new to the investment group. I advised them to work with the established family business, modernize the POS, update the menu to smaller plates, and remodel. Fish nets and ship's wheels are passé. But El Capitán's seafood was excellent, fresh, and well prepared. But Belle Époque had their own ideas. I'm not a stockholder. They ignored my expert opinion. *It's not like I'm a street food connoisseur or anything.* Did I tell you I was a food blogger for years? A *New York Times* food critic mentioned me once. My website crashed; it got so much traffic."

I closed my eyes and pinched the bridge of my nose to calm myself. My anger was real. I wanted to shake Jules. Okay, maybe not shake him, but at least yell at him. *My parents are out of a job with no notice, no plan, not enough savings, and I'm mad for them!* I exhaled slowly through pursed lips.

"Mr. Howard, did you or didn't you have anything to do with the sale of this place?" I whirled my pointer finger in the air.

"I honestly don't know who bought Punta Palma, but I'm going to find out. Actually, that's where I'm headed now. I'm meeting a friend of a friend. He's a real estate agent on the island. I hope he can find the name of the buyer for me. Please believe me. Your parents are so nice and kind. Your mother's arroz con pollo is the best I've ever had. What's her secret?"

I gave Jules a hard stare. *Also, carajo Mami, you fed the enemy.*

"I hate that this has happened to them with no warning." Jules stepped closer to his rental car.

Liar, liar, pants on fire.

"I swear. Scout's honor. It wasn't me," Jules said.

"Miriam," Sally shouted, waving from under the villa's bougainvillea arch. "Are you coming?" Sally was in a flowy resort-wear cover-up, as was Ana. Marie and Pepper were in bathing suits with sarongs around their waists.

"I don't believe you, but I have to go," I said to Jules.

"I'll prove it to you. I'm going to find out who it is, like I told your dad I would."

I threw Jules an angry *humph* and walked away.

270

"I promise," Jules said.

I heard his car start and the tires squeak on the pavers. I met my friends at the pool before I slipped into the house via the patio door to change. My family was at the front door about to exit.

"Where are you all going?" I asked.

"A pasear," Mami replied.

"Your parents want to show me the sights," Robert said. He broke from them to give me a kiss goodbye. "Enjoy your friends." Then he lowered his voice to a whisper. "We'll keep Manny entertained. I think we're going to a zoo or a petting farm. I don't know, something to do with animals. It's all good. I got this."

"Bye, Mami." Manny hugged my legs.

"No te preocupes por la cena. I will make dinner for you and your friends," my mother said. "Y tu papa put a cooler by the pool con cervezas y refrescos for your friends."

I thanked her and secured the door after them. I wiggled into my swimsuit and rinsed off in the shower before joining my friends in the pool. They'd already found the cooler with beer and drinks. Everyone had alcoholic beverages except for Pepper. She had a Coca-Cola.

"You smell better," Sally said. "I didn't want to insult you, but if that's a new perfume, you might want to get your money back."

"*Right*. No, it was a hex breaker cleanse from my aunt. My mother thinks it will rid me of my bad luck," I said.

Marie, who'd been listening, agreed. "That stuff works." She nodded and splashed some water on her shoulders. "Vodou is like a Wi-Fi connection to your ancestors."

Marie and I smiled knowingly at each other. While Vodou and Santeria weren't exactly the same, they were like cousins in the family of African diaspora religions.

"I thought most Haitians were Catholic," Pepper said. "I love seeing the Little Haiti ladies all decked out in their finest on their way to mass at Notre Dame. I *love* the bright colors. And the hats! Do you think I could pull off one of those hats?"

"Um, no," Marie and I said in unison.

"Too old-lady for you," Ana said. She was floating on her back, her blond hair making a halo, not unlike a Russian icon.

Maria and I exchanged looks. That wasn't the reason, but it would do.

Ana switched to her stomach and swam to the deep end.

"The two religions are not exclusive. We say Haiti is seventy percent Catholic, thirty percent Protestant, and one hundred percent Vodou." Marie laughed.

"Do you believe in it?" Pepper asked.

Marie mm-hmmed, and to my surprise, I did too. *Miriam, you need to examine your feelings about it. It's not just Tía's thing. It's your heritage too.*

"So, what happened? What was the bad luck?" Sally asked.

"Sorry to interrupt, but I think Alma's Uber has arrived," Ana said from her position at the pool's edge closest to the driveway.

"Gracias a La Caridad," I said. "Honestly, she needs a bad luck cleanse more than me." I got out of the water via the wide steps at the shallow end. I wrapped one of the rolled beach towels on the lounge chairs around my shoulders.

"What do you mean? What happen to Alma?" Ana asked.

"You all don't know, do you?" I asked. "It hasn't reached the US news, I guess." I waved to the car and directed them to park by the pool.

"What hasn't reached the news?" Sally asked.

"Let's wait for Alma so we can tell you together," I said, patting water droplets from my legs. "Uh-oh."

"*Uh-oh*. What-oh?" Marie asked.

"Alma has an FBI escort," I replied.

"*FBI*," the quartet said.

"It's a long story. I'll be right back."

Chapter Thirty-Nine

I met the car as it rolled to a stop. Agent González was in the passenger seat, and Welmo was in the driver's seat, with Alma in the back. The small SUV's hatchback had more luggage than just Alma's. *Ay, ay, ay. They're staying.*

"Welcome to Punta Palma," I said, a little self-conscious that I was in my bathing suit while Welmo and González were dressed for business. Alma hugged me and stayed beside me with her arm around my waist.

"Hello. Which one is Mr. Howard staying in?" Agent González asked.

"That one." I pointed. "But he just left."

"What do you mean he's gone?" Welmo's voice was incredulous.

"Not gone, just out." *At least, I think so. He could have been lying to me. Maybe he was headed to the airport, and all that talk about finding the buyer was misdirection.*

"Chica, is there a changing room by the pool? I want a beer in my hand and my friends around me. Estoy cansada de estos dos." Alma lip-pointed toward the two people she was tired of.

"Claro, change at my parents' place, and we'll take your bag to the villa later," I said.

Welmo unloaded Alma's suitcase and set it beside her.

"Thank you for bringing Alma. Bye," I said.

"We aren't leaving yet," Agent González said.

A chill ran through my body. *Are they Alma's security detail because she's in danger? Ay, Caridad, she is going to have to go into witness protection.*

"Oh, you're staying in Punta Cana. Duh, of course. You still have to interview Jules," I bumbled.

"No, we're staying here," the agent said. "It looks like there are two apartments available."

She showed me the website on her phone. The apartment above my parents' place and the one next to Jules were on the screen. My heart sank. There was no way to escape it. We were going to be under surveillance.

"I'm canceling our hotel in town," González said to Welmo.

Alma laughed sardonically.

The squad was eavesdropping at the pool's edge like Sea World dolphins waiting for treats.

"Miriam," Pepper called out. "Your phone is ringing." She was in the shallow end, looking at the folded towel where we had all placed our phones. Near enough for pictures but out of the splash range. "I think it is your mother."

I scurried over to answer it. *I hope Manny's okay.* "Hola, Mami. ¿Qué pasó?"

She hurriedly explained what I already knew, that there had been two late guest registrations. She asked me to welcome them and show them to the apartments. The places were clean, of course. But she hadn't put out the customary fruit basket and welcome gifts because she thought they'd be vacant until the next reservation, which wasn't until Tuesday. Mami told me where to find the keys and a few other must-dos.

I'm sure someday we'd all laugh about our girls' weekend with the FBI, but at the moment, it felt awful. I showed Alma where to change, put on a bathrobe over my wet bathing suit, then got the keys from the pegs in the kitchen.

"Okay, who goes where?" I asked Welmo and González. They'd stayed by their car.

"You take this one." She pointed to the one above my parents' place. "I'll take the other one."

"Perfect." *Miriam, watch your tone.* I was tone-policing myself. "Let's get you set up first," I said to Agent González.

The villa next to the one Jules was renting was similar on the exterior but had two units. I opened the front door to a tiled foyer. To the right was a staircase to the upper unit, which was out of service for a cosmetic repair. The lower unit's interior door was painted a sunset orange. I unlocked it, and we entered the living room. After turning on a few lights, I passed on the important information my mother had given me over the phone— mainly about the delicate plumbing, the Wi-Fi and cable, and the laminated list of local restaurants and attractions.

"When do you expect Howard back?" González asked.

"I don't know. He said he was having lunch with a business friend," I replied.

"Interesting." She exchanged looks with Welmo. "Do you know the name of the restaurant?" She picked up the restaurant list from the counter.

"No, I'm sorry. He didn't mention it," I said.

"Hmm." She looked at the window in the living room. It had a view of the grass and scrubs between the two villas and the driveway. "After you drop your bag, move the car to this side."

"Yes, ma'am," Welmo said.

We left Agent González and went back to the pool. My friends' animated conversations died down to whispers when the car door opened for Welmo to retrieve his luggage. There was silence once Welmo and I got to la piscina.

"I'll only be a minute," I said to my friends in the water. Alma, drinking from a pink can, was ignoring us. But Ana, beside her, had predator eyes on Welmo. As we climbed the staircase to the apartment's balcony, I noticed Ana kept her prey in sight, even moving to the shallow end for a better vantage point.

Inside, Welmo set his carry-on next to the sofa and turned on the overhead light. I repeated the information about the filtered water and delicate plumbing.

"Is the Wi-Fi code the same?" Welmo asked.

"I think so, but let me check." I looked around for the laminated info sheet. It wasn't where it was supposed to be, so I opened the kitchen drawers. Utensils. Tin foil and plastic wrap. The final drawer had a stack of menus and water sports rental pamphlets. I noticed the hard plastic edge of the Punta Palma info sheet and pulled it from the middle of the pile. "Found it." Stuck to it by static was a white paper flyer. I slid it off and handed the Wi-Fi code to Welmo. The flyer, printed on one side, was for a beach food event. The date had passed, so I went to throw it away, but the writing on the other side stopped me. "Ay, Caridad."

"What?" Welmo asked.

I showed him the writing. "This looks like the same writing that was on the back of the picture Manny drew."

"Okay. Why is that important to you?"

"Because someone bought this place, and my parents are out of a job, and it feels a little like what was happening in Old San Juan to the viejitos—you know, sell to me or something bad will happen to you." Anger, fear, or a baby hot flash overcame me. I took a small glass from the cabinet and found a pitcher with a filter in the fridge. I poured cold water from it. After I drained the glass twice, I returned the pitcher to its place. That's when I saw the pink four-pack of rosé. I picked it up and plunked it on the counter.

"Miriam, FYI, that's not soda. It's wine," Welmo said.

"Oh, I know." I ripped open the carton and pulled out one of the cans. "Yep. Same."

"It's time to share with me what you are thinking."

I sighed. There was no point hiding anything from him. He would find out eventually. "I saw the woman who was staying in this unit drinking this brand of wine last week."

"It must be popular. Alma was drinking a can of it in the pool," Welmo said.

He is so annoying. He's just like Detective Pullman. He notices everything but doesn't say a thing.

"Yes, she likes rosé, but that has nothing to do with this." I waved the flyer in his face. "I think that that woman sabotaged this place so the owner would sell. I think she broke pipes, faked a photo so that the pool looked like it had algae, and even put a rat in the shower. She wrote the note, and this is her practice sheet."

"Did your parents receive a note?"

I had Welmo's full attention. "I don't know. They are refusing to talk to me about the situation. But I bet I can find Manny's drawing downstairs. If the writing is the same, then that proves it."

"That doesn't prove anything, but I would like to see it for comparison."

Welmo followed me down and through the patio. I took the rubber hibiscus magnet from Manny's drawing and flipped the page over. "See." I laid the papers side by side. "Same."

"Similar, but you don't know if the woman wrote them," Welmo said.

"Argh! It's obvious she did."

He raised his eyebrow at me. "Does she have a connection to Brandon Pickles?"

"I don't know, but it's very convenient that a real estate broker is staying here. I'm just saying." I gave him a hard stare. *Come on, do something!*

"What's this woman's name?" Welmo asked.

"I don't know, but I'll find out."

Chapter Forty

Alma, Ana, Marie, Pepper, and Sally were drying off to go to the grand villa.

"What's up, chica?" Alma asked. "Is the FBI harassing you? You had nothing to do with any of it. Coño, neither did I, pero they are still on me like Velcro."

"Don't worry. Welmo is okay." I jerked my head toward him, ascending the stairs to the pool apartment. "He's helping me with something," I said.

"I'd like *to help him* with something," Ana said.

"Cálmate. He's married with kids," I said.

"All the good ones are taken." Ana sighed.

"Mi'ja, don't get me started," Alma said.

Pobrecita. I know she is making jokes, but Herbie, the Love Bug, really broke her heart.

"Miriam, you're coming, *right*?" Pepper tied her sarong on.

"I'll be there ASAP. I need to do something for the new guests," I said.

"Do you need help?" Marie asked.

"Thanks, but I've got it. It will be quick, I promise," I replied.

"This is a girls' trip. We need all the girls present," Pepper pouted.

"I promise I'll be right over," I said.

Sally pulled me aside and whispered to me. "Do you need legal counsel? I can get you someone within the hour. I know people." My sister-in-law had a law degree but was not a practicing lawyer. She was an advocate that worked with the courts.

"What? What makes you think that?" I asked.

"Robert mentioned it, and Alma alluded that something went down in Puerto Rico. *And* I can spot a federal officer a mile away."

"That guy?" I pointed over my shoulder. "No. He's my security guard from UnMundo."

"Not him. Her. She is a career Fed. I'd bet my house on it." Sally brushed a stray blond hair off her forehead.

I took a beat. *Alma hasn't told them anything.* "So, Alma hasn't said anything, huh?"

"She said she was waiting for you so we didn't have to hear the story twice. And that we need to be someplace private. Did you two sign an NDA?"

A nondisclosure agreement. "No, but yes, private would be good." I saw that Welmo was out on his terrace waiting for me.

Sally followed my gaze. "My offer is still good. I can have counsel on a video chat in fifteen minutes. Let me know."

"Thanks, but I'm fine. Go to the villa. I'll be there soon for story time." I shooed her toward the others, who were crossing the lawn.

I slipped into my parents' place to find their laptop. *I hope all the passwords are saved.* I quickly changed out of my bathing suit into a comfy T-shirt and loose sweatpants. After I'd twisted my hair into a messy bun, I put the laptop under my arm and grabbed a banana. "I hear you, mi sirena. You want potassium. Pero, you know what else is good? Galletas y chocolate. Maybe you could crave those occasionally."

"Miriam, who are you talking to?" Welmo asked. He was at the sliding glass door.

"I'm talking to the baby," I replied.

"My wife did that with our first." He stayed on the patio.

"Do you want one?" I wiggled the banana at him. He shook his head no. I kind of wished he'd said yes. I wanted to be in the kitchen. I wanted to chop vegetables and smell goodness cooking. *Mi'ja, you are stressing.* Cooking for others was a thing I did to soothe myself when I was worried. Roberto called it stress cooking.

Welmo and I sat side by side on the patio. It took me a few clicks, but I found the reservation's email notification, which led me to the admin side of the rental website. "Here it is. Her name is Kandace, with a K, Mills. She paid through PayPal. That's weird. Most people use a credit card. And her home address is in Las Vegas, Nevada." I looked at Welmo. "Do you think that's legit? Las Vegas?" *Miriam, no seas boba. Of course people actually live there. The casinos aren't run by robots.* "Where are you going?"

"To get González to run her name," Welmo said, pushing his chair under the table.

"I'm coming with you." I shut the computer and put it back where I'd found it. I ate the banana along the way.

Agent González was a little perturbed that I'd tagged along. *Is she, or is that just resting FBI face?*

Welmo explained my theory about the note and the sabotage.

"You think this person is working for Brandon Pickles," González said.

"*Maybe,*" I said. Her tone made me think I'd jumped to the wrong conclusion. "I mean, it is odd that Jules Howard, a real estate guy, is renting a villa at the same time as her. I don't care that he said it's not him but the company he works with that's involved with Pickles."

"So, you spoke to him about it." She was unpacking cables and devices from her black bag.

I sensed I was in trouble or at least in time-out.

"What's her name?" González had her fingers poised over the keyboard.

"Kandace, with a K, Mills," I said as I approached her station. Welmo gave me a silent *no* and jutted his chin toward a chair in the living room. I sat and listened to him give her the address that he'd memorized. During their clicking and ums and ahs, I did my own search. I went on Instagram and found her account, KandyCoin. Her page was full of Burning Man photos, luxurious pools in the desert, more music festivals, and the standard twenty-something living their best glamorous influencer life. Her signature look seemed to be her drinking from a straw in a tiny bikini with huge sunglasses on while on a supersized float. There were unicorns, dragons, swans, a Pegasus, and a yellow duck. "I know that dog!"

"Excuse me," González said.

"This dog looks exactly like Dill," I said.

Welmo came and looked at my phone. "It does look like her," he said.

"Where are you taking my phone?"

"I'll give it right back," he said. He was back in the no-go zone beside Agent González. There was more tick-tacking of the keys, pointing at the screen, and sidelong looks.

Welmo set my phone down on the table, immersed in whatever was on the screen. I quietly got up and took it back. KandyCoin had tagged people in her post. I followed them and found a few videos that looked to be at the same festival. And then I hit the jackpot. Brandon Pickles sans the golden pickle necklace with his arm around Kandace Mills. I lowered the volume on the phone and held it to my ear so that only I could hear it.

"I'm here with Brandon Pickles and his girlfriend, Kandy. Tell my viewers how to get rich." The off-frame voice was high in all senses of the word.

"Buy Bitcoin!" Brandon Pickles's voice said.

"Yeah, buy his Bitcoin," said a voice that had to belong to Kandace.

I muted the video and watched it again. It was taken two years ago. I went back two years on Pickles's page, and there was Kandace. But she was nowhere to be found currently. Had they broken up?

I heard a car in the driveway. I was out the door before my companions could stop me. Jules parked, got out, and looked at me over the roof with his foot on the car frame.

"I know who bought the property," Jules and I said simultaneously. His voice was jolly. Mine was stabby.

"Kandace Mills," Jules said.

"Kandy Mills," I said.

We'd talked over each other.

"How did you find out?" Jules asked, shutting the door and closing the distance between us.

I sensed my companions at my back.

"That's not important," I said. "I want you to finally tell me the truth. Did you sabotage this place so Pickles's girlfriend could buy it cheap?"

"What? His girlfriend? No. I'd never," Jules said.

"Ms. Quiñones, I'd appreciate it if you'd join your friends now," Agent González said as she and Welmo flanked past me. "Mr. Howard, we'd like a word with you."

I gathered the edge of my T-shirt into my fist as I watched them usher Jules into his townhouse.

"Great. Perfecto," I vented to the sky before I gave up and headed to the grand villa to join my friends.

I shook out my frustration and put on a smile before I entered. Everyone was in the living room. Maria, standing, was pouring a cloudy pink liquid from a pitcher.

"I made a mocktail for you," Maria said, seeing me before the others. "Pepper's drinking one too."

All heads swiveled to look at me.

"Money laundering," Sally said.

"Murder," Ana said.

"Guns," Pepper said.

"I thought you said you were going to wait for me to tell them," I said to Alma.

"I tried. Pero, you know I can't keep quiet when I have good chisme," Alma said, toasting with her rum punch cocktail.

Chapter
Forty-One

Alma and I each told our parts of the story. We both learned details about the other's adventure that we hadn't shared yet, like how Alma had become suspicious of Heriberto after she moved from the UnMundo guesthouse to his hotel.

"It was bien raro, weird, you know," Alma said. "He kept going to the closet, saying he had to get a pair of socks. How many sock changes did the man need? *Like, were his feet especially sweaty.* No sé. And, like, I wasn't going to go through his stuff, *pero* I swear he had two duffel bags when we got off the jet. But there was only one in the closet. Y he would get messages and phone calls at all hours where he would have to leave me to talk to the people. You know."

"Is that when you called Frank?" I asked her.

"Who's Frank?" Pepper asked.

"Frank Pullman, the detective from Coral Shores," Alma answered.

Pepper nodded a duh, of course.

"You are now *friends* with him?" Ana gave a you-can't-be-serious look to Alma.

Ana and Alma held Pullman responsible for Alma's house arrest last year.

"Friend-ly, not friends," Alma said.

"Come on, Alma, you need to forgive him. He was doing his job and protecting you from harm," I said.

"I reserve the right to—" Alma began.

She was interrupted by Pepper. "Were Jorge or his boyfriend hurt? Are they still in Puerto Rico?"

I looked to Alma for the answer. She shrugged. "I saw Jorge and Lucas last night. But we didn't get to talk. I think they put them on a plane back to Miami early in the morning. *Maybe.* I don't know exactly. You should ask Welmo." Alma elbowed me. "He might tell you."

"Or we could just text Jorge," I said while texting. A notification beeped. "Jorge says they're home. He needs his beauty sleep, and we'll talk tomorrow."

"I'm hungry," Marie said. "Let me see what's in the kitchen that I can make for dinner."

"Wait. My mom said she had dinner handled. Let me find out what time she wants us over there." I called Mami's number, and Manny picked up.

"Hola, mi príncipe, déjame hablar con Abuela." I told him to pass the phone to his grandmother.

"Hey, babe, your mom is busy cooking," Robert said, taking the phone from Manny. "But, if you and your friends want to come over now, I think it will only be another twenty or thirty minutes before we sit down."

I hung up and told them we could head over. Everyone put their empty drinks in the kitchen. Ana went to apply fresh lipstick. A few others went to the bathroom, including me. In ten minutes, the squad was out the door.

"I don't remember a table being there," Pepper observed.

The pool's lounge chairs had been moved and in their place was a long dining table. Two rectangular folding tables had been put end to end and covered with yellow tablecloths. White plastic stackable chairs and my parent's patio chairs were around it.

"Oh, something smells good," Marie said. "Pork. Chorizo. Maybe chicken. Definitely, garlic." She had her nose in the air. "I think I smell a sweet guava barbecue sauce."

Papi was by a shiny metal grill that I'd only ever seen covered. Ribbons of smoke curled up from the variety of meats. Mami was at the table. She squeezed lime over a sliced avocado salad. With Robert behind him, Manny came through the patio pass-through carrying a tower of plastic cups.

"Mrs. Quiñones, this looks delicious," Marie said to my mother.

"Thank you," Mami said.

"Can I help with anything?" Marie asked.

My mother thought for a second.

"Mrs. Quiñones, I'm a trained cook. I promise I won't mess up your dinner." Marie smiled.

"Maybe you help with the Yaniqueques? You fry in the kitchen. The masa is there and ready." Mami demonstrated making patties between her palms.

"Sure thing," Marie said.

Robert pointed the way to her.

"Everybody sit. Dinner will be *very* soon," Mami said, motioning my friends to the table. "Mi'ja, go tell the other guest to join us. Julie and the new ones too."

I raised my eyebrows at her. She gave me a do-as-I-say stare.

"I'll go with you," Robert said. He took my hand and kissed me on the temple.

"How was the zoo?" I asked him as I led him.

"*Well*, there were animals, *but* it wasn't a zoo. It was more like a farm."

"I bet Manny still loved it." I gave his hand a squeeze.

"With a butcher shop attached to it." Robert grimaced. "We were there to pick up meat for dinner."

I chuckled. "Teachable moment. The circle of life."

Robert mimed lifting an invisible Simba.

I laughed some more.

"So, who are the new guests?" Robert asked.

"Would you believe me if I told you an accomplice to sabotage, an informant, and an FBI agent?"

"*Really?*"

"Really." I sighed as I tapped my knuckles on Agent González's door. "I didn't want to make a scene, but I'm not thrilled about Mami's guest list." Welmo answered my knock. "My parents would like to invite you two to dinner."

"Is it dinnertime already?" Jules's voice came from within the apartment. "Carmen invited me earlier today. I'm looking forward to tasting some more of your mother's cooking."

My goofy-moment-with-my-husband mood evaporated.

"You're still questioning him?" I asked Welmo.

"Almost done. For what it's worth, I don't think he is involved in the sale," Welmo volunteered.

"Are you certain?" I asked.

Welmo nodded.

Agent González coughed.

"Please, tell your mother thank you, but—"

González piped up. "We'd love to join you. We will be over in just a few moments."

Welmo screwed up his face. "I guess we are going."

Robert and I slow-walked back so I could fill him in on Jules, KandyCoin, and my theory. The sky was moonless, and the landscape lights made patches of brightness.

"But didn't that guy—he's the security guard, ex-cop, FBI informant, right?—didn't he say the Jules guy isn't involved?" Robert asked.

"Yep. So, now I don't know what to think," I said.

"How about don't think? Just enjoy your time with your parents and friends."

We were in the dark about to step into the party. "Speaking of my parents, would you be okay if they stayed with us for a few weeks while they look for a place to live?" I asked.

"Of course. You don't even have to ask."

I tilted my head back, and Robert kissed me deeply.

"Oye, lovebirds. Dinner is served," Alma said, sauntering toward us.

"Psst," I waved her into our patch of darkness. "Are you going to get to keep your commission?"

"¿Qué sé yo? I doubt it," Alma said. "They've frozen Herbie's US bank accounts. And the FBI has a forensic accountant looking over Pickles's transactions. The sale was legit on my part, but the money probably will be tied up in court for years."

"I'm so sorry, chica. I'd hoped something good could come out of this for you." I gave her a hug.

"I know, I know. Pero that money has blood on it, better not to touch it, even though I would have done good with it." Alma shrugged. "I'll just have to work harder and sell more houses. We Cubans know how to work hard. Am I right?"

I nodded and smiled.

"Come on, your dad is taking meat off the grill and your mom is ordering Marie around like she is her hija." Alma walked away, waving for us to follow.

* * *

As we stepped into the light, Robert said, "Just so you know, your parents talked to me a little on the way to the farm."

"Oh yeah, and?"

"Someone named Julie is helping them find a new property maintenance situation," Robert said, letting go of my hand as he stopped ahead of me.

"¿Qué, que?" I grabbed his forearm to spin him to me. "Julie? My mom says Julie, but she means Jules. I'm still not one hundred percent convinced he's completely virtuous."

"I'm right here," Jules said a few feet away.

Welmo and González trailed behind him and stopped to listen.

"Miriam, you have to believe me. I had nothing to do with the sale of Punta Palma," Jules insisted.

"I'd like to believe you, Jules, but I'm having a hard time with it. You just happened to be at the UnMundo party and then at Fela's restaurant, *and* you're a partner in El Capitán *and*—"

Jules interrupted. "I am not a partner! I consulted on the project but nothing more." He brought his flailing hands into prayer form. "I swear I'm just a foodie in search of a good meal."

"To appropriate," I said. The level of Jorge sass in my tone shocked me. But it also felt good, so I went all in. "Stealing cultural dishes for some not-from-here chef to then adulterate and make big money while the locals get no credit is the worst kind of—Ugh!" I stomped my foot. The word I wanted was just out of reach.

Robert gave me a let-it-go-for-now look. I volleyed back a don't-tell-me-what-to-do glare.

"Ugh!" I waved a fist in front of my scowling face. "Gentrifier!"

"Ouch!" Jules put his hand on his chest. "Hurtful, but I agree." He exhaled. "That's a little true. Look, I know my track record isn't the greatest. I've helped make some deals that hurt small family businesses, but—"

I opened my mouth.

"Hear me out. I've taken off my blinders. I get it. I've taken advantage of low-income areas. But I'm trying to start something new. It looks like I'll have to stay in real estate to fund it, but that's whatever. I really want to help talented cooks get the spotlight they deserve. Cooks, not pedigreed chefs. Cooks. That's why I was at the UnMundo party. I asked my old college friend to invest in my new not-for-profit business. "

"Nonprofits are usually organizations, not businesses," Robert said.

I appreciated that my husband had my back.

"Okay, yes. That's fair. It is *an organization,* or rather, will be. My goal is to be like the SBA but for five-star family restaurants. I want to help them get low-interest loans to buy their buildings and equipment. Offer mentorship and business planning."

Someone from the party walked toward us. "Come, come," Papi beckoned. "Dinner is ready."

Our group condensed and moved as one.

"What's in it for you?" I asked.

"Good food," Jules replied. "I *love* good food."

I softened a little bit. He seemed earnest. And he did talk about food the way I talked about food history.

The five of us joined the table, filling in the empty spots. Ana made sure Welmo sat next to her. González sat next to my father, Jules next to my mother, and Robert and I on either side of Manny.

"Come, come. Eat. Eat." Mami dug a serving spoon into the moro de guandules, a Dominican rice and pigeon peas dish made with coconut milk.

"Here, everyone take a yaniqueque while they're still warm," Marie said, holding a basket of fried flatbread.

"What are they?" Pepper asked.

"A type of Johnny cake. But not like American ones made from cornmeal. Or the Bahamian ones that are fluffy like muffins," I said. "Mami, don't they usually eat yaniqueques for breakfast here?"

"Yes. But I like them con la longaniza. See, you make like a hot dog." My mother took the thin, spiced pork sausage and placed it in the folded Johnny cake. The visual gave taco vibes.

Jules prepared one and took a bite. Sounds of enjoyment emitted from him. "You have to show me how to make these," he said once he stopped chewing.

The guy does like food. I hope he's telling the truth about his new nonprofit.

"Claro, Julies, I will show you when you visit us at the new place." My mother continued to serve the plates that came her way.

"I think I found a place in Miami for you," Jules said.

I zoned in on him when he said Miami. "A place in Miami? Are you talking about a restaurant or an apartment?"

"A property management situation, kind of like this place. It's in Little Havana." Jules put a forkful of the rice into his mouth, chewed, and swallowed. "But it won't be ready for a few months, maybe six."

"What's this about Little Havana?" Alma asked. "There are a lot of apartment buildings being renovated over there." Alma then asked my mother in Spanish if they were planning on moving back. They exchanged a few sentences and then switched to English. "I can help you find a short-term lease while you wait. Golden Jules is not the only one in real estate."

I noticed Agent González turned her attention to that news. She was being as quiet as a wallflower and just as out of place. She'd left her uniform-issued jacket, but her rigid posture screamed *on duty*. Welmo at least seemed to be relaxed and off the clock. Ana was chatting him up. *Chica, I know you are probably just bored, but we need to respect that he has a family.*

"Welmo, so tell me, how old are your kids?" I asked from across the table.

"We have two girls, gemelos, twins. They turned four in February," Welmo said.

"I'm four, almost five," Manny said with pride. I kissed the top of his head.

Welmo smiled. "And we just had a baby. He is three months old. Here. I have a picture." Welmo pulled out his phone and showed us an image of him and his wife holding a swaddled infant.

"Very sweet," Ana said. Her flirting had fluttered away. She was being sincere.

"Don'tcha just love babies?" Pepper said. She twirled the end of a tress. "Um, and since we're on the subject of babies, I have news. I'm pregnant!"

Applause and blessings sprang from the table.

"Now I get why you haven't been drinking with us," Sally said.

"Miriam, can you believe it? We're going to have little ones at the same time," Pepper said.

"This is the best news. I'm so happy for you," I said. La Sirena decided to kick me harder than ever before. "Ay. Even my sirena is excited." I laughed and rubbed my belly where I'd been battle-rammed.

"Is that the name you've chosen?" Pepper asked.

"We haven't decided on a name." I looked at Roberto. "Sirena means mermaid. It's just something I've been calling the baby. It's better than *it*." I chuckled.

"I've decided my baby will be named Elliot, no matter if it's a girl or a boy," Pepper said.

I reached across the table and patted my friend's hand. She was honoring her best friend, who died recently. "That is beautiful."

Sitting beside Pepper was my bestie, Alma. The image of her being held at gunpoint flashed into my mind. I don't know what

I would do if anything happened to her. She had been so lucky. La Sirena kicked hard again.

I know, I know. Us too.

Maybe there was something to that watermelon offering Mami had made me do at the beach.

Sirena, we are lucky to be alive. Gracias, Yemaya.

Recetas / Recipes

Tamarind Juice

If you didn't grow up with tamarind, it might be an acquired taste. The pulp is sticky and unappealing, with a distinct tangy aroma. *I think it smells like boiled orange juice.* It tastes tart. If you enjoy SweeTARTS or Sour Patch Kids candies, you will likely enjoy tamarind. I remember walking to elementary school with my father and him picking a pod off a tree. He cracked the papery, brittle shell and offered the pulpy legume to me to try. He told me he and his childhood friends in Cuba would eat tamarind on the path to and from school. While I didn't love the flavor, I loved the symmetry of our personal histories.

The tamarind tree, probably originating from Africa and documented in 1300 BCE India, is now cultivated over most of the tropical and subtropical Southern Hemisphere. Tamarind has many known health benefits. It can help with diabetes, cholesterol, and heart health. It also has anti-inflammatory properties. Folk wisdom suggests using it for morning sickness and gastrointestinal issues.

Raquel V. Reyes

Servings: 1 pitcher

Ingredients:

Tamarind paste
Sugar
Water

Directions:

If you are using unprocessed tamarind: Remove the shell and seeds. Place in a small pot of water. Bring to a low boil. Cover and remove from heat. Let it steep for 20 to 30 minutes. Strain the solids from the liquid, then add water to the concentration until it is tea-colored. Sweeten to taste. Refrigerate and drink it cold.

If you do not have access to fresh tamarind (try an Asian or Caribbean grocer), you can order tamarind paste. It usually has added sugar, so read the label. Follow the above instructions, being mindful of the sugar, as you will probably not need additional sweeteners.

Miriam's Sorullitos

The Miriam, in this case, is my Puerto Rican mother-in-law. Yes, Miriam Quiñones is named after my angelic MIL, whom I adore. (The Quiñones last name is a family name on my father's side.)

Sorullitos are sweet corn fritters. They can be made with or without cheese and are usually served with mayo-ketchup. The name translates to little cigar because the shape resembles the small hand-rolled tobacco.

Corn was cultivated in Puerto Rico by the Taíno, and there is evidence of it in the pre-Arawak Antilles since at least 2950 BCE.

Servings: 8–10 sticks

Ingredients:

1 tablespoon butter
½ cup water
1 tablespoon sugar
½ teaspoon salt
1 cup masarepa (precooked cornmeal)
½ cup whole milk
Mild cheese (queso blanco or gouda or string-style mozzarella)
   optional
Canola or vegetable oil for frying

Directions:

In a small pot, heat water and dissolve the sugar and salt. Add the butter and allow it to melt. Add cornmeal and milk. Stir until smooth. The dough comes together quickly. Remove from heat. If you are making the cheese version, cut your cheese into 2-inch sticks.

Once your oil is hot, and your dough has cooled, it is time to form your "cigars." With wet hands, mold the dense mixture into shape. If using cheese, make sure it is completely encased in the masa. *I like to make some with cheese and some without.* Your sorullitos should be the length of the width of your palm. Lower them into the oil and fry until golden. *To me, they resemble a Twinkie in color and texture when they are done.* Let them cool on a paper towel. Enjoy with mayo-ketchup dip.

Pique

In the story, I describe pique as a not-hot hot sauce. Puerto Rican cuisine is a zero on the Scoville Heat Units (SHU) scale. But on most casual restaurant tables and many homes, you will find pique, a pepper and garlic–infused vinegar to be dashed onto habichuelas/beans and other side dishes like breadfruit tostones. The pepper used on the island is the Ají caballero. The slim pepper ranges in color from pale green to orange to red and hits about 30,000 SHU. If you cannot find this particular pepper, use a Thai chili pepper. Ideally, the pepper should be more citrusy than smokey. Pique varies from maker to maker. I've seen it with bell peppers and Scotch bonnets added. What keeps this hot sauce *not* hot is that the hot peppers remain whole. This recipe can be scaled up to suit your needs. The important part is the 2 parts acid to 1½ parts water.

Servings: 3 ten-ounce oil and vinegar bottles, the kind with a jigger. I get mine at the dollar store.

Ingredients:

1 cup white vinegar
1 cup apple cider vinegar
1½ cups distilled or boiled water
1 tablespoon salt
Whole peppercorns
Garlic cloves
Dried oregano

Fresh thyme or fresh (young) oregano *optional*
Aji caballero or Thai chili peppers

Directions:

Sanitize your bottles with boiling water.

In a glass pitcher, combine your wet ingredients. I suggest you dissolve the salt in the water before adding the vinegar parts.

Place into each bottle: 8–10 peppercorns, ¼ teaspoon dried oregano, 3 garlic cloves, 5 peppers with the stems pulled off, and one sprig of fresh young oregano or thyme.

Using a funnel, fill the bottles to the neck with the vinegar-water solution. Seal with the jigger top. Let the pique sit for one week before use. There is no need to refrigerate as long as the bottle is not in direct sunlight.

Titi Sandra's Arroz con Pollo

Arroz con pollo is a Sunday meal in many households. It was at my abuela's house. I remember many family meals at her Miami Beach home. She'd bring the caldero (large aluminum Dutch oven) to the table, and we'd all comment on how beautifully she'd decorated the rice with pimentos, (canned) asparagus, and peas. As the youngest in the family, I had the privilege of getting one or both drumsticks. I don't know if this was because it was easier for a child to eat or because they knew it was my favorite, but either way, I loved Abuela's arroz con pollo.

This one-pot rice dish has many variations across the Spanish-speaking Caribbean and Latin America. This recipe leans toward the Miami-Cuban style, which uses beer instead of vino seco.

Servings: 6–8

Ingredients:

Chicken thighs and legs (skinless with bone in)
Olive oil
Salt and pepper
4–5 garlic cloves, pressed
½ tablespoon culantro
1 tablespoon fresh cilantro
½ tablespoon oregano
2–3 bay leaves

1 packet sazón with azafran/saffron
Tomato sauce (small can)
1 bell pepper, chopped
1 yellow or white onion, chopped
Chicken stock
1 beer (Presidente or Medalla or other light-tasting beer)
1 12 oz bag Valencia rice
Green olives, sliced
½ cup frozen green peas
Pimento to decorate

Directions:

Season the chicken with salt and pepper a few hours before you plan to cook.

Coat the bottom of a wide pot (Dutch oven or caldero) with olive oil and cook the chicken on medium-high. Season with oregano, cilantro, and culantro. When you turn the chicken to brown on the other side, add the garlic, onions, and bell pepper. You want those latter ingredients to cook but not brown.

Once the chicken is cooked, lower the heat to medium. Throw in your sliced olives. Add the washed rice. Stir in the packet of sazón along with ½ to ¾ can of tomato sauce. (This is not a tomato-forward dish. Use it sparingly.) Pour in chicken stock to cover the rice. Add bay leaves and cook uncovered for 15 minutes. Stir once or twice to make sure the bottom isn't sticking.

Next, pour in the beer. This is by sight and feel. (Use about ¾ of the can/bottle.) You do not want the rice to be too wet, as that will make the dish mushy. Lower heat to low-medium. Add frozen peas. Cover and cook for an additional 20 minutes or until liquid is mostly absorbed. Saucy is good, but soupy is not.

Decorate the surface with pimentos (and asparagus) to your liking. Serve with maduros/fried sweet plantains.

Pastelón

This layered and baked dish is sometimes called Puerto Rican lasagna. And rightly so, because it supposedly was influenced by Italian-American lasagna. This dish is a twentieth-century update of pastel horneado. The cultural exchange between Italians, Dominicans, and Puerto Ricans in New York City led to the addition of cheese. The Dominican version is made with boiled plantains instead of fried ones. There is yet another version of this dish that is called piñón. It adds canned green beans and kidney beans to the picadillo mixture.

Pastelón is one of my spouse's favorite dishes. I feel it is a *special* dish, one you make when guests are coming over or for a celebratory occasion. If you've read the recipes in the other books in the series, you know I am not a fan of ground beef, so I substitute it with ground turkey. The same is true for this dish. Also, as a person with a day job (in addition to being a professional author), I love a cooking shortcut. I suggest you save yourself from the mess and cleanup by using precooked frozen maduros/sweet plantains.

Servings: 6

Ingredients:
Picadillo (Use the recipe in *Mango, Mambo, and Murder.*)
2½ lbs maduros (frozen) or 5–6 ripe/black-spotted plátanos
4 eggs

Cheddar cheese, shredded
Mild white cheese (mozzarella or queso blanco), shredded

Directions:

Preheat oven to 350ºF.
Oil (or use a nonstick cooking spray) a 9x13 baking dish.

If you are using frozen maduros, defrost and individually press them, so they are all the same thickness. If you are frying fresh plátanos, cut them into long strips of the same thickness.

Line the bottom of the dish with a layer of maduros. Beat two eggs and drizzle over the first layer. Spoon in a layer of picadillo. Sprinkle with shredded cheddar. This is not a cheese dish, so be conservative. Cover the picadillo with a layer of maduros. Beat the remaining two eggs and drizzle over the maduros. Top with shredded white cheese. (Again, this is not a cheese dish, so don't be heavy-handed.)

Bake for 40 minutes.

Crisp top under the broiler if that is your thing. Serve with a side salad of avocado or greens.

Author Notes

This story is set in Puerto Rico. Because it is a real place known to millions of people, I use actual street names and landmarks. El Convento is a modern hotel that was once a convent for Carmelite nuns. La Catedral de San Juan Bautista is an in-use cathedral with a history as far back as 1521. Even though the places and structures in this story are real, please remember the characters and their actions are not; they are fiction.

However, I did find inspiration for certain characters from living people. El Jibaro 2.0 was inspired by El Jibaro Moderno, Miguel Sanchez. Please look up his YouTube and Instagram accounts. He is a joyful ambassador of Puerto Rican foods. Lara, La Pastelera is modeled after Viña, La Gran Pastelera, and her take-out window. I encourage you to find her on social media. Her cooking demonstrations make you feel like you are being taught by a grandmother or auntie. She has free-range chickens and other fowl. Temblor, the rooster in the story, is an homage to her gallo, Terremoto/Earthquake.

Puerto Rico has a rich mélange of culinary traditions. María Dolores de Jesús, better known as Lula, has kept pre-contact cooking techniques and recipes alive at her restaurant El Burén de Lula. In the story, I mention a James Beard nominated video. There is one about Lula. Watch it! A quick internet search will lead to many articles and essays about her. (Make sure to read

Author Notes

Illyana Maisonet's 2019 piece at her EatGordaEat Substack.) The Instituto de Cultura Puertorriqueña published a cookbook by and about Lula in 2011. The first edition is hard to find on the island and used copies off the island even rarer. Thankfully, the Instituto has reissued El Burén de Lula recently. (Libros787 sells online and will ship from Puerto Rico to the USA.) Lula is a Puerto Rican treasure. In November 2022, she celebrated her eighty-fifth birthday. Her recipes and artisanal techniques continue with the help of her family and the community. El Burén de Lula is open most weekends. If you get the chance to visit Loiza, I hope it will be one of your stops.

¡Buen provecho!